Co]

The characters and events portrayed in this book are fictitious. Any similarity to real persons, living or dead, is coincidental and not intended by the author.

No part of this book may be reproduced, or stored in a retrieval system, or transmitted in any form or by any means, electronic, mechanical, photocopying, recording, or otherwise, without express written permission of the publisher.

ISBN-13: 9798714872181

Cover design by: Art Painter
Library of Congress Control Number: 2018675309
Printed in the United States of America

This goes out to anyone who opens this up and reads that first page, thank you, and if you read to the end- even more thanks!

WILDEST DREAMS
An Introduction

They say love is like a rollercoaster, full of ups and downs, thrills and fears, and spontaneous surprises that make your heart pound; but what they don't tell you is that sometimes those surprises can twist and turn your life around to a point where you wind up in jail. No, I'm not the one locked behind bars but maybe I should be.

Afterall, I never expected for one small thing to grow into something so big that it imploded my life, breaking it into a million pieces that I couldn't put back together. I never would have expected that I would end up in a position where I have to rat on my boyfriend, or go to jail myself. But it happened. All because I found myself involved with the Redneck Devils- and if you don't know who or what they are, you're lucky because you don't want to; but I thought I could handle it, I thought I knew what I was getting myself into, most of all I thought he was worth it: but I was wrong. So here I am, being forced to write an excruciatingly truthful statement, giving every detail of the last few months- including my involvement with Zander and the Redneck Devils- despite the fact that it could, and most likely will, get me killed.

CHAPTER 1

It started like any other morning, my phone waking me up as my alarm rang in my ear; I reached over to turn on the radio so I could listen to the morning traffic and news report, but it was that song, that damn song, that always played right before the news and I was sick of it. I reached over and slammed the power button off, not wanting to hear another second of that song, but it was inevitable. It was everywhere.

After rushing to get ready and running downstairs and out the door, I got in my car only to crank the engine and hear that same song playing. I lowered my head to my steering wheel and took a big breath, letting it out slowly before lifting my head up again and easing my car into reverse. I didn't change the station; not this time. What was the point when that song seemed to follow me wherever I went?

I pulled into the parking lot of my favourite book store, Novella, and waited in my car for the clock on my dash to turn to nine thirty when the doors would open for the day. I rolled down my window and pulled a cigarette out of my pocket, inhaling deeply as I lit the end. This was it. The day I had been anticipating for the last six months. The day James McCloud released his new novel, and I was going to be the first one to buy it.

As the numbers of the clock finally changed from 9:29 to 9:30 I opened my car door, dropped my cigarette butt on the ground, and walked towards the store's entrance, blowing smoke out of my mouth as I went. I smiled at Glenda, the owner of Novella, as I swung the door open and inhaled deeply, breathing in the smell of books; it was the best smell in the world.

"Good morning Ali." Glenda was an elderly woman in her sixties. This bookstore was her pride and joy and I'd been coming here for many years, finding solace in the pages of the novels on the shelves even when I couldn't afford to buy them myself. At first, when Glenda found out, she was furious with me. She called my grandmother but upon hearing my story she was overcome with so much despair for me that she forgave my actions and allowed me to find whatever comfort I could in the shelves of her store, and for that I was grateful. "I can only assume you're here for McCloud?"

"Oh Glenda, I'm here to see you too of course." I smiled. "But yes, essentially I am here for the book."

Glenda laughed and pointed me in the direction I knew the book was in. "Feel free to browse our other new sellers as well! There's a wonderful one about a young woman meeting her prince charming in a coffee shop."

I laughed and shook my head; Glenda was a romantic, she believed love could be found anywhere: a coffee shop, a park, and especially a bookstore. I, on the other hand, have had it proven to me time and time again that those who loved you would only leave you; but I wasn't about to burden Glenda with my cynical beliefs.

Then the music started, and once again that god damn song began to play. I glanced back at Glenda who shrugged and gave me an apologetic look as I raised my eyes up and sighed. I just couldn't escape it today.

I sat alone waiting by the phone
When you didn't call
I threw it at the wall
Your face clear in my head
And the words that you said

Echo in my ear, it's all I can hear
You wrecked me
Ripped me to pieces
This can't be the way
You want it to be
Baby why can't you see
I don't want to be free
Come back to me
Ali

I couldn't stand to hear the heartbreak that was so clear to me as he sang those words and when my name came up in the song I squeezed my eyes shut and turned towards the bathroom rather than the shelves. I needed a minute to take a few deep breaths and straighten my head. Those lyrics kept echoing, though, as I shut the door and locked it. That's what I get for dating someone in a band, I guess.

Nick was my first real boyfriend. He also happened to be the lead singer of Shattered Life, an indie rock band who played tons of covers while writing their own songs from their tortured teenage years. We had met back when I was in ninth grade and dated up until a few weeks ago. His band had recently been signed to a record label who insisted on getting an official single out, something new and not from any of their old EP's that they'd created and sold online. When Nick and I broke up, they still hadn't had a completed song. Three days later, though, they released "Come Back To Me", which blew up and debuted at number three on the charts, and I've been hearing it everywhere ever since.

That song, however, was a reminder of what I did and how much I had really hurt Nick, which had never been my intention, but there was only so much I could take. Back when he was getting noticed by the record label he never had time for me, or so it felt, and I did some stupid things. Like cheating on him.

I hadn't intended for it to happen. I knew the moment

I walked through the door that it had been a mistake to go to that party. You know that feeling you get when something bad is going to happen? A sort of clairvoyant premonition? I had that, but I was feeling lonely and rejected after Nick cancelled our date night for the third time in a row so he could meet with yet another PR agent from the label in hopes of getting the single completed. So I did what any teenage girl whose boyfriend was ignoring her would do: I got drunk.

It started innocently enough; I had a few drinks at my friend Gina's house before we decided to leave for the party. Gina knew a ton of people and she always got invited to the most outrageous parties; this one, in particular, was being thrown by some college guys she'd met the weekend before at the club. We called a cab and discreetly took some shots of vodka in the backseat- that was my first mistake. Vodka, as you'll soon find out, has never done any favours for me. It's the bane of my existence to be honest. And yet, I can't seem to stay away from it.

When we arrived at the party I had a decent buzz going on and I was feeling pretty good about myself. Until I checked my phone to see that Nick still had not texted me back. A dark feeling overcame me, but I decided I wasn't going to let it, or him, ruin my night. I walked into the party, head held high, determined to find another drink. Gina walked away, waving to a group of guys, leaving me alone in a room full of people I didn't know, and I weaved through the crowd trying to find the kitchen where I was positive the drinks would be.

The keg sat beside the counter, red solo cups littering the floor around it. I grabbed what I hoped was a clean one from the stack and poured myself a cup. It was warm and flat, typical keg beer, but I continued to chug it until the cup was empty before refilling it and stumbling away into the crowd. There were tons of faces, all blurred to me, and bodies pressed against me. I looked around, trying to find Gina, when I felt a hand brush against my ass.

"Watch it," I slurred, turning quickly- too quickly. The

room spun and I squeezed my eyes shut, hoping it would stop. I didn't even notice that my beer had dropped out of my hands during the process.

"Shit! I'm sorry," someone said. "I didn't mean to touch- I mean, it was an accident and- oh fuck. Here, just let me help you." I felt a hand on my arm and I shrugged away, my eyes still closed, and stumbled right into a body.

"Don't touch me," I snarled. I felt the hands grab hold of me again but I was too dizzy to shake them off. "Leave me alone."

"I'm sorry," the voice said again. Hesitantly I opened my eyes, just a crack, and tried to focus on the face in front of me, but it was impossible. "I really didn't mean to-."

"It's fine." I said, or I thought I said. I wasn't too sure how clear my words were as I squeezed my eyes shut again.

"Can I get you another drink?" Convinced the room had finally stopped spinning I opened my eyes again and tried to focus on the guy; it took a minute but finally a face came into view. A handsome face, with brown eyes and dark hair- and a beard. I never thought beards were attractive before, but at that moment it was the hottest thing I'd ever seen on anyone. Ever.

"Uh," I blinked, speechless.

"C'mon," he reached his hand out again but this time he waited to see if I would grab it. Any other time I would have walked away, made the right choice, maybe even gone home- but not this night. I was sad, I was lonely, and I was drunk. None of these are good reasons for doing what I did, but it happened anyways. I reached out my hand and took his.

CHAPTER 2

The water was cool on my face as I splashed it, trying to get my thoughts under control. *It's just a song. No one knows it's about you* I tried telling myself, but I knew that wasn't true. Anyone who knew about Nick and I could figure out who "Ali" was, even if he refused to speak about it in interviews. If there was one thing I was thankful for, it was that Nick and I had broken up before his fame blew up, but that doesn't stop reporters from prying into his personal life. I was certain that some day I would receive a phone call, and it would be from some reporter that had somehow managed to track me down.

I hadn't spoken to Nick in weeks, not since we broke up, but I felt like I knew everything about him and Shattered Life. I tried to stay away from the articles and news reports but our town was proud of that fact that a local band was signed by a big record label, and they were making it known. As I walked out of the bathroom I spotted a display of magazines and on the cover of the latest issue was Shattered Life, along with an 'exclusive interview with the band'. I sighed, shaking my head as I made a mental note to talk to Glenda about the content she chose to sell in her store.

I finally headed for the aisles, towards the fiction section, and down the row that James McCloud's books were. It was deserted as I approached the books written by authors who started with "M" and I scanned the row, my eyes instantly falling on *Hazard Wave*.

I swallowed as I reached my hand out to grab a copy. I've been reading James McCloud's books since I was eleven. When I first discovered his novels I didn't fully understand them, but there was something about his writing style that drew me in. I read five of his books within a month, and ever since then I'd been buying his books every year as he released them and they've become more relatable to me as I grew older. This was his tenth novel and it was supposed to be his best one yet.

However, as I reached out I realized his books had been moved up on the shelf since the last time I'd been in this aisle. I stretched up on my tip toes, yet the book was still too far away. With a frustrated sigh I jumped a little, hoping to bridge the gap and extend my reach, but all I succeeded in doing was knocking the book over and pushing it further away.

I grumbled, taking a step backwards in hopes that if I ran a little at the shelf I might be able to get enough momentum to jump high enough to reach the book, but when I stepped backwards I stumbled into something- or someone, stepping on what could only be their feet. Surprised I quickly stepped forwards, spinning around to see who sneaked up on me, for I was certain the aisle had been completely empty when I first entered it.

My mouth dropped open as my eyes landed on the culprit, and I'm almost certain I drooled. Deep blue eyes, sandy hair, and a brushing of stubble- hardly enough to be considered a five o'clock shadow but breathtaking just the same. And did I mention the smile as his lips slowly curled up and he revealed his brilliant teeth, which left me standing there speechless? I had never encountered a man as beautiful as him.

I finally managed to shut my mouth, which was now feeling dry from hanging open for so long. The man just stood there, amused, that wonderful smile still stretched across his face as he watched me try and collect myself. I felt my cheeks start to warm as a flush spread across my face. "I'm sorry," I finally managed to say.

"It's all right. Do you need a hand?" His voice was smooth, deep, and relaxing. I wanted to stand there and listen to him all day. Then I realized he'd asked me a question.

"Oh," I stammered, glancing back at the shelf. What had I been doing here again? Oh, right, the book. I cleared my throat, trying to compose myself. "That'd be wonderful, actually. It appears Glenda moved the shelves around a bit and I can't reach the James McCloud ones." I realized I was babbling and stopped talking quickly. Meanwhile, the handsome stranger glanced up at the row of books and I realized I hadn't specified which one I wanted. "*Hazard Wave*," I quickly added. "It's his newest novel."

"I know." I blinked, surprised, as he reached up and easily grabbed two copies, handing one to me and holding on to the other one himself. "McCloud is my favourite author. I wrote a ten thousand word essay on his writing style in university; it allowed me to graduate with honours."

I wasn't sure which part of that sentence surprised me more: the fact that he knew and loved James McCloud as much as I did, or the fact that he had just graduated university. My heart dropped knowing that if he had any idea how old I was he wouldn't be giving me the time of day. As it was I should have given up right then, knowing he was a lot older than me and way out of my league. But I was infatuated, and I wanted to see just how long it would take him to realize I wasn't as old as he clearly thought I was. Maybe it was wrong of me to string him along like that, but it had been a long time since I had connected with someone so deeply, and I wanted to hold on to it as long as I could.

"He's a wonderful writer," I admitted, hugging the book he'd given me tightly. "I've read all of his novels."

He paused, looking thoughtful. "You know, I would love to hear your thoughts on *Deep Down;* my professor thought my interpretation of it was a little excessive, however I'm sure anyone who knows James McCloud as much as I do would agree with what I said. Do you have some time?"

I considered him for a moment, wondering if it was worth the trouble or if it was a waste of time. But he was handsome and I was enjoying the attention he was giving me, and even though it was probably a huge risk on my part I wanted to do it.

"I'd love to." I said, flipping my dark hair over my shoulder and sending him my most flirtatious grin. I saw the playful sparkle in his eye as he reached his hand out towards me and introduced himself. It was this moment that I would turn back to later, when things got rough and complicated. This moment, where he and I both pretended to be someone we weren't because we were trying to hide the truth about ourselves. This moment because it was where I fell for him, even if I couldn't admit it to myself at the time.

"I'm Zander."

And it was this moment I wish I could change, if only because it was the beginning of our complicated relationship, and because it all started with a lie. "It's nice to meet you Zander, I'm Jade."

Walking up to the counter with Zander to purchase my copy of *Hazard Wave* was a little nerve-wracking: what if Glenda saw me, or us, and started asking questions? What if she blew my cover? What if Zander found out I lied to him? I was already regretting my decision to use the name on my fake ID but it was too late now, what's done was done. However, when we got to the counter Glenda was nowhere in sight and the cashier, who must have been new as I didn't recognize her, rang in my book, glancing at Zander who was standing in line behind me, and batting her eyelashes at him. I felt a sudden wave of envy rush through me. Zander, though, only had eyes for me and didn't even seem to notice the signals she was throwing his way. As she hit the total button he stepped forwards, setting his book down on top of mine. "Will you ring this in as well?" he glanced at me and smiled that breathtaking smile. "I was thinking, I would be honoured to buy you this copy of *Hazard Wave*, if that's all right? As a memento, if you will."

I felt another blush creep over me as I smiled at him. "I'd like that," I admitted.

"Great," as he handed the cashier his card he added, "I'd also be honoured if you'd join me for a cup of coffee while we discuss *Deep Down*? Coffee Cafe is right next door, and they serve-"

"-the best cup of coffee in town?" I finished for him.

"Exactly."

I laughed softly and nodded my head as the cashier handed us our books. "That sounds wonderful."

I glanced around the store as we headed for the door, wondering if I'd see Glenda, but she didn't appear to be around and I let out a small sigh of relief. For now my cover was safe.

Zander held the door to Coffee Cafe open for me so I led the way inside and over to the counter. I'd been here often enough that the barista recognized me, not by name but by face, and asked if I wanted my usual order. Zander raised his eyebrows in surprise as he added his drink and handed her his card. "You come here often?"

"I come here enough," I replied casually reaching for my drink as they called out our order. We found a table by the window and sat down, setting our books beside our cups. The sunshine felt warm on my face as it shone in the window and I closed my eyes for a moment, taking it in: it had been a long winter and although it was only the first week of March I was already looking forward to the impending warm weather.

"All right," I opened my eyes and looked at him. My breath caught as I again took in the beauty of his face and I sounded a little breathless as I said, "where do we begin?"

We talked for hours. Zander was an intellect, he had such in-depth views on James McCloud's novels that it almost felt like I was talking to the author himself as he explained his take on the characters, the plot, and the meaning behind each book. We shared a lot of the same opinions, and on the ones we differed we engaged in civil debate over it. Time passed quickly and before I knew it I was on my third cup of coffee and my stomach was growling. I knew I should get home and check in as I'd been gone far longer than I'd expected to be but I was sad to say goodbye.

"This has been an amazing morning." I stood up, tossed my cup in the trash can, and grabbed *Hazard Wave*. "But- and I hate to say this- I should get going."

"Yeah," Zander glanced down at his phone which had been buzzing nonstop for the last five minutes. "I probably should go too."

I couldn't help but wonder who was trying to get a hold of him so desperately, then reminded myself that I hardly knew him and that it was none of my business. For all I knew he had a girlfriend and had only invited me for coffee in order to engage in some intellectual discussion about a paper his professor disagreed with him on.

"Thank you for the book."

"It was my pleasure. I hope you think of me whenever you read it."

I couldn't help the smile that stretched across my face but all I could think to say was, "yeah, you too. I'll see you around."

I turned to go but he reached out and stopped me, grabbing my hand gently, and sending shivers down my spine. "Jade." I glanced back to look at him as my heart began to beat a little faster. "I'm glad I met you there."

"Me too."

He grinned almost shyly, "I don't know how to say this exactly but- would you like to have dinner with me some time?" My breath hitched as I took in his words. "I've had a really great time with you this morning and I- I don't want it to end. Not yet."

"I-," my heart was beating harder now as I considered my options. I could decline the offer and try to forget about him- regardless of the fact I liked him I had lied to him. I could confess that I'd lied and come clean about myself and hope he forgave me and still wanted to have dinner with me (which would be unlikely). Or I could just accept the offer and keep on pretending I was someone I wasn't. "I would love to." I finally said, deciding to go with the last option. After all I was curious to see where this would go.

The smile on Zander's face made my heart skip a beat- he looked genuinely surprised I'd agreed. "I have some things to take care of this week but would Friday evening work for you? I know the perfect place we could go."

"Friday would be wonderful."

"Where should I pick you up?"

I hesitated, trying to think of a way to avoid having him come to my house. Finally I shrugged and said, "would it be okay if I just met you there? Wherever 'there' is," I added with a small smile.

He looked surprised, but nodded. "That would be fine. I'm staying at the *Golden Daylight Hotel and Spa*, have you ever been?"

My mouth dropped open and I fought to close it before he noticed. "N-no," I stuttered. "But I've heard it's gorgeous!"

"It certainly is. I was thinking we could have dinner at the restaurant there. The food is phenomenal." I couldn't believe he was staying at such an expensive place. Who was this guy? Was this really a good idea? I swallowed, hard, but then he reached his hand out for mine and gave it a light squeeze, and my worries and doubt began to fade away as I looked up into his blue eyes. "Is that all right?" He lifted my hand to his mouth and brushed his lips against the back of my knuckles; my knees felt weak and my heart started beating quickly again.

My mouth was dry causing my voice to sound raspy as I said, "Yeah, of course."

He smiled and squeezed my hand one last time before letting it go, reaching to hold the door open for me. My legs were weak as I walked outside and to my car. Suddenly I was itching to have a cigarette, but I was afraid to let Zander see me smoke in case he thought it was a bad habit.

"I'll make the reservation tonight. Does six o'clock work for you?" I leaned against my door, clutching *Hazard Wave* to my chest as I nodded. "Wonderful. I expect you to have finished the book by then. It'll give us at least one thing to talk about." He winked and tapped my car gently twice before turning to leave. I stood there and watched as he walked down the street and reached the corner. Before turning he glanced back, saw me watching, and waved. The smile that crossed my face was the biggest and brightest smile I'd worn in a very long time.

When I walked into the door I was bombarded by my cousins who were home from school that day due to an appointment they had that morning. "Ali's home!" Lisa and Sarah cried, as if they hadn't just seen me hours before. I stifled a sigh as I wrapped my arms around them. I loved my cousins, truly I did, but I'd been living with them for almost a year now and their five year old personalities were getting a little irritating.

"Give me some room," I groaned as I tried shoving them gently away.

"Let Ali come in the door." I looked up to see my Aunt Patty standing in the doorway to the kitchen, a spoon in her hand. "They really do love you, you know."

I glanced back down at the girls as they took the smallest step back not letting go of my legs, and saw them smiling back up at me. I felt a tug in my chest and smiled softly back. "Yeah, I know."

Living with my aunt this past year hadn't been my first choice, but after my grandmother ended up in the hospital- and later recommended to move to a nursing home- I was left with few options. I was more than willing to live by myself at her house, after all she wasn't selling it in case my father decided to show up again, so it may as well get used, right? But according to the judge I was 'too young' to be living on my own, despite the fact I had the maturity level of an adult, even then at the age of sixteen. I was more than welcome to the house once I turned eighteen, but that was still a few months away. Aunt Patty stepped up and took me in; she gave me a fair bit of freedom, all she asked in return was that I be a good role model for the girls and continue my education.

"Your grandmother called," Aunt Patty said as I kicked off my shoes and set my purse down on the ground next to the closet. I was sure to keep *Hazard Wave* safe in my hand, lest the twins hands were dirty and grubby. "She says you haven't been by in a few days."

"School's been busy with midterms," I nodded. "I was thinking of going there tomorrow; I have a mid-term exam and then I'm off for the day."

"Are you excited to have the week off next week? I know the girls are excited for our trip to Florida!"

The twins ran off to watch some television as I followed my aunt into the kitchen and slid into a chair at the table as she returned to the stove to stir something in the pot. I suddenly caught a whiff of spices and chicken: Aunt Patty's famous chicken soup. My mouth watered as I sat down.

"I guess," I shrugged, placing the book in front of me. "I mean, after this semester school's done. Then it's off to university- if I get in, that is."

"You're a shoo-in Ali," my aunt said setting the spoon down and placing the lid on the pot. "You have a wonderful reputation at school. Good grades, class president, and lots of volunteer work. Any school would be lucky to have you."

"I guess," I repeated. "I should be hearing from them after break. No point in stressing about it until then, right?"

My aunt came to sit next to me at the table, set her hand on top of mine and patted it twice before removing it. "I see you got the book you wanted." She nodded at *Hazard Wave* and I felt my face flush as I recalled that morning and Zander. I hoped Aunt Patty wouldn't notice though as I opened the cover, hearing that fresh crack of a new book and taking in the smell of the pages.

"I'm excited to read it," I admitted. "I wish I didn't have to study tonight."

"School comes first," Aunt Patty reminded me.

"I know." But all I could think of was that I had to finish the book by Friday evening and studying for a midterm I knew I would ace was a waste of time. But my grandmother had taught me to always review my notes the night before a test, because you never know what you may be forgetting, regardless of how well you think you know the material.

With that being said I made a quick sandwich, grabbed a bowl of soup, and went up to my room to study. By dinner I had made it through all of my notes and felt fairly positive I'd get an A on my midterm, which happened to be at eight am the next morning; that meant that despite the fact I wanted to start the first chapter of *Hazard Wave* I couldn't, because I knew I'd get lost in it and wouldn't want to go to bed. There were other things I could do, though.

I hadn't touched my guitar since Nick and I had broken up. At first it was a painful reminder of what I had done, how much I'd hurt him, and how, despite the fact I'd broken up with him, I kind of wanted him back. After all, Nick had been the one who'd first taught me to play, going as far as to buy me the very guitar that sat in the corner. I'd practised all the notes he taught me until I got them right, even if it meant my fingers bled.

Music had always been an outlet and coping mechanism for the stressful events that went on in my life. Melodies and harmonies that synchronized together perfectly- that was my favourite kind of music. When Nick and I had first met he played that kind of music. His voice was so soothing and melodic, the sound of the acoustic guitar matching perfectly as he sang; however, once he and his friends formed a band his voice changed. His songs were no longer soothing, they were upbeat and catchy, the kind of music that made you want to get up and dance to. But when it was just the two of us, alone together in his room, he'd pick up that guitar and sing me those soothing melodies, almost like a lullaby, and I'd be taken back to the day we met. I'd insisted he teach me to play, determined to learn the notes; I wanted nothing more than to mimic the feeling I felt hearing those songs on guitar.

The first song Nick ever taught me was a song he wrote about me, the very first one: Everlasting. A song about how we met, the strength of our love, and the fact we thought it would last forever. For whatever reason it was that song that my fingers plucked on the strings as I picked up my guitar. When I opened my mouth the lyrics came flowing out, sounding as melodic as I remembered.

It was a sunny day
A year ago May
You had a smile on your face
You took my breath away
It was impromptu
The day I met you
But I knew it was true
Green eyes and blue
And the day was warm
As I took your hand
And led you away
You laughed when I asked
To kiss you
And said "Okay"
That was the moment
The moment we came together
The second I knew
We'd be forever
Oh we'd be one
Two hearts colliding
No doubt that we'd be
Everlasting

My hands slipped off the strings as I stopped playing,

squeezing my eyes shut and forcing myself not to cry. I hadn't thought about that day in a very long time and I couldn't, wouldn't, let it get to me now. Not when I was feeling so good about today. I slammed the guitar down on its stand and began to get ready for bed, determined to put that memory out of my mind for good.

CHAPTER 3

That entire week went by excruciatingly slowly. My two hour midterm felt like it took six, but I finished it confidently, feeling like I passed with at least a ninety. I visited my grandmother, as promised, and found myself taking the long way home many times that week, driving past *The Golden Daylight Hotel and Spa*, hoping to catch a glimpse of Zander, but every time I drove past he was nowhere in sight. I had no idea why he was staying there, whether he was here on vacation, or for business, or simply just a stop along the way to somewhere else. I don't even know why I cared so much, but I did.

There was just something about him I was drawn to. It didn't matter that we'd only spent a few hours together, I was infatuated and I wanted to get to know him better. I wanted him to get to know *me* better. The real me. But I didn't know how. I didn't know how to tell him I wasn't a mature young adult in university, like he was- instead I was a fairly mature teenager in her senior year of high school, and that just didn't sound as endearing.

There was a valet at the restaurant when I pulled up and I handed him my keys before asking for directions to the entrance. Today the March weather was cold and there was a light layer of snow on the ground. I shivered as the wind blew, pulling my long coat closer around myself as I opened the door. It was warm inside; I let out a sigh as I stomped my feet on the mat and looked around. The lighting was dim and I could see candles on the tables giving off a romantic glow. I spotted a hostess stand and, unsure if Zander was going to meet me here or at the table, I approached it.

She was standing there, back to me, and speaking to someone who I assumed was a waitress by the white shirt and black skirt she wore. They were in the middle of a conversation and I felt a little awkward interrupting them, so I stood there and listened, waiting for the right moment to announce myself.

"-back for the third night in a row. He's sitting at a table this time though."

"I'm going for it tonight," the hostess decided, squaring her shoulders.

"What if he has a girlfriend?" the waitress asked, reaching her hands back to tighten her blonde ponytail.

The hostess laughed, "if he was dating someone we would have seen her by now. Not to mention he's staying in that room, by himself. I asked Bill to check the system this morning."

"You know he's not supposed to give out guest information!" The waitress said, sounding shocked yet amused.

"He owed me one," the hostess shrugged, turning around towards her stand. "And anyways I-." She stopped, eyes widening slightly as she saw me standing there. I watched as her eyes scanned my outfit quickly, sizing me up- a beige trench coat with black knee high leather boots; under the coat I was wearing a deep green form fitting dress which accented my eyes and dark hair, but she couldn't see that. Her eyes narrowed slightly, almost threateningly. "Can I help you?" I opened my mouth, about to speak, when she interrupted me before I could even get a word out. "We're completely booked, so unless you have a reservation-." She trailed off as if waiting for me to turn around and leave. I decided I wasn't going to take any more of her attitude.

"I'm meeting someone," I said firmly, tossing my hair and rolling my shoulders back.

"Name?" She asked, sounding bored.

"Zander."

Her expression wavered for a split second and then she smiled. "I'm sorry, we only go by surnames," she smirked, smugly, not even bothering to look at the sheet of paper in front of her. I don't know what I did to offend this woman I'd never met before, but she was really beginning to piss me off.

"I don't-" I began to say when I felt a hand gently touch my back, and the hostess' mouth dropped open as her eyes widened, and somehow I knew Zander had appeared. The waitress, who had been hovering beside her, glanced at her friend in surprise.

"Mr. Dionne," the hostess stuttered, her hands moving up to flatten her hair and brush a stray piece behind her ear. "I thought you were sitting at your table. Is there anything we can do to help you?"

"Do you need another drink? Whisky on the rocks, correct?" the waitress added eagerly.

Zander's smile was tight as his hand rubbed my back gently, sending shivers down my spine. "My drink is fine, thank you. Actually I was hoping Rebecca could show my date to our table?"

The hostess, Rebecca, seemed speechless as she turned her wide eyes towards me. I watched as they narrowed, slightly, on my waist where his arm was now resting. "Of course," she ground out, forcing a smile. "Right this way."

Rebecca and the waitress shared a long look before she turned and walked into the dining room, blonde ponytail bouncing. Rebecca, though, led the way towards a small table in the back. The room appeared darker there and it took a moment for my eyes to adjust to the soft glow of the candles. Nick had never taken me to fancy restaurants, he always chose the quick and cheap places. This, on the other hand, actually felt like a date, and I liked it.

I shrugged off my jacket, draping it around the back of the chair and felt Zander's eyes on me. Glancing up I could see the appreciation in them as I slowly slid into my chair. After reluctantly ensuring we had everything we needed Rebecca left us alone to pursue the menu, walking quickly away. I saw her stop beside the blond waitress a few tables down, whispering animatedly to her. Clearly she was jealous. Shrugging I picked up the menu and began to look at the options. I couldn't help but notice the prices and swallowed as I saw how expensive some of the dishes were.

"Everything looks delicious," I said slowly. My eyes landed on the cheapest meal. "Perhaps I'll get the chicken and rice stir fry."

"Jade," I stopped, glancing up at Zander. "I have had the pleasure of trying many of the entrees on this menu. Trust me when I say the stir fry is not the best option."

"I love stir fry," I stated- it wasn't a lie exactly, but it wasn't what I really wanted to order either.

"Jade," Zander said again, placing his hand on top of my menu so it lay flat on the table. I had no choice but to look him in the eyes as he said, "please, order whatever you like."

"Okay," I whispered. Our waiter arrived, carrying a whisky on ice for Zander and a glass of water for myself.

"Can I get you anything else to drink?" he asked.

I paused, biting my lip, wondering if he would card me. "I'll take a screwdriver please."

The waiter glanced at Zander, then myself, before nodding, not even asking for my ID. I let out a quiet sigh of relief as I turned back to the menu.

"Vodka," Zander noted, taking a sip of his whisky.

"Yeah," I nodded, "it's my go-to drink."

Zander smiled softly as he set his menu down, "in my family Vodka is saved for birthdays and other special occasions. A tradition, of sorts."

"Why vodka?" I asked curiously as the waiter appeared with my screwdriver.

"No clue," Zander grinned. "Ready to order?"

I nodded, giving the waiter my request. After Zander gave his I saw the blonde waitress at a table next to us as our waiter left passing by her. "That Rebecca chick seemed into you," I stated casually as I lifted my drink to my lips. The vodka was strong but after a few sips I hardly seemed to notice.

"Yes she was." Zander confirmed. I looked at him. "She's been flirting with me for quite some time. She seemed to mistake my kindness as me flirting with her in return. I tried to make myself clear, but apparently she didn't get the message."

"Clearly," I mumbled as I saw her lead another couple to a booth. She glanced over at us, saw me watching, and narrowed her eyes at me. "Her friend didn't seem too kind either," I added as the blonde appeared, yet again.

"Tiffany? She's actually a sweetheart." I raised my eyebrows at him. "Don't take that the wrong way," he quickly said. "I have absolutely no interest in her. I promise you."

"It's fine," I shrugged, taking another large gulp of my drink- I could hardly taste the vodka now. "We've only just met. It's not my business what you do in your spare time."

"Maybe I want it to be," he said, sounding serious.

I was speechless as the waiter arrived carrying our plates, setting down my salmon in front of me; my mouth watered as I took a deep breath savouring the smell. "This looks delicious," I finally said.

We were quiet as we began eating our meals, forks clinking against the side of our plate and knives scratching. I took another sip of my drink and blurted, "I don't blame the hostess for wanting you."

Zander paused, a forkful of steak inches from his mouth, as he raised his eyebrows at me. "No?" My face flushed as I lifted a napkin to my mouth and shook my head. "And why is that?" he challenged, finally taking the bite.

I raised my drink for another sip before saying, "Well, for starters you're incredibly handsome." He chuckled and I felt my face warm even more. "And intelligent." I took another quick sip and felt myself getting braver as I continued, the alcohol giving me the encouragement I needed to say what was on my mind. "You're polite, charming, and well educated. Not to mention your eyes are breathtaking."

Zander grinned widely at me as he set his fork down. "You think my eyes are breathtaking?" I nodded, raising my glass to finish off my drink in a large gulp. "You do realize, Jade, that your eyes are the deepest shade of green I have ever seen."

I paused, my fork halfway to my mouth, a bite of salmon dangling from it as I took in his words. Nick had never said anything so deep and meaningful to me, ever, in the entire three years we dated. Yet here was Zander, someone I had only met days ago; he not only managed to take me to the most romantic restaurant in town on our first date, but he also saw me in a way that no one had ever seen me before. Maybe it was the alcohol that made me say what I did next, or maybe it was the lust that was so evident between the two of us, but the words I blurted out surprised me as much as they did him. "Would you like a closer look?" Zander's look of surprise quickly changed to one of desire as I got up from my chair and walked slowly over to him. Although I knew we were surrounded by onlookers I didn't care as I slid on to Zander's lap, turning my body so I could look straight into his eyes. His face was inches from mine and as his deep blue eyes bored into my green ones I felt my own wave of desire stir within me.

I leaned forwards at the same moment he did, our breaths mingling together, and as my eyes closed I felt his lips brush mine- but only barely before he pulled away, leaving me breathless. My eyes sprang open as the dark feeling of rejection started to overcome me and I leaned away from him.

"I'm sorry," I whispered, feeling embarrassed. I began to slide my body off of him but his hands grasped my hips to hold them in place. "I shouldn't have-."

"You have nothing to be sorry for," he whispered fiercely and as I turned my head to look back into his face, I saw that desire was still written all over it. Desire- and willpower. "You have no idea how hard I am fighting myself, trying to restrain from kissing the daylight out of you. I want you Jade, but this is not the time nor the place for that. We've only just met and I would really love to get to know you better before we take things further."

"Really?" I whispered in a quiet voice.

"Really," he insisted and there was something about the way he said it and the tone of voice he used that I knew he was telling the truth.

"Okay." I smiled shyly, and then remembered exactly where we were and the position we were in. "I should get down," I mumbled, cheeks flaring red. Zander laughed as he supported my hips, and assisted as I swung my legs off of him to land back on the floor. I walked back to my seat, half aware of the people surrounding us. How many people had witnessed that? Were they staring? What were they thinking? "So," I started as I finally got resettled in my seat and took the bite of salmon that was still dangling from my fork. "What do you want to know about me?"

He set his fork down, wiped his mouth, and leaned back in his chair as he sipped his whisky. "Tell me what you like to do in your spare time, other than read James McCloud."

I chucked at the joke, but then paused as I really thought about the question. A lot of my time was spent doing things for school- yearbook, newspaper, student council- but I couldn't tell him about any of that. "I like to write," I finally admitted, summarizing as much of those interests as I could into a single topic.

"What sort of things?" he asked, sounding genuinely interested. Another thing Nick hadn't had time for was to hear about my likes and interests: if I mentioned a poem I'd written or an article I published in the paper, he always had to top it with a song he'd written that day with the band.

"Poems, mainly. I attempted blogging once, but I found it difficult to keep up with."

"I majored in English," Zander stated. He set his fork and knife down on his plate and slid it to the side, finished with his meal. "English combined with a bachelors in education. I've applied for a couple teaching positions and am hoping for something in September when the new school year starts, but that's still six months away. I'll take whatever I can get until then."

I took the last bite of my salmon, also sliding my plate away from me as the waiter came and collected our dishes. "Can I get you another drink?" he asked glancing at both Zander's and my empty glass. I hesitated a moment, unsure if I should have another or not.

"I think some wine would go well with dessert," Zander said, looking at me. "Would that be all right with you?"

How could I possibly say no to that? "That sounds wonderful," I agreed. I let Zander choose the wine and dessert, being more familiar with the menu, while I surveyed the room. I spotted Tiffany handing a couple at a table two glasses of wine themselves.

"Tell me something else about yourself." I glanced back at Zander who must have been watching me the entire time.

"Like what?"

"Anything," he shrugged. "It could be a secret, like something you've never told anyone, or even your favourite TV show. I don't care. Like I said I just want to get to know you."

I took a breath and, before I could stop myself, blurted out, "my mother died while giving birth to me." The waiter arrived then, setting down two glasses of red wine in front of us before ensuring our dessert would be out in a couple of minutes. When he left I looked at Zander who was wide eyed, afraid of what he was going to say in response to that. When he still didn't say anything I picked up my wine glass as something to do and took a large gulp, mouth watering at the sweet yet bitter taste of the wine. "I'm sorry, I shouldn't have-."

"My mother died as well," he finally said in a quiet tone. "When I was very young. I was raised by my father."

I looked at him over the top of the wine glass, a sympathetic look on my face. "At least you had your father."

"Didn't you?" he asked quietly.

I smiled sadly as I shook my head, tipping my glass up for another sip before saying, "my father has been in and out of rehab my entire life. Half the time I don't even know where he is or what he's up to. I was raised by my grandmother."

"Jade," Zander replied sadly as he, too, took a sip from his wine glass. "I-."

I held up a hand to halt his words. "You don't need to say it, I've heard it all before, and I don't need sympathy. I've long since accepted the life I've been given."

"That must have been very difficult for you though," Zander insisted. "Children need stability in their life, but to have such an unpredictable upbringing must have been very challenging to adapt to."

"I found ways to cope."

Zander looked at me with an eyebrow raised, "How?" he challenged.

"Books, music, and-" I blushed as I reached into my purse, pulling out a pack of smokes. "Don't judge me too hard," I said as I set it down on the table. As Zander looked at the small pack he lowered his head and started to laugh. It was my turn to raise my eyebrows questioningly. "What?" Still laughing, Zander reached into his pocket and set something down on the table- a pack of smokes, identical to the ones I had. He laughed harder as I looked at him in surprise. "But- I- What-?"

"You don't honestly think," Zander stated, still laughing, "I could possibly judge you, do you?"

I shook my head as I felt a bubble of laughter rise from my own chest, and then the two of us were laughing together.

The waiter came over, a plate in his hand, and set it down carefully on the table, giving us a confused look. "I can come back-."

"No, no," Zander waved his hand as he picked up and pocketed his cigarettes; I did the same and accepted the spoon

Zander handed to me. "Thank you," he said to the waiter, who left us to eat. "Ladies first."

I smiled, looking at the dessert eagerly. I dug my spoon into the lava cake, savouring the delicious taste of the chocolate as it touched my tongue. "Oh my god," I groaned. "That is amazing."

"It is my favourite thing on the menu," Zander admitted taking a bite for himself. "And it pairs beautifully with the wine."

"It really does," I agreed, taking a sip. I could feel the alcohol buzzing through my body and knew I wasn't going to be able to drive home any time soon. "I know it's a little cold tonight and there's a dusting of snow on the ground, but would you take a walk with me after we finish?" I asked, taking another bite.

Zander grinned, sipping from his wine glass. "A walk?"

"There is a beautiful park with trails about three blocks from here. I thought it might be a nice way to end the evening."

Zander pushed the plate towards me, offering the last bite as he said, "I think a walk would be lovely."

I finished the lava cake and reached into my purse for my wallet, trying to hand him some money for my meal but he pushed it away, waving his hand at me. "My treat," he insisted as the waiter brought over the bill. He swiped his card without even looking at the total and even handed the waiter some cash as a tip. The exchange was done so subtly and once again I couldn't help but wonder who Zander really was.

CHAPTER 4

Zander and I did, indeed, go for a walk through the park. However, as we stopped to admire a fountain and some statues near-by, he glanced over at me, pulled me in, and kissed me. This wasn't a brushing of lips as it had been in the restaurant, nor was he in any way hesitant as he pressed his lips to mine. The kiss was filled with desire and passion as I brought my hands up to his neck and he wrapped his arms tightly around my waist. Our tongues met as the kiss deepened, and his hands moved up and down my body, sending shivers all through me. I'd never felt so many different emotions in a single kiss and as we broke apart, both panting breathlessly, and I stared deep into his eyes I blurted, "I am way too drunk to drive home."

Christmas lights were still wrapped around bushes even though it was March, and despite the late hour, the light posts that lined the trail lit the darkness like a nightlight causing the snow to sparkle like diamonds. I hoped Zander could read the meaning I threw into that sentence and prayed my eyes portrayed exactly what I was trying to say. The hungry growl I heard low in his throat answered my question as he pulled me in for another long, deep kiss which left me shivering with desire again. "Why don't we go back to my room to warm up a little bit," he whispered in a raspy voice. I wanted to tell him

I wasn't shivering from the cold but a part of me knew why, exactly, he was asking me up to his room. All I could do was nod as he took my arm and led us back to the hotel.

Zander held the door open for me and I smiled, walking past him. He placed his hand on my lower back and I slid my own arm around his waist, snuggling my head into him as we walked towards the elevator. Suddenly I felt like someone was watching me; I turned my head to look around and my eyes landed on Rebecca, the hostess from the restaurant, who must have been finishing her shift and getting ready to leave. Her eyes were narrowed as she took us in, jealousy clearly written all over her face. I felt my lips stretch into a smile as I tightened my grip on Zander's waist, just as the elevator doors opened. I leaned up to kiss him as we stepped inside, glancing back out as the doors started to close; the last thing I saw was Rebecca's face, red and furious.

Zander's room was spectacular. I'd never been in a hotel room quite as large as his- there was a sitting room which was separate to the bedroom, a bathroom with a Jacuzzi tub, and a balcony; I barely had the chance to take in any of these details, though, as Zander undid the buttons to my coat and slid it off of my shoulders, leaning down to kiss me again. My gasp turned into a moan as his hands brushed my hip, leaning me backwards onto the couch, his body on top of mine as our kiss intensified.

I'd never been one to sleep with someone so quickly, in fact Nick had been the only one I'd ever slept with. We'd been teenagers when we met and had taken a year before I agreed to take that step with him, but being with Zander felt natural, I was completely comfortable as the kissing began to heat up. Until I was suddenly overcome with a wave of guilt- guilt for lying to him about my age and my name. I couldn't do this, not like this. My eyes sprung open as his lips moved to my neck, sucking and nibbling gently; my hands reached up to slowly push him away and he pulled back, confused.

"Is everything okay?" he panted, licking his lips. "Are we going too fast? I thought-."

"No," I whispered as tears stung my eyes and I sat up, straightening my now twisted dress. "It's not that, it's-." I stopped, taking a deep breath and trying to collect my thoughts.

"Jade?"

My shoulders began to shake. "I need a drink," I mumbled standing up quickly. "I need-."

"Vodka?" Zander asked, holding up a bottle that was sitting on the table beside the couch. "I don't have orange juice but I do have club soda if you'd like to mix it with something."

"Could I just have the bottle?" I asked, blinking as I reached my hand out. I was trying my hardest to keep the tears in but my eyes were stinging. I wasn't going to have the nerve to confess my secrets, though, if I didn't get a drink in me first.

"Are you all right?" Zander asked as he handed me the bottle. I didn't answer as I unscrewed the top and tipped the bottle back, wincing as I felt the vodka burn my throat. "Jade?"

"My name isn't Jade," I blurted, and then started coughing. Zander reached over to pat my back and I shrugged away from him, tipping the bottle back again, feeling less of a burn this time. As I lowered the bottle I looked at him, feeling the tears sting my eyes again. "My name isn't Jade, it's Alessaundra."

Zander gave me a confused look, eyebrows knitting together as he opened his mouth, "wait, what do you mean? You need to explain because-."

I took another large gulp of vodka, setting the bottle down on the table and starting to pace the length of the room. "When we first met I felt instantly drawn to you, but I couldn't tell you who I was because- because-"

"Because why?" Zander asked, his voice sounding dangerous as if he knew what I was going to tell him wasn't going to be pleasant to hear. "What else aren't you telling me?"

"Because I'm seventeen!" I shrieked as the tears that

were stinging my eyes flooded over, running down my cheeks. "I'm only seventeen, Zander, and I knew if you had known how old I was that day we met you never would have thought twice about me, because to you I would have been 'just a kid', right? You never would have asked me out if you had known I was just a teenager."

"You lied to me." I stopped my pacing, face wet with tears, as I turned to look at him. He stood up, fast, and took three steps towards me as he nearly yelled, "You lied to me!"

"I had to." I insisted unconsciously taking a step back. "Can you honestly stand there and tell me you would have asked me out if you'd known I was seventeen!"

"It doesn't matter, because you lied to me instead!"

"I had no choice!"

"Yes you did!" Zander growled. "And you chose to lie." His face knit together angrily as he turned his body away from me. I watched as he cracked in knuckles and began to mutter quietly to himself.

"I wanted to know you, Zander." I whispered.

"But I didn't get to know you!" He screamed, reaching towards the table and picking up the bottle. Before I could blink he'd flung the bottle across the room at the wall, shattering it, glass and vodka spraying everywhere. I gasped, my eyes going wide as I stared at him in surprise. His shoulders were moving quickly up and down as he panted in rage. Slowly he turned back to look at me, his voice level as he said, "I never got to know you, because you lied to me about who you were."

"I only lied about my age."

"And your name!" he roared, face now red.

I flinched, taking a small step backwards and away from him. "I'm so sorry, Zander. I really am."

"Fuck." Zander growled, raising his hands to his hair and tugging at it. "Fuck!" He turned, stomping towards the balcony and slamming the sliding door closed behind him, leaving me alone with glass and vodka on the floor, and tears running down my face.

I took a few shuddering breaths as I went in search of a broom and dustpan. That didn't go as planned, but at least I told him before I'd let things get too far, I just wish they hadn't ended like this. *I can't stay here,* I thought to myself as I sniffled, bending down to sweep up the glass and inhaling the smell of vodka, *but I can't drive home, not like this.* Standing up, I glanced outside to see Zander pacing back and forth, a cigarette in his hand, his phone to his ear. He looked angry, but who could he be talking to? As I watched, he stomped on his cigarette butt and lit another one while simultaneously yelling into his phone, I couldn't hear the words but there was no mistaking the expression on his face.

I shuddered, recalling how he'd thrown the bottle across the room. I'd never been so terrified in my life, he'd looked so angry, his face so red. Tears were still falling down my face as I dumped the glass into the garbage and began to search for my things. My purse was sitting on a table by the door, my jacket on the floor by the couch. I had to leave, that much I knew, but I didn't want to. Despite how angry he was and the fear that had shuddered through my body in that moment, I knew I was the reason he had felt that way, I was the one who hurt him, and it hurt me to admit that because I didn't want to be the reason he was hurting.

With a sniff I glanced one last time at Zander, who was now off his phone and holding onto the railing, his back to me. I let out a large breath and turned towards the door, shrugging on my jacket. Best if I go now, before I changed my mind. I swung my purse onto my arm and reached for the door.

"Don't go."

I stopped, my hand grasping the door handle tightly, knuckles turning white. "I have to," I whispered without turning around.

I heard the sliding door close, gently, and the sound of his footsteps on the soft carpet as he approached. "I- I'm sorry I lost my temper." I squeezed my eyes shut trying to stop the tears from falling again. "Jade- Alessaundra- please. Don't go."

My breath hitched as I heard my name, my real name, come out of his mouth, and it was that, above all else, that had me lowering my hand and turning to face him. His eyes, which had looked so dark before, had dimmed back to their deep blue colour, and the grief that was written all over his face almost had the tears falling from my eyes again.

"Why shouldn't I leave?" I whispered, my eyes shining with tears yet to fall.

"I'm twenty three years old, Alessaundra. I just graduated university with honours in English and a bachelor degree in education. I could teach the classes you currently attend in high school! Yet despite the six year age gap, despite the fact you could be a student of mine, and despite the fact that society screams that this is wrong and illegal- my entire being is telling me to be with you.

"There was something about you, that very first day, that drew me to you. I haven't been able to stop thinking about you all week. I wanted to call you, but didn't have your number. I wanted to spend hours discussing James McCloud's life work that day at the coffee shop. And just hours before, at the restaurant, I wanted to kiss you so badly, but I knew if I had I never would have let you go.

"When you said you were seventeen I- I lost control because I felt as if my heart had been ripped apart, like there was no hope for us, and as crazy as it is to admit because we've only known each other a few days- I feel like I'm falling for you, and I hated to think that the person I was falling for had been a lie."

I couldn't hold the tears back any further as they began to flood down my face. I sobbed as I whispered, "so what changed?"

Zander rushed towards me, arms grasping my shoulders, his face inches from mine as he said, "I believe you when you said you only lied about your age- and your name," he added as an afterthought. "I believe that the person you've shown me is authentic and real. It was my mistake to assume you were older than you are, but in my defence you don't look or act seventeen; I never would have guessed-" he shook his head, "but that's besides the point. I shouldn't have made assumptions, but it doesn't matter because I still would have fallen for you. Besides, you're old enough to make your own choices in regards to the relationships you enter into and-"

"The age of consent is sixteen, what we're doing would be perfectly legal." I mumbled interrupting him. He gave me a confused look and I shrugged, "I may have looked it up after that first day."

Zander smiled softly, reaching out to brush a strand of my dark hair behind my ear, resting his hand on my cheek, "so innocent, yet so mature."

I smiled back, sniffling, but still confused. "What are you trying to say Zander?"

"When I saw you walking out that door- I panicked. I couldn't let you leave, not without first telling you how I feel."

"You told me," I mumbled, "so now what happens?"

Zander stood up straight, letting his hand drop slowly from my face, palm brushing my cheek the entire time. He stared into my eyes as he quietly whispered, "now you get to decide, Alessaundra."

I blinked, sure I'd heard him wrong. "I get to- what?"

"You get to decide what happens next, you call the shots. If you truly want to be with me, then we'll do this. But if at any time you want it to end, all you have to do is say so, and we'll stop. But you need to know what you're getting yourself into, Alessaundra. There will be consequences if word gets out about us and you need to be ready for whatever may happen from here on out."

"I'm ready," I whispered, tears shining in my eyes. "I don't care about the consequences, Zander. I don't care what people will say or think- I don't care about any of that. I just want to be with you."

"Are you certain?" His voice was insistent and I nodded, tears leaking from my eyes again. "You're sure?"

"I've never been more certain about anything in my life.

I want to be with you, Zander." I stepped forwards, wrapping my arms around him and bringing my face to his. He met me halfway, mouth already pursed and ready as our lips collided in a kiss so passionate it left me breathless. He swooped his arm under my legs, sweeping me off my feet as he picked me up and carried me towards the bedroom. I never let our lips separate as he lowered me to the bed. It was dark, but my fingers instantly went to his shirt, quickly unsnapping the buttons and pushing it off of his back. I gasped as he broke away with a growl.

"If we do this, Alessaundra, there's no turning back."

My breath was coming out rapidly, my chest heaving up and down, as my hands wrapped around his neck and I whispered, "I'm ready."

Zander shoved my jacket off, his hands all over my body on my bare skin, sending shivers down my spine as he explored. I never knew a man could make me feel so much by doing so little, yet as his hands brushed my breast I moaned, loudly, feeling desire stir within me.

"Are you certain?" he whispered again, this time in a husky voice.

I grabbed Zander's face, trying to steady it with my shaking hands. "Zander," I stated slowly, being sure to enunciate each word so he understood. "I want this."

He growled again, bending down to capture my now swollen lips. His hands began to roam some more, pushing at the straps of my dress until they became loose and started to fall off my shoulders. I gasped as I felt the air brush my bare skin, then moaned as Zander's lips took place, trailing kisses down my neck, shoulder, and collarbone, lower still until they reached my breast. As he captured it in his mouth my hands went to his hair and tugged, my body shivering below him. Never had foreplay felt so good.

My hands grabbed Zander's waistband and I tugged impatiently at his belt, trying to get it loose. He chuckled, moving away from my breasts in order to lean upwards and within moments the belt was opened and I was tugging his pants, and boxers, down. I saw a flash of passion and desire in Zander's eyes as he pushed the dress entirely off my body, leaving me in nothing but my panties. I didn't feel an ounce of discomfort or insecurity as Zander took in my body, there was something about the way he looked at me that made me feel confident in my skin. Slowly, agonizingly so, he brushed his fingers under the waistband and pulled my panties entirely off before lowering his body to hover over top of mine. I could feel his penis brushing over me, causing me to quiver in anticipation.

"You are the most beautiful creature I have ever seen," he whispered, holding himself up.

"Please, Zander, please," I begged, feeling his body shiver.

"As you wish." I gasped as I felt him enter me, crying out as he began to pump in and out. My hands reached around him, fingers clutching his back; I was sure there were going to be nail marks left behind from the pressure. He bent down, capturing my gasps in his mouth, and as he kissed me it made the sex that much better, if that were even possible.

Whenever Nick and I had been together his movement had always been so slow and uncertain; he'd never made me feel like this. Zander was skilled, knowing exactly where to touch me and how to move his body with mine, giving me the most pleasure possible. I hadn't known sex could feel this good until now. Zander truly made me feel like a woman.

Afterwards, as we lay next to each other passing a cigarette back and forth, I couldn't help but feel a sense of completion, as if I'd found a missing piece of myself. I couldn't say it aloud, lest Zander think I was crazy, but as I snuggled in close and he wrapped his arm around me I sighed, feeling happier than I'd felt in a long time.

Early in the morning, after Zander and I had dozed off, his phone began to ring waking me from a deep sleep. At first I was confused as to where I was and thought it was my phone, but reaching for it on the bedside table I found the screen black. Zander stirred beside me and I recalled where I was, blushing as the events of only hours before flashed through my mind. I reached my elbow over, nudging Zander gently. "Zander," I whispered. His phone stopped ringing and I sighed, leaning back again. I had just closed my eyes when it started up again. With an irritated huff I sat up and nudged Zander again. "Your phone is ringing."

Zander mumbled in his sleep, rolling over to a more comfortable position as he faced me. The phone stopped and I waited a moment to see if it would start up again. Sure enough the ringing picked up moments after it'd stopped. Clearly it was important.

"Zander!" I said in a louder voice, using both hands to shake his arm.

"Wh-." Zander blinked coming to and jumped up as he heard his phone. He picked it up and glanced at the caller ID. "Whatever you do, don't make a sound," he insisted as he hit the green button on the screen. "What is it?"

I could hear a voice on the other end talking loudly, male I was certain, but as to what they were saying I wasn't sure. Zander sighed, and in the dark I could just make out his face expressing annoyance as he reached for his pants, tugging them on, phone propped between his shoulder and ear as the voice continued to talk. "And have you-." He let out a breath, now tugging a shirt over his head as he walked out of the room and towards the balcony. I looked around, confused as to what I should do, and decided getting dressed was a good first step, flicking on the bedside lamp.

After pulling my dress on I glanced in the mirror and saw how mussed my hair was, spotting a few small bruises that covered part of my body- hickeys, another first for me. Shrugging I walked out into the open space, saw Zander pacing the balcony, still on the phone, and walked to the fridge for a drink of water, my mouth desperately dry. My phone read three forty two in the morning, but despite the fact I hadn't checked in with my aunt, I had no missed calls from her, only a few texts from Gina about some party she was at and had wanted me to join her. I deleted the texts without replying, setting my phone on the counter as Zander walked inside, still on the phone.

"I understand what you're trying to say but-." He bit his lip as his mouth turned down in a frown. "You're not listening to me, Danny." He threw his hands up, rolling his eyes. "Fine. Fine. Yeah. I get it. Okay. Yeah. I said okay. Goodbye." He lowered the phone from his ear, stared at it for a second, then threw it on the couch. "Fuck."

I jumped at the sudden rise in his voice, "Is everything okay?" I asked tentatively.

"Yeah," Zander mumbled, rubbing his face with his hand. "Just- my brother, worrying about the family business."

I glanced at the clock. "At this time?"

"It's a twenty four hour thing," he mumbled.

"It sure seemed important." I filled my water glass again, downing it in seconds.

"He seemed to think so." The resentment was clear in his voice and I thought it best to drop it as I filled the cup for a third time, this time handing it to him. "Thank you."

I nodded, crossing my arms. "I have a brother too, you know."

Zander paused, the glass half way to his mouth. "You haven't mentioned him."

"Nor did you mention yours," I pointed out.

He took a gulp and lowered the glass, wrapping both hands around it. "Some things are best left unspoken."

"I agree. However if your brother is a key part of your life, I'd like you to be comfortable speaking about him."

"Jade," he shook his head, "Alessaundra, I mean. Look, it's not that simple."

"Why not?"

"My brother- he isn't- good."

I raised my eyebrows, "What do you mean he isn't

good?"

"It's complicated." Zander mumbled while taking another drink from the glass.

"Okay," I drew out the word, hoping he'd elaborate. When he didn't I pressed on. "What about the family business? You never mentioned that either."

He pressed his lips together and took a deep breath, "You don't need to worry about that."

"But Zander-."

"Stop, Alessaundra!" I jumped as his voice rose again and took a step back. "Just stop. There are some things in my life I'd rather not expose you to, some things I don't want to discuss with you. For your own good."

I could feel tears stinging my eyes as I nodded, glancing around for my phone. "Okay." I took a breath, reaching for my phone as I spotted it on the counter. "Look, it's really late and I'm feeling sober enough to drive so I should-."

"Don't go." The change in Zander's voice was instantaneous as he pleaded, "please."

"I have to."

He nodded, setting the water glass down and picking up his phone. Holding it out to me he said, "Before you go, would you put your number in for me? I'd hate to lose touch with you after tonight. In fact, I'd love to see you again."

I hesitated for a moment before grasping his phone and swiping. I couldn't help but notice his display screen was of a horse, and wondered if it was a generic picture that came with the phone or if the horse was sentimental in some way. "Should I put it under Jade or Ali?" I asked. "Ali is short for Alessaundra," I explained. "You can call me that, if you want."

"Ali," he repeated slowly, a small smile curving his lips. "I like that." I smiled back and quickly inputted my name and number, wanting to take a few moments to snoop through his phone if only to find out more about him, but knew how disrespectful that'd be. I handed it back to him and watched him move his finger along the screen for a moment before feeling a buzzing from my own phone. A smiley face emoji appeared from an unknown number and I knew it was Zander. "Now you have my number as well."

"I really should go." I picked up my jacket from where it sat on the floor and shrugged it on, slipping my phone into the pocket and swinging my purse onto my shoulder. "I had an amazing time tonight Zander."

He reached for my hand, pulling me towards him and softly kissing my lips. "I did as well. I wasn't lying when I said I would love to see you again, soon."

I pressed my lips together, "I would like that- but I'm going away this week, with my family. We're going to Florida, and my aunt is insisting we leave our phones at home."

"Okay," Zander paused to think about it, "when do you get back?"

"Our flight gets in Sunday night around six."

"Dinner that night?" he asked eagerly.

I slowly shook my head, "I have school Monday morning."

"Oh right."

We were quiet, our fingers intertwined together as we both got lost in thought. "We'll figure something out."

Zander smiled, leaning down to kiss me again. "Of course we will."

As I turned to open the door I paused, glancing back at him. "I turn eighteen at the end of May. In case you were wondering."

"May?"

"May." I confirmed.

"That's not too long," he mused.

"Not long at all."

He grinned, leaning down to kiss my cheek softly. "I'll call down and have the valet get your car brought around for you."

"Thank you." I stepped out of the door, walking down the hall towards the elevator. I heard a door open and Zander's voice echoed down the hall, halting me in my steps.

"Oh, and Ali? I very much look forward to the next time we meet."

I blushed, glancing back at him to see a very suggestive look on his face, making my face flame hotter. I couldn't stop the wide grin that spread across my face as I pressed the down button and waited for the elevator to arrive.

CHAPTER 5

As the week passed I kept thinking back to that night. The connection between Zander and I was strong and it killed me not to be able to message him while I was away. While Aunt Patty toured Disney with the girls, I chose to sit in the hotel room and mope, re-reading *Hazard Wave* over and over again until I was sure I could quote the novel. I couldn't wait to get home.

However, Sunday evening I walked through my bedroom door and instantly picked up my phone to find no missed calls or texts awaiting me from Zander. Sure, Gina had messaged me a few times but Zander hadn't even sent a single 'thinking of you' message to me while I was gone. I debated messaging him to inform him I was back, but what was the point when he hadn't seemed to miss me? I tossed my phone to my bed and began to unpack, dreading the return to school tomorrow.

The smell of bacon always made me nauseous. The day my sister, Monica, left was the same day my dad had returned from one of his trips to rehab. That morning he'd woken early and decided to make breakfast for us, his favourite meal. He had pancakes on the griddle, bacon in the oven, and eggs frying in a pan, the smell so overwhelming it woke me up. I'd gone into Monica's room to wake her, only to find her bed empty with nothing but a slip of paper to be found.

By the time you read this I'll be long gone. You don't need to worry, I'm safe. But please don't go looking for me. You need to understand that I have to do this. I can't stand to be in the same house as him, not after everything he's done, and if he's decided to come back, then I'm going. I'm sorry.

I'm sure there was more to the letter but that's all I could recall. I remember screaming for my grandmother who walked into the room calmly, as if she expected this. She held me as I cried into her shoulder. Monica had only been fifteen years old when she ran away, yet she had managed to enrol in school, graduate, and go on to earn a college diploma, graduating last year with honours.

Ever since that day, though, the smell of bacon brought back the feeling of abandonment Monica had left me with. My Aunt, despite the number of times I'd asked her not to make it, continued to cook bacon on special occasions- like the Monday after March Break.

Groaning, I rolled out of bed and began to get ready for school. Mid-terms were officially over, which meant it was time to prepare for the final stretch- finals were only three months away, and I still hadn't heard from any of the universities and colleges I'd applied to. Not to mention I had a yearbook to finalize, a newspaper to edit, and a prom to plan with the student council.

Checking my phone I again felt a wave of disappointment to see no messages from Zander and I began to wonder if I'd done something wrong. Maybe he hadn't actually wanted to see me again? Maybe he met someone while I was gone, someone more appropriate for him, like Rebecca? Maybe I just wasn't good enough? Maybe he'd reconsidered how he felt about me and the age gap?

I reached to pull my long hair back, taking in my reflection. I'd chosen to wear a plaid skirt, white button up shirt, and black tights which matched perfectly with the high ponytail.

I glanced at the time to see I had ten minutes to spare before I had to leave, just enough time for a quick coffee. I walked into the kitchen to find the twins sitting and eating their breakfast, still dressed in their pyjamas. One of the biggest downsides of having to leave my grandmothers house and live with my Aunt was the fact that Baysin High, the school I attended, was now across town. I could have transferred to Collins, like my Aunt had wanted me to, but I fought her on it, insisting it wouldn't look good on my college applications to transfer mid semester and although she obliged and agreed to let me stay at Baysin, I knew she wasn't pleased about it.

"Have some bacon," Aunt Patty said, placing a few slices onto a plate and holding it out for me.

I made a face as I reached for the pot of coffee. "Aunt Patty you know I can't eat that stuff."

"Oh Ali," she shook her head, "it's been six years since then and-."

"And it doesn't change how I feel about it." I finished, grabbing a travel mug and pouring the coffee in. "I'm going to take this to go."

"Are you sure?" Aunt Patty asked as I walked towards the door, slipping on a pair of black boots. "You really should eat something."

"I'll be fine." I swung my bag over my shoulder and opened the door. "I'll see you later."

I sat in my car and took a deep breath before starting it. I turn eighteen in two more months, graduate high school in three months, and then I could finally move out on my own. With that thought in mind I turned the key and nearly groaned as I heard the opening chords that filled my speakers.

"I'm Maggie in the Morning and this is local legend Shattered Life with their now number one hit Come Back To Me! Turn it up."

You broke my heart and tore the world apart
Baby how could you
I thought our love was true

You left me there with a flip of your hair
You broke our trust
And that was the end of us

I rolled my eyes as I put my car in reverse and backed out of the driveway, then realized what the radio announcer had just said. Shattered Life now had a number one hit. Nick's song had made it to the top! A part of me wanted to be happy for him, but a bigger piece of me recalled how that song was about me, and everyone at school knew it. I had a feeling this day wasn't going to be a good one for me.

"Ali, Ali!" I sighed as I heard Gina calling my name in the hall. Snickers erupted around me and, with a roll of my eyes, I turned around to wait for her to catch up. "God where have you been?" she panted as she reached my side. "Didn't you get any of my text messages?"

"I've been away Gina," I responded in a patient voice. "I didn't have access to my phone, remember?"

"But you could have texted me back last night."

"I was tired," I shrugged, as we stopped at my locker. I spun the dial and opened the lock, withdrawing my english textbook. "What's so important anyways?"

"Everyone's talking about Nick and Shattered Life. Their song made it to number one! That's huge! They went to this school and they're basically famous now and-."

"And it's nothing I care about." I slammed the locker shut and snapped the lock back in place.

"But everyone's talking about the song, Ali."

"Everyone's been talking about the song for weeks."

"Not like this." Gina insisted, brushing a stray hair behind her ear. "Seriously, everyone's speculating about your relationship now, they think they know exactly what happened between the two of you, and why you broke up. Didn't you read the interview they released last week?"

I shook my head, but suddenly recalled the magazine I'd seen in Novella. "Wait, what did it say?" I asked, almost afraid to hear the answer. Nick had sworn he'd keep our relationship private, but that had been before we broke up.

Gina pulled the magazine out of her bag, "Here. He didn't mention you, exactly, but if you know Nick, and you know about your past- well it's fairly obvious who he was talking about."

I stared at the cover as I held the magazine tight in my hands. "I don't know if I want to read it," I admitted.

"Read it, or don't," Gina shrugged. "That's your choice. But you'll never know what everyone is saying about you if you don't."

"You could just tell me, you know." I pointed out as we reached our home room and walked towards our seats.

"Where's the fun in that?" Gina laughed.

I let out a breath, setting my textbook and notebook down on my desk as I awaited my favourite class to begin. My peers around me were chatting softly as the bell rang again to signal the start of announcements. I looked around, feeling slightly confused, as I noticed our English teacher still hadn't arrived. "I wonder where Ms. Roberts is." I mused.

"Oh man, haven't you heard?" Gina, the queen of gossip, said as she leaned towards me. "She was put on bed rest! Apparently her pregnancy took a turn and her doctor ordered her to stay off her feet for a while."

"What?"

"Oh yeah, you missed a ton being gone last week." Gina glanced down at her nails, perfectly filed and manicured, and shrugged.

"But there wasn't even any school last week."

"Gossip spreads, regardless."

"So do you know who's covering for her?" I asked, glancing at the door.

"No clue, but I heard he's young and hot."

It should have registered to me, then, what was about to happen, but the pieces just didn't click. As the announcements started and I settled in my seat, I pulled my phone out to see if

I had any missed messages. There were none and again I had a sinking feeling of rejection. Why hadn't Zander texted me?

Announcements ended and still there was no teacher to be found. Whispers were starting to spread around the room, many asking how long they had to stay before it was appropriate to just walk out. As student body president I knew it was wrong, but a large part of me agreed with them and hoped no teacher would show up. However, just as the class was getting restless, Mr Thorn, our principal, walked into the room. He was slightly breathless as he stood in front of us and all I could focus on was the bald head and the round belly that jiggled as he folded his hands in front of him.

He waited patiently for the class to settle and slowly the whispers seized as Mr Thorn cleared his throat to speak. "Ms Roberts has taken ill in her pregnancy and has had to go on maternity leave early. We fully respect this decision, despite the abruptness of it. I understand that as seniors in your final stretch of highschool this sudden change may be difficult for you to adapt to, however we will be here to support you in every way we can. I will admit, though, that it has been fairly difficult to find a supply on such short notice. He will be with us momentarily, but while we wait I was hoping Alessaundra could lend me a hand by setting up the projector? Today's lesson plan has been misplaced so you are going to watch the movie adaption of the next novel you will be studying."

"Sure thing Mr Thorn." I stood up and walked towards the front of the room to sign into the computer and enable the projector. Mr Thorn started talking about the supply teacher, saying how he was new to the field and inexperienced. I rolled my eyes at that as I clicked through files, trying to find the english department's collection of videos. I was so focused on what I was doing I didn't realize the class went unnaturally quiet or that Mr Thron had stopped talking so loud and was discussing something in a whisper.

"All right, seniors, as you can see your teacher has arrived, take it away Mr. Dionne."

It took me a moment for the name to register, and it wasn't until he started speaking that all of the pieces started to fit together. I whipped my head around, my eyes going wide as I saw Zander standing next to Mr. Thorn, shaking his hand.

"Thank you Mr Thorn." He looked at the class and smiled, and I swear I felt a soft breeze from all of the girls sighing simultaneously. I was surprised at the wave of jealousy that flooded through me as I took in every single girl staring at Zander lustfully and had to bite back an envious snarl. Mr Thorn walked out of the room, leaving us alone with Zander. He hadn't yet noticed me standing by the computer at the front of the room, but it was only a matter of time before my presence was made known.

"All right. Well, I'm Mr. Dionne and I will be covering for Ms Roberts for a little while." Zander's voice sent shivers down my spine as I recalled his voice in my ear whispering sweet nothings to me while we made love, which in turn made me remember having his hands all over my body. I gulped and squeezed my eyes shut trying to block out the memories.

"How long?" Gina asked with a purr. My eyes sprung open as I glared in her direction, not that she seemed to notice. Her attention was entirely on Zander and I quickly looked back at him, waiting for his response.

Zander shugged, smiling again, "I haven't been given an end date as of yet. Mr Thorn has asked me to do some lesson planning, so I'm anticipating an extended stay. Now, he told me the video should be set up and-."

I held my breath as Zander turned and I knew I had two choices- one was run and hide, diving behind the desk and out of his eyesight, or I could face him head on, for it was inevitable he'd find out I was in this class anyways. His mouth fell open, slightly, and a silent gasp escaped, one I was sure only I could hear as he finally saw me. I knew we were staring at each other longer than was appropriate so I cleared my throat and gestured at the computer. "The video's just about ready, sir." The steadiness of my voice surprised me.

"Oh," Zander cleared his throat, blinking. "Right. Thank you-."

"Miss Campbell," I quickly stated. "Alessaundra Campbell. Student body president."

"Right." Zander repeated. I hoped nobody else could see how awkward this exchange between us was as I took a step away from the computer.

"If you don't mind, I'll just return to my seat and-." I pointed at my desk, taking another step forward.

"Of course," Zander quickly replied. "Yes, please, return to your seat. I'll just get the movie started for us."

I sat down and let out a breath, my hands shaking as I opened my notebook. "What was that about?" Gina hissed, leaning over.

"What do you mean?" I asked, trying to sound nonchalant as I fidgeted with my pen.

"You two seem like you know each other or something."

"What? No! I-."

"Quiet down," Zander's voice floated back to me, sounding stern. A few of my peers glanced back at me, snickering: I almost never got in trouble, especially in class. I blushed, mumbling out an apology as Zander hit play on the movie. I found it difficult to focus though, my eyes constantly wandering over to him. He sat at the desk, flipping papers and making notes, occasionally shushing the whispers that would break out during a boring part of the movie. Usually I was a note taker, but today I hardly followed the storyline of the movie, my mind too busy thinking of other things- how could Zander be teaching at my school? Why hadn't he told me he had gotten a job? Had he known this was the school I attended? And, most of all, what were we going to do about this?

Gina flicked a note onto my desk and I opened it, glancing at what was written. *Mr D is an 11/10 ;)* I rolled my eyes and handed the note back to her without a response. "What?" she hissed, "You know it's true."

"Shh," I whispered, staring blindly at the screen. "I'm

trying to focus."

But I wasn't really focusing at all. My mind was too busy spinning, going through the odds of Zander and I remaining together after this. Was it possible? Could we do it? Would it work? I glanced over at him to find his eyes on me, quickly averting his gaze when he saw I'd caught him looking. It seemed he, as well, couldn't keep his attention solely on his work.

As the bell rang at the end of class I tried to take my time packing up my things, if only to have a word or two with Zander but Gina grabbed my arm and pulled me out of the room. I glanced back, quickly, but Zander avoided my gaze. Sighing I let Gina drag me out of the room.

"Mr D is fine," Gina sighed as we walked down the crowded hall. I swerved to avoid a group of girls who were giggling together as I tried to keep up with her. "I wouldn't mind a few tutoring sessions with him."

"Gina," I sucked in a breath, feeling my heart clench in anger. "He's a teacher."

"A hot one."

I rolled my eyes, "you're not his type."

"I'm everyone's type," she flicked her blonde hair over her shoulder and smiled flirtatiously. "Besides how would you know what his type is?"

"I don't," I quickly said. "But you're a student and he's a teacher and-."

"Blah blah blah," Gina waved her hand at me. "Whatever. I can still think he's hot."

I shook my head at her, "I need to get to my next class."

"See you at lunch?"

I hesitated but nodded, "Yeah, sure. See you then." As Gina walked away and I turned towards my next class all I could think about was the fact that I needed to speak with Zander as soon as I could, and lunch was the only time to do it.

I couldn't concentrate on my next class and as the

morning went on I started to feel nervous flutters in my stomach over the possibility of what would happen now between Zander and I. I liked him, a lot- no, that wasn't right. I loved him. I'd only known him a short while, and it had taken something this big and drastic for me to realize that I wasn't just falling for him- I'd already fallen, fallen so hard I crashed and broke into pieces, pieces he now held in his hands.

When the bell rang, indicating the start of our lunch hour, I rushed from my seat and towards Zander's English classroom. Panting I stood outside the door as students exited and took a few breaths to steady my breathing and my heart. After a minute I was sure the last student had left and the room would be empty; I grasped the door handle and stepped quietly into the room, glancing around quickly to ensure it was in fact empty before closing the door behind me. Zander was sitting at his desk, head bent down, glancing at a piece of paper. He looked up when he heard the door close and stared at me as I took three steps towards him.

"Ali," he paused, swallowed and instead said, "Miss Campbell. What can I do for you?"

I glanced around the room again before turning back to stare at him. "You can drop the formalities, Zander. There's no one else here."

Zander shook his head, "Miss Campbell-."

"Ali." I stated firmly, walking until I was standing in front of his desk. I bent down, placing both palms on it and leaned towards him;. "Even my teachers call me by my first name, Zander."

"Mr. Dionne," he corrected, eyes rolling down to glance at my chest before moving quickly back to my face.

I shook my head, "cut the bullshit, Zander." Suddenly I was angry. "Why the fuck didn't you tell me you'd gotten a job? How could you forget to tell me you'd be teaching at my school!"

"I didn't-."

"You haven't texted me in a fucking week Zander!" I

snarled. "Nothing. I returned from Florida expecting something from you! Yet there wasn't a single message from you the entire time I was gone!"

Zander took a big breath, "texting works both ways. Besides, do you have any idea how busy I've been the last few days, Ali?"

"Too busy to send me a single message?"

"Not everything is about you!" He snarled, surprising me enough to take a step away from his desk. "There is a lot going on in my life, Alessaundra. You- you don't know half of it."

I looked at him curiously as he raised a shaking hand to his face. "You could have told me." I said softly.

"You couldn't have helped."

"I would have tried."

"No." He stated firmly, fiercely, and my eyes widened. "Not with this, Ali. I don't want you to help me with this."

"With what?" I asked, walking back towards his desk. "Talk to me Zander."

He sighed, "there's a large part of my life that is far too complicated to involve you with." I opened my mouth but he waved his hand at me. "No, Alessaundra. I refuse to drag you into my problems. I already told you, you can't know about certain aspects of my life."

"Fine," I said, pressing my lips together. "Why don't we focus on the issue at hand then?" I crossed my arms. "How could you not tell me you got a job?"

"I just got the call last night." Zander sighed, setting down his pen. "And before you say it again, I had no idea you went to this school!"

"But you knew I was still in highschool." I hissed. "You should have at least asked me!"

"Like I said it was a last minute decision. Besides, what was I supposed to do? Reject the offer? I needed this job, Alessaundra."

"I know," I whispered as tears sprung to my eyes. "It just

sucks, Zander." We were quiet for a moment and I finally whispered the one question I was most afraid to hear the answer to. "What are we supposed to do now?"

"There's nothing else for us to do but end it."

I stared at him as the tears leaked down my cheeks. "How can you say that?"

"We don't have a choice Alessaundra. Either we end it or I quit, and I can't afford to quit right now."

"So I'm just supposed to pretend like I don't know you? Like we had nothing? I can't do that!"

"We don't have a choice, Ali."

"But I love you Zander!" I blurted, wiping my eyes. He sat back in his chair and stared at me, taken aback as I sniffled. After taking a few calming breaths I said, "I love you. How can I pretend like I don't?"

"You don't know me well enough to love me, Alessaundra." Zander said quietly, a hint of remorse in his voice.

"Don't tell me how I feel!"

Zander looked at me sadly, "if you really knew me, you wouldn't love me, Ali. You couldn't, it'd be impossible."

"What do you mean?" I asked, scrunching my eyebrows together in confusion.

He shook his head, "It doesn't matter. It doesn't matter how you think you feel or even how I feel, because we can't let this go on. Do you know the consequences there'd be if we got caught? Do you realize how much trouble I'd be in? I need this job, Ali, and I can't afford to lose it."

"I can't just let you go, though."

"You have to." His words were strong but I saw the regret in his eyes. Despite his insistence that this was what we had to do, he hated it as much as I did, which only made it harder for me to accept.

I took a few steps, walking around the desk until I was standing right in front of him, slowly reaching a hand out to cup his face. He closed his eyes and I saw how much this decision hurt him. "If we're going to end this," I whispered, "the least you can do is give me one last kiss goodbye."

"We can't." He squeezed his eyes shut. "Ali we can't. It's too dangerous."

"I don't care," I reached my other arm out and leaned forwards until our faces were an inch apart. I could feel his breath on my face and breathed it in. "I don't care."

Zander opened his eyes and stared into mine, a hungry look on his face. "Fuck it," he whispered, reaching up to close the gap between us and slamming his mouth on mine. I moaned as his tongue entered my mouth and I tried to push myself closer to his body, forcing him against the back on his chair. I felt my leg hit his desk but ignored it as I moved myself onto his lap, straddling his waist. Zander reached around my body and up my skirt to grab my butt, causing me to groan. That seemed to bring Zander back to reality as he pushed himself away from me, licking his lips and panting. "We shouldn't have done that."

"Now you regret kissing me?" I asked, leaning back but still straddling his waist.

Zander looked up at my lips, which were swollen and wet from our kiss, then raised his eyes to look into mine. "You wanted one last kiss, Ali, and you got it. Now leave." He pushed me away from him, forcing me to get up and off of his lap.

"What?" I asked, sounding hurt as I reluctantly stood up, straightening my skirt and shirt which were askew.

"You need to leave, Alessaundra." Zander stood up himself, taking a few steps back and putting some distance between us.

"How can you say that Zander?" I whispered. "How can you ignore everything we had? The chemistry that is clearly right there between us? Last weekend you said-"

"That was then," Zander stated firmly, turning away and looking out the classroom window where a brick wall was the only view. "That was before. Please, Ali, just go. I have work to do."

I stared, waiting for him to turn around or even acknowledge me- to say something, anything, to make this better. But the longer I stood there the more I realized he truly meant what he'd said. This was the end of us. Tears sprung to my eyes as I turned and opened the door to walk out, knowing there was only one thing I could do if I wanted to save our relationship.

I headed straight towards the counselors office. Ms Pike, the secretary at the desk, smiled when she saw me. "Ali, what can I do for you?"

"I need a transfer request."

"A transfer request?" Ms Pike typed something into the computer and scrolled for a moment. "Half way through the semester? Which class would you like to transfer out of?"

"Actually I was hoping to transfer schools."

Ms Pike raised an eyebrow at me, "with only three months left of your senior year?"

"I need to go to Collins, it's closer to home and-."

"That would be a mistake, Ali."

"Please," I pleaded leaning across the desk. "Ms Pike, I need to leave Baysin."

"Is this about the song?" she whispered.

"Song?"

"I understand it must be hard for you to have a song written so publicly about your break up, but it's no reason to transfer schools Ali."

I blinked, confused, then realized what she was talking about. For a moment I'd forgotten about 'Come Back To Me' going number one, forgot about the song being written about me, forgot about the rumours that had spread about Nick and I. Ms Pike looked sympathetic as she shook her head, "if students are bullying you we can help you."

"No ones bullying me." I stated firmly. "I just-."

"Transferring schools isn't going to help you either, Ali. If anything it will put you behind. Listen," she leaned closer to me and lowered her voice, "I shouldn't tell you this but I heard Mr Schimdt on the phone this morning talking about you. I didn't hear which university it was, but it was all good things. You don't want to ruin your reputation by transfering do you?"

My eyes widened as I took in her words. One of the schools I had applied to had called for a personal reference about me. That could only mean I was being considered for admittance. "Do you know if a scholarship was mentioned?" I whispered completely forgetting why I was there in the first place.

"Like I said I didn't hear the details. However, I am the one responsible for faxing information to financial aid offices."

"And?"

She lifted her lips in a smile, "Let's just say you're in good hands."

"Oh my god."

Ms Pike grinned, "Still want that transfer information?"

"What? Oh, right." I shook my head a little to clear it. "No, no I think I'll be okay."

"Have a good day Ali."

"Thanks Ms Pike." I walked out of the office in a daze as I went over what I'd just learned. One of the schools I applied to wanted me, and was likely offering me a scholarship. It was all I wanted. How could I have even considered transferring schools? "Because you want to be with the man you love," I sighed as I sat down on a bench in the hallway. It was impulsive of me to think that transfering schools was the solution though, besides there was no guarantee it would have worked-who's to say Zander even still wants to be with me? He'd made it pretty clear we were done.

The bell rang indicating lunch was over. I sighed as I stood, swinging by bag over my shoulder and heading towards my next class, wishing it was the end of the day instead.

CHAPTER 6

It was nearly impossible to get through the first week of school. Sitting in my first period class every day watching Zander, listening to Zander, and learning from Zander- it nearly killed me. Gina knew something was wrong but despite pestering me, asking me the same question again and again, I refused to tell her. She may have been my friend but we weren't that close. Besides, I couldn't tell her about Zander even if I wanted to.

Instead I threw myself into my school work, ensuring my homework was complete and my readings were done. When I didn't have homework to distract me I worked on the yearbook, the school newspaper, or finalized details for senior prom. I was in constant communication with the rest of the student council, so much so that they ended up blocking me from the group chat on Friday because they didn't want to think about school on the weekend.

With all the time I spent working, Gina insisted I had time to read the article about Shattered Life, but I was hesitant. Nick and I hadn't spoken since we broke up, what if this article made me hate Nick? What if he said something unforgivable? I still had Nick's number in my phone, would this article make me do something stupid like call him? I didn't want that, but I had to know what he'd said.

With a sigh I opened the magazine and flipped to page seventeen, gazing at the picture of the band at the top of the article. Nick looked as good as ever, the picture clearly photoshopped as there wasn't a single freckle in sight on his face. I took a big breath then proceeded to read.

The first part of the article was about getting to know the band and each member- their name and a little blurb about how they met and formed the band. I was actually bored reading it, until I came across a question about what inspires them to write, and Nick's response left me fuming.

Yeah it's been tough, but inspiration can come from anywhere, you know? When I was writing Come Back To Me all I could think about was my ex. She- she cheated on me, broke my heart. We'd been together for a few years but I guess the pressure got to her. She was younger than me and couldn't take all the attention I was getting. I guess it was too much for her, or something. But breaking up with me may have been the best thing she could have done, since Come Back To Me was the result of it.

The title of the song, Come Back To Me, reflects that you want her back. Is that still the case?

Yeah, you know, I loved her. I still do actually. You don't get over your first love very easily. So, yeah, if she'd have me, I'd take her back. There's a lot of things left unsaid between us, a lot to discuss still.

Do you ever feel guilty about using her name in the song?

[laughter] It was a bold move, I'll admit. But, no, I don't feel guilty about it. She had it coming, you know? Beside's, the song just wouldn't have flowed as nicely if I hadn't.

I slammed the magazine down on the bed, angrily. How dare he blame all of this on me? He was the one who hadn't had time for me. He was the one who cancelled date after date, just to record a damn single. He was the one who ignored me because he was so focused on making a debut album. And to say 'I had it coming' and feel no remorse about using my damn name in the song? Screw him.

I picked up my phone and sent Gina a quick message.

Nick is a bastard. She replied back quickly with a laughing face emoji and I rolled my eyes, turning to lay down on the bed. I shouldn't have read it. I've spent weeks ignoring articles and news stories, avoiding social media as much as I could so I didn't have to hear about Nick and the band. However I let a moment of weakness ruin all of that.

I pushed the magazine aside, watching it fall to the ground in a crumpled pile as I closed my eyes and tried to sleep.

I was driving home from my grandmother's nursing home on Saturday and thought I'd go to Coffee Cafe for a coffee before returning home. I sat in the lineup for the drive thru, tapping my fingers on my steering wheel as I waited for the car in front of me to finish their order. Out of the corner of my eye I saw him, walking up to the door. He looked just as good as he had the last time I'd seen him outside of school. I sat up straighter, my foot nearly slipping off the gas pedal as I stared at him going into the building. He was alone, thankfully, and for a split second I considered exiting the drive thru and entering the building so I could see him, face to face, outside of the classroom. A moment later I realized that'd be a big mistake. Zander wouldn't want to see me, beside's he was probably meeting someone, inside Coffee Cafe, just as we once had.

With a sad sigh I drove forwards to give my order to the speaker, and as I got to the window I could see Zander talking to the barista at the counter. "That'll be three eighty four," the woman asked leaning out of the window.

"Has he paid for his order yet?" I asked glancing past her at Zander.

"Who?" she asked, looking confused.

"The guy at the counter."

She lifted an eyebrow as she turned to look back and shook her head. "I think he's just ordering now."

"Here." I passed an additional five dollars through the window at her. She took it, looking confused, as she passed me my drink. "Thanks."

I drove away, leaving her holding the money, and parked in a spot at the back of the lot, facing the building. My heart started racing as I sat there, wondering if he'd come out looking for me. But I stayed there for ten minutes, sipping my coffee, and Zander never appeared. I could see him by a window, back to me but still alone, taking sips of his own drink every now and then, and I felt my heart clench in disappointment as I shifted into drive and left. I wasn't sure what I'd been expecting, but it hadn't been this.

Walking into school on Monday was hard. I sat in my car until the warning bell rang, if only to prolong having to sit in Zander's class knowing he'd ignored me the other day. I hadn't even wanted to leave my room yesterday, choosing to sit in the dark and listen to music rather than throwing myself into school work as I had been doing. It was the final nail in the coffin, as they say- the deciding factor, the sign I was looking for that clearly stated Zander was through with me, and it'd hurt.

I considered skipping his class but knew I couldn't ruin my attendance record, not for a boy. But, I thought as I got out of my car and began walking towards the school, he wasn't a boy, he was a man, the man I loved. And he'd rejected me.

"Alessaundra I'm so happy I saw you before you got to class." I looked up from my distracted musings to see Mr Thorn panting as he stood in front of me. "I wanted to talk to you about a few things."

"I have English," I pointed towards the classroom but Mr Thorn waved me off.

"I've already informed Mr Dionne you'll be late. Come, let's go to my office." Curious about what this could be about, I hitched my bag further onto my shoulder and followed Mr Thorn down the hall and around the corner until we reached the office. I could hear Mitch, the guy who was in charge of the announcements, as he read the latest update on our basketball team, apparently they'd won their third game in a row. Mr Thorn opened the door to his office and gestured me in. I sat down, sliding my bag off my back as I did so.

"So, what did you want to talk to me about?" I asked as Mr Thorn lowered himself to his own chair.

"I went over your proposal for prom, everything looks good. I approved the budget and already called to reserve the hall. I'm impressed with everything you and your team came up with."

I smiled, "I'm glad. It was a team effort really, everyone had some really good ideas."

"But the main thing I wanted to discuss with you- I noticed Ms Roberts was the faculty advisor on the yearbook and for the newspaper."

I hesitated, then nodded, "yes, she was a huge help. She always read over and edited everything for me before I published an article on the website or for the paper. She was supposed to approve a few things for the yearbook as well after the break but-." I trailed off shrugging.

"Well I have a solution for you. Mr Dionne has been approved by the board to remain on for Ms Roberts for the remainder of the semester. Despite being new to the field the board feels it is particularly important for the senior class to have stability as they finish out the year, especially as students should be hearing about acceptances any day now."

My heart began to beat hard but I tried to steady it as I slowly said, "Mr Dionne has been fantastic thus far."

"He has, hasn't he." Mr Thorn grinned. "I' m glad you think that, Alessaundra. I've decided he should be involved in some sort of student group and thought that since Ms Roberts was the faculty advisor he can just take her place on the yearbook and newspaper. You would be working closely with him to ensure everything is finalized within the next month in order to get the yearbooks printed in time for graduation. As for the newspaper, Zander- er, I mean, Mr Dionne has history in publication. He was actually highly involved in his university's blog! He was their editor, in fact."

My mouth dropped open slightly, "oh, wow. I had no idea."

"He is a wonderful addition to our school. We're very happy to have him." Mr Thorn beamed. I smiled tightly, my heart beating even faster as I realized exactly what Mr Thorn was saying- Zander and I would be working together.

"Is that everything?" I asked, wanting to get out of there so I could think.

"Yes, of course. Please, return to class."

I got up from my chair and picked up my bag, turning to go. I paused at the door though. "Mr Thorn, does Mr Dionne know about this already?"

"Why yes, I spoke with him this morning."

"And he agreed?"

Mr Thorn looked at me confused, his eyebrows knitting together. "Of course he did. He was thrilled actually."

"Really?" I asked, unable to hide my surprise.

"Why of course Alessaundra. Why wouldn't he have been?"

"No reason," I quickly said, shrugging my bag on to my back and opening the door. "Have a good day Mr Thorn." I rushed out of there quickly and found a deserted bathroom down the hall. Slamming the stall door closed I lowered the toilet seat to sit down, taking a few deep breaths to steady myself. My hands were shaking, and tears had sprung to my eyes. I wasn't sure why I was crying, exactly. Maybe it was because I was confused about what this all meant, or maybe I was scared that the only reason he so readily agreed to this arrangement was because he was able to move on and forget about everything we had together.

I rolled off some toilet paper and wiped my eyes with shaking hands, taking a deep breath to try and calm myself. There was no way I could go to Zander's class, not like this. He'd know something was wrong, and he probably wouldn't care. I started going through my options- I could go to the cafeteria, like many other students who skipped, or maybe I could drive off in my car and grab a coffee, but would I be back in time for my next class? No, I didn't want to risk missing two periods in one day. Instead I decided to go to the print room where the yearbook and newspaper were, I had a lot of work to do, and if Zander was going to be my faculty advisor I should at least prepare something for him to review.

"You weren't in class today."

I paused, my hands resting on the keyboard where I'd been typing, but refused to take my gaze off the computer screen in front of me. I wasn't surprised to hear his voice. I'd spent the remainder of first period in the print lab, as well as my entire lunch hour, and even returned after school. I knew that hiding in the lab, hoping no one would find me, wasn't the answer. But I didn't know what else to do. Of course he found me, though.

"I had a meeting with Mr Thorn." I replied after a moment, as I finally continued typing, changing the title of the front page article.

"A meeting which took all class?"

I still hadn't looked up from the screen. "We had a lot to talk about."

I heard Zander sigh as he closed the door and approached me. "Alessaundra-."

"Save it." I raised my hand to cut him off, finally looking away from the screen in order to look at his face. My breath hitched as I took in his beauty. "Mr Thorn told me you're going to be the faculty advisor supporting me on the yearbook and editing the school paper for me. Impressive resume, by the way. You never mentioned being editor for your university's blog."

"It never came up," Zander mumbled looking embarrassed.

"Not even when I was talking about how I dabbled in blogging?" I raised my eyebrow challengingly, but continued talking before he had a chance to say anything. "It doesn't matter, though. Here's what I need you to review." I picked up a stack of papers and handed them to him. "The paper gets printed tuesday afternoon. We only put out issues once a month now, but still publish stories on the schools website. With phones and technology being as popular as they are now we found it a waste to print school papers every week, since most people only want to read what's posted on the internet."

"Right." Zander held the papers, glancing down at them. "Ali-."

"Just stop, Zander."

He sighed, "Mr. Dionne."

I narrowed my eyes at him, "I refuse to use formalities when it's just the two of us."

"You're being stubborn." He pointed out. "You're acting like a child."

"And you're acting like this meant nothing to you!" I snapped pushing my chair away from the desk and standing up. I turned, raised my arm and pointed a finger at him. "After everything we had, after that night- how can you stand there and act as if I meant nothing to you?"

Zander sighed and set the papers down on the desk. "I have to."

"Why? Why do you need to act like I don't exist?" Tears brimmed my eyes but I refused to wipe them away. I needed him to see how hurt I was.

"I told you, I can't afford to lose this job." Zander pressed his lips together tightly. "This isn't easy for me, Ali."

The tears leaked down my cheek slowly and I raised a finger to wipe it away. "You sure make it seem like it."

He shook his head at me. "I am using every single bit of willpower I have, Ali."

"You're a hell of a lot stronger than me," I sniffled.

"You don't make it easy." I glanced at him to see him smirking. "Saturday, at Coffee Cafe? Buying me coffee from the drive thru?"

I blushed as I lowered my head. "I almost went inside." I admitted.

"You left the baristas very confused." he chuckled.

"I waited for you, you know?" I glanced at him again, brushing a piece of hair behind my ear. "I waited outside to see if you'd come find me."

"I know." I tilted my head, confused. "I was watching you through the reflection in the window. If you hadn't left when you did-." He shook his head. "I was this close to coming out there." He held his thumb and forefinger close together then laughed as my mouth fell open in surprise. "I'm strong, Alessaundra, but I'm not that strong."

I sighed, lowering myself back to my chair. "I miss you Zander."

He reached over for the chair at the desk beside me and pulled it over so he was sitting next to me. "I miss you too," he admitted. "But we can't be together. I would get fired, you could get expelled- I can't allow either of those to happen."

"What if I said I'd choose you over school, any day?" I asked quietly. "What if I wanted to take that chance?"

"You'd be lying." He smiled softly at me. "You're too good a student not to continue your education. Do you have any idea how highly you are looked upon here? Your teachers respect you, your peers respect you- hell, even Mr Thorn respects you."

"My peers think I'm a joke," I mumbled. "I'm sure by now you've heard what they say about me."

He paused and nodded. "Actually, I have; and that's something *you* never told *me* about. How could you forget to mention you dated the lead singer of a band? That there was a song written about you, playing on every radio station in town?"

"It's not something you talk about on a first date." I mumbled. "Usually the topic of ex-boyfriends comes up after a few dates."

He let out a big breath, "I wish you would have told me."

I shook my head as I rolled my eyes, "I never got the chance to."

Zander stood up off his chair and took a few steps over to me until he was standing directly behind me. I could feel his presence and my shoulders stiffened as I anticipated what he was going to do next. After a moment I felt him rest his hand gently on my shoulder, squeezing it slightly. "I'm sorry your peers say such things about you, Ali." I could feel his breath on my neck and it sent shivers down my spine. I licked my lips and opened my mouth, unsure what to say. But before I could get a word out, he continued. "But who cares what they have to say. What matters is what you think about yourself. I've seen the confident woman that you are, and it's-." He stopped for a moment before blurting, "it's the sexiest thing about you."

I swallowed, hard, then turned my head to look in his face. His eyes were steely blue and full of desire, and despite the fact he said we couldn't be together I saw how much he wanted us to be. Zander wanted to be strong, but I made him weak, I could see that now. His willpower, his strength, was wavering as he stood there touching my shoulder and looking into my eyes.

Slowly I stood up, causing his hand to slide off of me as I turned so we were face to face. I took one small step forward so that our bodies were millimeters apart and I could feel his breath intermingingly with mine. I watched his eyes flicker down to my lips as I licked them, saw his Adam's apple jump as he swallowed, and felt his fingers twitch as he restrained himself from reaching out to touch me. I knew he wasn't going to make the first move so I raised my hand and wrapped it around his neck, lowering his face until his lips were right next to mine.

"I don't care about the consequences." I hardly needed to whisper for him to hear me, we were so close. "I don't care about the danger. I'm tired of playing it safe and ignoring my feelings for you." I licked my lips again, my tongue brushing his mouth in the process eliciting a small moan from him. "I love you, Zander. I want to be with you. We will figure this out. We're both two very intelligent people and if we put our heads together we can find a solution to all of this. But only if you want to, Zander. The ball is now in your court. All you have to do is say the word."

I stared into his eyes, willing him to say something, anything that meant he wanted this too. He'd first given me all of the power, when he found out my age, but now the power laid with him. I could almost see his mind spinning through his eyes as he stared at me. I was starting to lose hope, though, as the time went by. It felt like hours, but I knew it had only been seconds, before he growled and pushed my face towards his, causing our mouths to crash in a hungry kiss. I gasped as he lifted me up and onto the desk allowing me to wrap my legs around his waist and he deepened the kiss, thrusting his tongue into my mouth and nibbling on my lower lip. For a moment we both forgot where we were as we got lost in the passion and desire driven kiss, but when my hand knocked something off of the desk we both jumped apart, panting and flushed. My lips felt swollen and sore as I glanced at the ground to see a computer mouse laying there, the batteries rolling away from it.

"That was stupid," Zander said sounding breathless. My heart sank as I took in his words and I hopped down off the desk trying to hide the tears that sprang to my eyes. "We could have been caught." I nodded, bending down to pick up the mouse and batteries and started replacing them. "We'll have to be more careful next time."

I paused, battery in hand, as his words reached my ears and my brain processed what I'd just heard. Slowly I turned around to face him, my eyes shining. "What?"

"I don't think I could stay away from you if I tried, Alessaundra. Do you know how hurt I was when you didn't show up to class today? I thought- thought I'd driven you to drop my class, or transfer, or something crazy like that. All I could think was- 'what if I never see her again?'. That's when I realized that despite the fact that this is extremly dangerous, not to mention stupid- I wanted to try and make it work in some way. I wanted to ask you to wait for me, three months isn't that long a time, right? But that would have been selfish of me to do. When I accepted Mr Thorn's offer to be the faculty advisor I knew it was tempting fate, that being alone in a room with you would be dangerous, but I wanted to take the chance and see what would happen because if we were truly meant to be together, then there was no point in fighting fate.

"But know this, Ali. This isn't going to be easy. We can't be seen together, do you understand that? We can't go out for dinner like a normal couple, we can't go for walks and hikes, we can't even hold hands in public. When we're in class together we need to act like teacher and student, when we pass each other in the halls we need to act like there's nothing going on between us. If I see a student flirting with you I can't punch them in the face, or when someone is talking about you and that damn song I can't defend your honour. Likewise if you see a fellow staff member talking to me you can't go into a jealous rage, you can't act like there is any sort of connection with us. Do you think you can handle that?"

"Yes," I said nodding quickly. "Zander, I can do it. We'll figure it out, we'll make it work."

"And another thing." He slipped his phone out of his pocket and scrolled down until he found my name. He clicked the edit button and deleted A-L-I and I watched as he inputed J-A-D-E instead. "It's better this way."

I nodded in agreement, "Thank you Zander. Really."

Zander reached up and gently placed his hand on my cheek, rubbing slow circles with his thumb. "Like I said, I couldn't stay away from you if I tried. Now, should we get to work?"

I blinked for a moment as I recalled exactly where we were and why we were there. I looked at the desk where Zander had left the papers and nodded at him, gesturing him towards his desk. "Let's get to work."

I hadn't thought that being in class with Zander could be any more difficult, however having officially decided to be secretly together, it made being in close proximity to each other every day that much more challenging. There were far too many times I would spot one of my female peers acting like they didn't understand the assignment just so Zander would lean down to their level. Whenever he read aloud to the class every female in the room was enchanted by his melodic voice. Gina, however, was the worse of all, dropping her pencil repeatedly in class just so she could bend down, showing off her cleavage as she picked it up off the floor.

The week passed by slowly. I anticipated the end of every day if only because Zander and I would get to spend some time alone together in the lab. We'd start off with a room full of students, all working hard to finish the layout for the yearbook or write about the latest in sports. However as soon as the last body left Zander and I would lock the door and take advantage of the rare time we got alone together.

Our relationship wasn't perfect but it worked, for now anyways.

Since we couldn't always be together physically we resorted to phone calls and texts whenever possible. Sometimes these texts came in while I was sitting in my Math class, when he should have been teaching his own class. Or while driving to school in the morning, preparing for the day that awaited us. Other times we'd text each other while laying in bed, after parting ways at school. We always tried to keep our conversations free of anything school related, though, lest someone happen to find them.

Despite all of these conversations I still felt like I didn't know much about him. He refused to talk about his family- the only thing I knew was that his mother had died when he was very young and that he had a brother named Danny who ran the family business. He refused to elaborate on either of those topics, though. I understood, there were some things that would be better left discussed in person, but we never had that chance. I didn't want to tell him about my addict of a brother Karson over text, or discuss how my sister abandoned me when I was eleven during a phone conversation. These were things you could only explain face-to-face, so I tried not to take his lack of sharing personally.

One topic I was more than happy to talk about was my grandmother. Zander thought it was wonderful how my grandmother had stepped up and raised me, and although he'd never met her he was heartbroken over the fact that she was on limited time.

"It's been so hard," I told him on the phone that Friday night as I laid in bed. I'd just finished having a relaxing bath, detoxing after the week we'd had- who knew that keeping a secret like this would be so taxing on the body? "The doctors say she could go any day. I mean, to be fair they've been saying that for two months and she hasn't gone yet. But the fact that it literally could happen at any time- I just hate not knowing."

"She has been a huge part of your life." Zanders smooth voice floated through the speaker of the phone and into my ear, and just hearing it made me relax a little more. "It's completely understandable to feel that way."

"I thought I was going to spiral," I admitted. "The day they told me she had six months to live- Gina had invited me to a party. At that time I wasn't into drinking, really. I'd had the occasional drink or two, but that was the first time I really got drunk."

"Let me guess, vodka?" I could hear the smirk in Zander's voice.

I laughed, "how'd you guess?"

"Just a hunch."

I smiled. "You'd think it would have made me hate the drink, but instead it made me adore it. Anyways," I said after a moment, "I had a crazy night that night. It was around the time Nick and his band were being spotted by some record company and they were playing a lot of gigs and-."

"-and he was too busy to be there for you?" The anger in Zander's voice surprised me. "That's just- inexcusable."

"He had a good reason," I shrugged.

"You should have been his priority, Ali." Zander's voice was firm. "If he truly loved you, he would have told his band that they had to reschedule their gig so he could be there to support you through that difficult time. That's what I would have done. I would have dropped everything to be there for you. Everything."

Flutters erupted in my stomach at his words and I swallowed hard, shifting on the bed until I was in a more comfortable position. I switched my phone to my other ear, "you have no idea what that means to me Zander."

"Have you seen your grandmother recently?" Zander asked quietly. "How is she doing?"

"I'm planning on visiting her in the morning." I replied. "I try to visit her every weekend when possible. Some days are good, some are rough. There are times she can't even get out of bed, and those are the hardest for me. Seeing her so frail, after knowing her to be so strong- it just seems wrong."

"I'm so sorry," Zander sighed. "You have no idea how badly I want to hold you right now."

"I appreciate that, but I'm okay. Really."

"I promise we'll think of something, Ali. Some way we can be together, without having to hide." The sadness was evident in his voice and it made my heart clench. This entire week we'd had to pretend we weren't together and at times, I'll admit, I'd wondered if what we'd been doing was a mistake. But hearing the honesty in Zander's words, I knew that despite the fact it was challenging, despite the fact we'd be tested trying to make this work, what we had was real and worth it.

As we disconnected the call and I snuggled into bed I was left with the feeling of hope- hope that Zander was right and that we'd find a solution to all of our problems.

CHAPTER 7

My grandmother was in the greenhouse when I arrived at the nursing home, which could only mean one thing- she was having a really good day. When my grandmother lived on her own and was capable of doing things without assistance she had loved to garden. I could remember walking out the front door and smelling flowers- roses, peonies, and honeysuckles to name a few. My grandmother always said that 'a flower made the world a little more beautiful' and she strived to make the world a more beautiful place.

Our house was the brightest, most colourful, and loveliest place on the street. Unfortunately, since moving out and leaving the flowers behind, a lot of those blossoms have withered and died. I did visit her house frequently, allowing a cleaner access to it once a month to keep the place somewhat tidy lest my father show up, but I'll admit to neglecting the plants- gardening was her forte, not mine.

"Ali, my darling." My grandmother's voice sounded so weak- the lung cancer had been harsh on her body affecting everything from her breathing, to her voice box, and even her digestive system. I could see the wires from her oxygen tank hanging from her nose as she extended her arms out to me for a hug. "How was school this week?"

I hesitated- I'd always been fairly open with my grandmother. She's been the only constant in my life, having lost everyone else in it. While Nick and I dated I confided in her and she always seemed to know exactly what to say. When I cheated on Nick, my grandmother was the first one I told and it was she who convinced me to stop and really think about our relationship; if it hadn't been for her I may not have come clean about what I'd done and ended things with him. "School was good," I finally said. "Busy. We printed this month's paper, and need to finalize the yearbook soon so that the printers have time to finish them before the end of the year."

Grandma studied my face closely, "that's wonderful to hear, but there's something you aren't telling me."

I sighed. I should have expected she'd know I was hiding something, grandma could read me like no other. "There is something," I paused and looked around the greenhouse. There was a nurse sitting in a chair by the door, scrolling on her phone- grandma always had a nurse close by in case something happened- but we were otherwise alone. I lowered my voice so the nurse wouldn't hear me and said, "you know how Nick and I broke up."

"Yes," my grandma nodded, raising her hand to her tubes and pushing them slightly in her nose before taking a deep breath, inhaling some oxygen.

"Well, I may have already met someone new."

"Oh?" Grandma replied with a raise of her eyebrows.

"An- an older someone." I confessed pulling a stool over to sit on it. I folded my hands in my lap. "A much older someone."

"How much older?" Grandma asked in a calm voice.

"Six years."

"Alessaundra," my grandma said, sucking in a breath.

I quickly raised my hand to cut her off before she could say anything else. "I know, grandma, I know. The age gap is sort of intense- right now. But in two, three years it's not going to be that big of a deal."

Grandma took another large breath of oxygen, "how did

you meet this young man?"

"At Novella. Glenda had no idea," I quickly added. "So don't go calling her and complaining!"

Grandma chuckled, "you know me too well, darling."

"And you know *me* too well too. You know that I wouldn't be with someone that much older unless I loved them."

"How long have you known him Ali?" Grandma asked curiously.

"Not very long," I admitted, "but he makes me feel- special. I do love him grandma."

"And how does he feel about you?"

I opened my mouth to say he loved me too, then realized he hadn't actually said it to me yet. "I think he feels the same way, he just hasn't told me yet."

"Be careful," grandma said, reaching over to pat my hand endearingly. "Love can make us do some crazy things sometimes."

"I am being careful, grandma." I wanted to tell her more about Zander, but I couldn't risk the nurse overhearing. Instead I squeezed grandma's hand gently, "I promise."

Grandma smiled at me before glancing at her nurse. "Carol? I think it's time for some tea, what say you, Ali?"

I nodded as the nurse stood up and brought grandma's walker over to her. "Tea sounds wonderful."

I followed grandma out of the greenhouse and across the lawn. As we walked grandma started coughing and my heart tightened in my chest as we stopped, waiting for her to recover. "Are you okay grandma?" I asked worriedly. The nurse handed grandma a tissue which she used to wipe her mouth with, coming away with specks of blood.

"I'm dying Alessaundra," grandma rasped out. "It's no secret."

"You're coughing up blood again," I said panicked, staring at the rust stained tissue.

"We should get you to the on-site doctor," Carol, the

nurse, quickly added. "You know what he said and-."

"No, no, no," grandma wheezed. "Ali is here. I want to spend time with my granddaughter while I still have the chance."

"Grandma, if the doctor wants you to go in-."

"No, Ali," Grandma pushed her tubes in and inhaled deeply again. "We already know I'm dying. What if today is my last day with you? Would you not feel remorse for sending me off to the doctor rather than having tea with me?"

"Don't say that grandma," I pleaded as my heart clenched and tears sprung to my eyes.

"I'm not seeing the doctor," my stubborn grandmother insisted. "Take me to the dining room. We're going to have a cup of tea."

Carol glanced at me but I sighed and shook my head. "All right," I said. "Whatever you say, grandma."

I lit a cigarette as I pulled up to my grandmother's house, then sat in my car staring at the stick of tobacco smoldering in my hand. How could I continue to smoke these deathsticks knowing they can cause lung cancer and make a person cough up blood? Regardless of what I knew I was addicted to the things and brought the tip to my mouth, inhaling deeply before blowing out a cloud of smoke. Through the smoke my eyes landed on one of grandma's old garden boxes, empty and muddy. Amazingly the month had gone by without any more snow, leaving the ground wet and mucky from the thaw. I opened my car door, dropped my cigarette butt on the ground, and approached the house.

Anxiety overcame me as I stood on the walkway staring up at the front door. Although my grandmother had given me a good life in this house I was constantly reminded of the horrors I experienced within. My parents had been living with my grandmother when my mother was pregnant with me. They'd been saving up for a new place, hoping that by the time I was born they'd have enough put aside for a house to suit a family of five. Then my mother died in childbirth from a postpartum hemorrhage- she never even got to hold me- and my father fell into such a serious depression that he turned to substances to cope, quickly becoming addicted. My grandmother had to take over the role of caregiver, while simultaneously watching her son destroy his life. Eventually she kicked him out of the house, not wanting my brother Karson or my sister Monica to see him in the state he was in. She was granted custody of the three of us and my father was forgotten about- at least in the eyes of the law. However, I could never forget about him. I grew up wondering why my father only came around a few times a year, and why I was raised by my grandmother when the rest of my peers had moms and dads, and as I got older I started wondering why my father didn't love me as much as the substances he so relied on.

 My heart stopped racing and slowed to a normal beat and I was able to walk up to the house and sit down on the front steps. My father was the only other person with keys to the house, but he rarely came here. It'd been over a year since I last saw him, he came to visit when grandma first got sick and disappeared soon after she was diagnosed with cancer. I had no idea where he was- he could be in jail, checked into a rehab centre, or dead for all I knew.

 I lit a second cigarette, then a third as I sat on the steps, staring out at the street. The house was located in a quiet neighborhood and as far as I was aware the crime rate was low here. I desperately wished I could live here, that the judge had allowed me to remain in this house, instead of sending me off to Aunt Patty's. It would have made things much easier.

 I jumped as my phone rang, digging it out of my jacket pocket. My heart leapt when I saw Zander's name on the screen and I quickly swiped to answer the call. "Hi," I breathed squashing my cigarette with my foot. I exhaled the remainder of the smoke in my mouth.

 "Hi," Zander replied in that smooth voice I loved so much. "How are you?"

"I-." I swallowed, crossing my legs over each other as I stretched out on the steps. "I'm okay."

"Are you sure?" Zander asked. I could hear the concern in his voice.

"Yeah," I shrugged. "I mean- I just came from visiting my grandmother and- well, I don't think she's doing very well."

"What do you mean?" Zander asked.

I sighed, "she started coughing up blood, Zander, and then she refused to see the doctor. I'm scared-" I swallowed, feeling a lump in my throat. "I'm scared she doesn't have much time left."

"Ali," Zander breathed. "I am- so sorry."

The sympathy was clear in his voice and it caused tears to spring to my eyes as I realized how much Zander truly cared about my grandmother, despite the fact he'd never met her. "I don't know what to do, Zander. If I lose her I-."

"You shouldn't be alone right now," Zander stated. "You need to be with someone."

"Like who?" I asked sniffling as a tear leaked from my eye. I reached up to wipe it away as I adjusted myself on the steps; the stone was getting cold and uncomfortable after sitting for so long.

"I-" Zander stopped and I sucked in a breath, holding it in as I waited for him to speak. Surely he didn't mean-. "Me." He finally said firmly. "You need to be with me."

"But how?" I whispered, more tears leaking from my eyes.

"I have somewhere we can go," he stated. "For today, at least. Do you think you can meet me at *The Golden Daylight*? I know it's risky but-."

"I'll be there," I quickly said, interrupting him. "Even if I see someone, they won't know I'm meeting you there and-."

"We won't be staying here," Zander said talking over me, causing my words to come to a halt. "I will inform the valet that you are coming and they will take your car and park it for you. We'll be taking my truck and leaving town."

This time I hesitated, thoughts spinning through my head- where would we be going, how far away, when would we be coming back? "Leaving town?" I finally asked wearily. "What does that mean exactly?"

Rather than answer my question Zander asked, "do you trust me?"

This time I didn't hesitate. "Of course I do."

"Then trust me with this. We won't be gone long, Ali, a few hours at most. I think you just need some time away. Is that alright with you?"

I licked my lips and nodded as I exhaled a large breath, stood up from the steps, and headed for my car. "I'll be there in twenty minutes."

"I should clarify," Zander said as we drove out of Baysin, past the highway on-ramp, and out of city limits. "When I said 'out of town' I didn't mean I was taking you far."

I glanced at him, taking my eyes off of the passing field out the window. The sun was bright as we drove and I was wishing I had my sunglasses. "Where are we going exactly?"

"Have you spent much time outside of Baysin, Ali?"

I shook my head and turned back to look out the window. "We didn't exactly have the time or the money to travel. Grandma worked hard to support us, she worked three different jobs, constantly leaving me with Glenda when she had to. The two of them connected and became pretty good friends because of me."

Zander chuckled, "I remember you telling me the story." His face then sobered. "Outside of Baysin there are many small towns. A lot of them declare themselves as part of the Baysin community due to their close proximity, however there are a few who stand alone."

I turned back to look at him, "I never really thought about what was beyond the city limits," I admitted.

"Most don't," Zander stated. "Which, believe it or not, has its advantages."

I scrunch my eyebrows together, "what do you mean?"

Zander smiled softly as he shook his head, hitting the blinker and turning left onto a gravel road. "Nothing." I opened my mouth to press him on it but he continued talking before I could get a word out. "Would you believe me if I told you I grew up only thirty minutes away from Baysin?"

My mouth dropped open, "Are you serious?" I breathed.

"Riverton is a very small community outside of Baysin's city limits. We're so small, in fact, we don't even have a police department- the closest OPP station is about fifteen miles down the road, but they don't regularly get themselves involved with us."

"Must be a pretty quiet town," I observed as Zander took another turn. He didn't say anything as we passed a sign that said **Welcome to Riverton**. We drove so quickly I couldn't make out what the symbol that was painted under the sign read, but I was intrigued by it. "You guys have a logo or something?"

"Something like that," Zander mumbled. I looked over at him but he was staring straight ahead at the road. I decided not to press him on it as I leaned back further in my seat.

"So what are we doing here?" I asked. "Are you finally going to introduce me to your brother?"

"No." The word was said so firmly it made my eyes widen slightly. "He's not around this weekend."

"So why are we here?" I was a little hurt. Why didn't he want me to meet his brother? Zander had once told me he wasn't 'good' but I still didn't know what that meant.

"I feel like you need to relax a little bit," Zander finally said, hitting his blinker again. I looked to see where we were turning and spotted a sign that read **Horse Shoes**, underneath was something else but I couldn't make it out but I did spot the same symbol that had been on the Welcome sign, now able to make out the circle and the R that was centered within it. The driveway was lined with trees as we drove down it, until we passed a thick treeline which opened up to three barns, an old farmhouse, and countless horses in the open field. I turned to look at Zander, my mouth hanging wide open. "I was hoping you'd join me on a trail ride, horseback style. You wouldn't believe how calming horses can be."

I didn't know what to say. Zander parked his truck and swung open his door, coming around to my side to help me out. It was late afternoon, approaching dinner time now, and the March sun was shining on my face, a breeze blowing across the field- I could smell hay, fresh air, and manure- as I stepped out of the truck.

"This- this is spectacular Zander," I breathed as my eyes took in everything around me. I turned on the spot, looking at the old brick farmhouse with the wrap around porch, across from it was an open field where I could see at least four horses standing around; there were two barns, one large and one smaller- inside the large barn I could see the stables, while the smaller barn's doors were closed. I spotted the third barn tucked away behind the house, but couldn't make out what was in there as we were too far away.

Finally I turned back to look at Zander who was watching me anxiously as if waiting for my reaction. I jumped, throwing my arms around him and holding his body close. My hands grasped his face and I brought my lips to his, kissing him softly, until a voice interrupted us.

"Since when does The Professor participate in PDA?"

I felt Zander smile, his lips still on mine, before slowly moving away from me, turning his body towards the female voice that had spoken, but keeping his arm wrapped around my waist, holding me close. "As pleasant as ever today, eh, Scarlet?"

I moved my head to the side, feeling suddenly jealous at the easy banter Zander was giving to this unknown woman. When I saw her, I almost stopped breathing- she was beautiful. She had blonde pin-straight hair, bright blue eyes, and a slim figure. I spotted the cowboy boots on her feet, her jeans tucked into them, wearing a blue and white plaid button-up shirt, the waist also tucked in. But when she saw me looking at her there was no jealousy on her face. There was, however, suspicion.

"Just trying to keep things interesting since everyone's gone today. Who's this?" she added nodding towards me.

I flinched, surprised at her tone, and glanced at Zander to see if he'd say anything.

"This is Jade." My eyes widened slightly but he didn't seem to notice. "Jade," he turned to me, raising a hand to gesture at the woman. "This is Scarlet. She's- like a sister to me."

"Sister?" I asked, finally opening my mouth to speak. I gave her a curious look. "Are you Danny's wife, or something?"

Zander and Scarlet turned to look at each other for a second before they both broke out in laughter. I didn't know why what I said was so funny, but clearly it had been something neither of them expected to hear. Zander reached over to hold his truck as he bent over laughing, while Scarlet raised a hand to her eye to wipe a tear away. "That-," Scarlet panted as she finally started to get some control of herself. "Oh God, that's a good one."

"I don't-." I glanced at Zander, still confused, and he stood back up, a smile on his face. "I don't get what's so funny."

"Danny and Scarlet hate each other," Zander finally said, his smile wide.

"But-."

"It's a long story," Scarlet replied with a wave of her hand.

"One we don't need to get into," Zander quickly added, sending Scarlet a look. I couldn't decipher what the look meant but she could, and for some reason that made me feel jealous again.

"So what brings you out here today, then?" Scarlet asked, placing her hands in the back pockets of her jeans. "I didn't expect to see anyone."

"Which is exactly why we're here." Zander glanced towards the barn. "I was hoping to take Jade, here, on a little trail ride. Maybe watch the sunset over the lake? We'd be gone by ten, at the latest."

"You two are going to need to eat something when you get back then. Guess we should get some dinner started," Scarlet stated.

"Oh, no Scar, you don't have to-."

"Hush," Scarlet said tapping his arm endearingly. "It's my job."

"It doesn't have to be," Zander said sternly. "I've told you, repeatedly, and-."

"-and I told you no." I felt as if I didn't exist as the two of them started talking. Scarlet lowered her voice. "You know what would happen to me if I-."

"Nothing would happen," Zander insisited. "I'd make sure of it."

"I won't let you risk it, Zander."

Zander bit his lip, irritated. "Scarlet-."

"Jade," Scarlet said in a louder voice, interrupting him as she turned to me. "You can't ride in those things." I squinted, confused to what she meant, so she nodded her head at my feet. "As nice as those boots are they will have no support in the stirrups of a saddle. Why don't I fetch you a pair of my boots? Trust me," she continued when I opened my mouth to protest, "You need a sturdy pair of boots."

I closed my mouth and nodded, "okay." Scarlet smiled at me, sent Zander a look I didn't fully understand, then turned to go into the house leaving the two of us alone.

"This way," Zander guided me towards the barn, his arm still around my waist.

"How long have you known Scarlet?" I asked quietly, stepping inside. The barn smelt much like outside- hay and manure but with the smell of old wood mixed in. The ground was soft and I saw the floor was littered with hay.

"A while," Zander shrugged. "Our dads were- friends. We grew up together."

"I see," I mumbled looking into the various stalls. They were all empty and I assumed the horses were all out getting some fresh air in the field.

Zander sighed, "Scarlet and I are practically family, Ali. There's nothing to worry about, I promise."

"You called me Jade." Zander turned to look at me, confused. "Back there with Scarlet. You introduced me as Jade. Why-?"

Zander let a big breath out, shaking his head. "I'm sorry. I just-."

"And she called you a professor." I added leaning against a door to one of the stables, kicking my foot nervously back and forth, eyes gazing downward.

Zander raised his eyebrows, "you caught on to that, huh?"

"What's going on here Zander?" I asked, raising my head to look directly at him.

"What do you mean?" he asked, trying to sound nonchalant, but I could detect the hesitancy he hid in his voice.

I shook my head, "I feel like there's something you're hiding from me but I just can't figure out what it is." Zander opened his mouth but I stopped him, raising my hand. "You also just *seem* different here. I can't put my finger on how though."

Zander let out another large breath and glanced around the inside of the barn. He was quiet for several moments until he finally said, "there's a lot about me you don't know, Ali, and I'm not going to lie to you- I don't *want* you to know about any of it."

That hurt. I felt my eyes sting a little but blinked rapidly to stop any tears from forming. "Why?"

Zander shook his head firmly. "No. We're not going to get into it. Not now."

"Why Zander?" I demanded. "What aren't you telling me?"

Zander and I heard the footsteps at the same time, both turning to look at the door where now Scarlet stood, a little awkwardly, holding a pair of old worn black cowboy boots. "I can come back," she said quietly.

"No," Zander stated, sighing. "Come on in, Scar."

"Your feet look to be about the same size as mine." Scarlet handed the boots to me and I took them, feeling a little uncomfortable. "They should fit you nicely."

"Thanks," I mumbled holding the boots in my hands.

"Try them on." Scarlet gestured to a bench down the wall outside one of the stables. Fully aware they were both watching me I walked over to the bench, sat down, and began to remove my comfortable yet stylish brown boots. I heard whispering between Zander and Scarlet as I did this, slipping on the black cowboy boots and feeling the firm leather material hugging my calves. I glanced up at them, saw Zander's annoyed expression, and looked back down, pretending to adjust the fit.

"-just leave it, Scar," Zander hissed.

"Zander-." I looked up, saw Zander wave his hand at her and Scarlet sigh, looking sad. Then she saw I'd finished with the boots and forced a smile to her face. "Those look great on you! How do they feel?"

"Good," I shrugged standing up. The boots felt stiff, yet comfortable.

"You can keep them, if you'd like." Scarlet offered.

"Oh no, I couldn't," I waved my hands in protest but Zander stepped in.

"Keep them. You never know when you'll need them next."

I glanced at Zander, curiously. "Really?"

"Keep them." He repeated firmly.

"Okay," I glanced back at Scarlet. "Thank you."

"Don't mention it, I have about a dozen pairs. I should go start dinner," she added looking back towards Zander. "You know where everything is. The thaw has left the far field very mucky, we've been detouring through the pasture instead. The river has been running fast too, so I'd stay clear of that as well."

"But the route to the lake is okay?" Zander asked.

"It should be fine."

Zander nodded and Scarlet waved her hand in farewell before turning and walking away. We watched her cross the driveway until she reached the front door and walked inside. Zander then turned to me and gestured towards the other end of the barn. "After you."

"I've had Rocky since he was a foal. His mother was, unfortunately, shot-." I sucked in a breath as my body bumped up and down in the saddle. "Yeah it was bad," Zander agreed, nodding. "Rocky was left defenseless. I bottle fed him, nurtured him- kept him safe."

"You basically raised him," I said glancing at the beautiful grey horse that Zander was riding on, which I recognized as the horse from the photo on his phone.

Zander chuckled, "my brother thought I was a wuss for caring so much about him, but I couldn't just leave him like that."

"How old is he?" I asked. "Rocky," I clarified.

"Fifteen."

"You were only eight when this happened?" I asked with a raise of my eyebrows. Zander turned Rocky to the left and I copied his movements, yanking my reins slightly in order to get Marbles, the brown horse I was sitting on, to follow. "You were just a kid, Zander."

"There was no such thing as childhood in my family Ali," Zander mumbled as he pulled back on his reins, bringing Rocky to a stop. "After my mother died- we all had to grow up fast."

"I know the feeling."

"We had two very different childhoods," Zander disagreed.

"Neither one of us had the childhood we should have had though." I argued.

Zander swung his leg over the saddle and I watched as he slid down effortlessly. He walked over to Marbles and looked up at me. Rather than respond to my statement he reached a hand out. "Need some help getting down?" I glanced at the distance from the saddle to the ground and nodded. "All you need to do is swing your leg over and slide down."

"Is that all?" I asked sarcastically.

Zander chuckled, "trust me, it's easy. I'll catch you."

I sighed and shook my head but tried to follow his instructions. As I pushed myself to slide off the horse I stumbled and fell into Zander- rather than catch me we both fell to the ground. Mud instantly covered both of us and I groaned, feeling sore from the impact, as Zander wrapped his arms around me. "Sorry," I whispered. I went to move off of him when I felt his arms tighten, holding me even closer.

"I'm not," he growled. My eyes widened in surprise as Zander moved one arm slowly until it was resting behind my neck, then he carefully, yet forcefully, brought my face down towards his until our lips met in a heated kiss. Despite the fact we'd stolen a few kisses over the past week we hadn't really had the chance to be completely alone together. Feeling Zander's body pressed against mine excited me and I felt desire stir within, my hands clutching his back tightly as I opened my mouth to deepen the kiss.

I jumped as one of the horses snorted, whipping my head around and my heart hammering in my chest. I'd almost forgotten they were there. Zander laughed at me and I smiled embarrassed. The sky was starting to change colours, a golden light spreading across the horizon, but in the distance I could see the colours start to morph and change, fading into oranges, reds, and pinks. Zander took my hand and led me a little away from the horses until we stood on a wooden dock overlooking a large lake. Directly across from us we had a clear view of the sunset.

"Wow." The word escaped my mouth in a hushed voice. "This is- beautiful."

"Not as beautiful as you are." I turned away from the setting sun to look at Zander as he took a step closer to me. "Listen, Ali-." He stopped and took a breath, letting it out in a big huff. I shivered, now that the sun was starting to set, the cool night air was setting in and my damp clothes were making me cold. "The reason Scarlet called me The Professor- the reason I introduced you as Jade- well, everyone around here has a nickname. It's- better- for you if you have one too."

"Why?" I asked. "Why can't I just be Ali?"

Zander paused, looking like he was searching for the right words. Finally he shook his head. "It's complicated."

"Complicated?" I asked in a flat voice.

"Yes."

"That's such a bullshit answer." I stated growing angry. He turned to me in surprise at my aggressive tone. "Zander you drag me to this place outside of town, introduce me to some random woman I'd never heard you talk about despite the fact you claim to have known her since you were kids, give me a nickname instead of using my real name- and you won't even tell me why? What are you hiding?"

The sky was now fading from its golden colours as the sun continued to sink lower, pink turning to purple and navy blue. "Do you remember when I told you I didn't want to get you involved in my problems, Ali?"

"That doesn't answer my question," I mumbled irritated, crossing my arms and turning away from him.

Zander sighed and reached over, pulling my arms loose. He took my hand in his and squeezed it gently. "I love you Alessaundra."

I froze, my body stiffening as the words he said reached my ears. Slowly I turned my head to look at him, sure I'd heard him wrong. "What?"

"I love you." He repeated. "It's because I love you that I've done all of this today. Ali, I want you to know where I come from, I want you to meet the people I care about, and I want them to know *you*. But there's a lot of really complicated things in my life that I'm not ready to expose you to. Not yet. Maybe not ever."

"But why?" I whispered. "Do you not trust me, or-."

"Of course I trust you," Zander breathed squeezing my hand harder. "It's because I don't want you to get hurt!" He stopped, biting his lip for a moment before sighing deeply and continuing, "maybe one day I can explain everything to you. But today is not that day." He pulled me in so he could kiss my forehead, wrapping his arms around me in an embrace. His body heat felt warm as I shivered again, this time more intensely. "Are you cold?" he asked, suddenly worried.

"A little," I admitted. "I didn't expect the weather to change so much once the sun set."

We both glanced over at the lake where the sun had officially disappeared, the navy sky now black. Glancing up I saw millions of stars stretched across the darkness. In Baysin there were so many city lights we never got to see the beauty of the night sky. "It's amazing."

"We should head back," Zander said after a moment. I nodded; Zander led us towards Rocky and Marbles, helping me up into my saddle. Once on his own horse he clicked his tongue, causing Rocky to start to walk. I waited a moment as Zander's silhouette began to disappear into the shadows, thinking- what was Zander hiding? What did he mean he didn't want me to get hurt? Why couldn't he tell me what was going on? With a frustrated sigh I kicked my heels gently, encouraging Marbles to walk as I followed him back to Horse Shoes.

CHAPTER 8

Zander had a few flashlights hanging from his saddle, lighting up the path, as we made our way back to Horse Shoes. It was dark when we arrived at the barn and Zander slid down off of Rocky, leading him with the reins into a stall before coming back to Marbles and I. He reached his hand up towards me, lending me assistance to swing my leg over the saddle and slip down without falling this time. Once down he grabbed hold of Marbles' reins and brought her to her stable as well.

"I need to find someone to give them their cool down." Zander stated as he closed the stall door. "Are you hungry? Scarlet should have dinner ready."

My stomach growled and I nodded. " But I don't want to impose."

"You aren't," Zander mumbled looking around the barn. "Why don't you go ahead inside? I'll find one of the stable hands to take care of the horses."

"I can help."

Zander looked at me and hesitated before shaking his head, "no. We have people to do that, it's what they're paid to do."

"I don't mind," I insisted, taking a step forward.

"I said no, Ali."

I blinked, surprised at the tone he suddenly used with

me. It was firm, strict, and demanding. "Okay," I mumbled in a quiet voice.

Zander sighed, "I'm sorry." He walked over to me and pulled me in for a gentle hug. "I didn't mean-," he shook his head and repeated, "I'm sorry."

I nodded into his chest and he held me tighter, then kissed the top of my head. I raised my arms, wrapping them around him as well and felt him relax as we stood together in the glow of the barn lights. Suddenly I felt Zander's body go rigid as his muscles tensed, his arms now tight around me. "Zander, what-." I stopped, hearing the rumble of what could only be a motorcycle- perhaps even multiple bikes. I glanced up at Zander's face, which was turned towards the driveway. It was difficult to make out his expression in the dark but from what I could see he was suddenly angry. "What's wrong?"

"Alessaundra I need you to get inside. Now."

"Why?" I asked quizzically, watching as the headlights from the motorcycles began to light up the parking lot. My mouth fell open as the bikes continued to roll in until I lost count of how many there were. Zander swore as the bike engines seized and everything became quiet.

"Go inside." Zander repeated without looking at me as he started to take a few steps away.

"Zander?" I called questioningly.

"Zander?" This time it wasn't me who called his name, but Scarlet, emerging from the house.

"Take her inside!" he roared pointing towards me, but still not looking at me, as his pace got faster and he strolled forwards. One of the guys took his helmet off and stood up, getting off his bike just as Zander reached him.

"Wasn't expecting to see you here," he said. Zander didn't say a word, rather lifted his arm and swung, punching the guy in the face. I gasped as the guy's face turned from the impact. He spat, blood flying out of his mouth, before turning to look back at Zander as if nothing had happened. "Feel better?"

"What the fuck are you doing here, Danny?" Zander spat. My mouth dropped open, realizing that this was Zander's brother- but who were the other guys, why were they here, and why were they dressed the way they were? My eyes slowly took in the leather jackets each of the men wore and my mind slowly began to put the pieces together, just as Scarlet reached my side.

"C'mon Jade," she said urgently, tugging on my arm. "You need to go inside."

"I'm not going anywhere," I stated firmly, wrenching my arm from her grasp. "What's going on?" Scarlet didn't answer, just reached out to try and grab me again. "Get off of me!" I roared, moving away from her and towards Zander, needing to know what was happening. If Scarlet wasn't going to tell me I'd find out myself.

"Jade, don't-" Scarlet yelled then swore as I ignored her and kept walking forwards.

Zander's back was to me but his brother, Danny, looked over at me as I approached. My stomach clenched as I started wondering if this was a good idea, and I stopped a few feet away but close enough to see and hear everything. "Who's this?" He nodded his head at me, his face emotionless.

I could see Zander's shoulders tense and he slowly turned to look back. He sent me a quick apologetic look before turning back to his brother and growling, "She's mine."

Danny smirked and took a step towards me, causing Zander to growl once more. "She got a name?"

"One that doesn't concern you," Zander stated, taking a threatening step forward. "Back off, Danny."

Danny chuckled low in his throat and took a few more steps, knocking against Zander's shoulder as he passed. My heart started racing as I took two small steps back. "What's your name sweetheart?" he whispered, his eyes scanning up and down my body, ending on my face. I felt a shiver go down my spine as he scrutinized me.

"I-," I glanced at Zander who sighed and nodded slightly

at me in return. I shivered as a cold wind blew. "Jade."

"And how do you know The Professor, here, Jade?"

I opened my mouth to answer but Zander stepped in before I could get a word out. "That's irrelevant Danny." He strolled over, knocking Danny's shoulder in the process, and wrapped his arm around me possessively.

"She could be a spy," Danny stated firmly. "Or a cop. How do we know we can trust her?"

"Because I trust her."

Danny laughed humorlessly, "your judgement isn't very reliable these days, now, is it? Not since you stepped away from this Club."

I started, glancing up at Zander for confirmation about that statement but he wasn't looking at me, his eyes were fixed on Danny and they were narrowed into thin slits. "She has nothing to do with this, Danny. Just let her go."

Danny raised his finger threateningly, "you brought her here, Zander! You're claiming her as yours! That speaks for itself, Professor. Whether you want her to be or not, you now made her part of this. Or is she just a Backwarmer to you?" The smile Danny gave Zander was meant to taunt him, and it worked as Zander tensed again.

"She's not," he hissed out, taking a single step forward without letting go of me. "I didn't bring her here for a good time, she's not one to be passed around to the next willing member! If anyone touches her I'll kill them myself."

Danny grinned, "that's the brother I remember."

"Fuck you, Danny." Zander spat.

"So if she's not a backwarmer, what is she?" Danny asked, ignoring his brother's anger. Everyone, including me, turned to stare at Zander and I saw his Adam's apple jump as he swallowed hard.

"She's my girlfriend." His words were clear, no hesitation as he said them, and I found myself smiling despite the fact I was surrounded by what was clearly a bike gang- we'd never truly defined our relationship in terms before but now

Zander had. He held me a little tighter as if he knew how I was feeling and tried to communicate without the use of words that he, too, was pleased with this next step in our relationship even if the circumstances weren't ideal. I felt a little warmer all of a sudden.

"Girlfriend." The smile quickly left my face as I looked over at Danny and began to shiver again. "So she already knows about all of this?"

"Leave her out of it." Zander's pleasure didn't last long as he quickly became defensive again, shoving me behind him. I stumbled but retained my balance. "I'm leaving, Danny. I'm taking her home. Nothing you say is going to stop that." He reached back for my hand and grabbed it, turning to lead us towards his truck. Danny's next words stopped him in his tracks.

"We have Kovach." Zander stood there, frozen, as I glanced back between the two of them. I had no idea who or what Kovach was, but clearly it meant something to Zander. "The Kovach. Eric Kovach. He's in the trailer. Six Inch is with him- but he's not doing too well."

Zander finally turned around to look at Danny, his face pale. "What happened?"

"He was stabbed." My eyes widened as Zander winced. When Danny spoke next it was in a demanding and carrying voice. "Open the door!" Zander and I turned to see the backdoor of a horse trailer, one I hadn't noticed had pulled in alongside the many motorcycles, lower to the ground revealing what was inside. Two of the men grabbed flashlights and shone them in and I nearly screamed when I saw all the blood on the ground. Zander, though, let go of my hand and walked forwards, seeming to forget about me as he stood directly in front of the open door.

"What happened?" he demanded in a voice I'd never heard him use before- it was full of authority and leadership, much different even then the voice he used as a teacher giving a lecture.

"We called upon The Satan's to lend a hand in tracking

him down," Danny stated. "We thought it would take all weekend, but we found him within hours. However, when we tried to capture him things went south and Six Inch, here, took the brunt of it."

The man inside the trailer, Six Inch, hissed in pain. "'S all right," he groaned. "It's just a scratch."

"You need stitches, man," Zander muttered, clapping him on the shoulder. "Scarlet will take good care of you. Get him inside," he ordered looking at two men beside the trailer who responded instantly, rushing inside and helping Six Inch up. With him out of the way I could finally see the bound man in the back, blood oozing from his head, rope tied around his wrists and fabric around his mouth. He wasn't moving. "Is he dead?" Zander asked the question I was thinking.

"No- not yet," Danny added. I gasped and stepped backwards away from the gathered crowd, suddenly feeling afraid as I realized what Danny was implying: they wanted to kill this bound and helpless man.

Zander whipped his head around and looked at me, recognition dawning as he realized I was still there. I watched as a hundred emotions crossed his features, finally settling on one of determination as he yelled out, "Vetta!"

A young woman with auburn hair stepped away from the crowd. She wasn't wearing a leather jacket, like the men were, but she did wear cowboy boots like Scarlet had been paired with a tight black dress and bore heavy dark makeup. "Yes, Professor?"

"Take Jade inside. Keep her there."

"What?" I asked, my eyes widening as I realized Zander was sending me away. I started to shake, not from the cold this time, and took a few steps away from the crowd. "No, Zander-."

"Now!" Danny demanded and Vetta nodded, walking over and grabbing my arm.

"Let go of me," I struggled, but she was surprisingly strong, keeping her grip on me despite my squirming

"C'mon," she murmured in my ear, pulling me towards the house.

"No, I need to stay with Zander." I tried to wrench my arm away but she wasn't letting go.

"You don't want to see this." I looked at her so surprised that I stopped struggling and she was finally able to lead me away.

"What do you mean-?" I finally asked but she just shook her head, opening the screen door of the farm house, passing the two men who'd helped the injured man, and ushering me inside. I'd forgotten about how cold I was during the chaotic scene, however as soon as the warmth of the house hit me I began to shiver again, my body adjusting to the temperature change. My eyes landed on Scarlet who was leaning over a bleeding Six Inch laying on the couch, his eyes squeezed shut as she dabbed at the wounded leg.

"Close the blinds," Scarlet stated as soon as the door was closed and locked; Vetta nodded walking over to the windows and shutting all the curtains and blinds within reach, covering any barrier that allowed me to possibly see what was going on outside. I stared around confused, listening to Six Inch hiss in pain. I didn't know what was happening, where Zander was going, or why I had to be away from him. I had a bad feeling, though, as my stomach clenched in fear and anxiety.

"You may as well get comfortable," Vetta stated as she returned, gesturing towards a brown recliner with a blanket hanging off of the side, setting down a glass of water and a bowl of beef stew that she had in her hands. "They may be a while."

Two hours later Zander finally walked into the house, covered in dirt and blood. I had begun to doze off in the chair, the blanket wrapped around me and the bowl of beef stew untouched in front of me; after all, how could I have been expected to eat when there was so much going on around me- so much that I didn't know about or understand? Vetta and Scarlet had given me no answers despite my nagging questions and eventually I'd given up and slumped into the chair to wait.

Not only was Zander filthy but he was also suddenly sporting a leather jacket- not a jacket, I now saw, but a vest, just like every other man outside had been including his brother- with various patches stitched onto it. From the distance I couldn't read what they said, but the mere fact he had it on made my stomach clench uneasily.

"Zander, wh-."

"Come upstairs." His voice was quiet, glancing at the couch where Six Inch was now sleeping peacefully, his leg wrapped in white gauze and bandages. I was a little hesitant to go after what I'd witnessed earlier, but followed him nevertheless as he turned and started up the stairs.

There had been no indication of the bike gang around the main floor of the house, however as I walked up I saw pictures of men wearing the same leather vest lining the wall- one man, in particular, looked almost exactly like Zander and I could only guess it was his father. Zander had once said that his brother was involved in the family business but he'd never once mentioned his own involvement in it. I looked at Zander's back, able to fully read the large patch that took up the entire back of his vest: Redneck Devils; under the title was a logo- a picture of a lumberjack riding a motorcycle and carrying a bloody axe. I swallowed hard as we reached the landing and turned right, opening the last door at the end of the hall.

Entering the room I knew immediately that it was Zander's- there were stacks of books covering every surface and I could pick out James McClouds within the piles; I wasn't surprised to see that Zander owned every novel just like I did. Zander gestured for me to sit down on the bed and I did so, sitting on the edge uncomfortably waiting for him to say something as I glanced down at my hands folded in my lap; they were still muddy from our earlier horse ride.

"I'm sorry." I raised my head to look at him and saw various emotions displayed: grief, remorse, and sorrow. "I'm so sorry you had to see that." I was surprised to see a tear actually fall from his eye and stood up, wrapping his dirty body in my arms and holding him close.

"What happened?" I finally whispered. "Zander what happened after you sent me away?"

"No." Zander moved away from me, shaking his head. "I can't- I can't tell you that."

"Please Zander," I whispered watching as he began to pace. "I need to- I need to understand."

He stopped and looked at me with sad eyes, "I never intended for you to find out about all of this."

"All of what?" I asked. "What, exactly, is going on here?" I pointed at his vest. "Are you part of this- this gang?"

Zander sighed, "club, Alessaundra, not gang. We're a Bike Club."

"What difference does that make?" I asked.

"We are not a gang! We have rules, protocols- respect for each other and a mutual love for riding. The sole purpose of a gang is to cause trouble and mischief- we may run into trouble but we don't go looking for it, at least not intentionally. Gangs are violent in nature and-."

"And you guys just killed a guy!" I blurted, then paled as he looked sternly at me. I swallowed, "didn't you? How can you stand there and tell me you aren't a gang when you just committed murder."

"You- you have no idea why- you couldn't understand- it had to be done." He paused, pursing his lips, before saying, "We protect this area, Alessaundra. You want to know why the OPP doesn't bother with us? Because we enforce the law here, we ensure people are behaving, so we can protect our town and those who live in it. Riverton is such a small community that the police frequently overlooked any criminal offence that took place. You wouldn't believe the number of robberies and theft crimes that took place around here and the police would do nothing about it. When my father started this Club he took matters into his own hands, and eventually the police came to realize that the Redneck Devils were here to help, not cause harm. We were their allies.

"You see my grandfather was a member of another Club in a district not too far from here- The Satan's. They used to patrol this area as well until my father started up The Redneck Devils and marked his territory. He had his own vision in mind for The Club, one my grandfather didn't approve of, one I don't even approve of."

"What is it?" I whispered, terrified yet intrigued.

"To control the Drug source." Zander looked me in the eye as he said, "The Redneck Devils transport and deliver various drugs throughout the community, ensuring nothing contaminated makes its way into this area." My mouth hung open and Zander nodded. "My father started it, patched in a few buddies who agreed with what he said, and Danny took over when he died."

"How did your father die?" I asked, almost afraid to know the answer.

Zander shook his head, "no, Alessaundra, I can't tell you that either." When he saw the hurt look on my face he added, "not now. It's far too complicated."

I nodded, trying to make sense of it all. "So have you been a part of this your whole life?"

Zander let out a big breath, reached into his pocket, and pulled out a pack of smokes. He lit one, handed it to me, then lit another for himself before answering. "Yeah, kind of. We've been exposed to the life since we were babies but we were too young to actually be members. A lot of our chores revolved around Horse Shoes, a legitimate business where we do, in fact, host trail rides and teach people how to ride. Some of our horses even compete in races- we travel all over the country, sometimes across the border, with these horses."

"So what's your role, exactly?" I asked, inhaling deeply and blowing out a large cloud of smoke. As terrifying as it was to hear about this life, I was intrigued and had to know more.

Zander hesitated, licking his lips nervously before saying, "I have seen so many lives destroyed because of this life- relationships shatter and fall apart and I didn't want that for myself. So when I was a teenager I decided I didn't want to be a part of it anymore. I wanted to be the rare one that graduated highschool, went to university, and made something of myself. But once you're a part of this life you can never truly leave it behind. I'd made a deal with my brother once he took over presidency of the club- if I put myself through school and found employment he couldn't call on me for Club business whenever he needed me. The catch was I'd agree to become a 'Weekend Warrior', continuing to support The Club in whatever way I could, but only on weekends.

"You see, Ali, that's why the job at Baysin is so important to me. Do you remember when I told you I couldn't lose it? When I said I couldn't take that risk? If I lost that job I wasn't going to find another one until September, at the earliest, which would mean I'd have to be a part of this Club, full time, until then. I couldn't have that happen."

"Danny's the president?" I asked once Zander stopped talking- it was the one thing he said that surprised me the most. "So he, what? Runs this Club?"

"He's been a member of this Club since he was eighteen years old. He was the youngest person to be inducted to a Bike Club. Before that he assisted on many runs as an unofficial member of The Club. Danny loves this life, The Club is everything to him."

"But what does this mean for me? For us?" I finally asked, pushing my cigarette into the ashtray sitting on his dresser. "Is Danny going to- kill me- because I know all of this?"

"What?" Zander's eyes went wide, "No! No Alessaundra, of course not." He put out his own cigarette and reached over to pull me into his arms. "No matter what happens next, Ali, no harm will come to you. Do you understand that?"

"How can you be so sure?" I asked, my voice muffled by his vest.

"Because I won't let it happen." He placed his hands on my face and tilted it up so I could look into his eyes. "I love you Alessaundra and I will do whatever is in my power to keep you safe. But I-," he hesitated and licked his lips again before continuing, "I can only do that if you accept every part of this life. I don't want to put any pressure on you Ali, but- I told you how complicated my life can be and I have an obligation to this Club still. If you are uncomfortable with all of this- if you don't think you can handle what this life has to offer you- it's going to be very difficult for us to be together." I blinked as tears stung my eyes and glanced down, away from his gaze. I knew he saw them, though. He leaned down to kiss my forehead, resting his lips there for a moment. "Take some time to think about it, if you want."

"No." I shook my head, reaching up to wipe my eyes. When I looked up at him again they were shining with tears, but I knew I had to see his face when I said what was on my mind. "I love you Zander and I want to be with you. I'm not going to stand here and tell you that I'm not terrified of what I've discovered today, because I am. I don't know how long it's going to take me to be completely comfortable with all of this, but I'm going to try. I'm going to try because I want to be a part of you- a part of your life- even if it means getting involved in something as- scary and crazy as this. You took a chance on me when you found out how old I was, and another when we discovered you were my teacher- now it's time I take a chance on you."

"It won't be easy, you know," Zander whispered, eyes shining.

"Life's not easy," I replied, reaching up to kiss him. His lips were soft and warm as they touched mine. I licked his lips, trying to slip my tongue in and he granted me access with a moan, rubbing my back with his hands and slipping them under my shirt. I felt tingles go down my spine as I felt his skin on mine and broke away panting. "I love you Zander."

"I love you too Alessaundra."

CHAPTER 9

We ended up staying the night at Horse Shoes. Zander had offered to drive me home but I was exhausted after the events of the day and wanted nothing more than a comfortable bed and something to eat. Zander had come up moments later with sandwiches for each of us and we curled up in bed to eat them before passing out. I'd forgotten to call my aunt but wasn't surprised to find no messages from her when I awoke in the morning. There were, once again, messages from Gina about some highschool party she was at and begging me to join her. I deleted those without a response.

Zander had woken me with a gentle kiss to the forehead, slipping out of bed quietly. We'd both been too tired to take a shower the night before and I was therefore unsurprised to hear the water turn on in the adjoined bathroom. I set my phone back down on the nightstand and sat up, yawning, only to catch a glimpse of Zander stripping off his filthy clothes and tossing them in the corner.

"I didn't mean to wake you," he said as saw me stretching my arms above my head.

"It's fine." Zander was now standing in nothing but his boxers and as he turned around and bent over his dresser to find some clean clothes my eyes spotted a large tattoo on his back. I must have made a surprised noise because Zander glanced over at me.

"What's wrong?"

"You- you have a tattoo." My eyes were wide and I couldn't take them off of his back. The tattoo took up a large portion of it and was a replica of the patch stitched into the back of his vest. "A very large one."

Zander turned to face me and I continued to stare unblinkingly at his chest as if I could see through it and to his back. "Ali, look at me."

"I am," I mumbled, still staring.

He sighed, "look at my face." Slowly I moved my eyes upwards so I could look into his eyes. "I got this tattoo in honour of my father when he died. It not only represents him, but this Club as well. Despite the fact I wanted to make something of my life- I knew I'd always be connected to the Redneck Devils and a part of me also wanted to have a piece of The Club with me in case, by some miracle, I actually managed to get out of this life- because although that's what I've always wanted my life has revolved around this Club and the people in it ever since I was born."

"How did I not know- how could I not have seen-?"

"The night we slept together, Alessaundra, the room was fairly dark. We didn't stop to turn on any lights, remember?"

I paused and thought back to that night- that wonderful, magical night- and slowly nodded. "I'm just surprised, I guess."

"I understand." He leaned down and kissed my forehead again before looking back into my eyes. "Care to join me in the shower?" Despite the sudden change of subject I couldn't help but grin as he smiled suggestively at me and wiggled his eyebrows. With a laugh I slid off the bed and followed him into the steamy bathroom, stripping off my own filthy clothes and tossing them into the corner along with his.

"ScatterBrain's back from the run."

These words meant nothing to me but clearly they

meant something to Zander as he jumped up out of his chair and rushed out the front door. I glanced over at Scarlet and raised my eyebrows in question but she just smiled and shrugged, turning back to the window she'd been looking out of, leaving me sitting there in confusion.

Once Zander and I had finished our shower, we'd gotten dressed- me wearing some of Scarlet's clothes- and headed downstairs to find some coffee and breakfast. Scarlet had a fresh pot brewed and ready to go as we settled into our chairs at the antique round table.

The farmhouse was old- the wallpaper was tacky, the hardwood floor scruffed, and there was a faint smell of mildew regardless of which room you walked into. Yet despite these unique characteristics the house had a very welcoming and homey feel to it, one I hadn't felt since living with my grandmother, and although I hadn't been there for even a day yet, I felt a strong connection to it.

As I'd observed the night before there were hardly any traces of the Redneck Devils throughout the house, with the exception of the photos on the wall going up the stairs. There were, however, many photographs of the family scattered about. When I asked about it Zander had said that the Club had its own headquarters in the mysterious third barn, and that the majority of their memorabilia resided there. They wanted to keep the house as separate as possible, lest the authority come knocking at their door. He still wouldn't elaborate much on the topic of family though, and I couldn't help but wonder what the story was there. I knew his mother had died when he was young, I knew his father had raised him, and I knew he had a brother- Danny; but other than that I didn't know much about Zander's family.

I heard Zander's voice, loud and excited, as the front door opened again and in he walked, arm around another man. Zander glanced at me, and he looked happier than I'd ever seen him. My eyes moved from his face to the man standing beside him, and a gasp escaped before I could stop it as my mouth dropped open. My eyes locked with his and he stopped in his tracks as recognition took place.

Zander didn't seem to notice. "Jade I'd like you to meet my best friend-."

"Markus?" I whispered, not taking my eyes off of him.

"Jade?"

My eyes flickered over to Zander who was suddenly blinking rapidly, the smile fading off of his face. "Do you guys know each other?"

Slowly I turned my gaze back to Markus and nodded, "You could say that."

"The name's Markus." The music was loud and he'd led me through the crowded party but despite my best efforts I still bumped into a few people as I stumbled to keep up. My hand kept slipping out of his until he finally locked our fingers together, opening the back door and stepping out onto a deck. It was cold and I shivered as I lit a cigarette using the large heavy lighter Markus handed me.

I exhaled, my breath mingling with the smoke in a white cloud. "Jade."

Markus took a deep breath as he inhaled his own cigarette. "You from around here, Jade?"

I shrugged, "might be."

Markus chuckled, pulling a flask from his jacket pocket and taking a large gulp from it. "You want some?" I snatched the flask without a thought, pouring the contents into my mouth and wincing. "Not a fan of whisky?" Markus laughed at my face.

"It doesn't mix well with vodka," I mumbled before taking another large gulp, this one going down a little easier.

Markus accepted the flask as I handed it back to him and finished my cigarette. "This doesn't seem like your type of crowd," he observed as his eyes glanced up and down my body.

"Oh yeah?" I slurred. "And why is that?"

"I don't know." Markus put out his own cigarette. "I just

don't get the feeling you belong here."

"Oh, yeah? So where do I belong then?" I asked, stumbling towards him. I tripped and he caught me, his arms wrapping around my waist to steady me. I glanced up and his face was close- so close- and before I could stop myself I was leaning forwards, our lips colliding in a sloppy kiss as my tongue slipped out of my mouth and his beard tickled my face. He laughed, reaching his hand around my neck to steady me and take control of the kiss. We stood there for a while, keeping each other warm as we made out on the cold deck. However, when Markus moved his hands around my waist and up to my chest I was suddenly reminded of where I was, who I was with, and who I was *not* kissing. Guilt washed over me as I pulled away quickly, gasping as tears sprung to my eyes.

"Jade?" Markus asked, taking a small step towards me. "Are you-?"

"Get away from me," I whispered but when he went to walk towards me again I shouted, almost hysterically, "get away from me!"

"Whoa." Marus raised his hands in defence. "Easy. I'll go, if that's what you want."

I nodded, collapsing to the snow covered ground in tears. I heard his footsteps fade and a door shut behind him as he walked inside. Ignoring the cold I curled into a ball and let the tears consume me, sobs wracking my body, and the weight of guilt heavy on my mind.

As the memory of that night flooded my mind I glanced back at Zander who looked worried and confused. He opened his mouth to say something but before he could I blurted, "we met at a party a few weeks back."

Zander closed his mouth, moved his gaze towards Markus, and then back towards me. "And were you dating-?"

"Nick? Yeah." I admitted, swallowing hard. "Markus and I- hooked up."

"You slept with him?" Zander asked, inhaling sharply.

I winced but it was Markus who answered him, "no, man. We just made out a little. I swear."

"But he is the reason I broke up with Nick. Well, that among other things." I admitted.

Zander let out a large breath and a disbelieving laugh. "This is crazy," he mumbled, bringing a hand up to his forehead.

"It didn't mean anything," I stated, glancing from Markus to Zander then back to Markus as I added, "no offence."

"None taken," he shrugged.

"It was a moment of weakness during a time I felt sad and lonely. How was I to know that someday I would be dating his best friend? The odds of that are crazy and-." I was babbling and Zander knew it. He dropped his hand and quickly walked towards me, capturing my mouth in a silencing kiss.

"It's okay," he whispered against my lips before kissing them again.

"Are you sure? I don't want to cause any problems between the two of you."

Zander chuckled, "ScatterBrain and I have never let a woman come between us before."

"ScatterBrain?" I asked, remembering who Scarlet had said had returned.

"The one and only." Markus grinned. "Not a lot of people call me by my name around here."

"Right. The whole nickname thing." I nodded.

Zander leaned down to kiss my forehead before standing up right again and turning to look back at his friend. "You should probably get some rest. That run was pretty intense."

Markus- or ScatterBrain as I would refer to him as from now on- nodded as he turned towards the main floor bathroom and shouted over his shoulder to us, "You have no idea how intense it really was Professor."

Zander took me on a tour of the farm- a real tour this time. The only place he avoided was the Clubhouse, which was sacred to Club members, prospects, and associates only- terms I was still learning about. Zander promised that one day he was sure I'd be inducted as an associate, someone close to The Club and privy to much of their secrets while still remaining on the outside of being a full patched member, and honestly that had made my heart race a little. I had never really thought about motorcycle clubs before and was therefore surprised to hear about everything that went into being a member: it wasn't as easy as being born into it, I soon found out.

We stood outside of the Clubhouse, staring at the front doors. The sun was shining, the warmth of it's rays soaking into my skin as a breeze ruffled my hair. The smell of spring was in the air and I inhaled deeply, listening to Zander speak.

"Danny and I were the rare lucky ones. We were raised around all of this and therefore we were automatically given membership status. Sure we had to go through an initiation phase, much like a prospect, but it wasn't nearly as taxing as they go through. We learned to ride when we were twelve, got our bike licence before we got our generic one- we sat in on meetings as early as sixteen even though we couldn't be patched in until we were eighteen. Danny loved it, but as I mentioned to you last night, I had a harder time adjusting to the life and would have prefered to go through all the steps, like ScatterBrain had, and maybe I would have been presented with a different outcome."

"What are the steps?" I asked as I watched Six Inch limp out of the Clubhouse, leg still bandaged.

Zander nodded at him as he waved then said, "First you start as what's known as a 'Hang-Around', someone who we've chosen as a person of interest, someone we can eventually see as being part of The Club. We would approach you, invite you to a few select events, and keep a close eye on you to ensure you are worthy of The Club. Once we've established that, you get inducted as an Associate.

"Once you're an Associate you are privy to a few details,

you may hang around a bit more, you get to see inside the Clubhouse. But official Club meetings, which we refer to as Church, are still closed to you. We may ask for your assistance on a run, but your role would be extremely minor.

"Once we're sure you deserve it we'd change your status to Prospect. If you're lucky enough to get this title it means we like you, and we feel you're truly worthy of being a member. It's the induction portion. You would be put through many tests to prove you can handle this life. You'd attend some meetings, but wouldn't get to vote on any issues that truly matter. The other thing about being a Prospect is you are worthy of a Cut, a blank leather vest with just your title on it. In order to earn yourself the official Club colours you have to pass all of the tests that The Club puts you through. It's hard, Ali. It can be gruesome. Only the strongest will get through, and the rest-." He trailed off and sighed.

"The rest what?" I asked quietly, almost afraid to hear the answer.

"The rest die." He stated emotionlessly. "They die during a run, or during a confrontation with another Club- or we'll kill you ourselves. If we thought you were strong enough to become a prospect but you're slacking in the position then you're out, and if you're out you are out, there's no turning back. At least not in our Club, every Club does things a little differently."

Slowly I turned to face Zander, who was staring hard at the Clubhouse in front of us. His face was blank, his eyes set on the door to the building. "You kill someone because they aren't worthy of being a member of The Club?"

Zander refused to look at me as he said, "I don't make the rules, Ali, I just enforce them."

"What do you mean you enforce them? I thought Danny was the President, doesn't that make it his job?"

Finally Zander turned to look at me and the intensity of his gaze caused me to gulp, it was so strong I felt as if I had said something wrong. "Danny and I share the role of presidency."

"Wh-what?" I whispered as the words crashed over me. I swallowed again, glancing at the Clubhouse for a moment before turning my gaze back to his. Despite the stern tone he'd used I could see the guilt and remorse that resided in his eyes. "But last night, you said-."

"What I told you last night was the complete truth," Zander stated firmly. "I swear. I didn't lie to you. I just-."

"-Wasn't completely honest," I finished for him as tears suddenly sprang to my eyes. I blinked, trying to force them back but it was useless as they started falling down my cheeks. "You said you were a Weekend Warrior, you said you weren't involved, you said-."

"I told you the truth, Alessaundra." Zander turned and grabbed my shoulders forcing me to look into his eyes. I let the tears flow freely as I stared back at him. "I told you the truth. I *am* a Weekend Warrior, but-" he stopped, licking his lips for a moment as he collected his thoughts. "-But that's not all that I am. I told you that Danny took over Presidency when my father died, and that was the truth. However, what I failed to mention is that my father requested that we both step into the role, as equals. The only reason Danny agreed to my request to try and live a normal life was because it meant he got to make all of the decisions without me. I would only be involved when my schedule allowed it, and if I couldn't make it to a meeting, his vote counted for two. All he ever wanted was to be President and he hated sharing that role with me. By giving me my freedom, he got everything he ever wanted."

"Why didn't you tell me that then?" I whispered hurt. "Why lie about it? Why-?"

"What was I supposed to say, Ali? I wasn't expecting to share this part of my life with you. I didn't want you to know-," he shook his head. "I didn't want this for you."

"Were you ever going to tell me?" I whispered as a breeze ruffled my hair. I slid a stray piece of hair behind my ear as I waited for his answer.

Zander closed his eyes and lowered his head in shame,

"No, Ali. I wasn't. I wanted out of this life, and dragging you into it would only have made it harder to leave."

I sniffled, reaching up to wipe tears away from my eyes. "Are you still going to leave?"

Zander let out a long breath and glanced around again, his eyes stopping on the Clubhouse for a minute. "I don't think it's an option anymore." He turned to look at me again. "I've brought you here. You know everything. I have no reason to stay away anymore, and if I did there would be some serious consequences for both of us. You know about us now and I can't- we can't, The Club can't- take the risk that word might get out."

"But what about what you said about wanting a better life, about getting away from-."

"You don't get it, Alessaundra." Now Zander sounded frustrated and he had to inhale deeply, trying to compose himself. He lowered his voice as he said, "yes, I wanted out of here. Yes, I wanted something more. But a large reason for that was because I didn't think I would ever find someone who understood me, who accepted me for who I was, when I was a part of this lifestyle. Until I found you. I have you, I have a steady job, and I still have the Club. If I leave here and allow Danny to take full control- this Club will be torn apart and I can't let that happen. I may disagree with what my father had turned this Club into, with what Danny continues to uphold- but it is still his legacy and I can't let my brother destroy it. I can't let my brother hurt *you*," he added emphasizing the word. "The consequences of us leaving- especially now that you've seen all of this and agreed to keep our secrets-." He shook his head in pain, "I can't even fathom it."

"You told me he wouldn't kill me," I whispered as my heart started racing. "You told me-."

"I said I would protect you, and that's what I'm doing. I'm protecting you by staying, I'm protecting you by ensuring you have all of the information necessary to keep you alive." My hands shook as I reached up to wipe more tears from my face. Zander noticed and nodded, "there's the fear I expected to see from you last night. Now do you realize how dangerous being involved with me is?"

I turned to look at him, my eyes feeling puffy from the tears. "Are you saying I should walk away now, before it's too late?"

"It's already too late, Ali," Zander admitted solemnly, taking my shaking hand in his. "That's why I asked you last night if this was what you truly wanted."

"My answer hasn't changed though Zander," I whispered, squeezing his hand. "I do want to be with you."

"Are you sure about that Ali? Because being with me means being here, around Danny and the rest of The Club. I could try and warn you about what that entails but you won't believe me until you really see it for what it is. I'm giving you one last chance to step away."

I sniffed and nodded, "I'm sure. I'm fucking terrified, but I'm sure."

Zander tightened his hold on my hand as he leaned in to kiss me. I could taste the saltiness from my tears on his lips, and as he reached out his tongue to deepen the kiss I moaned, wrapping my free hand around his neck and pulling him closer.

"Get a room!" Gasping I pulled away, whipping my head around as a familiar voice echoed in my ears. It was ScatterBrain, walking out of The Clubhouse with a wide grin on his face and heading in our direction. I felt my face burn in embarrassment, lowering my head to Zander's shoulder as he chuckled at his friend.

"How'd it go in there?" Zander asked, reaching his free hand out to slap ScatterBrains.

"It went." He shrugged and looked at me, studying me for a moment before saying. "This is where you belong, Jade."

It took me a moment to realize what he was saying and once I did I felt my face flush hotter, "you think?"

"I do." Zander glanced between us questioningly, waiting for someone to explain. "The party I met her at, man," ScatterBrain shook his head. "Not her scene."

"And this is?" Zander asked quietly, almost pleadingly.

ScatterBrain hesitated a moment before saying, "Maybe not. But you, Professor- yeah, she belongs with you. No doubt about it."

I glanced at Zander to see his lips twitch as he fought the smile from stretching across his face but he didn't say anything, only nodded at his friend in thanks before leaning down to kiss the top of my head.

CHAPTER 10

Monday was strange. It started with my Aunt expressing her concerns of me being gone all weekend without notifying her. I apologized, said I'd gone over to Gina's after visiting my grandmother, and that we lost track of time so I spent the night and had a girls day on Sunday. She accepted my excuse so easily and I felt a little guilty for lying, even more so when she asked how grandma was doing and I hesitated before lying once more and saying she was fine. I didn't mention the coughing or the blood. I didn't want to give her anything else to worry about.

The day got stranger when I arrived at school and saw Zander in class. After everything that had happened that weekend it felt surreal to go back to the role of student and teacher that we played, to pretend we weren't so deeply connected, for me to act as if I didn't know the secrets behind the mask he so carefully wore while at school.

"What happened to you this weekend?" I jumped as Gina's voice hissed in my ear, her body bumping mine as she passed me to get to her seat. "Are you too good to come to parties with me now, or something? I texted you at least a dozen times!"

I rolled my eyes and sighed as I pulled out my notebook. "Relax Gina, it's nothing like that."

"So what is it then?" she pouted slouching in her chair.

"I-," I paused, glancing at Zander who was writing on the board behind him. "I went to see my grandmother and- she wasn't doing too well."

"Oh god," Gina sat up straighter now and turned her body so it was angled towards me. "What happened? Is she okay? Fuck, I'm sorry Ali, I feel like shit now."

"She was coughing up blood," I admitted glancing down at my fingers as I twisted them together nervously. "She refused to see the doctor. I just have a bad feeling is all. I wasn't really in the mood to socialize."

"I get it." Gina reached over and pulled me in for a hug. I glanced over at Zander again who smirked, shaking his head as he saw the exchange before turning back to his desk. I sighed, pushing Gina away from me a little. "Look, don't feel obligated to anything, okay? But, it has been a while since we partied or even hung out together."

"Yeah it has."

"How about this? Once your grandma's feeling better we'll plan a huge celebration, we'll invite everyone! It'll be an opportunity for you to relax and enjoy yourself knowing she's okay."

"Gina." I bit my lip and shook my head. "It could be weeks- months even- before we know anything. She may never get better."

"Oh don't say that, she's going to be just fine." Gina waved her hand flippantly and I felt anger stir within me. She really had no clue what I was going through did she? Luckily Zander called the class to order before I could respond and I turned to give him my full attention, trying to forget what Gina had just said.

The exchange with Gina had left me in a bad mood all day. On my lunch break I'd gone to Zander's room to find comfort in his arms but he wasn't there, which caused my bad mood to grow. The afternoon dragged by and all I wanted was to go to the print lab and work on the yearbook, if only to take my mind off of everything.

When the final bell rang I grabbed my books and fled the room before anyone else, rushing down the hall and slamming the door to the lab closed and flicking the lock into position. I let out a large breath and took a step away from the door, switching the light on, then nearly screamed.

"I've been waiting for you."

"Oh my god," I breathed as Zander stood up from my desk and slowly walked towards me. "You scared the crap out of me."

Zander smirked as he reached a hand out to flick the light off again then leaned down to kiss me. I gasped, caught off guard, which caused my mouth to open and gave him easy access to slip his tongue in.

"Wait, Zander," I mumbled against his lips. He moved away, confused, as I tried to catch my breath. "This is prime time for the committee to come in, what if we get caught?"

"I'm sorry," Zander grinned, "I couldn't help myself. I've been wanting to do that all day." He leaned down and pressed his lips to mine again.

I turned my head away, his lips brushing my cheek instead. "I wanted that too, trust me, but we need to be more careful."

"What if I told you I sent an email to everyone saying the print lab would be closed today?"

"Did you really do that?" I asked stepping back so I could see his whole face.

Zander smiled again, "I needed to see you. It's been so hard pretending you're nothing more than a student to me, Alessaundra. After spending the entire weekend with you- I don't know how long I'll be able to keep up that role around you."

"But you have to Zander," I insisted, taking his hands in mine and squeezing them. "You need this job, remember?"

"Actually, I've been thinking," This time Zander

squeezed my hands as he said, "after seeing the way you adapted to everything in Riverton, how well you seem to get along with everyone- maybe I was wrong about wanting to distance myself from The Club. Maybe ScatterBrain was right when he said you belong there, because I belong there too and-."

"And you want to quit your job and go back to The Club?"

"It would mean we'd get to be together, Alessaundra. No more hiding."

"But all you've ever wanted for years was to distance yourself from them. Why the sudden change?"

Zander let out a breath, "I guess I just thought it would be easier that way. If we didn't have to pretend all day and hide in a print lab just to steal a few moments alone. Wouldn't you want that too, Ali?"

"Of course I would, Zander, there's nothing I want more. But..." I let his hands slip out of mine as I stepped away, glancing around the room. He followed me as I moved, waiting for me to continue speaking. Finally I spoke, my back to him. "But I refuse to let you sacrifice everything you've worked so hard for- just for me."

Zander was quiet as he processed my words. I glanced back at him as he nodded and let out a deep breath. "I guess I'm just being impulsive."

I walked back over to him, reaching up to brush his arm comfortingly. "Let's just see how things go. Maybe we'll find the balance we need to make this work."

"Like visiting Riverton on weekends?"

I raised an eyebrow at Zander, "is that your way of inviting me up there again?"

Zander chuckled, "Scarlet wanted to know if you'd join us for our Easter celebration this weekend but it would mean spending the entire four days with us. Think you can handle it?"

I blinked, taken aback. "I don't know what to say."

"Say yes," Zander pleaded.

I nodded quickly, "yes, of course I will. I just- wasn't sure if everyone liked me, is all. I'd only just met them. They really want me there for the whole weekend?"

Now Zander hesitated and I got the impression there was something he wasn't telling me. "Of course they do, Ali."

"Who does?"

"What?"

"Who wants me there?" I repeated, now growing angry as I crossed my arms. "Or rather, who doesn't?"

"It doesn't matter," Zander mumbled.

"It's Danny, isn't it?" I asked, feeling hurt. I dropped my arms to my side, my hands slapping my thighs loudly, as I turned my back to him. "God, Zander, your own brother doesn't even want me there. So why should I go?"

"The thing you should know about Danny," Zander said quietly coming up behind me and placing his hands on my shoulders comfortingly, "is that he has a hard time trusting people. The reason we- kill- those who don't make the patch is because Danny doesn't believe anyone is capable of keeping our secrets once they've seen too much. He's got trust issues, Ali. Besides, why would you want an asshole like Danny to approve of you anyways?"

I turned to face him, tears shining in my eyes, "because he's your brother, Zander. He's the only family you have left. You don't have a mother for me to impress, or a father for me to charm- but you do have a brother, and if he doesn't like me then how could we ever have a future together?"

Zander reached to pull me into his arms, rubbing my back with one hand as he held me tightly with the other. He kissed my forehead then rested his chin on the top of my head. "You just need to give him some time, Ali. Give him time to get to know you, give him time to see you for who you are. He'll come around."

"How can I be myself when I don't even know who I am when I'm there?" I sniffled looking up at him. "Who is Jade?

What is her role? Am I her or is she me?"

"I'm so sorry I've made things so confusing for you." I could see Zander's eyes shining and felt guilty for making him feel that way. "If I could go back and change things-."

"No," I shook my head. "No, things are perfect, maybe not ideal but who cares? If we can make it work the way we're doing it, then that's all that matters right." I took a big breath and let it out, trying to relax myself and prayed I wouldn't stutter as I said. "Of course I will come to Riverton this weekend, Zander."

"Are you sure?"

I nodded and leaned up to kiss him. "I'm sure." He smiled and leaned down, meeting me halfway but as our mouths met my phone started ringing. I contemplated ignoring it but decided it was best if I checked who was calling. With a sigh I broke away and slipped my phone out my pocket, seeing Aunt Patty's name on the screen. "I should take this," I mumbled, swiping to answer it and holding up a finger, indicating Zander should keep quiet. "Hello?"

"Oh Ali, I'm glad you answered! I wasn't sure if you'd be driving or working, or what."

"I'm just in the print lab working on the yearbook," I half lied, again feeling that sense of guilt. "What's up?"

"Well, I just got home and saw a rather large envelope in the mail with your name on it."

"Envelope?" I asked, my heart starting to race. "Wait, from the university?"

"Yes," Aunt Patty said excitedly. "It's fairly large, that could only mean one thing, right?"

"I don't know." I bit my lip, suddenly feeling nervous as I glanced around the room. My hand reached up to play with my hair as I twisted it anxiously in my fingers. "You have to open it."

"Right now? Wouldn't you rather wait and open it yourself?"

"No, no, I need to know!" Zander glanced at me with a

raise of his eyebrows and I covered the speaker and whispered, "I have mail from the university- it could be an acceptance."

Zander silently walked over and grabbed my hand holding it tightly as I listened to my Aunt rustle papers in the background. I could tell by the echo of the sound that she'd turned on the speakerphone. "All right, I got it open. Let's see here… Dear Miss Alessaundra Campbell, it is with pleasure that we offer you acceptance to-."

"I got in?" I shrieked and Zander squeezed my hand in pleasure as I beamed, dropping my hair and letting out a large sigh of relief.

"There's more," Aunt Patty continued in a loud voice. "It seems… they're offering you a full ride!"

"I got a scholarship?" I nearly dropped the phone. "Oh my god. I can't believe this."

"Congratulations sweetie," Aunt Patty cried and I could tell she was smiling.

"Thank you," I turned and bit my lip wanting nothing more than to kiss Zander. "Um, I'll be home in a bit, there's not much left for me to do here today. I'll see you when I get home."

"All right, Ali. The girls will be so excited for you!" I hung up, dropped my phone to my desk and threw my arms around Zander as he held me close. He kissed my forehead, my nose, and finally my mouth, his soft lips calming my racing heart.

"Congrats," he mumbled against my mouth.

"I can't believe it," I breathed, my forehead brushing his. "A scholarship, Zander. A scholarship!"

"They would have been fools not to accept you."

I smiled and kissed him once more before moving away to look around the print lab. I scratched my head for a moment then sighed, "Well, I guess I won't be able to concentrate on any of this now."

"No, I gather you won't."

I smiled and reached for his hand, "I'm glad you were

here to celebrate with me when I got the news."

"Me too."

We kissed one more time before departing from the lab and walking towards the parking lot. It was nearly deserted as we parted ways, Zander going to the staff lot while I went to the student zone. I watched as he got in his truck and pulled out of his spot. He had to pass me to exit the parking lot though and as he drove by he raised his hand. I waved feeling overly ecstatic at the events that took place within the last hour. My grin was wide as I finally started my engine and left.

"-Oh and Saturday I was thinking we could go shopping, maybe go out for lunch to celebrate your acceptance?" Aunt Patty was rambling on about her plans for the long weekend and it took me a moment to realize what she'd just said.

"That sounds great Aunt Patty, except-." I hesitated, taking a bite of roast beef to bide some time. How could I explain I wasn't going to be around all weekend? Do I lie, again? No, the guilt I was feeling from the last few lies I told was starting to weigh on me. Maybe it would be best if I was honest. "You see, the thing is I've actually been- sort of- seeing someone for a few weeks now and-."

"You're seeing someone?" Aunt Patty frowned, cutting me off, "But I thought that you and Nick-."

I dropped my fork and wiped my mouth as the twins screamed beside me- I ignored them. "What? That we might get back together?"

"Well, yes," She mumbled, taking her own bite of roast beef. "You two were so great together."

I sighed and shook my head as Aunt Patty reached over to stop their fighting. "No Aunt Patty, we weren't. Nick was a neglectful, selfish guy who cared more about his music career than his girlfriend. Beside's, after that song-," I swallowed and shook my head again, "we weren't going to get back together."

"I liked Nick," Lisa quickly said.

"He was cute," Sarah added.

I ignored them again as Aunt Patty sighed, "He was just so sweet."

I laughed humorlessly, "you have no idea what he was like Aunt Patty." I shoved my plate away from me, my fork clinking against the plate, having suddenly lost my appetite. "I'm done eating." I stood up, setting my napkin down on top of my food. "Look, I won't be around for the long weekend, Aunt Patty. I promised my boyfriend I'd spend it with him and his family." I turned ready to storm away from the table when her next words halted me.

"But what about your grandmother, Ali? Don't you visit her every weekend? Won't she be expecting you?"

I bit my lip for a moment considering my options. I'd been so excited about spending the weekend with Zander that I hadn't stopped to think about my routine trip to Grandma's- but it was just one weekend. I'd make it a priority to visit her the next Saturday and spend all morning with her, that'd make up for missing this one, right? "It's just one day, Aunt Patty. Grandma would understand." Before she could respond I turned and fled to my room.

I hardly spoke to Aunt Patty all week. I avoided her as much as I could, staying late into the night at school working on the Yearbook which I was fairly confident was almost complete, other than last minute additions that were happening during the month of April. Luckily the week was short and Thursday evening came quickly. I didn't even bother going home after school; instead I headed straight for *The Golden Daylight* and handed my keys to the valet, who already recognized me by face. He had a spot right next to Zander's reserved just for me, thanks to him. I often silently questioned how Zander could afford to stay at such a place for an extended period of time but knew I didn't want to know the answer. He'd admitted to me already that The Club dealt in Drugs; I could only imagine he saw a cut of those dealings.

Zander was waiting for me in the lobby talking to, much

to my surprise, Rebecca. I stopped in the entrance, glaring at her as she flipped her hair to the side and tilted her head. When she reached her hand out and touched his arm endearingly I found myself storming towards them. Zander's back was to me but Rebecca saw me, her smile slipping from her face instantly as she took a step away, her hand sliding back down to her side.

She narrowed her eyes for a second before smiling at Zander again. "Anyways, I guess I'll see you later. Thanks for the chat. Feel free to come for another drink tonight."

Zander raised his hand in a wave then turned and saw me standing there. "Hey...what's wrong?" he asked as I glared at Rebecca's retreating form.

"She's a bitch," I muttered.

Zander raised his eyebrow at me, "for talking to me?"

"You said you didn't like her!" I snapped.

"I don't," Zander replied. "She was asking me a question and-."

"And flirting with you!"

"Are you jealous?" Zander asked, sounding amused.

"No!" I yelped, then said more calmly, "well, maybe- yeah, okay, I am."

"Oh Ali," Zander grinned and pulled me in for a hug, one I reluctantly returned. "You are the only one for me. I swear."

I sighed as he pulled away and glanced back at the entrance to the restaurant, where Rebecca was nowhere to be seen. "I don't trust her."

"You don't have to," Zander shrugged. I turned to look at him, eyebrows raised. "You only have to trust me."

"I do trust you," I insisted. "It's just-."

Now Zander sighed and I could tell he was getting annoyed with me. "Sometimes I forget how young you are Ali."

I blinked, taken aback as Zander grabbed my hand and led me towards the valet station where his truck was awaiting him. I would have resisted but was too shocked at what he'd just said. Yes, I was seventeen- almost eighteen- but I was far more mature than the majority of the people in my place. I'd even argue I was more mature than half of the members of the Club. I was young in age, yes, but not young in heart. Was that how Zander really felt about me, though?

It took me a few minutes after we were on the road to finally find the right words to express how I was feeling to Zander. We'd just pulled out of Baysin and onto one of the many side roads that took us into Riverton when I said in a quiet voice, "I'm sorry for acting like a child Zander."

Zander looked over at me quickly before returning his eyes to the road. "I never said you were a child Ali."

"No, you didn't," I agreed as I let out a breath. "But you implied it." I angled my body towards his, which was difficult to do while wearing my seatbelt. "Look, I may not be in my twenties yet, but the experiences I have gone through in my life had me growing up a lot quicker than most people my age. I mean yeah I'm only seventeen and although that doesn't make me an adult in the eyes of the law, I feel like I am older than everyone who surrounds me. Sure, I may lash out in anger or jealousy sometimes but that's only natural and it's not fair to categorize me in the same group as those my age. If you truly thought of me like the rest of them you wouldn't be with me right now, right? Could you ever see yourself with someone like- I don't know-," I flipped my hand in the air as I thought. "Someone like Gina?"

"I-," Zander opened and closed his mouth, stunned into silence for a moment before shaking his head. Finally he admitted, "No, Ali, I'd never date Gina."

"And why's that?" I asked. I needed to hear him say it, had to know how he truly felt about me.

He sighed, "because she is far too immature to be in a serious relationship like this- unlike you."

"Exactly." I stated feeling relieved. "My age does not reflect my being." My voice got quiet as I adjusted myself to sit comfortably in my seat again and began to twiddle my thumbs. "It hurt when you said that to me Zander. It made me feel like I wasn't good enough for you just because I'm 'young'."

Zander let out another breath, glancing over at me again while still paying attention to the road in front of us. The heat was blasting out of his vents and hit my face feeling like a warm breeze on this cooler spring day. "I'm sorry Alessaundra. I didn't mean to make you feel that way. It wasn't my intention. I will try to be more careful with my words next time. And for the record," he continued looking over at me again, "you're far more mature than I was at your age."

I thought being at The Club all weekend would be awkward, but instead it was completely comfortable. Scarlet really enjoyed having my company and quickly showed me the ropes of being an 'Old Lady' to a biker. When she first said the term I felt a little offended- I didn't like being considered 'young' but I also didn't want to be considered 'old' either- however she quickly explained that it was a term used by bikers to identify their significant other and that it was an honorable title. Our job was simple: cook, clean, and ensure our man is taken care of. I almost felt like a housewife, and when I expressed that feeling to Scarlet she chuckled and nodded.

"Clubs are very traditional: they value traditions and reject change. When the Redneck Devils was first founded there was a huge uproar in the community due to the complete disregard for rules they seemed to show. Donald, Zander's father, didn't care though. He knew what had to be done in order to make The Club successful and he was willing to risk everything in order to implement his ideas. In the end, though, everything worked out in his favour. Not only are The Redneck Devils successful as a Club but they created recognition nationwide. Donald ensured they made their mark in this world."

"Did you know Donald well?" I asked as I accepted a glass from Scarlet as she rinsed it. I used a towel to dry it before replacing it in the cupboard beside me.

"Yeah, sort of. My- husband- was a member of this Club."

I turned to face her, my mouth open. "Your husband? Who is it?"

She cleared her throat uncomfortably before handing me another glass, refusing to look at me. "His name was Patrick."

"Was?" I asked, leaving the glass sitting in her soapy hand. "You mean-?"

"He died a few years ago." Scarlet set the glass down on the dish tray and turned to face me full on. "A drive by. He was shot and killed almost instantly."

"Oh my god," I breathed, reaching out to pull Scarlet in for a hug. "I didn't- I mean I'm sorry-.I didn't know-"

"It's fine," she whispered, accepting my embrace as her wet and soapy hands held my back. "You couldn't have known."

After a moment we separated and I picked up the glass she'd set down and finished drying it, lost in thought. My heart ached for Scarlet, if only because I had no idea what I would do without Zander. We'd only been together a few weeks and already I knew I couldn't live without him. But Scarlet had been married to Patrick, meaning they'd been together far longer than Zander and I had been- the hurt she must have felt, must still be feeling, had to be indescribable.

"What else can you tell me about The Club?" I finally asked once we finished the dishes. "It'll be helpful to know as much information as possible if I want to secure my spot here."

Scarlet smiled a little sadly at that as she folded some bed sheets. "Are you sure that's what you want Jade?"

"It can't be that bad, you have your spot after all." I picked up a towel from the basket and folded it, adding it to the pile in front of me.

Scarlet's smile looked even sadder as she said, "it's different for me." I paused, the towel dangling from my hand.

I wanted to ask her what she meant but didn't get the chance to as she started speaking again. "The first thing you should know is that nobody goes by their real name here, at least none of the members do- Vetta and I don't have a nickname, anyway. Members use what's called a Road Name and are only referred to as that name whilst in the presence of The Club. Take ScatterBrain for instance; you know his real name-."

"-Markus." I nodded, setting the towel down.

Scarlet's voice suddenly turned stern. "Don't let any of The Club members hear you calling him that. Especially here. This is sacred ground for The Club. Only Road Names should be used."

"But Zander-."

"Is different. He's practically family. But during Club business, you will only hear members call him Professor. In your case, since you're his Old Lady, you can refer to him by his name, but for the rest of us- it's seen as disrespectful. There are consequences for things like that."

"What's Danny's Road Name?" I asked hesitantly, reaching for the fitted sheet Scarlet was holding so I could help her fold it.

"Danny is, to no one's surprise, The Prince." My mouth dropped open and Scarlet nodded, completely serious as she grasped the corners I was holding. "He is The Prince of this Club after all. He's the founding father's son, he was the youngest member to be inducted, and he's been around this Club since he could crawl."

"So has Zander," I pointed out. Scarlet took the sheet entirely from me and finished folding it before placing it into the basket.

"True, but we both know Zander hasn't always wanted this, not like Danny has. Oh, and another thing you should know about The Redneck Devils is that almost every member is under thirty, which is highly unusual when it comes to Bike Clubs."

I raised my eyebrows, "I hadn't really thought about

that, to be honest."

Scarlet pushed the now folded laundry aside and sat down on the couch. "When Danny and Zander took over The Club, the older members were hesitant about trusting them. So they were given a choice- patch over to The Satans, or remain with The Redneck Devils and live by Danny's rules. Needless to say they all patched over leaving Danny and Zander to build their own Club."

"But why?" I asked, coming to sit beside Scarlet.

"Because Danny's way of running The Club is unorthodox. But, it's worked. Say what you will about him, but Danny knows this world. He's done The Club well."

I glanced out the window and saw Vetta walking by, a tight black dress and black cowboy boots on her feet. As she walked she flipped her auburn hair over her shoulder. "And what about Vetta?" I asked curiously, watching as she disappeared around the corner of the house and towards where The Clubhouse was. "What's her story?"

"Vetta," Scarlet murmured leaning back on the couch. She lifted her feet and rested them on the coffee table in front of her. "Well, technically Vetta is Danny's Old Lady." I turned and stared at Scarlet, my eyes wide. She nodded, "yup. Crazy, huh?" She lowered her feet and turned her body towards me. "Vetta is obsessed with this lifestyle. She would give anything for The Club to patch her in, but that's one line they haven't crossed yet, maybe not ever. Traditionally Clubs only consist of men, and the rare Club who does have a female patched in, that female hardly gets seen or respected as a true member. It's a little sexist, but it's the way The Club works."

"But Vetta and Danny? It just doesn't make sense." I looked back out the window in the direction Vetta had disappeared.

"Maybe not right now, but it will." I looked back at Scarlet who shrugged. "Eventually you will see how well they work together. Vetta completes Danny in a way no other woman could."

"I guess I just don't see Danny as a 'one woman' kind of guy." I admitted, leaning back on the couch myself and crossing my arms.

"Oh he's not." My eyes widened as Scarlet said, "the two of them have an open relationship. Vetta, though, wouldn't dare associate herself with another member. Danny's the top of the food chain and that's all she's ever wanted."

"But Danny can do whatever he likes?" I asked affronted, my mouth open wide.

"It doesn't make sense to me either, but it's also not my business," Scarlet shrugged. "If that's what makes them happy, so be it." She jumped up off the couch and picked up the basket of laundry. "Now, we still have work to do. I'll put the laundry away, would you start cutting up some carrots for dinner?"

Time passed slowly here and I sort of loved it. The four days I was at the Club felt like a week instead. I was so busy while there- helping Scarlet cook and clean, and even assisting in grooming the horses- but it never truly felt like work to me. In the evenings, when I finally got some alone time with Zander, we'd spend it curled up in his room reading together. We'd take turns reading aloud from various James McCloud novels, and, of course, making love.

When we weren't locked away in the bedroom we were in the living room socializing with everyone else. The house was shared by Scarlet, Zander, and Danny and Vetta. I later learned that The Clubhouse had a few rooms where members could crash if needed, but I'd yet to see inside the sacred space.

Danny seemed to be coming around to me, though, if only a little. The first night he hardly spoke to me, choosing to speak to Zander about business and isolating me from the conversation completely. Zander could tell I was frustrated but couldn't do anything about it at the time. Friday, after helping Scarlet prepare dinner, The Club gathered around a fire and passed around a bottle of vodka. I remembered Zander telling me that vodka was reserved for birthdays and celebrations, and although I didn't know what was being celebrated I was invited to participate in the festivities. Danny was skeptical of me downing vodka straight, and was therefore surprised when I not only took the shot that was passed to me, but that I also slugged the bottle without wincing. I knew that earned a little respect in his eyes even if he didn't say it aloud.

It wasn't until Sunday morning, though, as I slid a plate of eggs and bacon onto the table in front of him, that I got the first real compliment. "These eggs are cooked perfectly," he'd said as he cracked the yolk and dipped his toast in. It was a small one, but that compliment, I knew, was his way of showing me he accepted my presence here, even if he hadn't completely accepted me yet.

I was sad to depart The Club on Monday even though I knew I'd be returning the next weekend. Beside's Riverton was a short half hour drive from Baysin, I could return any time I wanted to really.

Next weekend was big though and I was excited for it. The weekend after Easter The Club usually throws a huge party to celebrate the beginning of the "bike season". Although the weather has been fantastic this year and The Club has already had their bikes out a few times, this is the time they usually take their bikes out for a ride together. Old Lady's get to ride on the backs, associates are included in the festivities, and oftentimes the Hang Arounds are invited to partake in the celebrations. I wasn't exactly sure what to expect, especially since I'd never ridden on a motorcycle before, but Zander assured me I'd be completely safe.

I think the anticipation of the weekend made the following week go by slowly, even though there were only four days of school. Tuesday and Wednesday dragged on and on, I felt so exhausted by the end of the day I didn't stick around to work in the print lab on either day, choosing instead to go straight home and sit in my room all night until I passed out on my bed.

Thursday morning I was driving to school when a familiar voice came on the radio. I was so surprised that I almost crashed into a car in front of me, who'd slowed for a red light. As Nick's voice filled the speakers of my car I pulled into the school's parking lot and sat there listening to every word he said.

"The album drops next week! It's been a lot of work but we're finally in agreement that it's done. The hardest thing was choosing a name."

"And you're satisfied with what you decided on?"

"Oh yeah, yeah. You know, there was only one thing we all agreed upon, but I was a little hesitant at first."

"And why's that?"

"I've always tried to keep my personal life separate from that of the band, but that all changed with this record deal, you know? I learned that sometimes sacrifices have to be made. Like with 'Come Back To Me', I'd never thought using a name in a song could change the way it sounded, but it really impacted the end result."

"And that's the title of the album, right? 'Ali'?"

My eyes widened as I stared at my dash, praying it wasn't true. But the next words Nick spoke echoed throughout the small space and my heart felt like it stopped beating. "Yeah, yeah, that's the album. Turns out there were a lot of songs influenced by that one relationship, that one woman. It was only fitting to name the album after her."

I slammed my hand on the radio controls, shutting it off as my breathing came out rapidly. How dare he, how dare he name the album after me! The song, that god damn song was bad enough but now Shattered Life is releasing an entire album that was apparently inspired by me, or at least my relationship with Nick?

The silence of the car felt too loud though and with a frustrated sigh I hit the radio controls again.

"-that was Nick from Shattered Life. Here's their newest single from their album Ali: this song's called Rage."

Loud guitar chords filled my ears and I winced, reaching

to turn off the radio again. Then the words began to play.

> *Thunder crashes*
> *Rain falls*
> *It's the calm before the storm*
> *The words you said*
> *All I can hear*
> *Echoing in my ear*
> *The earth shakes*
> *The air cracks*
> *My fists shake with rage*
> *Memories flash*
> *Through my head*
> *As I break through the cage*

I couldn't believe what I was hearing. Come Back To Me had been such a sweet, yet heartbreaking song. But this? This was anger. This was hatred. This was rage. No wonder they named the track that. I couldn't help but wonder, though, how the band felt about Nick naming the album after me. Nick may be the lead member of the band, but Kevin and Aaron had been with him for a long time. Surely they weren't as pleased about all of this as Nick was.

As I sat in the student parking lot and watched my peers exit their cars and walk into the school I was suddenly filled with anxiety- the last time Nick and Shattered Life had released a song about me the whole school couldn't stop talking about it. I was mocked, I was bullied, and I was harrassed non stop for weeks. Things had finally started to settle, and now this? My hands began to shake as I reached for my keys to start the ignition. There was no way I could handle this today.

CHAPTER 11

I ended up at Coffee Cafe, in a booth by myself with my second cup of steaming coffee sitting on the table in front of me. I'd already heard Rage three times since sitting there. It seemed like everyone was promoting Shattered Life. I didn't know what to think or how to feel. Did I have a right to be angry about this? Afterall, Nick was allowed to name his album whatever he wanted, Nick could write about whatever he felt like writing, and Nick could express himself in whatever way he saw fit. But did it have to be at my expense?

Sighing I reached for my coffee and took a sip just as my phone buzzed. I pulled it out and saw Zander's name. My hand shook as I slid the screen to reveal the message. *Call me if you need to talk.* So, he'd heard. I guess it was expected he'd find out considering everyone was probably talking about it, which only made this worse. But if Zander had already heard that meant the rumour mill was going strong; the whole school probably knew by now.

I hit the power button, turning off my phone, before sliding it into my pocket. I was sure Zander wasn't going to be the first to message me about my absence, I hardly ever missed school afterall, and I didn't want to be bothered by Gina or anyone on the student council about this.

The door opened as I took another large gulp of my

coffee. I didn't pay any attention to it, customers had been coming and going the entire time I'd been sitting there, but there was something about the way the coffee shop fell quiet that had me glancing over my shoulder towards the door. I didn't gasp loudly, at least I hadn't thought I did, but nonetheless Nick's head turned my way and our eyes locked; I couldn't blink. I hadn't seen Nick in months and other than hearing his voice on the radio I hadn't heard from him. My fault, of course, for I was the one who ended things. Seeing him standing mere feet from me, though, felt a little surreal. It took me a moment to realize why he was even here, that the interview he'd been giving was local, and therefore he would likely be around town. What were the odds he'd come in here though?

Nick hesitated then leaned over to whisper something to the guy with him. I had no idea who he was but he glanced at me and nodded. Nick smiled politely at the customers around him who greeted him excitedly and even stopped to sign an autograph and take a selfie with a young woman's phone. The entire time this was happening my mind was racing, begging me to flee, but my body felt frozen to the chair and I still had yet to take my eyes off of him.

Finally he made his way to my table and stood there, hands in his pocket, a small grin on his face. He looked different even though it'd only been a few months since we'd last seen each other. He rocked back and forth on his heels for a moment then gestured to the bench across from me. "Mind if I sit?" I shook my head slightly and I saw him let out a big breath, looking relieved, as he slid in. I didn't know what to say so I sat there, still staring, as he got comfortable. "Ali, I-."

"How could you?" I finally blurtred in a whisper. He stopped, mouth open, and cocked his head to the side confused. "How could you do that to me? How could you expose me that way? How could you use my name in your song? How could you name your album after me? How could you-." The more I talked the louder I got and Nick reached over to grab my hand, trying to shush me.

"Ali, please, you need to be quiet," he hissed as I stopped to take a breath. "Please."

I pursed my lips, breathing heavily, and glanced down at where his hand rested on mine. I wrenched it away, replacing it in my lap as I narrowed my eyes at him.

"Look," he let out a large breath and glanced around the coffee shop. I suddenly noticed there were a few more customers walking in the door than would be normal for ten o'clock in the morning, and they were all looking our way. "Can we go somewhere else to talk? Please?"

"Why?"

"Well," Nick swallowed and glanced around again. I did too and watched as someone pulled their phone out of their pocket to take a picture of us. My eyes widened in surprise. "I'm not exactly discreet."

"That's not the right way to use that word," I pointed out, sounding every bit the straight A student he knew I was. Then I shook my head as I picked up my, now cold, coffee and took a sip. "Besides, I don't even know if I want to talk."

"Please?"

I tapped my fingers on the table anxiously as I brought my cup to my mouth again. Giggling and the flash of a camera from the corner of my eye made me realize I had to get out of here, and soon. "Fine," I muttered standing up and tossing my cup in the trash can beside me. I glanced back at Nick who's eyes were wide in surprise. "Where did you have in mind?"

"That's Scotty, our manager," Nick explained as we managed to sneak out the back door of Coffee Cafe undetected. We got into a black SUV with tinted windows, Scotty sliding into the front seat next to the driver. "He escorts me everywhere."

"Only you?" I asked, noticing Kevin and Aaron's absence.

"The others decided they didn't want to explore town." Nick shrugged looking out the window. "Kevin wanted to be with Jocelyn, and Aaron stopped in to see some friends."

"I don't blame them for not wanting to go out," I mumbled as the car drove a little ways away until we were in a deserted alley. Scotty and the driver got out leaving Nick and I alone. I reached into my purse for a cigarette and my lighter.

"What's that supposed to mean?" Nick asked, sounding defensive, staring at me.

I lit the cigarette and opened the window a crack. "Don't take this offensively but I haven't kept up with the band that much," I shrugged as I inhaled. "But what I have heard seems to revolve around you, Nick, and not the band as a whole."

Nick looked taken aback. "What? That's crazy, Ali."

"Really?" I turned to face him angrily, my cigarette dangling out the window. "The song? The album title? You can't tell me the guys were okay with that! The band has always been a group effort, Nick, but lately it seems like it's all about you. The articles? The radio interview? They all revolve around you. Kevin and Aaron are hardly even mentioned."

"Scotty thought-."

"Oh so Scotty makes the decisions does he?" I snapped flicking the cigarette out the window and closed it.

"He's our manager, he does what's best for the band."

"And naming your album after me is best for the band, is it? And what about that 'exclusive article'? C'mon Nick, explain to me how that benefits everyone and not just you?"

Nick sighed, "look, I'm sorry about all of this, Ali. But, Scotty told me to say those things. That article in the magazine? The radio interview? Scotty prompted what I should say." When I just started at him and remained silent, he shook his head, "you just don't get it, Ali. You were never interested in any of the band stuff-."

"That's because you never made time for me while you were doing it! The band was all you cared about, Nick. Why would I invest my time in something that was the reason for your neglect?"

"Neglect?" Nick whispered, sounding angry. "You think I neglected you?"

"You cancelled so many dates on me, Nick, and spent hours at the studio or in meetings, leaving me alone. The only time I got to see you was at a gig, and even then you were so busy with sound check, the show itself, and the fans that you hardly had time for me. Why do you think I went out with Gina that night? Why do you think I cheated on you? You stopped caring about me."

"I never stopped loving you, though Ali. You have to believe that."

Tears were in my eyes and I blinked rapidly, trying not to let them fall. "If you loved me you wouldn't have used my name in a song. Do you have any idea how humiliating that was for me, Nick? The second that song was released, the second it got airplay, the entire school was talking about it! Talking about *me*! Speculating about our relationship! It was horrible Nick. All of that drama had finally started to settle and now you do this? How do you expect me to believe you love me when you break my trust like that? You promised you'd never disclose our relationship if you became famous, and all you've done is use it in your music. You've betrayed my trust, Nick."

"I'm sorry Ali," Nick reached for my hands, squeezing them as he pleaded, "I'm sorry. I never wanted to- I didn't think it was- but Scotty thought it would be good and-."

"And you let your manager decide something like that rather than agreeing as a band?"

"You have no idea what it's like, Ali. This life- it's not what I thought it would be like."

Was he looking for sympathy for being famous? I scoffed as I wrenched my hands away from his again. "You chose this life, Nick. You threw everything away- your family moved away to BC, your friends were abandoned, and me?" I scoffed not even bothering to elaborate further on how I felt. "You threw it all away for this because this is the life you wanted."

"Ali, please, just listen-." he paused and reached into a bag at his feet withdrawing a USB stick. "This is an early copy of our album. You need to know that I regret everything that happened to us Ali. I regret ignoring you, regret neglecting you- I should have told you how much you meant to me while I still had the chance! I acknowledge the mistakes I made. All I ask is that you give the album a listen before you decide I'm not worth a second chance. Please."

He closed the small stick in my hand and I felt the hard plastic dig into my skin. "I'm seeing someone else, Nick." I stated flatly, his hand warm in mine. "There is no second chance for you."

Nick's hopeful face fell, but he kept the stick closed within my hand anyway. "Just listen. Please."

I sighed as I nodded and felt Nick remove his hand so I could slip the USB stick into my pocket. I glanced at the time seeing it was now late afternoon. "I should get going."

"I'm surprised you're missing school," Nick stated slowly. "You've never been known to skip before."

I glared at him, my eyes flashing dangerously. "When I find out my ex boyfriend named his debut album after me and announced it on local radio, a station I know everyone at school listens to? I'm not very inclined to attend school."

Nick looked down at his hands, "I'm sorry," he said, actually sounding remorseful. "Seriously Ali, I am."

"It's too late now," I mumbled reaching over to grasp the handle of the door.

"Let us at least give you a ride back to Coffee Cafe!"

I shook my head as I opened the door, "you've done enough Nick. I'm sure those photographs are already all over Instagram, Facebook, and Twitter." My stomach clenched as I realized that Zander had probably seen, or at least heard that Nick and I were together. My face fell, wondering what was going through his head right now. "I don't need anymore shit to deal with today."

I started to get out when Nick's voice stopped me. "Hey Ali? Did you ever hear from any of the universities you applied to?"

I paused, one leg out the door and one in before glancing back at him. "I got into my number one choice."

The smile that lit Nick's face was genuine as he nodded. "Congrats. I knew you would."

"Thanks," I whispered, finally dropping my other leg to the ground. "I'll see you around Nick."

"My number hasn't changed- if you want to talk. I'm in town until the album drops. Please, just listen to it. Okay?"

I swallowed and nodded as I pushed the door shut. I took two steps away and instantly Scotty and the driver appeared around the corner and opened their doors. Scotty paused, though, and looked towards me. The way he stared at me without blinking made me nervous but I refused to break eye contact. Finally he got into the SUV and I turned, walking out of the alley as the SUV pulled away, exiting from the other end as I made my way back to Coffee Cafe and my car.

By the time I finally turned my phone back on I had half a dozen missed calls from Zander and at least ten text messages from Gina. I deleted all of Gina's messages without even looking at them and hit Zander's name, hoping he'd be on break. The phone rang three times before going to his voicemail and I let out a sad sigh and sat back in my seat.

After retrieving my car from Coffee Cafe I drove and drove until pulling into the parking lot of the city park where I could sit in peace and think. My phone started buzzing and I saw Zander's name; my heart raced as I swiped to answer. "Hi," I breathed.

"Do you have any idea how worried I've been?" he hissed. "You didn't reply to my message, you didn't answer or return any of my calls, and then I hear students talking about how you skipped school to be with Nick and-."

"I didn't miss school to be with him," I interrupted defensively. "I missed school *because* of him, him and that damn album!"

Zander let out a breath, "yes I heard about that as well. I

assumed that was why you weren't at school but I hoped you would at least text me and let me know you weren't coming. Instead I heard about it through the other students and then when you didn't answer my text and I heard-."

"Were you jealous?" I interrupted with a smirk.

Zander sighed again, "I wasn't particularly happy about what I heard, but I wouldn't say I was jealous exactly. I trust you Ali."

I smiled softly, "I'm sorry you had to hear about all of that from everyone else. You should have heard it from me."

"Was all of it true, Ali?"

Air came out of my mouth in a puff, "do you really want to know Zander?"

"Of course I do."

"All right. Yes, I was with Nick, but I didn't go looking for him, if anything I wanted to avoid him; that didn't seem possible though. I went to Coffee Cafe and he just- appeared. I was so surprised I couldn't move. When he asked to talk to me- Zander I couldn't say no, I should have though. These- people- started taking pictures of us and I got so anxious about it that when Nick asked to speak somewhere private I agreed, if only to get out of there.

"We took his car to a deserted alley to talk, and that's all we did. We talked."

"Alone, in an alley?"

"We weren't alone, not really," I countered, drumming my fingers on my steering wheel. "His manager was there and so was his driver. Apparently Nick can't go anywhere by himself these days. Anyways, we talked, he gave me a copy of his album, and I left. I also made it clear I was seeing someone else and I was no longer interested in him."

Zander was silent for a moment and I was growing nervous the longer the silence lasted. Finally he said, "these photographs- Ali they may ruin everything for us at The Club if they somehow get to them."

My stomach dropped as fear overcame me. "I hadn't

even considered that."

"The chances of anyone seeing them at The Club are slim, but not impossible."

"So what do we do?" I asked nervously, glancing around the park. I could see a few young kids playing on the climber with their parents, but the parking lot I was in was deserted.

"Honestly? I don't know. As your boyfriend I want to protect you, say we'll keep it a secret and deal with it when the time comes, but-."

"But what?" I asked. "But what Zander?"

He sighed. "But as a member of The Club I know the consequences of keeping secrets is bad. I know the outcome is horrible."

"So what do we do?" I repeated, this time with tears in my eyes. I think Zander knew I was on the verge of crying.

"We wait." He decided. "I'll find a way to explain things if the time ever comes. Until then we remain oblivious and keep on pretending. Nobody has to know who you are, Ali."

I nodded and blinked rapidly even though I knew he couldn't see me. "Okay," I whispered. My phone beeped, indicating another incoming call and I pulled the phone away from my ear to glance at the screen. Grandma's nursing home flashed across the caller ID and I paused before putting the phone back to my ear. "I gotta go Zander. Call me later?"

"Of course."

With a small smile I hung up and swiped to answer the call from the nursing home. "Hello?"

"Alessaundra Campbell?" Tears instantly sprung to my eyes as I heard the waiver of the nurses voice. I knew what she was going to say before she even got the words out and the tears started falling as my heart began to pound. "This is Cynthia Gourds, I'm the director here at the Baysin Care Retirement Centre. I'm afraid I need you to come down here immediately."

"Is she okay?" I whispered in a broken voice.

Cynthia hesitated before saying, "I can't disclose any information over the phone. We need you here as soon as possible."

"I'm on my way." I sniffled, hanging up the phone. I broke down, tears flooding my face and my hands shaking, as I cried. After a moment I forced myself to take a deep breath, wiped my eyes with a napkin from my middle console, and placed my car in gear. I couldn't allow myself to lose control, not yet, not when my grandmother needed me.

"I'm so sorry Alessaundra." I was sitting outside of my grandmother's room with my eyes swollen and my arms were wrapped around my legs as I cried into my knees. The voice was the same as the one who called me and I lifted my head with tears streaming down my face to stare at her through half closed eyes. "We did everything we could but- we couldn't save her. Not this time."

"It's my fault," I sobbed. "I knew-," I sniffed, "knew she w-was coughing bl-blood. B-but sh-she w-wouldn't see a doctor. I- I sh-should have made her!"

"Alessaundra it's not your fault," Cynthia knelt down and placed an arm around my shoulders. "Your grandmother knew she was sick, knew she was on borrowed time. Her doctor was amazed she made it as long as she did. You had so much more time with her than you should have and-."

"Is that supposed to make this easier?" I snapped.

"Of course not."

I shook my head and moved away from her comforting arm. "Just tell me what you need from me."

Cynthia hesitated, "your grandmother had you down as her emergency contact, however you are not yet eighteen, is that correct?"

I sniffed, "not until May."

"I'm afraid we need someone else in the family to come sign a few papers. Your father perhaps?"

"Good luck finding him." I mumbled.

"Do you have any siblings?"

"You knew nothing about my grandmother did you," I laughed humorlessly as I hiccuped. "It was just grandma and I."

"There has to be someone, Alessaundra. Who have you been living with?"

I sighed as I realized exactly who I needed to call, someone I should have called from the beginning. "Patrica Campbell."

By the time Aunt Patty got to the nursing home I'd already gone through most of grandma's possessions. She didn't have much, just some clothes, pictures, and a few pieces of jewelry; the majority of her important items remained at her house. Aunt Patty gave me a hug, which felt stiff and awkward, and I quickly pulled away as I closed up the last box.

"They need you to sign some papers. Apparently I'm too young to do it," I grumbled as I picked up the box.

Aunt Patty watched me worriedly, tears in her eyes, as I balanced the weight of the box in my arms and turned towards the door. "Ali, are you all right?"

"Peachy," I mumbled walking out of the room. I heard her sigh behind me but kept walking until I reached my car and placed the box inside of it. A few tears leaked down my cheek again but I wiped them away, too tired to cry anymore. I reached into my pocket for my lighter but accidentally pulled out the USB stick Nick had given me instead. I let out a long breath and placed it back, unable to process the mental stress it would no doubt cause me.

Finally I found my pack of smokes and my lighter and lit one, inhaling deeply. The past few hours had felt like an eternity. It had taken Aunt Patty forever to find a sitter and I had been starting to grow anxious, which was why Cynthia suggested I pack up grandma's room. I almost snapped at her, thinking it was way too soon, but quickly realized I needed something to distract me while I waited and beside's, they probably needed the room empty as soon as possible so another resident could move in.

Zander had tried calling me twice, but I didn't have the nerve to answer it, knowing I'd break down the second I had to say aloud the inevitable truth: grandma was dead. Thinking this my phone buzzed again and Zanders name appeared for the third time. I knew I couldn't ignore it again, he was already pissed about me skipping school and being with Nick, so reluctantly I answered, trying to sound as casual as possible. "Hey Zander, what's up?"

Silence met me for a moment and I questioned whether he hung up on me, but then he spoke. "What's wrong?"

"What do you mean-?"

"I can hear it in your voice. Have you been crying?"

Just like that the tears started again. I leaned against the side of my car, sliding down until I was sitting on the dirty asphalt driveway. "She's dead," I whispered brokenly.

"What? Who?"

"G-grandma." Sobs wracked my body and I dropped the phone, unable to hold it anymore. Distantly I could hear Zander calling my name, asking if I was okay, but I didn't have the energy to answer him. I just sat there crying, leaning back against the cold metal of my car, as he called out my name.

It was late when Aunt Patty and I finally returned to the house. She relieved the babysitter, checked on the girls who were both asleep in bed, then retired to bed herself. I walked up to my room and sat on my bed, before curling into a ball and shedding even more tears.

I wasn't sure why grandma's death had hit me so hard, we'd known it was coming after all. It wasn't like I hadn't just seen her two weeks before either- but maybe that was why I was so sad, because although I'd seen her a few weeks ago, I hadn't stopped in to see her as I had promised I would last weekend. Not only that, though, but I knew she was unwell, I knew she was coughing up blood, and I did nothing to help her. If I'd only encouraged her to see the doctor rather than sitting in the dining room having tea, maybe she'd still be with us today. Cynthia said I had no one to blame, that there was nothing I could have done to prevent this, but that didn't change the fact that I felt immense guilt for not even trying.

With swollen eyes I found Zander's name on my phone, ignoring the fact that it was almost midnight, and hit the call button. He hadn't hung up; despite the fact I'd broken down in the parking lot of the nursing home, he'd stayed on the phone and listened to me cry until I was able to get up again. Then, and only then, did he let me go, knowing I was okay- for a while. But now that I was home I desperately needed to hear his voice.

"Ali," he breathed, not even sounding remotely tired. "I was hoping you'd call."

"Have you been waiting up for me?" I sniffled.

"That and grading papers. Well done, by the way, I just finished yours. You really captured the essence of the book."

"Thanks," I let out a soft breath and sniffed again.

"How are you doing? Really?"

"I don't know," I admitted playing with the frayed edge of the blanket on my bed. "I'm sad, I'm hurting... but there's a small part of me that feels- relieved, and I feel like that makes me a horrible person."

Tears started to leak again but Zander's words slowed them as he said, "she was in pain, Alessaundra. It does not make you a horrible person for being relieved that she is finally at peace."

"Thank you," I whispered, taking a tissue to my face and wiping it. "You know what the worst part of all of this is though?"

"What's that?"

"I have to contact my brother- and my sister- and attempt to track down my father."

"Shit," Zander breathed and I heard him set down his pen. "How are you going to do that?"

"I don't know," I admitted. "I have my sister's number but we never talk. We were never that close, actually. When she ran away- it was the biggest betrayal. She abandoned me, left me alone in a house with my fucked up father and my grandmother who worked more than she was home. I- was alone. She tried to make amends a few years back but I wasn't willing to listen. I don't even know if she still has the same number, actually, but it's all I have to go with."

"And your brother?"

"Last I heard he was in rehab, much like my father. He was arrested for possession and the lucky bastard got off with court mandated rehab."

"Do you think he's still there?"

"Who knows," I shrugged, flopping back on my bed, "but it's a starting point. I'm sure someone will be able to get in touch with him."

"I wish I could help you with all of this," Zander sighed. "You shouldn't have to do this alone."

"Aunt Patty is finalizing the funeral arrangements. Lucky for us grandma had everything planned. The only benefit to knowing you're dying is you can prepare for the outcome."

"Let me know when the funeral is and I'll be there."

I sat up quickly. "No, Zander, you can't-."

He cut me off, "I spend enough time with you as your faculty advisor on the yearbook and the newspaper, no one will question my presence as a supporting figure."

I smiled softly, "thank you."

"You should get some sleep. You've had a long and emotionally draining day. You must be exhausted."

I yawned, loudly, and Zander laughed. "I am."

"Call me tomorrow, okay? I assume you won't be going to school?"

I sighed, "no, which makes the fact that I skipped today even worse."

"No one will question why you missed today. You can just tell them you knew your grandmother was sick."

"How do I explain the pictures then?"

Zander hesitated before saying, "you stopped at Coffee Cafe on your way to the nursing home. You knew your grandma was unwell but didn't realize the seriousness of the situation."

I blinked, "that's- that's good."

"Get some sleep."

"I will. Thank you Zander."

"Of course. I love you Alessaundra."

"I love you too."

I turned off the lights after hanging up with Zander and crawled into bed, but my mind kept racing. A lot happened today, too much, and my mind wouldn't settle down. I began to recall the events that had taken place and as I remembered Nick handing me the USB stick I crawled out of bed and dug through my pockets until I found it. Plugging my headphones into my laptop I inserted the memory stick and opened the file marked "ShatteredLife.Ali.album". Instantly eleven icons appeared. I immediately recognized "Rage" and "Come Back To Me" as two of the tracks, but the rest were foreign; either the band had written an entire album in two months, or Nick had recorded songs while he was with me that he never shared. I clicked track 2, skipping past the first track which was their first single, and leaned back as smooth guitar notes filled my ears.

I place my hand on your cheek
Bring your face close to mine
But then all I can see
Is her eyes on your face
And no matter how hard I try
I can't stop these tears I cry
I pull away from your embrace
I just can't forget her, my dear

I never thought about how Nick might have felt after our breakup, never stopped to consider the pain he may have been feeling. Had I really ruined him so much that he couldn't even kiss another girl without thinking of me? Or did it just make for good lyrics?

    I listened to a few more tracks, but the next one to jump out at me was titled "The Pain"

> *I'm addicted to the pain*
> *The girls screaming my name*
> *Don't change anything*
> *I just wanna feel okay, again*
> *Oh why'd you have to leave me here*
> *Alone and tired*
> *I've cried out all the tears*
> *I'll just keep on waiting for you*
> *Tell me you feel the same way too*
> *I can't go on with someone new*
> *I need something to help me get through*
> *The pain*

As I listened I felt the tears start to fall for the umteenth time today. If these lyrics were true then Nick was hurting, badly. He hadn't seemed to be in that much pain when I saw him today, but maybe he was just hiding it? I finally reached the last track and pressed play. Soft melodies filled my ears, melodies that brought me back to the first songs Nick used to write, the melodies that harmonized with his voice, the kind of melodies that made me fall in love with him and his music.

> *I will love you until the sand runs out*
> *Yeah let me tell you what it's all about*
> *The love you give me will live longer*
> *And continue to grow stronger*
> *My heart will beat day by day*
> *Through the ups and the downs, we'll be okay*
> *As long as you're there by my side*
> *I know everything will always be fine*
> *Oh, all I want is you*
> *To hold, through and through*
> *The days seem so dark and grey*
> *I need your light to make it through the day*

    I ripped the earbuds out and closed my computer as

tears pooled in my eyes. Why did I torture myself by listening to these songs? Songs written by the guy I used to love? What did I think it would accomplish? I was happy with Zander- wasn't I? Nick hadn't been good for me, he'd been a neglectful boyfriend who only cared about becoming famous, as was proven by him today; he all but admitted it! Did I owe it to him to listen to the album? No, but I had anyways, and all it had done was produce more tears, tears I was tired of crying, tears that I thought I had emptied from my body hours before, tears that I never wanted to cry again.

I tried to ignore the songs replaying in my head as I closed my eyes and went to sleep.

I didn't make it to The Club's celebration that weekend. Zander said he'd cover for me but a part of me knew that Danny and the others would be pissed. But I couldn't worry about that right now, I had enough on my mind.

Monica's number hadn't changed. By some miracle the call went through and she even answered on the second ring. She obviously had no idea it was me who was calling, and as I spoke I could almost picture her face falling as I delivered the news. "Oh Ali," she'd breathed when I was finished. "I'll be there as soon as I can be."

"You don't have to come, I just thought you'd want to know."

"Are you kidding me? Of course I'll be there."

I got up from my bed and began to pace across my room. "I just thought that-."

"I'll be there Ali," she said in a firm voice.

"Okay." I paused for a second, looking out my window, then asked, "have you heard from Karson by any chance? Last I heard he was in rehab but they said he left a few weeks back." I resumed my pacing as I waited for her answer.

"Uh, actually I have. He's- here."

"What?" I stopped, standing in the middle of my room, frozen.

"He's only been here for a few days. He promised he'd be gone within a week. He just needed a place to stay and-."

"And he somehow got himself checked out of a court mandated rehab clinic, Monica! You realize he's probably wanted in some way, right?" I scoffed as I resumed walking back and forth.

Monica sighed, "he's our brother, Ali. I couldn't just turn my back on him in a moment of need."

"Last time you tried to help him he stole from you." I pointed out angrily. "He stole mom's necklaces, her wedding rings- how could you take him in again after he did that?"

"You need to calm down, Ali." Monica let out an irritated huff. "He's clean, Ali. He swears it."

I stopped at my window again and gazed out of it as I bit my lip and rolled my eyes, not that she could see- I trusted Karson about as far as I could throw him. "He's not staying at the house." I decided.

"Where else is he supposed to stay then?" Monica asked annoyed.

"I don't care, Mon. I'm not having any of grandma's things going missing for drug money! Not while we're planning and attending her funeral."

"But he's clean!" She insisted. When I didn't answer she sighed. "Fine." Monica snapped, then asked in a quieter voice, "But what about dad?"

I let out a breath of my own, "I haven't called him yet."

"You have his number?" She sounded so surprised and I honestly couldn't blame her. We all shared the same feeling about our father.

I walked over to my bed and glanced down at grandma's address book, which I'd found in a stack of papers from the nursing home. "Maybe," I admitted. "Grandma seems to have a pretty recent number written down in her book. I- I didn't even know she was in contact with him."

"Will he be staying at the house?"

"It's his house now, Monica," I pointed out reluctantly- I

desperately wanted the house to be mine.

She growled, annoyed. "Well if dad's staying at the house, then Karson and I will get a motel room or something. I can't be under the same roof as him, Ali."

"I know," I whispered, eyes watering as I stared at his number. "I know."

Before hanging up Monica assured me she and Karson would be here in a few hours, and that she'd call me when they got to their motel. I hardly listened, my eyes gazing unseeingly at the phone number in front of me. I wasn't sure how I'd get the nerve to dial his number, but I knew I had to.

So I took a deep breath and dialled, raising the phone to my ear in anticipation. I held the breath I took until the phone rang four times and I heard my dad's familiar voice echo through the speaker and into my ear as his answering machine picked up. "This is Jonathon." The phone beeped and I removed it from my ear to stare at the screen, surprised that was all there was to his machine message. Then I realized that I was currently leaving a message filled with silence and quickly said, "hi. Uh, dad. It's me- uh- Alessaundra, your daughter." I stuttered and took another breath as I shook my head. "Look, I don't really want to leave this in a message but- well, I have some- bad news. Uh, grandma- your mom?- she, uh, she's gone..." I took another breath as I blinked a few times to stop the tears that instantly sprang to my eyes. "She passed away yesterday and, uh, I thought you'd want to know. The funeral is in a few days, and I th-thought maybe you'd want to attend." I sighed as I realized I was rambling. "Anyways, you probably won't even hear this message thanks to the silence at the beginning of it, but if you happen to get it, you can call me back at this number. Bye, dad. I- I love you."

I groaned as I hit the end button and flopped back on my bed, throwing my arm over my face. I hadn't told my father I loved him in three years, not since I was a young teenager, so why had I ended my message with it?

I jumped as my phone began to buzz and my heart

began to race, but it wasn't my father returning my call it was Zander. "I got things sorted out with Danny," he said when I answered. "He's not- pleased- you're missing the celebrations but he accepted it."

"What did you tell him?" I asked, closing my eyes as I lay back on my bed again.

"The truth."

My eyes sprung open, "what?"

"I told him you had a death in the family."

"But Zander-."

"It'll be fine, Ali."

"We never should have lied about who I was, Zander." I sighed, rolling over to my stomach. "Lies make things that much more complicated."

"It's too late now," Zander said. "Besides, I can't tell them about you, Ali. Not yet."

"And now not ever. I'll forever be this character you made me into."

"You were the one who created Jade, Alessaundra, remember? The day we first met? Besides, didn't you say this was okay? I thought you were fine with all of this."

"Yeah, well, if I could go back and change it..." I trailed off as I sighed again.

"But you can't." Zander's voice was stern. "We made a choice and now we have to live with that, otherwise the consequences would be-."

"I know." I interrupted him and I heard him let out a frustrated breath. "Look, I'm sorry, I'm just super stressed and upset. I've just finished leaving a message for my dad, I talked to my sister, and-."

"Come here."

I blinked, "what?"

"Come to the hotel. I took a half day today, hoping to make it to The Club early, but I feel like you need me right now."

"Zander," I paused, bringing my thumb nail to my mouth

and nibbling on it for a moment then shook my head, "there is nothing I want more than to be with you right now but- well, my sister and my brother will be here shortly and I need to go to my grandmothers house and make sure the cleaners did a good job last week. Besides, I'm still waiting to hear back from my dad and-."

"I get it."

He sounded annoyed and I instantly felt guilty. "I'm sorry Zander, I really am. Trust me, I want to be with you, but I just feel like I need to be with my family right now." He didn't answer and a silence fell. I swallowed and said, "I'm off school for all of next week. Mr Thorn called my Aunt this morning and said to take as much time as I needed to grieve."

"Yes he passed the message along to me as well." His voice sounded flat and emotionless and my stomach clenched feeling guilty.

I nodded, not that he could see. "I should go. Call me tomorrow?"

"Tomorrow is the celebration, Alessaundra. I doubt I'll have time."

"Oh. Right." Silence fell again and this time I felt uncomfortable about it, as if I'd done something wrong. My stomach clenched harder, making me feel a little nauseous. I took a breath to calm it and said, "I love you Zander."

"I love you too Ali." Then he hung up. After all of the tears I'd shed the past few days, I honestly didn't think I'd have any left for something as silly as a disagreement with my boyfriend, but there they were. I sniffled as my phone began to buzz again. At first I thought it might be Zander calling me back to apologize, but when I looked at the screen I realized it wasn't Zander who was calling me, it was my father.

My hands shook and my stomach felt even more nauseous as I swiped at the screen to take the call.

"It's good to see you kid." The hug my father gave me was entirely awkward but I accepted the embrace and even wrapped my own arms around him. We only stayed that way for a couple seconds before he moved away and glanced around the house. "I can't believe she's really gone."

I studied my fathers face, and although he certainly looked sad I noticed the absence of tears in his eyes. "How long you here for?" I asked without replying to his statement.

He looked back at me, his face set in a serious expression. "I'm here to stay."

I raised my eyebrows in disbelief. "Really?"

"I'm clean, Ali. I swear." He insisted. I studied his eyes, not seeing the tell-tale signs of him using, but that didn't mean he was actually clean. "With your grandmother gone someone needs to take care of you."

I turned away unable to hide the look of disbelief on my face. "I've heard that one before," I muttered, resentfully. "Beside's, I don't need you here to take care of me, Aunt Patty's been doing just fine, and in two months I'll be eighteen. I can take care of myself."

"Whatever you say, kid."

Despite the fact he didn't look like he was using I could still smell a different sort of substance on him. "You smell like a brewery, by the way."

"A few drinks isn't going to hurt me," he defended shrugging, "but I haven't touched a single drug in two weeks."

"Doubtful." I scoffed.

"I promise you, Alessaundra. This time I mean it, I'm clean. Rehab worked. I'm here to stay."

I didn't answer him, instead I turned to pick up my backpack and walked away, carrying it up the stairs. I hadn't stayed in my childhood bedroom in almost a year, not since I was forced to leave the house and move in with Aunt Patty. It was a little strange to walk over the threshold and stare at the walls covered in posters, posters of people I hardly even liked or cared about anymore. What was more, there were still pictures of Nick and I all around the room.

After setting my bag on my bed I walked to my old

dresser and picked up a framed picture of Nick and I at the beach from three years ago, the first summer we dated. His arms were around my waist as I sat between his legs, leaning back into his chest. We were both wearing sunglasses and sitting on a towel. The sky was blue without a single cloud in the sky, and the water behind us almost blended perfectly in with the skyline. We looked happy and I could almost smell the salt from the water as I thought about that day.

The next picture I saw was stuck in the edge of the mirror and it was of me holding Nick's guitar as he placed my fingers on the strings, teaching me chords. Kevin had taken this one after a show, we were back stage and empty beer cans sat around us. My head was thrown back, laughing over something that had been said, but I honestly couldn't recall what it was now.

The last picture in the room was of me and Nick kissing, the night of Nick's graduation. He wore his gown and cap and I had stolen his diploma from him as I leaned in to kiss him. His parents had taken the picture, it was the last time I'd seen them as they moved to BC that summer, allowing Nick to choose his own path and follow his dreams. I remember being so proud of him, though, and in that moment thought we'd be together forever.

"Ali!" My fathers voice echoed up the stairs making me jump. I set the picture back down on the dresser.

"Yeah?"

"I'm ordering pizza! Is bacon okay?"

I grimanced, thinking of the last time my father made bacon for me, the day Monica left, but instead of reminding him of his past mistakes I pushed the memory aside. "Sure. Sounds good."

"I already told you, Alessaundra, I can't be around him."

I groaned into the phone at Monica as I walked into the kitchen, "can't you put your hatred and anger aside for one day? This is for grandma. We need to be united and look like a family. She would have wanted us to be together."

"She would have understood," Monica disagreed. "Beside's, how can you act like he's done nothing to you! The way he abandoned you, time and time again-."

"You want to talk to me about abandonment?" I hissed, grabbing the milk and slamming the fridge door closed. "You left me- you! When I needed you most. I was used to dad leaving me, Monica, but not you. Karson had already left us, grandma was always working- you were all I had! And you just left."

"I had to!" Monica pleaded into the phone. "Ali, I couldn't be around him anymore. He wasn't a good dad, Alessaundra. He was neglectful, abusive, and-."

"Abusive?" I asked, pouring myself a glass of milk. "He was never abusive."

"Maybe not physically, but mentally? He was the worst. Maybe you were too young to remember, Ali, but he was the worst with you."

"I know he blamed me for moms death, Monica. I know he hated me, despised me even. But I would never call it abusive."

Monica let out a long breath. "I spent years in therapy, Ali. I've discussed our family dynamic to five different professionals and they all agree that I had made the right decision in leaving. That house was a toxic environment and I couldn't live there any longer."

"But you were willing to leave me in it?" I stated coldly, my voice even.

"Grandma took care of you, like I knew she would."

"Until she got too sick."

"Ali-." Monica let out a sad sigh, "Okay, fine. I'll meet you at the funeral house at two. We'll stand together. For grandma."

"Thank you." I whispered.

A silence passed between us, then Monica asked, casually, "so what's with Nick's music these days?"

I groaned as she laughed, the tension easing between us a bit. "Don't get me started."

"I had no idea you two had split up."

"That's because you hadn't reached out in three years." I pointed out.

"I'm sorry, Ali, I truly am. I've thought about you so much, though. Grandma kept me informed too, you know."

"What?" This surprised me almost as much as finding a current number for my dad and I almost choked on the sip of milk I'd just taken. "You guys kept in contact?"

"Of course we did," Monica stated. "I mean, we didn't talk often, but we kept in touch."

I smiled sadly, "I can't believe she didn't tell me."

"We both agreed it was best to let you come around when you were ready. We knew one day you'd be ready to talk- possibly even forgive me?"

I could hear the desperation in her voice and although a part of me wanted to hold on to the anger, a larger part knew that life was too short to hold on to the resentment. "I do forgive you Monica."

"Really?" She asked in a quiet voice.

"Really. I'm not a child anymore, I understand why you did what you did. It- it wasn't easy for me, not at the time, but I know you had to get out of here if you wanted to live your life freely."

"Wow, that's really mature of you Ali."

I finished my glass of milk and got up to rinse it in the sink. "I may only be seventeen, Monica, but I'm not your average seventeen year old."

"I know you aren't, Ali. Not after the life you've lived."

"I wish everyone else would see me that way," I sighed leaning against the counter thinking of Zander and the rest of The Club- how we lied to them about who I was simply because of my age.

"What do you mean?" Monica asked and I could hear the curiosity in her voice.

"I-" I paused and bit my lip. "Nothing," I decided, shaking my head. "Just forget I said anything. I should go," I added, "lots to do before the funeral."

"All right. I'll see you at two."

"See you." I hung up and sighed, then pulled up my text messages. It'd been two days since I'd last heard from Zander. Looking at the messages I sent him I felt a wave of sadness wash over me. *Dad's back, things are weird. I miss you.* No response. *Hope things are going well at the celebration. Sorry I can't be there. Call me when you get a chance.* No reply. Then, the last text I sent him, the one I really wanted him to reply to. *Visitation is at two tomorrow, funeral is monday morning.* He'd said he'd be at the funeral, but that was days ago, before we had our disagreement. I hadn't heard from him since and I was starting to get worried I'd really done something wrong.

My fingers hovered over the keyboard, but I didn't know what else to say to him. With my heart feeling heavy I hit the lock button on my phone and slid it into my pocket. If he wanted to contact me, he would, I wasn't going to chase him anymore.

CHAPTER 12

I chose a simple black dress that I found in the back of my closet, slipped on the black cowboy boots Scarlet had given me, pulled my hair back in a simple bun, and wore nothing but a bit of eye liner and mascara on my face; today didn't seem like the day to put too much effort into my appearance, I'd probably just cry and smear my makeup anyways.

My family had stood by my side at the front of the room as we greeted those who arrived. My dad had spent a minute alone with grandma when all of this began, Karson had said a quick goodbye, and Monica had stood there quietly staring at the open casket. Me? I hadn't been able to step foot in the room, hadn't even found the nerve to walk up and see her. I wasn't ready to say goodbye yet.

Most of the guests that came were grandma's friends from all the jobs she worked at or made throughout her life here in Baysin. Glenda had shown up, hugging me tightly and crying as she walked up to the casket. But besides that I didn't really know anyone else. I hadn't given the details to any of my friends, despite the fact Gina had texted me asking about it, and other than Nick no one had even met her.

I hadn't expected anyone to come, but Nick walked through the door around three thirty, during the last half hour of the visitation. I still hadn't stepped foot in the room and was therefore standing in the small lobby waiting for four o'clock to come and trying not to cry as I fixed myself a cup of coffee. When he walked in the door nobody noticed, nobody openly stared at the lead singer of Shattered Life- except for me. I almost poured hot coffee onto my hand, unable to take my eyes off of him as he walked towards me.

"Careful," he said quietly, reaching for the pot and setting it onto the table. "The last thing we need is to take you to the hospital for burning yourself on coffee." When I still didn't say anything he murmured in a quiet voice, "I am so sorry about Caroline."

"What are you doing here?" I finally asked, looking down at the table for some cream. I found it and poured a bit into my cup.

"I loved her, Ali. Why wouldn't I come pay my respects to her?" I nodded, tears brimming my eyes as I raised my cup to my lips. "I'm going to go in and see her," he pointed at the room where the casket was, "would you care to join me?"

My eyes went wide and I shook my head, setting my cup down. "I can't. I- I just can't." I took a breath, "and honestly? I haven't been able to go in there at all."

"I can go with you, if you like?" Nick offered, raising his hand and placing it on my arm comfortingly.

I shook my head as I felt the warmth from his hand. "No, no, it's something I need to do on my own- when I'm ready."

Nick nodded in understanding, rubbed my arm a few more times, squeezed, then removed it. "Okay, well, I'll be right back then."

I watched as he walked into the room and sighed; if I was honest with myself I was thankful he had come. It was nice to have someone who actually cared about me here, but it wasn't who I wanted to see.

"Am I too late?"

I nearly spilled my coffee as Zander's familiar voice reached my ears. I spun around quickly, my dress twirling out around me, as my eyes landed on his face. I couldn't take my eyes away from his, those blue eyes boring into mine. His brushing of stubble was thicker, a sign he hadn't trimmed it in a while, and there were wrinkles around his eyes from exhaustion. I knew The Club had to have partied late into the night and he looked pretty rough, but he was here and I was beyond thankful for his presence.

"You came," I breathed, not daring to move.

"Of course I did. I couldn't let you go through all of this alone."

My eyes brimmed with tears again as I reached up to hug him and his arms wrapped tightly around me as he held me close. Over his shoulder I spotted ScatterBrain and Butch, another member who Zander was close to, standing awkwardly in the doorway unsure of themselves. "Hey guys," I sniffled.

"Jade," ScatterBrain murmured, hugging me.

"Sorry for your loss," Butch whispered as he held me quickly.

"We're going to give you guys a moment. We'll be outside." Zander nodded as the two men left. For the first time I noticed they weren't wearing their cuts, which made them look completely different, almost like regular people.

"They wanted to make sure you were okay, but I asked that we not draw attention to ourselves by wearing our colours," Zander explained. "I hope you don't mind that I brought them?"

"Of course not," I whispered reaching up to wipe a tear away.

"Nice boots by the way," Zander winked, causing me to laugh softly. I reached out for his arm and rubbed it softly, picking up my coffee with my other hand. I saw my father walk out of the viewing room and look around as if he was searching for something, then he saw me and headed my way.

"Hey kid, I just saw Nick in there! You didn't tell me he was coming."

"Uh," I glanced at Zander who was eyeing my father suspiciously, eyes narrowed. "I didn't know he was."

"Great kid he is," my dad exclaimed. "We were just talking in there. Did you know his album drops on Tuesday, and that he named it after you? He gave us tickets to this exclusive show Wednesday at Shakers, said he'd love for us to go. What do you think? It'll be fun!"

"He- what?" I asked, my eyes wide. Zander still hadn't said anything but as I glanced over at him I watched his frown deepen. I turned back to my father. "Dad, I don't know-."

"Oh c'mon, his music's not that bad. Besides, we don't get enough bonding time. It'll be something to help get your mind off all of this death stuff." My mouth dropped open as his words reached my ears and my eyes began to water again but I wasn't given the chance to respond. "I think we should go, okay? Anyways, I'm going out for a smoke, I can't stand being around all of these people. I'll be outside if you need me."

Zander and I watched as my father walked out the door, pulling a cigarette out of his pocket as he did and lighting it the second the door closed. I turned slowly to look at Zander, my heart racing, unsure what to say. "I- I'm so sorry you had to meet my father like that."

"He's charming," Zander said sarcastically staring outside after him.

"He's honestly not that bad," I tried defending him but Zander gave me a hard look and I shook my head, defeated. "Okay, so he's an asshole."

Zander grumbled and glanced towards the viewing room. "I'm a little disappointed I never got to meet your grandmother."

I was thankful at the sudden change of topic and smiled softly, bringing my cup to my mouth for a sip. "She would have loved you."

"Which part of me? The teacher or the biker?" He challenged me.

I smirked, "both."

Zander laughed and placed his hands in his pockets, "would it be okay with you if I paid my respects?"

I nodded as I took in a deep breath and set my cup down again. "You are more than welcome to go in there."

"Would you like to come with me?"

"I-," I swallowed a gulp of air as my heart began to race. "I don't think I can," I finally admitted looking down at the ground in shame. "I haven't been able to say goodbye to her yet."

Zander reached forwards and pulled me in for another hug. As he held me I looked around and realized that the room was nearly deserted now, most of the guests had left, and those that were still there had no idea who Zander was- we didn't have to hide here. I closed my eyes and held Zander close, taking comfort in his embrace. "If you need me to come with you, Alessaundra, I will. Let me be your rock."

I smiled and pulled away, looking up at him with tears in my eyes as I made a decision. "Thank you Zander. I think I'm ready to see her now." I reached for his hand and took a deep breath as we headed into the viewing room. Monica and Karson were sitting in a corner whispering, Aunt Patty was leaning over the girls, both of which were sleeping on a couch. Nick was on his way out but paused when he saw me enter, a smile starting to spread across his face.

"Hey, are you ready to see her? I can come with you-." His smile slipped as he looked past me and spotted Zander, his eyes lowering to our enclosed hands.

"I'm okay, thanks though," I forced a smile and kept walking. I could feel his eyes on me as I headed towards the casket but refused to look back at him. Suddenly my feet felt heavy and I stopped, five feet away, unable to move any closer.

"Ali?" Zander whispered, squeezing my hand.

"I can't do it." From where I stood I could just see my grandmother's hands, folded across her chest. "I can't."

Zander let go of my hand, moving until he was directly behind me and placed both of his hands on my shoulders. I was starting to shake as sobs overcame me and the tears fell freely. Zander never let go of me though and slowly I was able to take a few steps closer and through my tear blurred eyes I was able to see my grandmother's body resting peacefully.

"I am so sorry grandma," I whispered. "I should have done more for you. I should have-." my words shook as I gasped, unable to say anything more. "I'm sorry." My knees were starting to grow weak and I felt like I was going to collapse, but then Zander's arms were around me again, supporting me, and I turned into his chest letting the tears flow freely and wetting his shirt as I cried. His hands smoothed my hair and I felt his lips discreetly brush the top of my head before I pulled away, eyes swollen and face wet.

"You should go clean yourself up," he whispered quietly.

I sniffled and nodded, unable to respond as I turned and headed for the bathroom. I heard my sister call my name but ignored her as I closed the door. I splashed some cold water on my face and watched as the makeup I carefully applied ran and smeared across my eyes. Wetting a cloth I rubbed gently until it was off, then looked at my face. Without any makeup on I actually looked as young as I truly was. Makeup did a lot to enhance my features, and although I always had a fairly mature look to myself, I never realized how much makeup emphasized that. But standing here, naked and vulnerable, I looked like the sad seventeen year old I was. That fact almost had me in tears again as I thought about Zander, who was standing right outside waiting for me.

I squeezed my eyes shut to repress the tears and reached for the door handle, swinging it wide open and stepping out, my eyes instantly searching for him. I didn't see him and panic rose within me, my heart pounding hard as I glanced around, scared he had left without saying goodbye to me. Then I heard my sister laugh from the lobby, and somehow I knew she was with him.

I rounded the corner and watched as my sister reached out her hand and rested it on Zander's arm, sending him the biggest, most flirtatious grin she could as she rubbed it up and down intimately. Instantly my stomach flared and I felt a rush of anger, and as I continued to watch she flicked her head to the side, swishing her hair, and leaned in closer to him. I could tell Zander was uncomfortable with the exchange but he was too kind to say anything. I, however, wasn't going to let it go on for another moment longer.

Zander saw me and took a small step backwards trying to put distance between him and Monica but she just stepped closer, leaning in until she was nearly hanging off of him.

"-just so funny, you know? So how long have you been teaching?"

I stopped, my eyes widening slightly as Zander shook his head at me a little. "I graduated just last year. I've been teaching at Baysin for a few weeks now. It's been an amazing opportunity."

"You're lucky. I have a friend who's a teacher and she can hardly get work and she graduated three years ago!"

"Baysin was desperate. But I never would have met your sister if I hadn't started there. She is an exceptional student." He nodded at me and Monica spun, eyes wide in surprise as she saw me standing there. "Are you okay?"

I nodded, glancing back and forth between them. "I see you met my sister."

"He is fantastic, Ali! You didn't tell me your English teacher was so handsome." She brushed his arm again and I watched as he inched back, trying to create some space between them.

"Well, he is my teacher."

"I was just telling your sister what a fantastic student you are and how lucky I am to be your teacher and your mentor for the yearbook and paper."

"Mr Dionne has been incredible." My lips felt numb as I spoke, unsure how to proceed.

"You two seem very close." Monica pointed out. "You act more like friends than teacher and student."

"We work very closely together. We've put a lot of work into the yearbook." Zander smiled at me. "Miss Campbell would always talk about her grandmother, I felt almost like I knew her myself. When Mr Thorn said she'd passed I felt obligated to pay my respects."

"I-," I swallowed past a large lump in my throat. "I appreciate it. Thank you."

Zander reached out to rub my arm, "I should get going. Would you walk me out?"

I nodded and glanced back at Monica. "I'll be back in a sec."

"Take your time." She waved, winked at Zander, and turned back into the viewing room. The lobby was completely deserted now and as Zander reached to open and hold the door for me I realized that nearly all the cars from the street were gone as well.

I hadn't seen my father since he left for a smoke. Thinking this I reached into my purse for my lighter as Zander, almost reading my mind, handed me a cigarette. "Thanks," I mumbled.

"You looked like you needed one."

"I can't believe my sister," I said, blowing out a cloud of smoke. "She was all over you."

"She's- unique," Zander nodded, inhaling his own smoke. I waved at ScatterBrain who was leaning against his bike and we walked over to join him.

"You okay Jade?" he asked, reaching out to hug me again with one arm. I nodded as I wrapped my own arm around his back in a quick embrace. "We missed you this weekend."

I nodded, "I was disappointed to miss the party. How was it?"

"Typical," ScatterBrain shrugged.

"I wouldn't know what that looks like," I pointed out as I finished my cigarette and stomped it out.

"You will." ScatterBrain finished his own smoke and sat on his bike. "One of these days Zander will get you on his own bike." I glanced at the empty bike beside ScatterBrains.

"Is that yours?" The bike was black and sleek. I recognized the make as a Harley Davidson but beyond that my knowledge of motorcycles was limited. I did notice, however, that the name 'Professor' was painted across the side in small lettering.

Zander nodded, "what do you think?"

"Impressive."

Zander glanced around quickly before pulling me in for a hug and kissing my forehead. "You going to come up to The Club this week?"

I hesitated, then mumbled, "my dad got tickets to Shattered Life's show at Shakers on Wednesday. Besides, I should probably stick around for a few days. I'm not sure what he'll do, you know, since his mom just-." I trailed off, swallowing again.

"I get it," Zander mumbled. "I'm not happy about it, but I get it."

"Next weekend, I promise."

Zander nodded and kissed me again before climbing onto his bike, placing a helmet onto his head. "I wish I could be there for you tomorrow, but I have to work."

I nodded watching as he got settled. "It's okay. Thank you for coming today."

"By the way," Zander asked, glancing over at Scatter-Brain. "Where'd Butch go?"

He shrugged, playing with a few knobs and buttons on his bike. "Said something about Club business and that we'd see him later. He took off about fifteen minutes ago."

"Odd, I don't recall there being any business to attend." Zander looked thoughtful for a moment then shrugged, hitting a few switches and buttons himself. The engine roared to life making me jump at the sudden sound. "Anyways, we should get going. Call you later?" This was directed at me and I nodded, raising my hand in farewell as they both lifted their feet off the ground and drove away. My sister suddenly appeared at my side, eyes on their retreating backs.

"And he drives a motorcycle? Damn. Do you know if he's

single?"

My father showed up to the funeral with a black eye and a deep cut bleeding across his eyebrow. He wouldn't tell me how he got it or even where he'd been, but he stank of alcohol and I suspected that although he had seemed to be clean these past few days, he no longer was. I didn't have proof but the way he had been acting was a little too familiar and, I admit, I was a little scared for him.

He was so late showing up I almost had the service start without him until he stumbled in battered and bruised. I rushed over to him, pulled him into the private room adjoined for families of the deceased, and began questioning where he'd been and what had happened. Of course he wouldn't answer me and eventually Monica popped her head in and said we had to get started. I had sighed, angry and frustrated, and left my father alone. Five minutes later he joined us in the front row and sat for the service but he seemed restless, constantly twirling his thumbs and drumming his fingers on his knee.

My grandmother had specifically requested I give her eulogy, and as I was called to the podium my hands began to shake. I desperately wished Zander was there but he'd texted me just before the service started, sending me love and good wishes. I took a deep breath as I gazed out at the crowd.

"My grandmother wanted me to be the one to speak to all of you," I said, my voice shaking slightly. I swallowed and continued even as the words wavered. "She was a wonderful caring woman who raised me for most of my life. Caroline Campbell was the strongest and bravest woman I ever knew. She didn't shy away from life when she heard she was dying of cancer, she embraced it. She lived life to the fullest. She did whatever she wanted to, no matter the consequences." Tears had slowly begun to fall, but I kept going, trying to be as strong as grandma had been.

"All these flowers you see around here, they came from the greenhouse at the nursing home. She loved flowers, loved the colours, the smells, and the look. She said one flower could brighten up even the darkest of rooms. She believed that flowers made the world more beautiful and colourful. She'd spend hours in her garden, weeding and pruning even as the sun burnt her skin." I was slowly growing more confident as I spoke and my words began to come out clearer and stronger, the tears weaker.

"My grandmother was an inspiring woman. She made me who I am and for that I say thank you. Thank you for taking care of me. Thank you for being there for me when no one else was. I wouldn't be the person I am today if it wasn't for you.

"But it wasn't just me she inspired, she also touched many lives. All of you here today have been impacted by my grandmother in some way and although we are all heartbroken that she has left us, I want you to remember the good things she taught you, the lessons she showed you. And the next time you see a flower, don't shed a tear, smile. Smile because life is far better when we don't hold on to the bad, but embrace the beauty and the good."

Nobody clapped, nobody congratulated me on my speech, and nobody praised me for being so strong. We all sat and listened as final goodbyes were said, and then the pallbearers came to collect the casket. My brother and father were among those carrying grandma to her final resting spot, and neither one seemed upset as they grasped their handles and walked around to the back of the church where the cemetery was. There were a pile of roses, roses I recalled being in the greenhouse the last time I saw grandma, and as the casket was lowered to the ground we all picked one up and tossed it in. I waited, wanting to be the last one, and as the red petals floated down to land on the pile I allowed myself to shed a few more tears before standing up straight and being the first to walk away knowing grandma was finally at peace.

CHAPTER 13

Monica and Karson took off later that night and suddenly it was just my father and I again. Although we didn't spend much time together, having my brother and sister around for a few days almost made it feel like we were a family again, even if they hadn't stayed with us. Now, with their absence, I was reminded of what life was truly like and how unusual our situation was.

My father still wouldn't talk about his injuries. As the days passed the bruising around his eyes darkened and I was fairly certain the cut on his eyebrow should have had stitches but he refused to let me take him to the hospital. I knew there were injuries he was hiding from me as well, for I spotted him holding his sides occasionally and wincing, but he wouldn't admit anything to me. I also observed an odd pattern in his behaviour, finding him staying up all hours of the night before crashing at around four in the morning. He never seemed to eat, either, despite the fact I did my best to provide him with meals. I knew he was using again, but what type of drug he was on this time I couldn't say.

Meanwhile Nick's album had dropped. The songs I'd listened to in the confines of my room back at Aunt Patty's were now being publicly played all over town. Everywhere I went that day I heard their music, saw their album being promoted, and repeatedly listened to various interviews being played on local radio stations. I recalled the tickets my father had obtained for the next night and inwardly groaned at the thought of seeing Nick again. We hadn't spoken since we saw each other at the visitation and I dreaded running into him at the show for I knew he was going to ask about Zander and I wasn't quite sure what to say to him about it.

The first thing my father did as we arrived at the club was head straight to the bar. I watched him wearily as he spoke to the bartender and ordered a drink- or two, I sighed, as I saw the bartender hand him two pints of beer. Shaking my head I turned to find a table. Shakers was the bar the boys first played their live shows at. I had a lot of memories here, watching Nick up on stage, playing songs he wrote with his friends. Although the club catered to a 19+ crowd Nick always managed to get me in; it helped I had a fake ID as well.

The bouncer that night was one I recognized and he didn't even blink as I handed him my fake ID along with my ticket. My dad raised his eyebrows and I just shrugged walking in along with the rest of the line.

As my dad joined me at the table he slid a shot across from me: vodka, of course.

"What's this?" I asked, eyeing the clear liquid.

"For you."

"I'm underage," I pointed out.

My dad rolled his eyes, "the way you got in, I'd say you do this often enough."

I raised my eyebrows, offended. "I came here a lot with Nick, the only reason I have a fake is because of the band, and-."

"Just take the shot." I swallowed my retort and picked up the small glass, throwing it to the back on my throat without a wince. "You're a natural, just like your old man."

"Is that supposed to be a compliment?" I asked accepting the next shot he handed me.

"Would that be such a bad thing?"

I stared at him without blinking, "is that a serious question?"

He let out a breath, "okay, so I haven't always been the greatest dad. I'm trying to change that, kid. I'm here aren't I?"

"Yeah, but for how long?" I challenged. "A week? A month? How long are you going to stay clean this time?"

"I am clean."

"Dad," I shook my head, "c'mon."

"You don't believe me? I'll prove it to you."

I thought about his behaviour the past few days but decided not to bring it up. "Prove it to me by really sticking around."

Before my father could respond the lights dimmed and the music started. Girls all around us started screaming and I watched as the band slowly made their way onto the stage. There was smoke, there were lights, and there was a lot of theatrics that the band had never needed before. I personally thought it was all a little too played out and dramatic but the crowd seemed to love it.

My father was nodding along to the music but he wasn't paying attention to what was happening on stage, his head was bent down and he was staring at his phone. I watched his facial expressions change from worried, to angry, to annoyed. I wanted to ask him what was wrong, but I doubted he'd share his problems with me.

The band sang three songs, one was from their early stuff and the other two from their album, when my father suddenly yelled, "I'm going to the bar. Be right back," and left before I could respond to him. I stared at his retreating figure, then jumped when I heard another voice say, "enjoying the show?"

I whipped my head around to see Butch and Yankee, another member from The Club, standing beside the table in full gear and their Redneck Devil cuts clear on their backs. I glanced around but saw no one I recognized.

"What are you doing here?" I yelled over the sound of guitar blasting from Kevin's electric.

Butch leaned down, "we were sent to watch over you. We heard this could be a rowdy crowd and The Prince wanted to make sure you'd be safe here."

"The Prince?" I paused, and Danny's face came to my mind. I shook my head to clear it. "Why is Danny so concerned about me? What about Zander?"

"The Professor wasn't the one who sent us." Yankee shrugged.

"Look, Jade, you're family now and we keep our family safe. The Professor wants us to respect your privacy, but The Prince wanted us to watch over you."

"Watch over me." My voice came out flat and cold. "Because he doesn't trust me?"

"It's not that," Butch tried to say but Yankee interrupted him.

"You're still new, sweetheart. You've yet to prove to The Prince that you can be trusted. You're out, at a club, without The Professor- The Prince found that a little suspicious."

"I'm here with my *father*," I emphasized looking around the club again. Butch and Yankee shared a look, one I couldn't identify. I sighed, starting to get frustrated. "Look, if you want to keep an eye on me or whatever, that's fine, I have nothing to hide. But could you be a little more, I don't know, stealth about it? I don't feel like answering questions to my father about why two bikers are hanging around me."

"I don't-." Yankee started but Butch cut him off.

"Fine. We'll be over there if you need us," he pointed towards the wall across the room. "C'mon Yankee." He nodded his head away and Yankee, looking unsure, followed but not before glancing back at me. I wasn't entirely sure why Danny was so worried about me or what he'd have to be suspicious about. Besides, Zander knew exactly where I was and who I was with and he was fine with it. Wasn't he?

Shaking my head I turned back to the stage where Nick was wrapping up the forth song, Rage. I winced as the last note rang out of the electric guitar and the crowd screamed wildly.

"We're going to slow it down a little bit and play a classic from our early years. Ladies, and gentlemen," he added with a wink at the crowd- there weren't a lot of men there but there were a few. "Here's Everlasting."

Nick knew I was there, he'd been the one who'd given my father the tickets after all, but it was almost as if he searched the crowd for me as the opening chords to the song began. He found me and our eyes met as he leaned a little closer to the microphone and softened his voice; instantly a thousand memories flashed through my head as I recalled all the good times we'd had together, years of memories I'd tried to repress over the last few months. Tears were slipping down my face as Nick sang, and as he reached the end of the song I watched him wipe a few tears away from his eye as well. His gaze was on me as the song ended and the lights faded to black for a moment, then the guitars picked up again and Aaron banged on the drums as the lights flickered on and they moved into another one of their songs from the album.

For the rest of their set, though, Nick couldn't take his eyes off of me. My father had returned at one point, handing me another shot of vodka which I took gratefully, before disappearing yet again moments later. It came as no surprise to me when Shattered Life closed their set with Come Back To Me, the now familiar notes ringing in my ears as the crowd screamed louder, if that were even possible. I watched as Nick took a step towards the end of the stage and stared right at me as he sang the last verse of the song. Around me things went dark for a moment and all I could hear was Nick and those words as they echoed in my ear.

Come back to me, my baby
Come back to me, my love
Come back to me, my everything
Oh come back to me, Ali

Kevin, Aaron, and Nick exited the stage to cheers and screams. I could see Kevin and Aaron exchanging high fives, but when they turned to Nick he was gone, already halfway across the club walking towards me. They looked at each other, shrugged, then turned and opened a door beside the stage which I assumed led to their dressing room just as Nick reached my table.

"You came."

"You gave my dad tickets," I pointed out, reaching for the glass of half finished beer my dad had left on the table as something to do. It tasted flat on my tongue as I took a large sip.

"Which is what surprises me the most. You don't typically do things with your dad."

I forgot how much Nick knew about my family, forgot that he'd been around for a large portion of my dad's betrayal and abandonment. "He says he's clean this time."

"And you believe him?"

I shrugged and took another gulp. "I thought he was, but now? I don't know, to be honest."

Nick nodded and looked around, saw a few girls staring at him and waved, making them blush. He turned back to me, "how'd you like the show?"

"What were you doing Nick?" I asked, looking him in the eye as I spun the glass in my hand. "Why would you sing to me like that? Especially that song? You know what that song meant to me."

Nick looked down, ashamed. "I'm sorry Ali, but I miss you. I thought that writing about you would help me get over you, but seeing you these last few days made me realize how much I still love you."

"I thought I made it clear to you that I was seeing someone."

Nick shook his head looking frustrated. "Who? That guy from the funeral? He's way too old for you Ali!"

"You don't even know him, Nick." I spat as I grabbed the beer and downed it. "Besides, it doesn't matter who I'm seeing, the point is I'm seeing someone, I've moved on, and you should as well." I stood up and gathered my purse in my hands, turning to walk away from the table.

"Ali, wait," Nick reached out and grabbed my wrist to stop me. I caught movement from the corner of my eye and saw Yankee and Butch move to walk away from the wall they were positioned at. I quickly shook my head and they relaxed back, keeping their eyes on me. Nick, having spotted this exchange, paled as his eyes widened. "Do you know those guys Ali?"

"It doesn't matter." I shook my arm free from his grip and turned to face him full on. "Look, I need to get out of here. If you see my dad, tell him-."

"Tell him what? That you went off with two sketchy looking criminals?"

"They're not criminals," I snapped. "And no, just tell him I left."

I turned to go but he stopped me again, this time with his words. "Ali wait. Are you okay?"

I glanced back and smiled a little sadly at him, the concern evident in his eyes. "I'm fine Nick. Have a good night." Without waiting for a response I walked away heading straight for Butch and Yankee, stopping in front of them. "I've had too much to drink. Would you give me a ride?"

The two men exchanged looks. "We only have our bikes," Yankee pointed out.

"And I don't think you've even ridden on The Professors bike yet," Butch added.

"Please? I have to get out of here."

The men exchanged one more lasting look before finally Butch nodded his head towards the door. "Let's go."

Zander was walking out of The Clubhouse when we arrived and I ran into his arms as he held me tightly, a small smile gracing his lips. "Are you okay? I didn't expect to see you."

I glanced at Yankee and Butch who were parking their bikes. "A few friends gave me a ride."

Zander eyed them curiously, "I know, but I don't understand-."

"Danny sent them," I shrugged. Zander narrowed his eyes as he looked towards the door where Danny appeared, now speaking in quiet tons to Butch and Yankee. Whatever conversation they were having seemed serious by the expression on their faces. "Hey," I whispered trying to bring his attention back towards me. "It's okay. I'm actually glad they were there."

"What happened?" He asked, taking my hand and leading me towards the house. We stopped outside the barn so I could pat Marbles, a horse I felt had turned into my own over the past few weeks. It was hard for me to believe how much I had missed being here.

"My father got drunk, got me drunk, then Nick pissed me off. I had to get out of there but I couldn't drive myself."

Zander paused as he considered all of this but nodded as a smirk slowly graced his lips. "How did you feel on the back of the bike?"

I chuckled as I shook my head, my hair falling in front of my face. I reached up to brush it away. "Honestly? I closed my eyes and held Butch a little tighter than I ever imagined I would. I'd like to try it again, but only if you're the one driving."

Zander laughed and pulled me close, kissing my forehead, then grabbed my hand as we walked towards the house. As we stepped onto the wrap around porch the door opened, ScatterBrain pausing with his hand on the handle. Scarlet saw me and jumped up from her chair, pushing Zander out of the way so she could wrap her own arms around me. "I'm so sorry you lost your grandmother, Jade! I wanted to be there for you but Zander didn't want you to feel crowded. I've been thinking of you so much. How you holding up?"

I laughed softly at Scarlet's rambles as I held her close. "Thank you Scar, and I'm okay, really."

"I need to get going," ScatterBrain said, stepping aside so

we could walk into the house. "Will we see you tomorrow?" he asked, glancing at me.

"Uh," I looked at Zander who shook his head.

"I have to work tomorrow. I was getting ready to head out but then I got the call saying you were on your way- if we stay we need to be up by six so I can be back in Baysin, unless you wanted to stay here yourself?"

I shook my head, "I abandoned my car at the club and should probably pick it up first thing."

ScatterBrain nodded. "Where did Yankee and Butch go? I wanted to touch base about a few things before I leave."

Zander shrugged, "last I saw they were talking with Danny and-." We all turned to look out the door as the sound of bikes filled the air and saw three of them speed past, presumably Danny, Butch, and Yankee. Zander and ScatterBrain looked at each other.

"Want me to follow them and see what they're up to?" ScatterBrain asked slowly, his foot already halfway out the door.

Zander hesitated, glanced at me, then shook his head. "It's not worth it, man. Whatever they're doing can't be that important."

"Do you have any idea what it is though?" ScatterBrain looked intensely into Zander's eyes.

He sighed and shook his head, "nah and right now I don't care."

"You're just as high ranking as he is, Zander." ScatterBrain pointed out. "Whatever he's involved in-."

"Just leave it," Zander insisted, reaching out for my hand. "Jade and I are going to go to bed. Go home, ScatterBrain, and get some rest."

We headed towards the stairs and I glanced back at ScatterBrain who was biting his lip, worriedly. When he saw me looking he tried to relax his shoulders and raised a hand to wave. "Good night, Jade."

"Night," I whispered, allowing Zander to pull me up the

stairs after him. I couldn't explain the sinking feeling that suddenly came over me, my stomach feeling like it was knotting, squirming, and tightening. But I felt wholly uneasy as I heard ScatterBrain's footsteps and the sound of the door closing as he left.

Walking into my house I found it dark and deserted and that same bad feeling I was having last night returned. "Dad?" I called out, my voice echoing but there was no answer. I knew he'd been having late nights, but usually there was some sign of him- his shoes by the door, a few empties scattered around, even his sweater draped over the railing of the stairs. But the house looked too clean to me. "Dad?" I called again walking up the stairs, my hand brushing the railing. I passed the bathroom at the top and saw his toothbrush missing, and my stomach sank. "Dad?" I tried once more finding the door to his room open. I looked around, found the bed still made, his closet door thrown open and empty, and his dresser drawers half open as if he'd packed in a hurry.

I pulled my phone out of my pocket and hovered over my fathers number- was it worth it to call him? He was clearly gone. No note, no message- nothing. So much for sticking around this time. I shouldn't have felt the weight of disappointment, but for some reason this time felt worse than any time before. A part of me had honestly believed him when he said he was clean and wanted to stay and take care of me. I sighed, closing my contacts list and glancing at the time. It was early and I knew Zander would be arriving at school soon. My dad was gone, my siblings were gone- maybe I should just go back to school, where I'd at least be surrounded by other people? If nothing else, at least I still had Zander.

That turned out to be a mistake though. I pulled into a deserted parking lot as it was so early still. Students wouldn't be arriving for at least twenty more minutes, and although there were a few cars that belonged to other staff, it was still fairly empty. The sound of a motorcycle caught my attention and I recognized Danny's bike pull into the lot and speed towards the staff zone. My heart began to race as I inched away from my car and rushed over there, trying to stay hidden- something told me this wasn't an encounter I should be seen witnessing.

"What the hell are you doing here?" I heard Zander hiss as Danny got off of his bike and removed his helmet. "Are you trying to get me fired?"

"Relax, brother," Danny smirked, taking a few steps forwards. I ducked down behind a minivan, which was the only other vehicle present, peeking up in order to see the two of them. Zander glanced around, worriedly, then stepped closer to Danny. "This is Club Business."

"It couldn't wait?"

"Not this time, it's urgent."

"Is this about last night?" Zander asked quietly. "Where did you go? What happened?"

"I had business to attend to, but it got me thinking- about Jade," I sucked in some breath, then raised my hand to cover my mouth hoping they hadn't heard me. They didn't appear to as Danny kept talking. "I don't trust her."

Zander growled and took another step towards his brother. "Oh yeah? And why's that?" I could tell he was trying to stay calm, keep his composure, but his brother's words had pissed him off.

"How long have you known her, brother? How do you know we can truly trust her?"

"Where is this coming from Danny?" Zander's voice sounded dangerous as he took one more step towards his brother. He was only a few inches away now and his face looked angry. "The two of you seemed to be getting along just fine the other day."

"That was before-."

"Before what?" Zander snapped, reaching up to shove his brother. Danny stumbled backwards a few steps but steadied himself, narrowing his eyes at Zander and fixing his Cut, which went lopsided. "What's changed your mind? What has she done to make you question her loyalty?"

"She hasn't done anything, Zander, and that's the problem!" Danny shouted causing me to wince and I looked around the parking lot myself to make sure no one was around. "She's done nothing to prove she cares about this club, she's done nothing to show me she's serious about committing to us! She can't even show up to the things that matter most to us, Zander! Where was she during our biggest celebration, huh?"

"Her grandmother had just died," Zander seethed, "She had other things on her mind, priorities-."

"The priority should be The Club."

"She never asked for this, Danny," Zander argued, face red, "and I think she's doing a damn good job for someone who was thrown into this life."

"She has to do better." Danny stated standing up straight. "Do you want her to become an associate? Do you want her to be trusted by The Club?" I held my breath as Danny spoke, afraid to see where this conversation was going. Zander and I hadn't discussed whether or not I'd want to be a part of The Club in that manner. I'd always imagined that maybe someday I would take that step, but I hadn't expected it to happen any time soon.

Zander was hesitant now, as well, as he bit his lip for a moment before saying, "we hadn't talked about it yet."

"What is there to talk about, brother?" Danny sneered. "If she wants to be with you, it means being a part of us. You can't have one without the other, brother. You know that. You claim she's trustworthy, you claim she's loyal? Then make it official." Zander and Danny both turned as a red car pulled into the parking lot and parked in the student zone. Danny took a few steps back, towards his bike, and picked up his helmet. Before he slid it on he glared at Zander again and said, "You have a choice you need to make. Either induct her in, or cut her loose. There's no in between." Without waiting for Zander to respond Danny straddled his bike, slipped his helmet on his head, and took off out of the parking lot, just as a few more cars began to pull in, some heading towards the staff lot.

I watched as Zander shook his head slightly and reached into his truck to pull out a few books before turning and heading into the school as if nothing had happened. But me? I was a little shaken up after everything I'd just heard. Danny didn't trust me. Danny wanted Zander to choose between me and The Club. Danny wanted me out, and I knew that only meant one thing to him.

I most definitely wasn't ready to go back to school today.

I sat on the couch, alone in my grandmother's abandoned house, staring at a blank TV contemplating what to do next. I'd been there for hours, Danny's words spiralling around in my head *Induct her or cut her loose. Induct her or cut her loose. Induct her or cut her loose. There's no in between.*

Zander and I had only been dating for about a month, but after everything we've been through it felt like we'd been together for years. The connection we had was strong, real, and undeniable- there was a reason the universe put us together and has challenged us with such difficult obstacles, but we've managed to come out on the receiving end of each and every one of them so far. This would be no different.

If Danny wanted me to prove myself to him, I would, even if it meant inducting myself into The Club. Would it really be any different, though, than what I already did now? After all Scarlet was an Associate and all I ever saw her do was cook, clean, and bind the wounds of the men when they got injured on a run. Zander himself said that associates hardly got involved in runs and Club Business, it was the Prospects that handled the dirty and difficult things, so the odds of me getting tied up in Club Business was slim. So why did this decision make me feel so uneasy? Was it because it was being forced upon me, rather than letting me make the choice when I was ready? Was it because Danny was basically threatening me?

Or was it because Danny didn't even really trust me and only wanted me inducted so he could keep me under his thumb?

I felt as if becoming an associate meant throwing my life away. How could I balance being a part of The Club with school? How could I go to university in the fall and still be connected to The Redneck Devils? Danny basically said I hadn't contributed to The Club, but what did I truly have to offer them? What could I offer them from a dorm room in university? Was there a point in even going?

My phone rang and somehow I knew it was Zander before I even looked at the caller ID. I wanted to ignore it, but Zander had no idea I had been there in the parking lot and saw what had happened this morning. I couldn't let him know I was there, so I answered the phone with my heart hammering anxiously. "Hello?"

"Hey, everything okay?"

"Yeah," I said, trying to make myself sound nonchalant. "Well, actually," I took a breath realizing Zander also had no idea my father had taken off. "No, it's not. My dad left again."

"What? When?"

Air came out of my mouth in a huff, "good question. My guess would be last night some time. I feel so guilty- I mean clearly something was bothering him last night but instead of talking to him and helping him I took off, and so did he."

"You can't blame yourself," Zander countered. "You tried to help him, remember? You were there for him. You supported him. But he didn't want your help, he denied and ignored your questions, just as he's been doing your whole life. I know he's your father, but maybe it's best that he's gone."

I knew what Zander was saying was true but it was still difficult to hear. "You're right," I whispered trying to swallow past the lump that was forming in my throat.

Zander cleared his throat into the phone, "so, listen. I'm heading out to Riverton tomorrow and was wondering if you'd like to join me. I was thinking about riding out there and giving you a real experience on the back of a bike. I promise it will be a lot more fun than it was the other night riding on the back of Butch's."

I laughed as I recalled the way I clung, terrified, to Butch as he raced to Riverton from Baysin- I was thankful the vodka shots had numbed my body, otherwise I'm fairly certain I would have been shaking by the time we'd reached Horse Shoes. Then I remembered why Zander was actually asking for me to join him at The Club, and my heart began to race again. I licked my lips and picked up my lighter off of the coffee table, flicking it on and off, my eyes trained on the flame. "Okay," I finally managed to say.

"Okay?"

"Yeah," I mumbled, "I mean, why wouldn't I?"

"No reason," Zander said a little too quickly, "I guess I just thought you may need some more time or something, and-."

"I don't need more time, Zander. You know I love you, and I love Scarlet, and ScatterBrain- even Butch showed me a fair bit of loyalty the other night by respecting my wishes. I enjoy being at Horse Shoes, and as crazy as it sounds I enjoy being around all of The Club as well. They've become my family."

"I'm happy to hear that," Zander admitted, sounding a little relieved.

"I've actually been thinking," I took a big breath and spat the next sentence out before I could stop myself, "that maybe I should come around a little more often? Maybe be a little more hands on? Kind of like Scarlet, you know?"

Silence met me on the other line and I held my breath, waiting for his response. "Are you saying you want to be an Associate? Ali, that's a serious decision to make."

It was the first time he'd spoken my name while on the phone, and considering I knew he was on his lunch break at work and could be easily over heard, I knew I'd hit a nerve. "I'm ready for it, Zander. Besides, The Club is basically the only family I have left. With my father gone- I just feel like we may as well make it official, you know?"

"But do you really think this is the answer? Once you're in-."

"I know." I stated firmly. "I know that the only way out is-."

"Death, Ali, it's death. Are you certain this is what you want to do?"

"Do you not want me to be an Associate, Zander?" I asked, feeling a little hurt. Wasn't this what he and Danny had just been discussing this morning? "I thought you'd be happy-."

"I am thrilled you want to be more involved, I'm ecstatic you love and care for my family and friends so much that you'd be willing to do this for yourself. But I don't think you've truly stopped to consider the consequences of this decision."

"I have been thinking about this nonstop for a long time Zander," I snapped angrily into the phone. "Do you really think I would make a choice like this without weighing my options? Without considering all of the side effects? But guess what? My love for you outweighs them all! My respect and loyalty are worth more than anything else I have to offer. I am ready to pledge myself to them- are you ready to accept me into your life one hundred percent?" I challenged. "This will only work if you are completely on board with it."

Zander was once again silent and for a moment I actually worried he'd deny my request, that our relationship wasn't as strong as I thought it was. Then he laughed softly and whispered, "you have no idea how happy I am to hear you say all of that Ali."

"Really?" I asked as my heart leapt, both in excitement and in fear.

"Really. This- well, it just makes things a whole lot easier for everyone."

"In what way?" I asked, trying not to sound like I knew what he was getting at.

"It's nothing," he said, avoiding the topic all together. "Look, I have to get back to class. But I will call you later and we will finalize some details, okay? I love you."

"Love you too." We hung up and I slowly set my phone down, my hand shaking slightly. There was no turning back now, I'd made my choice. I was going to dedicate my life to The Redneck Devils, I was going to induct myself into this Club, I was promising myself over to them. A single tear slipped from my eye but I didn't reach up to wipe it away, instead I let it fall, leaving a small wet trail all the way down from my eye to my cheek.

"Take this." I looked at the black helmet Zander held out to me skeptically. It was small, round, and didn't look very strong.

"I don't really think that'll protect my head if we crash."

"Ali," he shook his head in exasperation. "You're not getting on this bike without a helmet. Besides, you wore one when you rode with Butch, right?"

"I was drunk," I pointed out, as I thought back to that night to clarify that I had, indeed, worn a helmet. "But yes, I did. I would have worn anything." He continued to hold the helmet towards me and I sighed, reaching out to take it. "Fine." I pulled my hair back into a low ponytail and slipped the helmet on, clipping the buckle under my chin then turned to look at the bike, a little wearily. "Are you sure it's safe?"

Zander laughed softly, "You've ridden one already, remember?"

"I know, but again, I was drunk."

Zander chuckled again smiling at me. "Don't you trust me?"

"Of course I do."

"Then get on." He walked over to the bike and swung his leg over the side until he was sitting on the seat. I still hadn't moved so he looked over at me, grinning mockingly. "Are you coming?"

With only another moment of hesitation I finally marched over there purposefully, stepping onto the little bar and swinging myself on, using Zander's back as a clutch. Once I was finally settled I looked around, feeling a little off balance. This had been much easier when I was drunk.

"Happy?" I asked sarcastically.

Zander just looked over his shoulder at me with a smirk, pulling his own helmet off of the handlebars and sliding it onto his head. "I'll give you instructions as we go around turns, but you should be fine. As long as you hold on tight." With that he hit a few buttons and switches and I felt the bike start to vibrate as the engine roared to life below me. After a few revs of the engine Zander lifted the stand up from the bike, placed his feet up, and took off speeding down the road. I screamed as I clutched onto him tightly.

Riding with Butch had been a blur- I had been angry at Nick, annoyed with my father, and buzzed off the vodka. Everything seemed to happen so fast that I hardly took the chance to experience it. This time, though, I was living fully in the moment.

In the beginning my stomach had been flipping nervously and I felt completely unsteady. However as we rode I slowly became a little more comfortable, and the fear changed to excitement and exhilaration- I'd never experienced anything more thrilling. Zander made sure to yell back for me to lean with him into the turn as the bike sped around a corner, and for a moment I thought I was going to fall off and held his waist a little tighter, but then we straightened back out and continued down the road until we passed the sign for Riverton, The Redneck Devil's tag standing out brightly on it. By the time we pulled into Horse Shoes my smile was wide as I hopped off of the bike and threw my arms around Zander, reaching up to pull his face towards mine in a passionate kiss.

When I stepped back away from him I saw someone out of the corner of my eye standing in the driveway waiting for us: Danny. My smile slowly faded from my face as I reached up to unfasten the helmet strap and took it off, tossing it to the ground. I turned my attention towards him, my hand reaching back for Zander's, but suddenly Zander wasn't there. When I glanced back to see where he would have gone I found him standing away, frowning and his eyes looking sad and apologetic, as more members of The Club slowly circled around me. I was nervous and my heart began to race as I swallowed and looked back towards Danny. I squared my shoulders and stood up a little straighter, tossing my hair over my shoulder to try and look more confident, despite the nervous flutters I was feeling. I hadn't expected this to be such a serious display.

Danny took a step forward and narrowed his eyes a little, studying me. Finally he spoke. "Jade." I tilted my chin up a little more and folded my hands together in front of me. "The Club has come to the agreement that you have earned your place here as an Associate to The Redneck Devils." My lips twitched, whether because they wanted to smile or frown I wasn't entirely sure, but I fought to keep a straight face. "However, before such an initiation can be conducted there are a few- questions- I want to ask you first." I heard something behind me, something that sounded like a gasp and feet struggling. I wanted to look back and see what was going on but I couldn't move my eyes away from Danny. His face looked so serious, his eyes set angrily, and I felt my confidence begin to waver as he took another step towards me. That was the first time I noticed he was holding something in his hand- a magazine.

He dropped it on the ground where it slid, landing inches from me. My eyes followed it and I saw Nick's face on the cover, along with a photo of me and him at Coffee Cafe. I stared at it, my mouth opening in a silent gasp, as tears filled my eyes. My confidence had completely disappeared and was replaced with fear.

"Care to explain this?"

"What the fuck are you doing?" I heard Zander yell, then the sound of more scuffling. This time I turned my head slowly and saw Yankee wrapping a hand around Zander's mouth, Six Inch struggling to hold one arm, while Butch grabbed the other. Zander's eyes were narrowed and I could tell he was fighting them with all of his strength. Whatever was happening right now, Zander had had no idea about it, and he was angry.

My hands shook as I turned back to face Danny and I swallowed hard as tears sprang to my eyes. I blinked rapidly and glanced down at the magazine again, my eyes landing on the headline. *Shattered Life's Lead Singer Nick Meets With Ali In Coffee Shop*

My voice wavered as I finally opened my mouth and said, "what do you want to know?"

"The truth." Danny took another step towards me and I couldn't stop myself from taking a small step back wanting distance between us. "Who are you, Jade?"

I glanced back at Zander who had finally stopped struggling, but he still looked pissed. He tried shaking his head at me, but I knew what I had to do, I didn't have a choice, not anymore. Turning back to Danny I whispered, "Alessaundra."

"What?"

In a louder voice I stumbled out, "my name is Alessaundra."

"So you lied?" Danny asked in a loud voice, a sneer sliding across his face. "You lied to us all?"

"No!" I shrieked, "no it's not like that."

"Then what is it?" Danny roared.

"I-," my voice faltered as it shook and I gulped. "I just wanted to be with Zander! I never asked for any of this."

"You want to know what I think?" Danny asked in a low, dangerous voice as he took another step towards me; I was frozen to the spot now, unable to step away. "I think you knew exactly who Zander was when you met him. I think you knew exactly what he was a part of. I think you knew exactly who we were!"

"I didn't!" I insisted.

"And you pretended to be someone else, pretended to be oblivious to this whole life, just so you could help your father."

"N-no," I stuttered, then squinted my eyes and drew my eyebrows together in confusion. "W-wait. My- my father? What does he have to do with this?" My heart started pounding harder as little pieces started to click together. My father, his drug addiction, and the fact The Redneck Devils controlled the drug source around here. Was it possible, could it even be realistic for him to have been involved in any of this?

"Jonathan Campbell," Danny stated coldly. "Is your father, correct?"

"I-," I swallowed and nodded. "Yes." I heard a few members around us whisper among themselves for a moment, but when I glanced back at Zander he looked just as confused as I felt. I turned back to Danny. "What does he have to do with any of this?"

"As if you don't already know," Danny sneered. "Your father was one of our biggest clients three years ago! He owed us thousands of dollars in merchandise! I assume my dear brother has shared our main business with you?" I nodded, swallowing nervously. "Of course he has. I can only assume you took all of that information back to your father, didn't you?"

"No!" I insisted again, my hands trembling.

"Lies!" Danny roared, causing me to flinch. "All you have done to us since day one is lie! You had this Club wrapped around your manipulative little finger. Jokes on you, though, isn't it, Jade."

"What do you mean?" I asked, tears in my eyes. My lips quivered as Danny took another step towards me. All I wanted to do was turn and run, but I couldn't move.

"Your father came here begging us to settle his debt, tossing us ten thousand dollars and promising to get the rest of it to us in a week. That was Sunday night." Flashes of my father's bruises appeared in my mind- his black eye, the cut on his eyebrow, and the way he winced as he walked which I was certain now were bruised ribs. "We thought we made ourselves clear to him, but then Butch and Yankee saw him at that club with you, carelessly spending money he should have been giving to us! When they told me what they'd seen I knew you couldn't be trusted, knew he couldn't be trusted. Zander tried to convince me you were loyal-," Danny moved his eyes from me for the first time to look over at his brother. I turned too, and watched Zander start struggling again as Danny said, "but you were wrong, weren't you, brother! I knew what had to be done."

"What did you do?" I whispered facing him again.

"We took care of business."

I felt queasy as his words hit me and I had to swallow to stop bile from rising in my throat. "Meaning what?" I asked, but I knew the answer. There was only one way Danny dealt with traitors.

"We killed him, Alessaundra." My hands started to shake uncontrollably and my knees felt weak, I wasn't sure how much longer my body could support my weight as his words crashed into me. "We found him trying to flee town, with another five thousand dollars hidden in his bag and no intention of paying us the remainder of his debt. Do you realize how many drugs he stole from us over the years? He's been in hiding for the last six months, hiding because he knew what would happen to him if he showed his face around here again. Then you come along- it seemed a little too convenient to me."

"I didn't-," I tried to blink back the tears that were flowing down my face. "I didn't know, I swear."

"I don't believe you," Danny snapped. "Why should we trust anything you have to say?"

My legs finally gave out and I crumpled to the ground. I heard Zander call out my name, but that was all he managed to say before his mouth was covered again. I felt the hard ground under me as I rolled into a ball and began crying in the middle of the driveway. I had never felt a strong connection to my father but I had always hoped that some day, maybe, he'd come back and be the father he never got to be. The fact he had been here at all to help and support me through my grandmother's death had been the first step in proving to me he could, in fact, be a loving father. Now I'd never know if he was actually capable of it.

"Get up." Danny demanded but I couldn't move. My body shook as sobs overcame me and I cried harder. I heard Danny's footsteps then felt his foot nudge my body, rolling it over until I was forced to face him, rocks digging into my back as his foot held me down. Zander tried yelling out again, his screams muffled by Yankees hands. I looked up at Danny through blurred eyes as he bent down to stare into my eyes. "You don't deserve to become a part of this Club."

"That's enough Danny!" Zander's yell had Danny looking up towards his brother. A shadow passed over me and the next thing I knew Zander was tackling Danny to the ground, reaching up and swinging his fist in his face. Danny growled, throwing Zander off of him and rising up to punch him in return. I could barely move, too overcome with grief and fear, but the fight was quickly broken up as ScatterBrain pulled Zander back and Yankee grabbed Danny to restrain him. "Let me go," Zander growled.

"Not until you're calm," ScatterBrain muttered.

"I'm going to kill him," Zander seethed, "you son of a bitch!"

Danny's laugh was a little hysterical as he said, "you can't touch me!"

Zander thrashed out harder but I just continued to cry. I could hear voices around me, but it was ScatterBrian's quiet voice saying, "don't worry about your brother right now, man. She needs you," that penetrated my ears.

"She can't be trusted!" Danny yelled. "Do you all see that now?"

"Fuck you, Danny," Zander yelled. "You have no idea what you're talking about, you know that? It was *my* idea for her to lie! I introduced her to Scarlet as Jade, I told her to lie to you all, and do you want to know why? It's because she's only seventeen years old! It has nothing to do with her fucking father!"

Danny laughed even louder, "seventeen? You've got to be fucking kidding me."

"She's a minor," Zander stated, "and what's more, she's one of my students!" Suddenly the voices that were whispering around us were quiet, and Zander's was the only one speaking. "We met in a book store in Baysin. I had no idea her age- and she had no clue who I was. I swear to you all, on my patch," he emphasized, "that Alessaundra was just as surprised to learn about me as I was when I learned about her. She wasn't infiltrating the club, she hated her father! If you'd done your research, brother, you would know that her father was a deadbeat drug addict who was never around! And Ali? She's a straight A student, top of her class, student body president! Does that sound like someone who was trying to learn The Club secrets for her father?"

As Zander talked the tears began to subside and my body stopped shaking. I was able to open my, now swollen, eyes and watch as he approached each member of The Club sounding every bit the leader he was meant to be.

"We have had to keep our relationship a secret in Baysin, for if anyone ever found out I would get fired and Ali, herself, could face some serious consequences. The day I brought her here was the first time we had been able to go out in public. I wasn't expecting anyone from The Club to be around! But you all showed up, because you'd found Kovach, and to be honest I don't regret it. I don't regret it because it allowed Ali to see my secret, the one I had been hiding from her, the one that had been killing me because I didn't know how she'd react to it. But Ali proved to me that day that she was stronger than any one I had ever known. She proved to me that she could be trusted, and relied upon to keep our secrets. Alessaundra found out some scary shit that night, yet here she remains, despite the fact she is only seventeen! Yet you want to believe Danny when he says she's been spying, that she's been trying to help her father all this time?

"The fact that Alessaundra is Jonathan's daughter is a complete coincidence, and therefore irrelevant. Not to mention the fact that he's supposedly this big, important client yet I had no idea who he was, or the fact he was connected to Ali until today. How is it that this guy was such a big deal to The Club, yet he hasn't been discussed in months?"

"You gave up The Club," Danny sneered. "You traded in your declared title for that of a Weekend Warrior! You said it yourself, all you cared about was Kovach. You wanted nothing more to do with us. You didn't deserve to know all the details of this Club!"

"And in the last month I have been here, I have thrown myself back into this Club, and proved to you all that I am more than that of a Weekend Warrior, yet you still kept this from me! We're supposed to be equals, Danny! Yet you've withheld vital information. You're trying to say Ali can't be trusted, but maybe it's you we shouldn't trust."

"Speak for yourself!" Danny growled. "You, the one who's never wanted this life. The one who's tried to get out of it on multiple occasions. The one who kept one toe in the door just in case he needed help-."

"Because you made me!" Zander retorted.

"You just don't want to admit to yourself that you've secretly always loved this life. You can go around and act like you hated it and wanted out- but the truth is, you got scared! When our father died, you got scared that the same thing could happen to you, so you fled instead." I had never heard either Zander or Danny talk about their dad, and as the conversation turned towards him I found myself slowly sitting up, pushing myself on weak arms until I was able to shift my weight enough to sit comfortably. Zander was only feet away from Danny, who was still being restrained by Yankee. The two were staring at each other now almost as if they forgot they even had an audience.

"I didn't get scared," Zander stated coldly.

"Yes you did. You got scared and you ran, withdrawing yourself from this life as much as you possibly could."

Zander was quiet as he stared at his brother. Finally he shook his head, taking a step towards him. "It doesn't matter one way or the other. What matters is that I'm here, I'm back, and I deserve to be treated as the President that I am. Which means," he added, finally turning to address the gathered crowd, eyeing each member of The Club as he looked at them, "you all need to show me the same respect you show him." He raised his arm and pointed at his brother without looking back at him. "If there's a problem, tell me. If you have something to share, find me. I'm done being the good guy, I'm done being the outside guy. I'm your fucking president and it's about time I fulfill that role."

Without waiting for anyone to respond Zander turned and strolled over to me. Our eyes met and I saw the worry that was hidden behind the anger as he bent down, wrapped one arm around my legs and the other around my back as he lifted me up off the ground and held me close. "I'm taking Alessaundra upstairs to my room. I expect everyone to respect our privacy for the next few hours. Church will commence at eight o'clock tomorrow morning- mandatory attendance."

ScatterBrain stepped aside to make a space for Zander to pass through and as he carried me towards the house he bent down and kissed my head gently before whispering, "are you okay?"

I nodded, nuzzling my head into his chest but unable to speak any words aloud. I think he understood though. Scarlet swung the door open as she watched us approach but she didn't say anything, just stepped aside and let us pass. Vetta was sitting on the couch and she turned narrowed eyes on us as we walked through the living room. Zander didn't pay her any attention, though, but I couldn't keep my eyes off of her. I knew Vetta was close with Danny, and I was fairly certain she and I would never have the chance to become as close as she was with Scarlet.

"I hate this," I mumbled into Zander's chest as we laid in bed early the next morning. I didn't sleep much, too busy tossing and turning, my mind whirling as I tried to sort through the events that had happened hours before. I don't think Zander had slept much either for he was a little too still and I heard a few deep sighs escape from him. But throughout the night neither one of us had spoken. I'd felt Zander crawl out of bed early, around five, to call in sick to work- there was no way he was going to be able to make it to school today.

"Which part?" Zander asked, pressing his lips softly to the top of my head.

I raised my head so I could look up into his face. "I hate that my loyalty is being questioned. I hate that everyone seems to be arguing and picking sides when The Club is supposed to be about unity and family. I hate that Danny has basically made me out to be some sort of liar-."

Zander frowned, "you can't worry about all of that right now."

"It's my fault all of this is happening Zander. If I hadn't come here with you- or if I'd never lied about who I was- if we were just honest in the beginning-." Tears had formed in my eyes and they began to leak down, sniffling I reached up to wipe them away. "Not to mention my father's dead- at the hands of your brother, no less. How can I ever trust him or The Club again, after all that?"

"You don't have to," Zander murmured, "there is nothing keeping you here."

"You are," I stated firmly. "You are what keeps me here. You are the reason I want to be involved in The Club, you are the reason all of this means something to me. I love you Zander. This is your home, these people are your family- they matter to you and so they matter to me. I want them to like me, I want them to trust me."

"Are you certain?" Zander asked, staring deep into my eyes. "Are you sure this is what you really want?"

I sniffled, reaching up to wipe my nose with my sleeve. "I've told you many times, Zander- I want you, and if that means being a part of this, then yes, it's what I want."

He closed his eyes as if in pain for a moment but nodded, raising his head to look at me again. "Okay. Then we're going to have to prove your loyalty to The Club."

"How?" My voice was desperate as I pleaded with him.

He paused for a moment, glancing at the wall deep in thought. "We could modify a few of the initiation tests to suit you. They won't be easy, though."

"This life isn't easy, so why should the tests be?" I grumbled.

"I'm serious, Alessaundra. These tests will be- extreme. They could pertain to illegal activities, activities that might get you into trouble. Are you sure you're ready for this?"

A moment of panic passed through me, my heart racing as I closed my eyes and took a few deep breaths in order to settle it. Once I got my heart rate under control I reopened them and stared directly into Zander's as I said, "I'm ready."

The look he gave me was sad, but he nodded, acknowledging and respecting my decision. "Okay. I'll bring it up at Church, I'll get everyone on board- and then we'll get started. Immediately."

CHAPTER 14

"If you want to be a trusted member of The Redneck Devils, you're going to have to prove your loyalty to us." Danny's words were cold and hard- emotionless- as he stood in front of me, his eyes boring straight into mine with an intensity that had me unable to blink as I kept eye contact. His arms were behind his back and he was standing so straight I felt as if I had to straighten my posture as well, so I sat up in the hard wooden chair I was in, squared my shoulders, and continued to lock my gaze on his. "The Professor has plead his case to us and we've agreed to put you through a few tests in order to give you the chance to prove yourself. He can have no part in the planning of these tests and therefore I will have full control over them. Are you ready to hear what your first test will be?"

I swallowed but nodded, took a deep breath and stated clearly, "I'm ready."

Danny's lips twitched, but I wasn't sure if it was from fighting to smile or frown. "Alessaundra Campbell. I hereby declare this the beginning of your initiation. Are you prepared for the consequences that will proceed these tests if you shall fail?"

"I am."

"Then let's begin. Come with me." Glancing around the

room as Danny turned towards the door I caught Zander's eye briefly. He nodded slightly but didn't say a word- now was not the time to speak- and I slowly stood up from my chair and followed Danny out the door. We'd been sitting in the house but now he led me towards the mysterious third barn- their sacred space- the one I had yet to step foot in. A few bikes were parked outside and I could spot Zander's next to Danny's as the first two bikes there. Danny stopped outside, looked back to make sure I was there, then reached for the door and swung it open. It was dark as we stepped inside, footsteps echoing behind us as the members of The Club joined us. My hands were shaking slightly now, my heart beating hard in my chest, my breathing coming out rapid and shallowly. Danny finally flicked on a light and I blinked, my eyes adjusting to the sudden change as I studied the space around me.

"Welcome to the headquarters of The Redneck Devils. There's no going back now. Once you've stepped foot inside this building- you can't ever leave it. Do you understand?"

Gulping I nodded, my voice shaking a little as I said, "I do."

This time I detected the smirk that flickered across his lips. "Tell me, Alessaundra, how do we earn our profit?"

"Club dues," I stated.

Danny rolled his eyes, "how else?"

I licked my lips slowly, glancing around the barn again. The room I stood in was fairly bare with a few motorcycles tucked away in the back and some wooden crates stacked beside some hay bales. I knew the barn was far larger than the room we stood in, but I wasn't sure what else resided behind the other doors. My eyes stopped on the hay bales and a conversation I once had with Zander echoed through my head, then I remembered what Danny had said about my father, and how he owed them money. I looked back at Danny and stated loudly, "you control the drug source around the area, ensuring nothing contaminated passes through."

"How do we do that?" This time I didn't know the answer. I shook my head slightly, lowering it down in shame. "Professor, why don't you enlighten her?" Danny sneered. I whipped my head up, my eyes widening as they moved from Danny and I turned back towards Zander who was standing behind me. Since Zander was pledging me he was supposed to remain silent throughout the initiation and even he seemed caught off guard by this request.

"Well," Zander cleared his throat and stepped forwards. Watching his face I knew his mind was spinning, wondering exactly what, and how much, he should say. "Each month three members of The Club are assigned a run up to the North of the province, when they return they come back with a trailer full of hay bales. Inside these bales are bricks and bricks of cocaine. These tend to be the runs where we also participate in and rig a few horse races, bringing some of our best runners and betting on them at the tracks. We also have a barn with three horses up North so we don't always need to transport them back and forth. A few friends take care of them for us.

"On a weekly basis various Club members will go on runs outside of town where they will meet with our suppliers- these runs are less discreet as we aren't using the Horse Trailer and trying to keep up with our cover story. Members must always travel in pairs, or groups of three to ensure our safety and well being. There's always a chance we will run into a rival Club during these outings. No man should ever be alone during one of these runs. At times a Prospect will accompany a member if no one else is able to. Rarely will The Prince or I attend one of these runs, unless it is with one of our higher suppliers.

"Occasionally we go across the border to obtain higher quality supply. We have friends in various Clubs who will provide a place for us to stay. We value their hospitality while we are there, and are always willing to lend a hand in whatever troubles they are having at that time. The American Clubs, though, tend to be involved in some more dangerous situations. But they supply us with more than just drugs."

I narrowed my eyes in confusion, wanting to ask what other supplies they may provide but afraid to say something wrong. Danny must have seen my confusion though.

"Weapons." I turned my head to look at Danny, my mouth dropping open a little as the word reached my ears. "They provide us with weapons, Alessaundra. You see, it's far easier to obtain firearms in America than it is here in Canada."

"What kind of weapons?" I whispered. Danny smirked and nodded towards Zander and I quickly turned to look at him.

"Guns- hand guns, rifles, shot guns, anything we need basically. We stock up on ammo while we're there. They sometimes sell us bow and arrows as well, and knives-."

"They particularly like The Professors custom knife," Danny called out and when I glanced at him he was smirking.

"What knife?" I asked turning back to face Zander.

With a straight face Zander bent down, lifted up his pant leg, and withdrew a knife from what I could only guess was a hidden holster in his cowboy boot. He dropped it on the ground where it spun a few times as it slid towards me, stopping inches from my leg. I could see the details clearly, how perfectly the handle was etched with The Redneck Devil's logo- how the maker was able to create it so perfectly on such a small space I didn't know but I wasn't able to take my eyes off of it as I studied the precise detail.

"Are you ready to hear what your test will be?" Slowly I turned my body so I was facing Danny again, my back to Zander. As beautiful as the knife was, I was still surprised he even had it and hadn't told me about it. How many times has he had that knife in his boot while we were together? "Other than picking up drugs from our suppliers, we also need to deliver them to our dealers. Tonight we've been given an opportunity to provide a very respected dealer with our merchandise. He is not someone we have dealt with before in this manner, but he is more than willing to compensate us- and compensate us very well. But, there's a catch. He wants two women to bring him the drugs. Vetta has already agreed to come along, but we need someone else."

"What about Scarlet?" I asked without thinking. I quickly pressed my lips together once the words slipped out, but I didn't regret asking.

"Scarlet can't be a part of these things, she's too well known in our community." Danny stated, sounding a little annoyed.

"What do you mean?" Again I spoke without thinking, and I saw from the corner of my eye Zander wince as Danny stepped forwards angrily.

"Who do you think you are?" he asked, taking a few more steps towards me. I unintentionally took a step back. "You don't get to ask questions, do you understand? You do what you're told, or this ends now."

I opened my mouth to respond when I felt his hand hit my cheek and swing my head to the side. I cried out in pain and surprise as my cheek suddenly felt hot and began to sting. I heard a quiet growl from Zander but he didn't move, didn't come to see if I was all right. He knew I'd stepped out of line, knew I was basically disobeying Danny by speaking freely and there was nothing he could do about it, despite the fact he wanted to.

Tears were stinging my eyes as I blinked and swung my head towards him to look him in the eye. Slowly I bowed my head in submission, standing there as I blinked rapidly, forcing the tears away as I awaited Danny's next move. I hated what was happening right now, but it was my only option if I wanted The Club to trust me.

"Look at me." I raised my head, feeling my cheek sting some more, as I looked Danny in the eyes again. "You and Vetta will deliver the drugs to the dealer this evening around six. You won't be unaccompanied of course. The Professor and I will be alongside you, we just can't enter the building without an official invitation. Vetta will know what to do, just follow her lead and you'll be fine. Do you have any questions?"

I swallowed hard, feeling a lump in my throat. When I spoke my cheek felt tight where I'd been hit. "How are we going to do the exchange? I don't imagine we will be carrying a brick of cocaine in our hands."

Danny smirked, "oh you won't be handling cocaine. Nah, this dealer likes things- a little easier to swallow."

"What do you-?"

"Opioids." Zander said and I glanced back at him. I could see the pain and anger in his eyes as he stared at my face, seeing the redness that remained, but he didn't betray these feelings to his fellow members. "This guy deals in opioids- heroine, fentanyl, codeine, and even some morphine. We deliver them to him in pill form and he takes care of the rest."

"Those are some dangerous names," I mumbled, my mouth feeling dry.

"You won't be touching the drugs directly," Zander promised.

"Well, she'll be wearing them." I turned back to Danny and raised my eyebrows in confusion. He chucked, "ever see that Gossip Girl episode? The one where the chick puts pills inside a dress? Yeah, sorta like that."

"How is that even possible?" I asked as suddenly two dresses, handbags, and shoes were brought out on a clothing rack by Vetta. The black fabric was covered in big, silver gems and jewels that sparkled in the dim lighting.

She smirked at me as she gestured towards them. "One of my many talents."

"Vetta has ensured the product is secured inside your entire outfit." Danny stated.

"But won't it be suspicious when we enter into this place wearing one outfit, then leave wearing another?"

Vetta laughed, "oh darling. Nobody's going to notice."

"But-."

"We're attending a masquerade party. Even our masks are covered in the product." She raised a mask to her face and

I could see a few gems stuck to the side of it next to the eye holes. I looked at the entire outfit uneasily and gulped.

"Think you can handle it, princess?" I turned my attention back to Danny, not liking the nickname he'd just given me. There was no way I was going to start being called 'princess' when he was 'The Prince', it just didn't feel right to me.

I stood up straight and tossed my hair over my shoulder. My stomach was in knots and I felt sick about the entire situation, I honestly wasn't sure if I was going to be able to do it. But I did know I wasn't going to let Danny see how nervous I really was. "The name's Jade, not princess. And yes, I can do it."

A flicker of respect passed over Danny's features, but he hid it quickly as he nodded and looked past me at Zander. "All right, Professor. The initiation has officially begun. Let's see how long she's going to last."

Vetta looked amazing in her dress. The fabric clung to her body in all of the right places and I couldn't stop staring as the light caught the gems and glistened like diamonds. Next to her I felt as if I was a pale imitation of her- we were posing as sisters, personally invited to attend this party by the host himself- the owner of the club- as a cover so he could obtain his product from us. Apparently his brother was a police officer, and the party was in honour of him celebrating ten years in the field, and therefore there would be a heavy police presence- as if I hadn't been nervous enough about the entire situation, that single fact had me visibly shaking.

"Calm down," Vetta hissed at me. "You do realize the police are going to be able to smell your anxiousness and become suspicious, right?"

"She's right," Zander mumbled from the other side of me. We were sitting in the back of a fancy black car. Danny was in the front with the driver, behind heavily tinted windows. Zander had slid into the back beside me, holding my hand and squeezing it sympathetically the entire time. He gave it another tight squeeze as he said, "they will be able to detect something is off the second you walk in those doors if you don't get control of your feelings."

"If we get caught-."

"You won't."

"But-."

"Ali, you can do this," Zander whispered, bringing my hand to his mouth and kissing it softly. The warmth of his breath and the softness of his lips on my hand helped calm me as I released a deep breath and nodded. "Just let Vetta do all of the talking."

"This isn't my first rodeo, sweetheart," Vetta smiled.

"Shut up," Danny stated from the front seat as we pulled up to the curb beside a club. There was a line of guests waiting to get in, each person baring a mask and dressed in their finest clothes. I took a deep breath and leaned over to kiss Zander quickly. There was something that passed between us in that moment, almost as if he was saying goodbye, and I gave him a quick questioning glance as we separated and the driver opened the door for us. Vetta got out first, then it was my turn. I reached for the driver's hand, glancing one last time at Zander, who had turned to look forwards, face emotionless. I didn't have time to think about what it meant before Vetta took my arm and led me away from the car and towards the door.

A tall man with a clipboard stood outside the door accepting names and checking them on the list in front of him. Some people he let in right away, others he brushed aside asking to wait. Vetta surpassed the line and stopped, me at her side. I watched as the security guard glanced at both of us. My long dark hair had been twisted up on my head, a chain- which I could only guess had more drugs hidden within the gems- wrapped around my hair in a decorative piece that accented the outfit perfectly. My long legs were bare and my feet stood in four inch black heels, decorated in more gems. I was certain that even the jewellery I wore had drugs hidden in them in some way.

"Jodie and Jessica," Vetta declared. "Guests of Mr Burrow himself."

The security guard studied us for another moment, taking in our entire outfit, before looking at the list and nodding, opening the door behind him- thumping music instantly flooded my ears.

"Mr Burrow is in the VIP lounge. To the left and up the stairs."

"Thank you." Vetta reached out and brushed his arm affectionately before reaching for me again and guiding me inside. Once the door was closed behind us I could feel the vibrations on the floor from the music and I could hardly hear anything except the bass blasting from the DJ stand. "Flirting goes a long way," Vetta shouted in my ear, steering me to the left. "But only if done right. You don't want to give the impression you're going to take them home, but you want to make them think they're appreciated. Got it?"

Confused, I nodded as we reached the stairs. Another security guard was standing there holding a phone in his hand. He studied us as we approached, his eyes moving up and down my body, then Vetta's. I was sure these men all worked for the mysterious Mr Burrow, and therefore knew who we were and why we were there. However I also knew there would be cops present, and we couldn't be too careful with who we trusted.

"We're guests of Mr Burrow." Vetta shouted.

"Names?" Vetta opened her mouth to respond but he shook his head and pointed at me. "Not you, her. What are your names?"

"Uh," I swallowed, almost forgetting our cover. "J-Jessica and J-Jodie."

"You don't seem too sure about that."

"I am," I said, a little wobbly.

"You better be more sure when you get up there." He removed the rope from the stairs and gestured us through. "People are watching."

"Fuck," Vetta whispered as we started up the stairs. The

music grew quieter- still loud but at least now I could hear myself think- as we climbed. "Fuck."

"I'm sorry," I mumbled.

"You need to stop worrying so much about- everything! You need to be sure who we are, right now. You pretended to be someone else for weeks with us, and you can't pretend to be someone else right now, when our lives depend on it?"

"I-."

"Get your shit together," she hissed. Once we reached the top she smiled, grabbed my arm, and led me into the room. Here, it was a completely different scene. We could still hear the music from below, but it wasn't blasting in my ears anymore, and the crowd seemed more composed, standing around and talking. A waiter was going around with glasses of champagne and what appeared to be wine- not a shot of vodka in sight, and I sighed, desperately wanting a shot to help me gain my composure.

"Where's Mr Burrow?" I asked as we walked through the crowd, smiling and nodding at those around us.

"No clue," Vetta shrugged, reaching for a glass of champagne. "I've never met him."

"But you said-."

"I said I've done this before," Vetta pointed out taking a sip, "I never said I met this particular client."

"So what do we do?"

Vetta reached for a glass of wine and handed it to me, "linger and enjoy yourself, at least until Mr Burrow shows himself to us. We're supposed to meet him at six and it's only five thirty. We have some time. Relax, have some fun, and drink. You look like you need it."

Fifteen minutes later I'd had three conversations with men who I was fairly certain were cops. They all wore suits, and although they also bore a mask, there was something about the way they held themselves that screamed authority. Two of them were married, their wives clumped together in their own group, gossiping away, and the third was single and had definitely been flirting with me. I'd politely declined his offer to buy me a drink but he hadn't left my side despite my efforts to sneak away.

"So how do you know Mark?"

"Huh?" I asked, blinking at him.

"I feel like Mark would have mentioned you to me, he's always trying to hook me up with his friends. We've been on the force together for five years now, you know. So who are you? A friend of his girlfriends? A cousin? Are you his sister from BC that he never talks about?"

"No, I'm-."

"Jessica!" I looked and saw Vetta standing beside me suddenly, reaching for my arm. "I'm so sorry, sir, but I need my sister for a moment. You don't mind, do you?"

"Oh, I-."

"Thanks so much." Vetta pulled me off of the stool I had been sitting on and away from the bar, walking fast.

"Thanks," I muttered. "He-."

"I don't care," she hissed pulling me along. "I found Mr Burrow."

"You found-?"

She nodded and pointed to a man talking into his phone in the corner. "He said his name was Mark Burrow. How many Mr Burrow's could there be here?"

I sighed and shook my head as I recalled the guest of honours name. "Mark is the cop, not the dealer."

Vetta studied the guy and looked at me suspiciously, "are you sure? He doesn't look like a cop."

"Fairly sure. Unless you want to go up to that guy and inform him we have his drugs-."

Vetta groaned and glanced around the room again, "fucking Danny."

I raised my eyebrows in surprise, "what?"

"That bastard gave us an impossible mission. Usually when I go on these runs the guy knows it's me. But nobody has come up to me, nobody has asked for their package, nobody-."

"This has nothing to do with you, Vetta," I pointed out as my stomach sank. I took a breath and let it out in a puff. "This is because of me. He wants me to fail. He wants me to ruin this- possibly even get caught- so that he doesn't have to worry about me anymore."

"True," Vetta admitted and my eyes widened in surprise- I'd had my suspicions but I hadn't expected Vetta to confirm them. "However, if you fail, I get taken down with you and I don't think Danny would do that to me."

"Really?" I asked, sounding skeptical.

"Despite what you might think Danny does love me. He might show it in the strangest ways but-." Suddenly Vetta stopped talking, her eyes narrowing in on something behind me. "Hang on, I think- I see something."

"What?" I asked turning around slowly, but I didn't see anyone or anything suspicious.

"Wait here."

"What? No, Vetta-." Before I could stop her Vetta had disappeared into the crowd- even in four inch heels that girl could move. I groaned, raising my head to look up at the ceiling in frustration. What was I supposed to do now? We had less than five minutes until six, yet we were no closer to finding Mr Burrow then we were when we arrived. I glanced over at the corner where Mark stood, still on the phone, and wondered if I could ask him where his brother was? Maybe there was some excuse I could make up- I worked for him, needed the key to the office- something?

I took a step in his direction when a voice spoke from behind me. "I wouldn't." I jumped, spinning around to see a young man sitting on a couch, legs crossed, drink in one hand, the other resting on his knee. He had brown hair, cut short, and a clean shaven face- and he wasn't wearing a mask. "My brother's on a very important phone call. You see, he was going to propose to his girlfriend tonight- but the ring hasn't arrived, and the cake was mistaken with a baby shower one, oh and his girlfriend isn't even here."

I blinked a few times, then took a step towards him. "Your brother? That makes you-."

"Mr Burrow, in the flesh." He stood up and reached his hand out for mine. I slowly placed it in his and he raised it to his lips- they weren't as soft nor as warm as Zander's and I felt a flutter of guilt go through me at the fact that another man was kissing my hand. "Jodie, I take it?"

"Jessica," I corrected. My heart began to race as I looked around for Vetta. "I really should get my sister-."

"Relax," the guy waved his free hand- for he was still holding mine with his other. "Take a seat." With a gentle tug I had no choice but to sit down on the couch next to him. He rested one hand on my knee and wrapped the other around my shoulder. "Your boy Danny tells me you have what I need but there's no way you have it on you right this second."

Vetta was nowhere in sight and if I wanted to prove my capabilities and loyalty to The Club I had to handle this myself. I raised an eyebrow and turned to face him, "want to bet?" He looked taken aback as I grabbed his hand and stood up. "I need to get out of this dress. I was promised there would be a change of clothes awaiting me."

Mr Burrow's lips stretched into a slow smirk as he glanced up and down my body in appreciation. "Right this way."

Taking a deep breath I allowed him to lead me through the crowd, towards another set of stairs that led down into the dark and quiet. I gulped, my heart racing but knew I couldn't turn back now. If only there was a way to get a message to Vetta about where I was though, just in case? But I wasn't allowed my phone, and that was the only way I knew I could contact her. I only hoped she'd seen me disappear.

At the bottom of the stairs was another door which Mr Burrow opened. Reaching for the light I winced at the sudden brightness after all of the dim lighting from the club. He held the door open and gestured for me to enter. "Thanks," I mumbled stepping inside. It looked like a regular office- a desk with a chair, a couch, a few filing cabinets, and two other doors. I wondered where they led as Mr Burrow closed the door and I heard a click- had he just locked it?

"So, Jessica," Mr Burrow smiled at me, placing his hands in his pockets as he leaned against his desk. "Have a seat, get comfortable."

"Don't you want your merchandise?" I asked, forcing myself to smile. "It's very valuable, I've been told."

"We'll get to that," he chuckled reaching over into his desk. He withdrew a bottle- whisky- and two glasses. "But I thought you might want to have a drink with me first. Surely working for a man like Danny can't be easy."

"No, he's not," I admitted taking the glass from him. "How well do you know The Club, Mr Burrow?"

"Not too well," he admitted taking a sip from his glass. "This was a test, so to speak, to see if they'd be willing to get my stuff to me, regardless of the circumstances."

"So you threw a party and invited half of the police department?"

"Pretty bold move, isn't it?"

I smirked and raised my glass to my mouth, swallowing the entire contents in one large gulp. "I had my drink, Mr Burrow, now where's my change of clothes?"

"Now, Jessica, we've just begun to have a little fun, haven't we?" He set his glass down and approached me. I hadn't sat down when he offered me the couch, and as he got closer I took a few steps back until I hit the wall and came to a sudden stop. Anxiety and fear began to stir within me, more than before, and my hands began to shake, the glass slipping from my fingers and crashing to the floor. That didn't stop Mr Burrow as he got closer, raising his hands until they pressed against the wall around me, enclosing me- I couldn't move, stuck within his cage. He leaned down and I turned my head, avoiding his lips as they landed on my cheek instead of my mouth. He laughed, throwing his head back for a moment like a child. "Oh, Jessica, you are a tease. I can see why Danny sent you."

"I- I'm not the one you want, Mr Burrow," I stuttered, my sentence sounding broken. "J-Jodie, she's the experienced one. I- this was my first job, and-."

"You've done marvellous, my dear."

"Jodie has the merchandise," I blurted. "She's the one who created these dresses, she's the brain behind this operation- I don't even know if my dress contains any drugs!"

Now Mr Burrow leaned back away from me, his expression concerned as his lips drew downwards and his eyebrows crinkled together. "That can't be right."

"I swear. Two dresses. Two pairs of shoes. Two masks-." I ripped the mask off of my face and thrust it towards him. "Two hand bags- they're all encrusted in these gems, the drugs should be hidden within them, but-."

"You don't think they're in there?" He studied the mask in front of his face, his eyes narrowing as he reached for it and brought the mask closer and closer to his face. I watched as he sniffed it, a big breath in through his nose.

"I don't know, sir," I admitted my heart pounding in my chest. "I swear, I- I don't know anything. Jodie is the brain behind all of this. Please."

"That is very disappointing to hear, Jessica." He muttered quietly, dropping the mask to the ground. "I was having a lot of fun with you."

"If you just let me go find Jodie-."

"No, no," Mr Burrow shook his head, "I'm afraid that's not an option, my dear Jessica."

"Wh-what d-do you mean?" I asked, my voice shaking and my hands trembling. I was starting to feel afraid now, trapped.

"I can't just let you go, not until I get all that was promised to me."

"I can find Jodie-."

Mr Burrow shook his head, "no that won't do. I need it,

now."

I glanced at the ground where the mask had landed, my eyes taking in a gem that had fallen off upon impact with the ground. With a wavering voice and a shaking hand I pointed to it, "maybe my d-dress did have s-something in it. After all."

Mr Burrow turned his head and looked down, staring at the pill that had clearly fallen out of the gem. He let out an excited sound and reached down for it, and I let out a small breath of relief that there was finally some distance between us. "You play a good game, Jessica."

"Wh-what?"

He stood up and showed me the white pill. "Have you ever tried opioids, Jessica? It's quite a thrill."

"N-no," I stuttered, watching his movements carefully, the terror evident on my face. I was terrified of being locked in this room, alone, with a drug dealer. Sure, there was a large police presence upstairs, but nobody knew I was here and with the volume of the music in the club, nobody would hear me if I screamed.

He grinned, walking towards his desk where he retrieved a bowl and a wooden stick. Dropping the pill into the bowl he began to crush it into powder. "It's a rush. Of course you have to be careful with it. Too much can kill you, as can mixing them together- you really have to know what you're doing. Lucky for you, I'm an expert." My eyes widened as he came over to me with a few lines of white powder, "Now, typically I prefer to inject heroin directly, but snorting can be just as effective."

"No, I can't," I cried, shrinking away from him as I pushed myself further into the wall. I wanted as much distance as I could get, but he continued to advance. All I could think of was my father, and my brother, and their addictive nature- I'd stayed away from drugs for the majority of my life because of them, because of the fear that I would become just as addictive as they were.

He reached towards me and I closed my eyes flinching

away. Something crashed against the wall on the other side of the room and when my eyes sprung open I saw Danny and Zander storming in. Zander reached for Mr Burrow and tossed him on the ground as Danny reached for me, pulling me away from the scuffle. I watched with wide eyes as Zander punched the guy, repeatedly, withdrawing his knife from his boot and cutting the guys face, leaving a red line down the middle of his cheek. Mr Burrow screamed out and I had to fight the urge to cover my ears from the sound. Once finished Zander spat on him, kicked him one last time in the ribs, and stepped over his whimpering body. He reached for me, pulling me into his arms where I broke down, tears streaming down my face as my body shook heavily.

"Did he hurt you? Did he make you take any drugs?" I shook my head into his shoulder and he smoothed my hair down, kissing the top of my head and held me close. "Thank God, we must have got to you just in time. You need to take the dress off," he added as he whispered in my ear. "Can you do that?" I nodded, turning so he could undo the zipper. Quickly the dress fell to the ground and I stood in nothing but a strapless bra and my panties. Zander handed me a new dress- where he'd gotten it I didn't see- and I quickly slipped it on. I kicked off the shoes, dropped the hand bag, and ripped out the chain that decorated my hair as well as any other piece of jewellery I wore. Vetta had appeared, already changed and waiting at the door when I was finally ready.

"Let's go," Zander said, gesturing for the open door. I glanced back at Mr Burrow who'd stopped whimpering, but was laying in a small pool of his own blood. My stomach twisted but Zander turned me away and pushed me towards the door. "Not now, Ali. We need to get out of here."

Danny reached for my arm and pulled me away as Zander followed behind, swinging the door shut and rushing me outside- I guess now I knew where one of those doors led.

The black car was waiting for us in the alley and Zander ushered me inside quickly slamming the door as I settled into the seat, tears still streaming down my face. Once we were all in Danny demanded the driver to go. Tires squealed and we sped away as I crumpled into Zander's lap and cried.

Danny got a phone call an hour later from Mr Burrow. I didn't hear what was said but when Danny hung up he looked grim. "He's going to pay us, but he's not pleased with how things were handled. However, he's willing to continue to work with us. He admitted to liking the way Jessica handled herself-." He stopped and looked at me. My eyes were swollen and bloodshot from the tears I'd cried, but as Danny studied me he smiled. "Good work."

"Really?" I was so surprised I couldn't move, just blinked a few times.

"You were successful, regardless of the events that took place. Overall the client is happy, and you didn't get caught."

"I-," I swallowed, my mouth feeling dry. There was a lot I wanted to say but I knew I couldn't, so I nodded, taking Zander's hand in mine and holding it tightly. I think he knew how I was really feeling and he returned the gesture without looking at me. "What's next?"

Danny reached for a bottle of vodka beside him and twisted off the lid, holding the bottle out to me. "Have a drink, relax, and celebrate passing your first test. Then get some rest. Tomorrow's test begins bright and early."

I accepted the bottle and tilted it back, taking a few large swallows and fighting the urge to spit it out as the liquid burned in my throat. After the third gulp, though, the feeling became numb.

"Easy," Zander murmured quietly, easing the bottle away from me. I coughed, wiping a few drops away from my mouth as he took a large gulp himself and passed the bottle back to Danny. We were the only ones in the small room of the barn, the rest of the members either at home or in one of the bedrooms hidden elsewhere in the building. Danny had excused Vetta back to the house when we arrived, escorting only Zander and I in where they both stood and watched me cry. Danny wouldn't let Zander comfort me during that time, I'm sure it was some other test he was putting me through. It hadn't been easy, but I had finally composed myself enough to sit down and await new directions.

Now Danny left us alone, disappearing down a hallway beside the bikes- I couldn't help but wonder where it led?

"We should go back to the house," Zander said quietly, taking my hand. "You need to get some rest."

"What's tomorrow's test?" I asked as I allowed him to lead me out of the barn lighting a cigarette as we walked. It was late, approaching midnight now, and the night air was cool as a wind blew, ruffling my hair which was out of the fancy up-do I'd sported earlier. I could hear crickets, and horses snorting, and even an owl hooting in a tree, but the rest of the night was silent. Glancing up I spotted a sky full of stars and I stared at them as we walked until they were hidden by the overhang of the wrap around porch. I placed my butt into the can in front of the door.

"I don't know," Zander admitted. "I've been dismissed from making those decisions. As your sponsor it would be a conflict of interest- remember?"

I nodded as he opened the door. Scarlet was sitting on the couch, a bowl of popcorn in her hand, and jumped up as we walked in. She rushed over to me, throwing her arms around me and holding me tightly. "Oh my god Jade, I've been so worried. Vetta wouldn't say anything when she got back- I thought the worst!"

"I'm okay," I whispered as I shook, tears brimming my eyes again.

"God, you're not," Scarlet breathed, reaching up to wipe my tears. "You can't possibly let her go through any more of these tests, Zander!"

"We have no choice," Zander sighed, "you know how these things work Scar."

"It's not worth it, Jade," Scarlet said holding my arms

and rubbing them. I swear she had tears of her own in her eyes.

"I have to do this."

Scarlet shook her head then looked at Zander pleadingly. "Don't."

"It's not my choice, Scarlet." He replied sadly.

Scarlet sighed and pulled me in for another hug, kissing my cheek softly. "I'll pray for you Jade. You need to pass these tests- otherwise-."

I nodded, feeling a tear slip from my eye and down my cheek. "I know Scarlet, I know."

The vodka was starting to hit me now and I stumbled when I started walking up the stairs. Zander wrapped an arm around my shoulder to guide me until we were in his room. Without taking the dress off I fell onto the bed and closed my eyes. The last thing I felt as I drifted off to sleep was Zander's lips on my forehead, and the warmth of his hand as he rubbed my temple softly.

CHAPTER 15

When Zander and I walked into the barn we found the entire Club gathered around a single motorcycle. I stared at the black bike, my stomach tightening as we stopped in front of the group. Danny stepped forwards and gestured towards the motorcycle.

"Welcome to your second test, Jade."

The fact that he used my nickname, and not my real name, registered with me but only briefly and I took a single second to hope that it meant I was coming around to him, if only slowly. I glanced at Zander, nervously, as I went to take one step forwards towards the bike. Zander grabbed my arm, stopping me, his gaze on his brother.

"This isn't happening."

"Lucky for me, this isn't your choice." Danny grinned showing all of his teeth. It sent a shiver down my spine.

"She's not doing this." Zander growled, leaning forwards. "Not today."

"She has to," Danny said firmly, voice loud. "She wants to be a part of this Club? Then she needs to learn how to ride. Get on the bike Jade." He turned back to face me, sounding angrier than before.

"This isn't happening Danny," Zander repeated, squeezing my arm harder to keep me back. I flinched, but he didn't notice as he was too focused on his brother.

"It is," Danny ground out between his teeth, and I was sure it was because Zander had refused to use his road name in the presence of The Club. "Whether you want her to or not, she's getting on that bike."

"Over my dead fucking body," Zander snarled, thrusting me backwards and blocking me with his body.

I swallowed, terrified, as Danny smirked dangerously and took a step towards his brother. "I will have you removed, Professor." He emphasized the nickname, making Zander growl. "I don't care what your patch declares, I don't care if you're her sponsor in this crazy initiation! If you won't follow protocol then I will have no choice but to kick you out."

I could tell Zander was angry, could see the tension filling his shoulders the more Danny spoke. I wasn't sure why this particular test was bothering him so much, why he was so angry about me learning how to ride- but he was. He stepped forwards, fist raised, and swung at his brother. Danny anticipated the move and ducked before tackling him to the ground. Instantly three other members were there lifting the two of them up and separating them.

"All right," Danny shouted as Yankee held him back, but whereas Zander was still struggling against his captors, Danny was calm. After a moment he was let go of and he shook his vest to straighten it before taking a step back towards me. "Now. Get on the bike Jade."

I glanced at Zander who was still trying to break free. "Don't," he ground out, but I shook my head at him, silently begging him to stop fighting his friends.

"It's okay," I whispered, swallowing against the dryness in my mouth. "I'll be okay."

Zander looked pleadingly at me and I could see the pain that was written clearly all over his face as he finally gave in to his captors and stopped struggling. I gave him one last long look before taking a deep breath and walked towards the bike. I'd only ever ridden on the back of a bike twice, and although

I'd tried to learn a few things from watching how a bike was driven, I was no expert on riding.

"Get on," Danny demanded nodding towards the seat.

"Where's my helmet?" I asked quietly, remembering how insistent Zander had been about me wearing one. "I'll get on, but only if I'm wearing a helmet."

Danny smirked and nodded towards ScatterBrain who was standing closest to me. He looked regretful as he handed me a slick black helmet with a heavily tinted mask- a much sturdier helmet then Zander had given me to wear- which I slid onto my head before slowly climbing onto the seat. My hands were shaking as I gripped the handlebars and I turned to look at Danny. "Now what do I do?"

He talked me through the steps, sounding surprisingly calm, and as I followed his direction I tried not to think about the fact that this could go horribly wrong: it was one thing to ride on the back of a motorcycle with someone else in control, a whole other thing to be the one to drive it. But as the engine purred to life and I felt the rumbling below me my nerves switched from one of fear to one of anticipation, and I took the opportunity to glance at Zander again- only to see he was gone. I wasn't sure exactly when he'd left but sighed nonetheless, fighting the wave of sadness that overcame me as I glanced back at Danny for my next instructions. "Now what?"

"Drive," he said easily, taking a step back.

"What?" I asked, surprised, my hand nearly slipping off the handlebar.

"Drive. You have the bike started, now you drive it."

"I-"

"Drive!" he demanded. He took one side of the bike while ScatterBrain came to stand on the other and together they pushed the bike forwards. Panicked I hit the break on the handle, causing my body to jerk up and the bike to skid and tilt; if Danny hadn't still been holding on to it, it would have fallen, but as it were he caught the bike and heaved it upright again.

My entire body was shaking as I took a deep breath and turned the bike off and just sat there, head lowered in shame and embarrassment. I blinked rapidly, trying to stop the tears that desperately wanted to fall.

"Get out," Danny demanded quietly. At first I thought he was talking to me so I went to throw my leg off the bike, but he placed a hand on my shoulder, stopping me. "Them. Not you. We aren't finished here yet. Unless you want to give up?"

I leaned back until I was sitting again, my heart pounding but didn't make a move to get off. Finally silence fell and it was only the two of us alone in the barn.

"Where's Zander?" I asked softly.

"He left," Danny shrugged. A few tears leaked from my eyes, and my nose was starting to drip but I didn't want Danny to know I was crying so I fought the urge to sniffle; luckily the helmet's mask hid my face. "Why are you so afraid to ride?" He finally asked me. His words weren't cruel or harsh, but genuine.

I raised my head and looked at him. "I'm not."

"You are. I can see it in the tension of your shoulders. I can see it in the way your hands grip the handlebars. If you're afraid you'll never be able to ride."

"Who says I want to learn?" I spat, frustrated at how easy he was reading me.

"I do." He stated coldly. "You want to be a part of this Club, don't you? Isn't that the whole point of this?"

"I want to be a part of Zander!"

"Zander IS The Club," Danny growled. "You want to be with him? Then you become a part of us, but you'll never be a part of us if we can't trust you."

"Why does it have to be that way?" I asked angrily.

"It's the life he chose."

"He didn't choose this. It was chosen for him." I argued.

"You're wrong, Jade."

"He told me so!"

"He was lying to you."

"Zander wouldn't lie!"

Danny laughed humorlessly, "then you don't know my brother Jade. Every day he goes to that school and he lies. Every time he shows himself in public without his cut, he lies. Every time he pretends he isn't a member of this Club, he lies. Hell, every time he hides his relationship with you, he's lying! Zander is made up of lies, it's the life he lives!"

"He's only trying to survive." I argued. "It's not the same thing."

"Zander has tried too hard to separate himself from us. He thinks he can live a double life, but he's wrong and I think he's finally starting to realize that. Sooner or later he's going to have a choice to make, and if you want to be with him you need to be prepared to make that choice along with him. This bike, right here, is the first step in being prepared. Do you want to be prepared to help him Jade?"

I nodded, slowly, as I took another big breath.

"Then start the engine again and this time- drive."

It took me fifteen minutes to make it five feet across the barn, but finally I was able to drive the bike. It wasn't easy for me, but Danny was a surprisingly good teacher, despite the fact he was extremely intimidating and frightening. Before long I was able to drive a lap around the barn without stalling. I certainly wasn't ready to go driving down the road, or take my driver's test but it was a start. All I wanted to do was share my achievement with Zander, but he had still not returned.

"You're a fast learner," Danny complimented and I couldn't help but smile.

"Thanks, even if this was against my will- at first."

Danny nodded and turned to go but before he could make it to the door I stopped him. "Zander does care about this Club, it's all that he has left in this life. That's why he cares so much about this initiation, even if he doesn't agree with it."

Danny glanced back at me, studying my face. "Then you better not screw it up."

Before I could say anything in return he opened the door

and stormed out. With shaking hands I lit a cigarette and inhaled deeply before walking out of the barn myself and heading towards the house.

"Have you seen Zander?" Scarlet was standing in the kitchen making breakfast. Danny had basically demanded I be in the barn at six thirty, meaning there hadn't been a chance to eat breakfast. Now that my second test was over Scarlet was trying to get food ready for the entire Club. Except for Zander, who remained nowhere to be found.

Scarlet turned from the stove where she'd just finished stirring some scrambled eggs, looking sad. "He-," she sighed and shook her head. "He needed some space, Jade. He saddled up Rocky and took him out for a ride."

"How long ago?" I asked, turning to head back towards the door.

"About an hour ago, but Jade-."

"I need to go find him."

"He wants to be alone." Scarlet stated firmly, rushing to block my way to the door, spatula in hand.

"Why?" I pleaded, "I- I don't understand why this particular test upset him so much."

Scarlet bit her lip and glanced out the window, "I shouldn't be the one who tells you."

"Please."

Scarlet sighed before reaching over to the stove for the pan of eggs. "Fine, but first help me get breakfast ready. The Club is getting hungry."

Nodding I reached for a few plates and held them as Scarlet scooped eggs onto them, then reached into the oven and withdrew some bacon. Finally she set toast on top and we carried the plates out to the dining room where most of The Club sat drinking coffee and laughing at something neither Scarlet nor I had heard. They mumbled their thanks as they dug in and Scarlet nodded her head towards the doorway.

She led me to her room which was the most modern

looking room I'd seen in the house yet- her bed was covered in a floral set with matching pillows, the walls were painted a pale pink, and I saw a few photographs hung up: Scarlet and her husband, Patrick. I walked towards one, studying it as I took in Scarlet in a white wedding gown riding on the back of a motorcycle, head thrown back in laughter as her husband drove.

"We had our wedding here," Scarlet whispered as she watched me study the picture. "I rode into the ceremony on a horse while he drove in on his bike. It was perfect."

I smiled softly, then frowned as I thought about my own relationship. "Scarlet, what's happening with Zander?" I turned to face her, crossing my arms over my chest. "He- he was so angry in the barn. He saw the bike and basically lost his mind."

Scarlet sighed and patted the bed beside her, "Come sit." I walked over and sat down, nearly sinking into the comfortable mattress. When I looked over at Scarlet she was nibbling her lower lip. "I wish I didn't have to be the one to tell you this."

"Please, Scarlet, please just tell me."

She closed her eyes and blurted, "Zander's mother died while driving a motorcycle." My mouth fell open but words wouldn't come out, I just sat there and stared, speechless. "After this happened their father drilled it into their heads that a woman should never- ever- ride. It was to be a man's job. But Danny-."

"Oh my god," I breathed, lowering my head into my hands.

"I haven't even told you the worst of it," Scarlet admitted in a quiet voice.

"It gets worse?" I asked. My stomach sank, my hands shook, and my mouth was dry. "How could that be any worse?"

Scarlet looked at me with tears in her eyes. "Zander was three. He'd gotten outside when he should have been inside.

He was crossing the driveway when his mother came flying down the driveway. He saw her, stopped, and began to wave- but she didn't see him until it was too late. When she hit the brakes she lost control of the bike and flew off of it, her body crumpling and rolling until she knocked into a tree. She wasn't wearing a helmet and she hit her head, hard, and-."

"Oh my god." My stomach clenched and I felt as if I was going to get sick. Bending over I took a few breaths trying to calm myself and settle my stomach. "Oh my god." I recalled the look on his face when I told him my mother had died in childbirth, my birth, and how I felt responsible for killing her. He hadn't said anything, but now that I thought back on it, there was anguish on his face, anguish he'd hidden well. Why hadn't he ever told me about this? Why did he keep it a secret?

"Zander is haunted by many things that this life has given him. Guilt weighs heavy on his shoulders from murder, theft, and countless other crimes he's committed as a member of this Club. However, none of that comes close to the weight he carries knowing he was responsible for his mothers death."

Tears were now flowing freely down my face and there was nothing I could do to stop them. "You don't understand Scarlet," I breathed. I sniffled, wiping the tears with the sleeve of my shirt. "I- I was also responsible for my mothers death. Zander and I had talked about it." I gasped as more tears overcame me, flowing steadily. "But he never mentioned this to me. Why would he keep it a secret?"

Scarlet reached over and rubbed my back in soothing circles, "Zander has a hard time opening up to people."

"But he should be able to trust me." I cried.

"It has nothing to do with trust, Jade. This- this is a hard thing for him to talk about. Do you like talking about your mothers death?" I shook my head, wiping more tears away- my sleeve was getting fairly damp now. "I don't know how your mother died, Jade, but I do know how Zander's did, and I know why he doesn't want to talk about it."

"I killed my mother in childbirth," I stated flatly, looking up at Scarlet with blood shot eyes.

"But that wasn't exactly your fault," Scarlet whispered, "you can't blame yourself for something like that. It could happen to anyone."

"My father spent his entire life blaming me for her death," I grumbled. "Not only did I cause her death, but her death was the reason for his addiction- I was the reason for his addiction."

"There is no one to blame for that, except for him," Scarlet stated firmly. "God, Jade. I'm so sorry you've had to go through all of this your entire life."

"You'd think that I'd be happy he was dead," I sighed, wiping my eyes again. The tears were beginning to slow, but my eyes still stung. "But, despite the shitty childhood he gave me- I can't bring myself to hate him, not really. I miss him, Scarlet."

"The Club killed him, didn't they?" I looked at her, raising my eyebrows questioningly. "I'm not privy to all of the going-on's in The Club, Jade. My relationship with The Redneck Devils is fairly unique, but I do hear things."

I nodded, sniffling. "Yeah, they killed him. That's why Danny doesn't trust me, that's why I'm going through all of these tests- to prove myself, to prove I'm loyal and trustworthy. I had no idea he was involved with these guys, but the coincidence of it all is a little too much to believe, I'll admit."

Scarlet hesitated a moment, stood up from the bed and walked over to the window. Looking out of it she said quietly, "I don't think you should be going through all of these tests just to prove yourself to Danny. I know you want to be with Zander and therefore you're willing to sacrifice a lot for him, but this life isn't all that it's made out to be Jade. I- I can never get out of it, I don't have a choice, but you do."

"But Zander-."

Scarlet shook her head and I could see the thoughtful expression on her face through her reflection in the window. "This has nothing to do with Zander. It has to do with you.

This is a dangerous life, Jade, and I won't lie to you, you could very well die just by being associated with The Redneck Devils, by simply being with Zander. The Club has a lot of enemies, there are many people Danny has pissed off through the years- and Zander? I won't sugar coat it for you, Jade. Zander's killed countless people- members from rival clubs, suppliers who tried to steal from The Club, prospects who turned on The Club- and so many others. Every time he kills someone, he creates more enemies for himself."

She turned around to face me, and now her expression was sombre- her lips tilted down in a frown, a wrinkle between her eyebrows, and her eyes looked sad. "Zander may seem like a good guy, Jade, but he has a lot of demons he's tried to suppress. He's tried to hide who he really is, he pretends to act like this perfect school teacher- but clearly he's not, otherwise he wouldn't have fallen for his student."

"Scarlet-," I gasped, offended. "I-."

Scarlet waved me off, "I'm not trying to insult you, or your relationship. I think you two are wonderful together, and Lord knows Zander needs someone stable in his life." She shook her head. "Look, all I'm trying to say is that there is a lot more to Zander than you could possibly know. You've only been dating a few weeks, right? That's not nearly enough time to truly know him, that's not enough time to make a decision as drastic as this one. Once you commit yourself to this Club, it's over Jade. That's it, that's going to be your life. Take it from me."

I closed my eyes, threw my body backwards on the bed, and raised my hands to my face to cover my eyes. Groaning I said, "I don't know what you expect me to say, Scarlet. It's already been done. My decision has been made. I've already passed two of these crazy tests- there's no turning back now."

"I know," Scarlet sighed and I opened my eyes, sitting up a little so I could see her. There were tears glistening in her eyes as she whispered, "I know. I just wanted you to know what you were truly getting yourself into. You deserve to know."

I nodded, "I appreciate it."

"You should also know that Zander returned about five minutes ago," she pointed her thumb out the window behind her. "He's in the middle of cooling down Rocky. I'm sure he's expecting you."

Without a second thought I swung my body up off the bed and rushed out the door, running through the house, ignoring the calls from The Club, who were all still sitting at the table, empty plates surrounding them. I didn't stop until I made it to the barn, panting, and watched as Zander exited Rocky's stall. As soon as he saw me he stopped, his hand still resting on the gate as he closed the door.

"Ali," he mumbled. I watched his shoulders heavy up and down as he sighed.

"I'm sorry, Zander," I blurted, taking a small step towards him. "I didn't know- I never would have-."

He raised his hand to stop me, halting my words. "I should have told you. It's my fault."

"No, it isn't," I insisted, taking another step forward. "It's Danny's. How could he- why did he-."

"This test was as much for me as it was for you. And I failed it, Ali."

I frowned, "what do you mean?"

"Danny was trying to get a reaction out of me, he wanted to see if I would disobey his orders- he wants to make me look bad so he can take my title away from me and have complete control over The Club."

"What?"

Zander shook his head and glanced away from me, "When I was a Weekend Warrior Danny had control of everything, and he was happy. Sure, I still had a right to vote, but ultimately he made the decisions. Ever since I returned and took back control of my position, he's lost some of that control and he hates it. He wants The Club to turn on me."

"They wouldn't do that, would they?" I gasped. "They-."

"I don't know, Ali," Zander sighed, closing his eyes. "I don't know." He opened them again and stared hard at me. "I do know that I made a mistake, though. I shouldn't have defied him. I broke protocol. I insulted him."

"Zander," I took another step towards him but he shook his head, halting me in my tracks. "I wish you would have told me about your mother."

"I know."

"I never would have got on that bike."

"Yes you would have," he insisted. "You would have had to. If you didn't get on that bike today, it would have been the end of this, the end of us. I wouldn't have let that happen, Ali. I hate this, I hate all of this," his hands clenched into fists and I watched as they shook, angrily. "But it doesn't matter how I feel because you've made your choice and I will support you in that decision, no matter what."

I ran towards him, throwing my arms around his neck and pulling him in for a passionate kiss. My hands grabbed his hair, trying to pull him as close to me as I possibly could. His hands wrapped around my waist, holding me tight. "I love you," I whispered against his lips. "I love you so much." He didn't respond, just brought our lips together again.

"Welcome to your final test, Jade. This one is a little bit more-unique- than your others have been. Are you ready to hear what it is?" Only three hours had passed since Zander had returned from his ride and I finished my second test. Danny had said the next one would be soon, but I hadn't expected it to be this soon. I was tired, exhausted from the events that had unfolded within the last forty eight hours, but there was no time to rest.

"I'm ready." We were once again gathered in the Clubhouse, the entire Club standing around me in a circle. Danny and I were in the middle and Zander, after making a formal apology to Danny in front of everyone, was welcomed to attend the final test. During his apology I watched as Danny smirked triumphantly, as if he was getting exactly what he wanted- to make Zander look weak. I'd hated it and it had only made me that much more determined to pass this final test.

"Can you tell me, Jade, what is the one thing, above all else, that members of The Club do to express their loyalty to this Club?"

I tilted my head to the side and narrowed my eyes in concentration thinking over the question carefully. "You wear your cuts to declare who and what you are."

"What about when we can't be so obvious about our ties?"

I slowly turned my body around in a circle, studying each and every member carefully, taking in the details of them- some of them were in t-shirts, others in a hoodie, but they all wore their cuts regardless. Butch reached up to scratch his arm and I watched the movement, his fingers brushing the ink on his arm, and I recalled the tattoo that covered Zander's entire back. Finishing my rotation I turned back to face Danny and said, in a loud clear voice, "you always bear the mark of The Club. Each and every member has a tattoo of The Club in some form on their body. Butch has one on his forearm, ScatterBrain has it on his bicep, and Zander's entire back is covered in The Clubs logo. Despite the fact you can't always wear your cut, you are always true to The Club by the marks you bare on your body."

Danny nodded his head once and my eyes moved towards Zander, who was off to the left of me. His lips twitched and I knew he was proud- and worried. That's when my own words penetrated my ears and my brain began to realize what Danny was asking me, and what this test would entail. I swallowed, feeling a lump in my throat as I truly stopped to consider this test- was I ready to get a tattoo? Was I ready to declare myself, in ink, as an associate to The Club? Was I truly ready to take that step? Scarlet had warned me about the possible consequences of truly tying myself down to The Club, and there was no doubt about it, marking myself with ink was certainly a sign I was dedicated to them. But did I want that on my body, forever?

"This is the true test to show your loyalties to us," Danny said quietly, as if he knew what I was thinking. He took a step closer to me, not removing his eyes from mine. "This will prove to me, to all of us, that you belong. By marking yourself, you are declaring to everyone that you belong to us. You want us to believe you had nothing to do with your fathers connection to us? Do you want us to forgive you for lying to us for weeks about who you really were? If you want us to forget everything that has happened, sweep it under the rug, and move on- if you want to be a part of this Club, then you will mark yourself as one of us." His words got louder as he talked and by the end he was nearly yelling, but I didn't flinch, didn't blink, as he moved his face until it was right in front of mine. "Are you ready to take that step, Jade?"

His breath was warm on my face and I felt a few drops of spittle land on my cheek as he spoke. I didn't reach to wipe it away nor did I shrink back in disgust. I tilted my head up higher so that we were truly eye to eye and spoke in a clear, confident voice. "I'm ready."

The smile he gave me sent shivers down my spine, he looked a little too pleased that I'd agreed to do this. I felt his arm go around my shoulder, pulling me close to his side- something about the interaction felt wrong and my shoulders stiffened, but he didn't seem to notice. "Let's begin! Come," he turned my body, leading me towards one of the doors to the right of us. I'd seen him disappear into that room before, but I had no idea what lay behind the door. The way he was holding me I couldn't look back to see if Zander was following but, by the sound of the footsteps behind us, I had a feeling he was there.

The first thing I noticed was the door, which was black and bared The Redneck Devil's logo right in the middle. Danny swung the door open and flicked the light on. I saw a long table with chairs, a few filing cabinets, and many pictures and logos of The Club surrounding the walls. My eyes narrowed in on the tattoo machine sitting at the table, the plastic wrap over a chair, and the smell of disinfectant.

"I bet you didn't know I was a licensed tattoo artist," Danny smirked walking over to the machine and starting it up. Instantly the sound of buzzing filled my ears.

"You're going to tattoo me?" I asked in disbelief.

"Did I forget to mention that?"

I blinked, unable to move as The Club crowded into the room. It was as if they had assigned seating, knowing exactly which chair was theirs, as they sat around the table.

"If you can't trust me with this, Jade, how do we know we can trust you? You have to give trust to get trust."

"I-." I licked my lips, which were very dry. "I don't even know what I want to get."

"You don't get to choose, Jade. We've chosen for you." He picked up a piece of paper and dropped it on the table in front of me. I stared at the image: an R and a D surrounded by a circle with little devil ears and tail- the tag that I'd seen countless times on the Riverton and Horse Shoes sign. I'll admit it wasn't nearly as bad as I imagined it would be.

"Do I at least get to position it on my body?"

Danny shook his head, "again, you have to trust me. Can you do that?" It was yet another challenge. Even when I thought the tests were over they never seemed to be. Swallowing I nodded, moving to sit down in the chair. "Oh you don't need to sit, you'll be lying on the table. You'll need to remove your shirt, as well. I need access to your back."

Quickly I glanced at Zander who nodded, the slightest bob of his head, and I sighed lifting off my t-shirt revealing my black bra beneath. A few of the guys whistled and I blushed, trying to ignore them as I crawled onto the table and laid on my stomach, closing my eyes, my heart pounding in my chest. I couldn't believe I was about to do this, couldn't believe I was letting Danny place a permanent tattoo on to my back. I held my breath as I felt him shift and knew the needle would be touching my skin at any moment.

I flinched as I finally felt the impact of the needle and unintentionally shifted away. "Don't move," Danny growled and I felt the needle move away from my skin momentarily. "If I screw this up it's going to be hard to fix."

"Sorry," I mumbled laying flat again, trying to relax my shoulders. I took a big breath in, held it for a second, then released it feeling the tension in my shoulders release as I did so. The next thing I felt was the needle again, but this time I didn't flinch, in fact I found it a little relaxing. Closing my eyes again I tuned everything out around me, even the feel of the needle. The light vibrations actually felt good and I'm certain I began to drift off when Danny proclaimed he was done.

"What?" I mumbled peeking my eyes open.

"It's done," he repeated and I heard the sound of chairs scraping as everyone stood at once. They gathered around me as I laid still on the table unable to move. My back felt numb from where Danny had inked me- right between my shoulder blades. I felt something cold and wet on my back, then saw a flash of light.

"Here," Zander's soft voice sounded in my ear. Turning my head he held his phone out to me so I could see the picture he'd taken. The skin around the tattoo was irritated and bright red, but the black ink stood out brightly against it. I couldn't take my eyes off the screen. I heard a ripping sound then felt something applied to my back.

"This is a clear bandage that'll help with healing. You'll need to change it in the morning, gently clean it, allow it to dry, then apply another bandage. Wear loose clothing and for the love of God avoid scratching it as it heals- I don't do touch ups." I wasn't expecting the hand he offered as I went to sit up but accepted it nonetheless, slipping my shirt on as he handed it to me, then sat there unsure what to do next. Were we done? Were the tests over? Was I free to leave?

"Alessaundra Campbell." Uh oh, we were back to using my full name. Was that a good thing? "I hear by officially declare you An Associate of The Redneck Devils Motorcycle Club. Congratulations. From here on out you shall be known as Jade whilst in the presence of The Club. Are we in agreement?" I jumped as the entire Club shouted out "aye" at the same time. Danny looked back at me, and once again he was smiling. "Welcome to The Club, Jade." As everyone gathered began to clap and cheer I couldn't hold back the smile that stretched across my face and the burst of laughter that escaped. I'd done it, I had passed the tests. It was over.

A bottle of vodka appeared and was passed around; when it got to me they began to cheer me on, encouraging me to "chug chug chug"- I knew it was stupid, reckless even, but I tilted the bottle to my lips and took a few large swallows, ignoring the burn. They cheered again as I removed it and passed it to the person next to me, who happened to be Danny.

"I'll admit," he took a swig, "I didn't think you'd pull this off."

"Which part?" I asked accepting the bottle as he passed it back to me. The circle of members split up and congregated in small groups, crowding the small meeting room.

"The first test," Danny admitted. I held the bottle out to him but he shook it away, lighting a cigarette instead. "I thought you'd fail for sure."

"Thought? Or hoped?" I challenged, taking another gulp.

"You can't blame me for wanting to be careful in this matter," Danny stated ignoring my question. "This Club is my responsibility. If anything goes wrong, it's my fault."

"Not only yours," I countered. Danny looked at me, confused. I took another big swallow and said, "it's Zander's too."

Danny shook his head and grabbed the bottle from me before I could lift it to my mouth again. Shrugging I reached for the pack of smokes sitting beside Danny and lit one. Looking around at the gathered group I spotted Zander talking with ScatterBrain; when he saw me watching him he nodded and smiled, then turned back to his friend. I wanted him to come over to me, but it seemed like he was keeping his distance; but why? Was it because I had gone through with the test? Did he see me differently now?

"He's respecting me," Danny stated, catching me staring. He stubbed out his smoke and immediately lit another one.

"In what way?"

"Well," Danny inhaled deeply and passed the bottle of vodka back to me. "You make a good point, Jade, as much as I hate to admit it- Zander has a large role in this Club as well. But in this particular event he had to step back and let me take over, completely. That wasn't easy for him to do. But he has to remain in that role until this celebration is finished- he is your sponsor until this night is over. Therefore, I am the sole standing President for the night. No one should interrupt the President while he is having a conversation, unless it is important."

"So you're taking full advantage of this night." I slurred putting out my own smouldering smoke and tipping the bottle back; I'd lost count of how many gulps I'd taken.

"Exactly." Danny grinned, removing the bottle from my hand again, and setting it down beside him. "I think you've had enough of that." He added finishing his smoke.

"I can handle my vodka," I protested, but even to my own ears my words didn't sound clear.

"Go." Danny reached out and helped me off the table. It was the first time I'd stood on my feet and I swayed, nearly falling over. Danny reached out to catch me as my body fell into his. "Easy."

"That's some strong shit you have," I mumbled.

"Only the best is reserved for these types of celebrations." He nodded towards Zander who instantly rushed over, taking my unstable body from Danny. I collapsed into his arms, giggling. "Sorry man," I heard Danny say.

Zander ignored him as he swung my body up into his arms. I snuggled my head into his shoulder, nibbling his neck and giggling harder.

"How much did she have to drink?" Zander snapped, twitching away from my mouth.

"Just a few sips." A moment of silence, then, "okay, maybe, like, seven shots or something? I don't know, man. She said she could handle it."

I felt Zander take a big breath in, but my eyes were starting to close. "Do I have permission to take her inside?" He growled forcing himself to be calm and patient.

"Yeah, yeah, go ahead." Zander went to take a step but was stopped as Danny called, "oh yeah, and brother?" I felt him turn around, presumably to face Danny again. "It's good to have you back."

There may have been more said, but that was the last thing I remembered. Between the vodka, the exhaustion, and the craziness of the last few days I wasn't able to hold onto to consciousness anymore. Sleep enveloped me as I relaxed into Zander's warm, comforting arms.

CHAPTER 16

"I don't think I can go back to school."

The words escaped my mouth before I could stop them and surprised even me. I felt Zander stiffen below me, my head resting on his bare chest, his arm around my naked shoulders. I had been far too drunk the night before to celebrate with Zander but we made up for that this morning. Now, we lay cuddled in bed enjoying each other's presence, but my mind wasn't as at peace as my body was- and it wasn't because of the hangover.

"What are you talking about, Ali?"

I turned so I could look him full on, holding the blanket up to cover my chest. "There is no possible way I could go back to such a mundane life, Zander. How- how could I sit in a classroom, day after day, listening to you, or Mr G, or even Ms Dimonde? Writing tests, submitting papers, and for what? So I can go to University in the Fall? How would that work, Zander? How could I possibly go off to University and leave you here, with The Club? It's just not realistic. I may as well stop now."

"You want to drop out?" Zander sat up now, looking concerned. "You can't do that, Alessaundra. You've worked so hard to get where you are- you can't throw it all away now."

"Why not?" I challenged.

"Because all of that work would have been worthless. Do you really think your grandmother would want you to drop out of school so easily?"

My mouth fell open and a small gasp escaped. "How- how dare you bring my grandmother into this!"

"I'm sorry," Zander apologized quietly, reaching out to rub my back. I shied away, pulling the blanket up to cover my body a little more. "You know I'm right, though, Ali."

"My grandmother wouldn't approve of what I've made of my life now anyways," I grumbled, "so what does it matter."

"What about your Aunt Patty?" Zander asked, inching towards me again. "How would you explain this to her?"

"Aunt Patty was never made my official guardian. Grandma was still living, I only resided with her, she was like a foster parent, a place to live until I turned eighteen."

"But you haven't turned eighteen yet, Alessaundra." Zander pointed out. "You won't be for a few more weeks." His hand rested on my shoulder again and this time I let him, sinking into his warmth. "I understand why you want to make this decision, but perhaps you should wait a little longer, until you're sure. Remember when you said you wouldn't let me sacrifice my hard work for you...?"

"This is different," I argued. "Besides, I just don't think I'm ready to go back yet."

He didn't say anything and when I looked over at him his gaze seemed blank, as if he was lost in thought. Finally he said, "then take another week off. Email Mr Thorn, tell him you're still grieving and you just need a little more time. You can even stay here, if you want. But I can't remain, I have to go back to work. It'd be a little too suspicious if we both started taking time off of school.

"Does your Aunt know that your dad is-."

"No." I shook my head before he could finish. "No, I haven't told her anything. As far as she knows, I'm still staying at the house with him."

"Let her think that. We can't have anyone knowing-."

"I know." An awkward silence fell between us and I shifted to look at him. "I'll give it another week. I'll consider all my options. But, Zander-."

"That's all I ask, Ali." He leaned over and kissed my forehead, his lips soft and warm.

I groaned, "okay. All of this thinking and talking is making my head pound more than it was before." I reached up and rubbed my temple. "How much vodka did you say I drank last night?"

Zander chuckled, the atmosphere of the room relaxing. "A fair bit. You and Danny seemed very- cozy."

I detected a small hint of jealousy in his voice. "Zander, were you-?"

"No." He cut me off before I could finish.

I started laughing, throwing my head back. "You were!"

He smiled, shaking his head, "I wasn't jealous- exactly. Actually, as hard as this is to admit- I kind of liked seeing the two of you get along."

Briefly I recalled the conversation the two of them exchanged last night while I was passing out in Zander's arms. "I think he's happy to have you back as well."

"We've never been super close," Zander stated, wrapping his arm around me then pulling me slightly so we were laying down again, my head resting on his chest. I could hear his heart beat a soothing rhythm in my ear: boom-boom, boom-boom, boom-boom. "We've always had a very strained relationship. He blamed me for my mothers death- and rightly so-."

"You were three Zander," I interrupted, "it's not fair to blame yourself."

"Do you ever listen when people tell you not to blame yourself for your mothers death?" I was silent because, no, I didn't. Essentially it was my fault. "Exactly."

"Sorry."

He ignored me, "growing up there had always been a bit of separation between us. I've told you before, Danny idolized my father and The Club, he tried to be around everything they did. I, however, preferred to help out with Horse Shoes, take care of the horses, and study. We were home-schooled, never given a real education- it's a wonder I ever made it into University, to be honest.

"As we grew older, I didn't really have a choice but to become involved in The Club. I had friends, like Scarlet, and other kids my age whose fathers were members of The Club. We got ourselves into trouble a lot- but my father and the rest of The Club utilized us to their advantage. After all, who'd suspect a thirteen year old to be in possession of a brick of cocaine?

"By that point Danny was being patched in, he'd gone through all of these tests to prove he was capable of handling the membership at his age- a lot of the members didn't agree with my fathers decision, but he knew how dedicated Danny was and managed to gain the vote. He wanted the same thing for me, which was why he was so determined to make me Danny's equal. I think, somehow, he knew how I felt about the family business, but he also knew he couldn't leave Danny solely responsible for The Club. Despite the fact I was so young, I'd only just turned nineteen, just been patched in myself the year before- he chose to lay all of this responsibility on me. I mean, he hadn't planned on dying, but-."

"What happened, Zander?" I whispered laying my hand on his arm, comfortingly. "You once said you couldn't tell me, but surely I'm ready to know by now."

I could feel his body tense up and didn't expect him to answer me; therefore I was surprised when he started talking. "As you've been told many times by now, this life isn't easy. There are consequences to everything we do regardless of how minor we think it is. When my father was starting up this Club he made a lot of little mistakes, mistakes that he brushed aside and tried to forget about; not to mention he called in a lot of favours- and favours are never free, not in this life.

"One of his biggest 'little' mistakes was not returning

a favour to one of The Clubs who helped him. He had connections to other Clubs thanks to his father, my grandfather, being a member of The Satan's. He used these connections to get the word out about The Redneck Devils. He was indebted to this Club, but when they called on him for help he ignored them. Not only did he refuse to help them, he also turned on them by helping their rival Club- for they also helped my father gain traction in the community.

"My father wasn't the brightest. His biggest flaw in life was how disorganized he was. What he should have done was keep a list of everyone he owed favours to, and keep track of those he had asked for help from. By asking two rival Clubs to assist him, he basically doomed himself. He couldn't help both, so he chose which Club he thought was more powerful.

"He didn't think the other Club was capable of redemption, but they were. However, they didn't factor in just how much protection my father had secured for himself. He called in a few more favours, begged his father and The Satan's to protect him, and when the inevitable came-" I held my breath, thinking Zander was going to say that his father was killed. Instead he said, "my father came out on top, killing the president and over running the club. He basically destroyed them.

"For a while everything was okay. The Redneck Devils became established, my father got his Club running exactly the way he wanted it to- and eventually he let his guard down. He became too comfortable with the life he'd built, and seemingly forgot about the fact that the president of that club had had a son, a son who was biding his time, waiting to strike.

"Four years ago my father went out for a run. It was supposed to be easy, it was supposed to be quick. He hadn't expected to be ambushed by Eric Kovach and the small club he'd rebuilt in honour of his father."

"Eric Kovach?" I whispered, my eyes wide. "Not-."

"Yes, Alessaundra," Zander stated. "The Eric Kovach I killed that night."

"So when you said it had to be done-." I trailed off recalling the conversation Zander and I had had that first night, the night I discovered his secret, the night I found out about The Club.

"It was our turn for redemption. We'd been hunting down Kovach for three and a half years, but every time we got close he'd slip away. It was the one thing I had been one hundred percent invested in, even as a Weekend Warrior. I had wanted to take you away that night Ali. I wanted to take you home, keep you away from all of this- and Danny knew if I left that night, I might never come back, and he couldn't let that happen.

"My brother is a very confusing man, Ali. As much as he wants total control over this Club, he doesn't want to get it because I decide to turn my back on it. He knew the only thing that would have kept me here that night was Kovach. He suspected I hadn't told you about any of this, and he was right, and therefore by keeping me here, by ensuring I had a hand in Kovach's murder- he knew you'd find out and that would do one of two things. It would either frighten you enough to run- which it should have done- or it would bring us closer together, thereby ensuring my return to The Club.

"Danny found it disgraceful that I limited myself to a Weekend Warrior. He wanted me to choose- either accept my title for all that I am, or leave The Club completely. He took a risk that night- nobody could have guessed how you'd react and you surprised them all by agreeing to this life without flinching. And then, later, with everything coming to light about your father-." Zander shook his head. "Danny thought he made a mistake, he was starting to doubt his choice. But you proved him wrong. You passed all of his insane tests and, I think, gained his respect, something he never thought would have happened. He wanted to hate you, Ali, he tried to hate you- but in the end you won him over, and secured my place back in The Club."

"That is a lot to take in," I breathed. I could feel my own heart beating and I was surprised it wasn't racing after everything I'd just discovered; instead it was almost in sync with Zander's, still beating that same soothing rhythm. "How could you possibly know all of this?" I finally asked, dumbfounded.

"During Church The Club has one rule: no lies." Zander stated, his chest rumbling as he talked. "The other day, when we met to discuss your initiation, I didn't hold back Ali. I plead your case, laid out all of the facts... and attacked Danny with as many questions as I possibly could think of in order to get to the bottom of why he seemed to despise you so much. It was then that he confessed how he felt about my position as a Weekend Warrior. It was then that he made me decide whether I would stay or go."

"And what did you say?" I asked, almost holding my breath as I waited for him to answer.

"I told him if you passed all of your tests and proved yourself to be loyal and trustworthy- then I'd live up to my title, one hundred percent. No more hiding who I am, or where I come from-."

"Except for at school." I sat up, turning to stare at him. "Right?" When he didn't say anything I began to get scared, my heart finally starting to pound a little harder. "Zander?"

"There's only two more months of school left-."

"And?" I shrieked, my voice coming out higher than I intended.

"They can find someone else to finish off the year." Zander finally admitted sounding exasperated. He sat up himself now, grabbing my hands and holding them tightly. "That's why you need to return to school, Ali. I can't quit at the same time you drop out- it'd be too suspicious. It wouldn't matter if I was no longer your teacher, if we got caught together there would still be severe consequences due to the simple fact that I was your teacher, and you still aren't eighteen."

"So your solution," I began starting to feel angry. My face was growing warm and my mouth was going dry, "to all of this, is to go back to the way things were before? We continue to hide away here, at The Club, for another two months until I graduate high school?"

"It's what we have to do."

"I don't accept it," I snapped, swinging my body off of the bed. I reached down for my shirt, which was wrinkled from being tossed carelessly to the ground, and pulled it over my head, feeling the middle of my back tighten from the bandage there. As I put my pants on I said, "even if I return to school there's going to be a lot of questions asked, Zander. How could we possibly pull this off? I'm not going to be able to go back to school and act like there's nothing between us! Too much has happened, Zander, too much."

"So what do you propose we do?" Zander asked watching me as I reached back to pull my hair into a messy bun.

I sighed in exasperation, lifting my arms and dropping them against my legs in a slap. "Exactly what we have been doing, Zander. Live here, together- you quit teaching, I'll drop out of school, and we can support The Club in whatever way we can."

"Is that really the life you want?"

I leaned down on the bed, my palms digging into the mattress. "It's the life I chose, Zander, because it means I get to be with you." I lifted my knee up, crawling across the bed until I was sitting in his lap. He was still naked under the blanket and I could feel his penis react to my body as I straddled him, fully clothed. "How many times do I need to say it to you Zander? I swear I have repeated myself, again and again." I leaned in until our mouths were barely a breath apart and whispered, "I want to be with you, Zander, even if it means living this life."

I could feel Zander react to me as I pushed forwards and pressed our lips together, but before he could try and rip my shirt off of me- again- I pulled back, grinning wide, like a devil. "We're expected downstairs in twenty minutes," I pointed out trying to swing my body off of his.

"That's enough time," he groaned, reaching for me again.

I giggled, rolling away and managed to get off of the bed

and away from his arms. "It's really not," I pointed out. Reaching down I picked up his pants and a shirt and tossed them at him. "We'll figure this out, Zander, I promise. Now get dressed. Otherwise you know they'll come up here looking for us and I'd rather not be discovered in a compromising position."

Once again we found ourselves in the headquarters of The Redneck Devils; I hadn't realized how much business was actually conducted in this building, never knew there was always at least one or two members in the building at any given time as a security measure, never saw The Prospects that always guarded the doors. I guess that's what happens when you're on the outside looking in, you don't see what's truly going on inside.

I was surprised to see three Prospects present today, not at the door but camouflaged within the group, blending in like they belonged. I'd seen them in the background many times before, lingering and waiting for orders, but none had been included in any of my tests. Maybe it was because The Club hadn't wanted them to see examples of the tests they could go through, or maybe they didn't want to mislead them into thinking the tests could be 'easy'; the tests I had gone through were modified versions of what they'd be put though after all.

One of the prospects was studying me as I stood there next to Zander, his eyes narrowed almost angrily. He hadn't taken his eyes off me, standing across the circle, mouth pressed together in a straight line for the entire duration of the gathering. I was trying to pay attention to what Danny was saying but it was hard to focus when you were being glared at for no particular reason. I'd never met this Prospect, never talked to him, never gave him a reason to hate me- so why did he keep staring at me like he wanted to kill me? It unnerved me and sent shivers down my spine.

I tried to ignore him and looked around at the group gathered there today- ScatterBrain was next to Zander, nodding along to whatever Danny was saying. Butch stood at attention, his hands folded in front of him, grinning in agreement. Six Inch, who's leg was almost fully healed now and was back to business, was standing next to Yankee, the two of them studying Danny seriously as he talked. Of course there were other members present, but I hadn't become as close to them, wasn't as invested in them.

The one thing I did notice, though, was that neither Scarlet nor Vetta were present for this gathering- but I was. Me, the newest addition to the family, the one with the least knowledge or experience, the one who knew nothing about The Club until a month ago. It didn't make sense to me, why was I here and they weren't?

I wasn't even sure what Danny was saying, couldn't follow along to his speech, and every time I did my eyes would wander back to that damn Prospect who was still staring at me. How had Zander not noticed? Why wasn't Zander saying anything? He was really starting to freak me out.

I felt Zander move beside me and thought *is he finally going to do or say something to this guy about staring at me*? But all he did was move to stand beside Danny, grinning happily. I'd never seen him smile like that in the presence of his brother. What had I just missed? I really should be paying more attention to what is being said around me right now.

"Thanks for that Danny." He said as he reached out for his brother's hand; they slapped their hands together then brought each other in for a brief hug. Thanks for what, though? I should have been paying attention, damn it. Zander began to walk around looking at all of the members and I finally turned to follow his movement, taking my eyes away from The Prospect, determined to ignore him. "As Danny was saying, I have a formal announcement to make and I have asked for everyone to be present for this particular gathering so that you all get the message at the same time.

"As of tomorrow I am handing in my resignation at Baysin High School in order to return to Riverton full time and resume my rightful role, next to my brother, as the other half of your President." He paused as the gathered members cheered and had to raise a hand to silence them, which they did so instantly. "Many of you are aware of the fact that I traded in my role a few years ago, stepping back so I could explore the world around me, keeping one foot in the door as a Weekend Warrior but distancing myself from The Club in order to find some normalcy in my life.

"I wasn't ready to accept the role, I wasn't ready to be in the position to make decisions, to lead alongside my brother. My time away brought clarity to my life, for I realized that no matter where I was or what I was doing, this life would follow me, I couldn't just have one foot in the door, just in case. I had a choice to make.

"I won't lie to you, I was ready to walk away, ready to leave this life behind me and throw away my title. Then I met Jade." I inhaled a short gasp of air and he turned to look at me, a soft smile on his face. Every other head in the room turned as well. "Jade, if it wasn't for you I never would have realized that this spot, right here, is where I belong. Thanks to your love, your support, and your loyalty- this Club is finally complete again. The hierarchy has been restored and you, yourself, have proved your dedication to all of us.

"To thank you, we'd like to present you with a few gifts, from all of us here at The Redneck Devils." He gestured towards the door where Scarlet and Vetta appeared, holding a few boxes wrapped in black wrapping paper; so, that's why they weren't here. Everyone was silent as they walked towards me, Scarlet smiling happily, Vetta with a straight face. They stopped a foot away, waiting for me to reach out and accept their offerings.

"I don't know what to say," I whispered, tears glistening in my eyes as I turned to look back at Zander and Danny, who was now standing beside him.

"You don't need to say anything," Danny shrugged. He reached out and grabbed the gift Vetta was holding and handed it to me. "Just open the damn gifts."

I chuckled as I accepted the box, tore open the paper and held a plain white box, a little bigger than a shoe box in my hands. When I lifted the lid I gasped, my eyes taking in the delicate details of the black cowboy boots that were nestled in the box. "These are beautiful."

"You can't keep wearing my grubby old ones," Scarlet grinned and simultaneously we looked down at the old, worn boots Scarlet had given me that very first day, which I wore every day I was here at Horse Shoes. "It'll take a few days to break them in, but they'll look killer on you."

"Thank you," I whispered. I reached up to wipe a single tear from the corner of my eye and carefully set the box down at my feet. Before I could move to hug any of them Scarlet thrust the next box into my hands.

"There's this one too," she grinned.

Smiling, I accepted it. This box was more square than rectangular, but wrapped in the same black paper. After ripping the paper off I discovered another white box but when I opened the lid, cowboy boots weren't inside. My eyes widened as I looked up to stare at Zander and Danny, "Are you-."

"You deserve it," Danny stated seriously.

"But-."

"Try it on," Zander urged, reaching forwards for the box and withdrawing the garment that was inside. He unfolded a black leather jacket, a small patch on the left side of the chest with my nickname stitched into it JADE.

"Wait!" Zander and I both turned to look at Scarlet, who appeared almost giddy. "There's one more."

Even Zander looked confused, his eyebrows knitting together. "What do you mean there's one more?"

"This one's from me." Scarlet stated, rushing towards the door and coming back, seconds later, with another package. This was the largest of them all, and when she handed it to me it felt light in my hands compared to the two before it. "I thought if we were going to present Jade with some welcoming gifts, we may as well have a real celebration, and if we were going to celebrate, she needed to dress the part of 'guest of honour'."

"What celebration?" I asked, refusing to unwrap the gift.

"The celebration of The Club being back together," Scarlet stated excitedly. "I've got some steaks for an early dinner, we'll have a few drinks- and yes I'm aware you have to work tomorrow, Professor," Scarlet winked. "This isn't going to be a big, crazy party. I just thought it'd be nice to have an actual celebration for Jade. She hasn't had the opportunity to participate in one yet and-."

"I think it's a wonderful idea," Zander said, wrapping an arm around Scarlet's shoulder. "Thank you."

She smiled, then nodded at me, "open it, Jade. Go ahead."

With everyone's eyes on me again I ripped the paper off of the final gift and opened the lid. I had to push aside tissue paper but once I finally cleared a path and lifted out the contents my eyes widened and I once again gasped. Flowing green material, soft and silky, draped down; I couldn't take my eyes off of it.

"I saw it, and all I could think about was how well it would go with your eyes." I looked at Scarlet, who was biting her lip nervously. "Do you like it?"

"I-," I swallowed as my eyes stung with tears. "I love it. Thank you."

"Oh good," she sighed, her shoulders relaxing. "I wasn't sure, you don't really wear green and-."

"Scarlet, stop." I blinked, trying to suppress the tears. "It's perfect."

"So why are you crying?" she asked, genuinely concerned.

I chuckled, reaching up to wipe a tear that was slipping down my cheek. "My grandmother was the last person who bought me a green dress- I was thirteen years old, graduating eighth grade, and she thought a velvet green dress would be just wonderful on me. I didn't have the heart to tell her I hated it, that the velvet was uncomfortable and stiff, and I was boiling while I wore it. Instead I forced a smile, let her take a million pictures, and then hid the dress in the back of my closet until I outgrew it."

"So those aren't sad tears?" Scarlet asked, moving out from under Zander's arm and reaching out for my hand, giving it a squeeze.

"No, Scarlet. They aren't sad tears, not exactly." I sniffled, laughing to myself as I reached up to wipe my eyes. "Oh God, look at me, I'm a mess."

"It's okay!" Scarlet turned to look at Danny. "Why doesn't Jade go get herself changed and cleaned up? Steaks are due on the grill at three. Sound good?"

Danny nodded, looking at Zander. "What do you think?"

"It sounds wonderful, thank you Scarlet."

Scarlet beamed, "I'll bring these upstairs to your room, okay Jade."

"Thanks," I whispered, wondering how long they've considered Zander's room 'my room'. "I'll be up in a minute."

"Take your time."

As Scarlet left Zander turned towards Danny, "I think that's everything. I guess everyone just heard that Scarlet is throwing a celebration for Jade. Everyone's invited. You've got a few hours, get yourselves ready and we'll see you soon."

Danny nodded, "I hereby end the unofficial group gathering. Thanks everyone."

The group broke up and I couldn't help but glance across the room to where The Prospect had been standing but he was gone. I contemplated bringing it up to Zander but decided I didn't want to deal with any of that negativity, not now, not today. I had enough on my mind from my earlier conversation with Zander and didn't need to be stressing about anything more.

"I need to stay and discuss a few things with Danny. Are you going to be okay getting ready by yourself?"

Zander's concern made me laugh softly. "I'll be okay."

"I can't wait to see you in that outfit," he growled quietly. "That dress, those boots, and that leather jacket." I watched him gulp and when he spoke next, his voice sounded hoarse. "You're going to look amazing." He leaned down to kiss me, a long lingering kiss which he was reluctant to end.

"You should go," I mumbled against his lips. "Danny's waiting."

"He can wait."

"No he can't." I jumped, not realizing Danny was, in fact, still standing there. "Let's go, Professor."

"Coming." Zander gave me one more quick kiss before turning to follow Danny towards their meeting room. I stood and watched until the door closed behind them, then left the barn to head towards the house and get ready for my celebration.

I stood in front of the full length mirror in Zander's room, which Scarlet had given me the second night I stayed there- it was an essential item, she said- and took in my appearance. I'd showered and styled my hair, blow drying it and straightened it with the tools I'd taken from my dad's house- they were older, but worked nonetheless and I'd wanted to ensure I had what I needed here. As I studied the reflection of the vanity counter in Zander's bathroom, though, I realized just how many items I'd accumulated- the makeup, my toothbrush, and even one of my bras could be seen hanging off of the door handle. If anyone stepped foot in this room, they'd certainly think I lived there.

Scarlet's words came echoing through my head again. *I'll bring these upstairs to your room. To your room. Your room.* My room. Our room. Zander's and mine. I truly had a place for myself here.

"Whoa." I blinked, clearing the haze of thoughts that clouded my mind as Zander appeared in our room. He stood in the open doorway staring, eyes wide, unable to move. I watched his tongue slip from his mouth, gently licking his lips. "You look-." He trailed off, his voice sounding faint.

"I have to admit," I stated clearly, turning away from the mirror so he could see me full on. "Scarlet wasn't lying when she said this would make a killer combination."

"You look incredible." He walked towards me slowly, reaching his hands out for my body, gliding them across the silky fabric of the dress. I shivered as his hands brushed my chest- a bra wasn't possible with this dress and I could feel every movement- and he grinned, seeing my reaction. "We could be a little late, you know," he murmured, finally resting his hands on my waist. "It is your celebration after all."

"It's our celebration," I pointed out stepping closer to him and tilting my head up, my dark hair cascading down my back. "This is as much for you as it is for me. Actually," I paused, "it's sort of for everyone. It's been a little stressful around here lately and I think this is just what we all need in order to relax." He leaned down to capture my lips in a kiss but I leaned back, giggling. "You'll smear my lipstick."

He groaned and placed his forehead on mine. "You're killing me, darling."

I breathed out a soft laugh, "don't blame me, blame the outfit." I moved away and pointed at the clothes I'd laid out on the bed, "I picked you out an outfit. I thought the grey t-shirt would look good under your Cut, and compliment my dress the best. I also found these in your closet-," I pointed at the cowboy boots at the end of the bed. "You always wear your tan boots, but these black ones will match mine and-."

"It's perfect, Jade." I blinked and was caught off guard. Hearing Zander call me Jade, when it was just him and I in the confines of our room- it felt wrong. He almost always called me Ali or Alessaundra, hardly ever referred to me by my nickname unless we were discussing something official, or if we were in the presence of The Club.

Zander didn't seem to notice though as he moved towards the bed and began to get changed. "You know, you weren't thirteen the last time you wore a green dress." Zander stated, slipping on his pants.

I reached for the pack of cigarettes on the dresser and lit on, my lipstick staining the filtered end red as I inhaled, blowing out the smoke in a cloud. "Oh no? And how would you know that?" I held it out in offering to Zander but he shook his head, pulling the shirt over his head and shrugging his Cut onto his back.

"You wore a green dress on our first date." He stated with a smirk, turning to look at me. "You made everyone jealous that night- Tiffany, Rebecca- everyone."

I took a few more puffs and then pressed the cigarette into the ashtray as he came to stand next to me. "I'd forgotten," I admitted. "I was so nervous that night- I'd forgotten what I'd worn."

"I didn't," Zander murmured, voice thick. "I ripped that dress off of you so quickly-." He stopped and swallowed hard and I could see desire stirring in his eyes again as I leaned up to kiss him quickly, this time not caring if I smeared my lipstick.

I quickly turned to the mirror to fix it, Zander coming up to stand beside me. As I stared at our reflections Zander said, "We look good." He raised his arm and placed it on my back, rubbing it soothingly, just below my tattoo. I studied us, taking in every detail: Zander's sandy hair was slightly mussed, his once five-o'clock shadow now a full on beard (when did that happen and how had I not noticed until today?), even his piercing blue eyes looked more serious than they once had and had taken on a more grey hue, and just a hint of lipstick could be seen by his mouth.

I couldn't deny that next to my long dark hair and deep green eyes, which were currently encircled in heavy dark makeup- we did look good. The two of us in leather jackets, black boots, and his grey shirt accenting my green dress- it was perfect. So why did it suddenly feel so wrong to me?

"Ready to go?" Zander asked, completely unaware of the confusing thoughts that were suddenly spinning around in my head.

I swallowed, trying to push the negativity aside and forced a smile as I nodded, accepting the hand he offered me. "Let's do this."

Music was playing softly, the smell of steaks filled the air as they were placed on the grill, and everyone was standing around in small crowds talking with a drink in their hand. The atmosphere was light, easy, and I had forgotten all my worries from before. I was determined to enjoy myself; this was a celebration for me after all.

My head was thrown back in laughter as ScatterBrain told a story about some girl he'd met on a run last year who had apparently been married and he'd had to sneak out in the middle of the night when her husband returned unexpectedly. He was explaining how he was in nothing but a pair of boxers, dangling from the window sill, when we all froze at the sound of bikes approaching quickly.

ScatterBrain and Zander exchanged fearful looks which had my heart beating a little quickly. "What's wrong? Isn't that more of our guys, or-."

"No," Zander stated firmly. "We're all here."

"But-."

"Get the girls inside!" Danny hollered from where he was standing, which was closest to the driveway. "Vultures!"

"Fuck," Zander growled, turning to me. "Ali, go, now."

"What's happening?" I shrieked, panicked as the sound got louder, and suddenly gun shots sounded. I screamed, covering my head as I ducked. Zander grabbed me by the shoulders and spun me towards the house, giving me a little shove. "Zander!"

"Go!" He yelled. As I started running I looked back at him to see that he'd grabbed the knife from his boot and was holding it steadily, ScatterBrain at his side with a gun. Shots continued to sound as five bikes entered the clearing that made up the Horse Shoes parking lot, with more sounding in the distance. I turned back towards the house and saw Scarlet waving me forwards, while Vetta was standing at the door, looking calm, a gun in her hand. As soon as I got onto the wrap around porch, panting, Scarlet grabbed my arm and pulled me inside. As the door closed I heard another shot sound and the window beside the door shattered. I screamed again, tears starting to flow down my face hysterically as glass rained down to the floor.

"To the basement," Vetta ordered, sticking her hand out the now broken window and firing off two shots. Scarlet grabbed my arm again and pulled me through the living room and kitchen, opening a door that I hadn't really noticed before. I paused at the top of the stairs, hesitant to go down.

"Go," Scarlet cried, pushing me slightly. "Hurry!"

I took a deep breath and began to descend the steps quickly as Scarlet flicked on a light at the top, following behind me. Vetta closed the door and locked it with three separate locks, the clicking sound of each one echoing in the empty room.

I looked around the space, my mouth open a little in shock. The walls were covered in shelves with books and DVDs, a TV and an old couch, with even a mini fridge in the corner. A microwave sat on a counter by the wall with a coffee maker next to it. I saw the small windows lining the top, but they looked a little distorted to me.

"Where are we?" I asked my voice shaking as I reached up to wipe tears from my eyes. Everything appeared a little too quiet down here for what must be going on outside.

"A safe place," Scarlet explained as Vetta sat down on a chair that was facing the stairs, the gun sitting casually in her hand. "They transformed the basement into a bomb shelter so wives and children would have a safe place to go in case of attack."

"Does it get used often?" I asked, sniffling, scanning the shelves. I noticed some of the shelves had cans of food, snacks, and even a few boxes of cereal.

"No. But we keep it stocked, just in case." I heard what

sounded like a rock ricochet off of the window and spun quickly to look at it. "Bulletproof, soundproof glass," Scarlet explained. "We'll be fine down here."

I swallowed, my mouth dry. "What about the men?" I asked worriedly.

"They'll be okay," Scarlet reassured me. "They know what they're doing-."

"Scarlet don't sugarcoat things for her," Vetta drawled, turning to look at us. She narrowed her eyes at me, in particular. "The Club is trained for surprise attacks- but there's never a guarantee that everybody makes it out alive."

"Vetta," Scarlet gasped, "don't say stuff like that!"

Vetta rolled her eyes, "you've gone soft, Scar. Ever since Jade came along, you've changed. You know this life better than any of us, so therefore you know what I'm saying is true."

"But we shouldn't jinx things." Vetta shook her head and spun back to face the stairs. Scarlet sighed and looked at me. "Jade, don't let Vetta scare you. Zander's going to be okay."

"But what if he's not?" I whispered the tears returning as they stung my eyes.

Scarlet wrapped her arms around me and I leaned into her, resting my head on her shoulder. "Zander can take care of himself, Jade. This is your first attack- but it isn't his. You have to remember that. I know this is all still so new to you but he's been around this stuff his whole life. He knows what he's doing."

"Okay," I whispered leaning away and wiping my eyes with my hand which came back black from all the makeup I'd been wearing. I groaned, "I should have worn waterproof mascara."

Scarlet laughed and pointed towards a door across the room. "There's a bathroom in there. It's not very big, but you should be able to clean yourself up a bit."

"Thank you." I turned to go when Scarlet called my name, halting my steps. I glanced back. "Yeah?"

"You really do look killer in that outfit."

I forced a smile and nodded before resuming my walk to the bathroom. Scarlet was right, it was small. There was a sink and a toilet, nothing more, not even a window. But all I needed was a bit of water to wipe away the smear of mascara and eyeliner that was currently all over my face. I couldn't get all of it off, not without my makeup remover, but I wiped enough away to make me look decent again.

Vetta hadn't moved from the chair, still holding her gun and facing the stairs as if she was anticipating someone to break in, but Scarlet was sitting on the couch and she touched the spot beside her, patting it with her hand. "May as well take a seat, Jade. It's going to be a while."

I wasn't sure how much time had passed while we were down there. Scarlet had explained to me that as a rule there were no clocks, that way the wives couldn't become paranoid and overly worried at how long they were down there for. I understood, but it almost made me more anxious not knowing. I didn't have my phone (the dress had no pockets and my phone wouldn't fit in the small pockets the jacket had) and therefore had no way to communicate with Zander to see if he was okay.

Scarlet had put on a random movie, Vetta continued to sit in her chair facing the stairs without moving a muscle, and I drew a random book off of the shelf and attempted to read it, all the while I could hear random ricochets on the window from what I could only guess were bullets- every time it happened my head would start spinning about what could possibly be going on outside. I could hardly take in any of the words to the book I was trying to read, but still somehow managed to get half way through it before a tapping sound caught my attention. Vetta and Scarlet jumped up simultaneously, rushing towards the stairs.

"That's the secret knock," Scarlet shouted over her shoulder at me and I threw my book down and ran after them, my feet thumping up the stairs. Vetta quickly undid the locks and threw the door open jumping into Danny's arms, who held her tightly. Scarlet, I was surprised to see, pulled ScatterBrain in for a big hug. My heart was hammering, waiting for Zander to appear. That's when I realized that despite Danny and ScatterBrain standing there, they looked very grim, and Zander was nowhere to be seen.

I started to panic as I shouted, "Where is he? Zander? Where is he? Tell me!"

"It's okay," Danny whispered, "he's okay."

"Where is he?" I asked, my breath coming out short and my heart pounding in my chest.

Scarlet moved away from ScatterBrain, her mouth dropping as I saw tears spring to her eyes. "Who was it?"

It took me a moment to realize what she was asking- although they said Zander was okay, Scarlet knew there was something they hadn't revealed yet- someone had been hurt.

Danny took a breath and let it out slowly. "We'll get to that later. Scarlet, we need you-."

"I'm on it." She instantly turned and left, presumably to collect her medical supplies.

"Everyone's in The Clubhouse," Danny called down the hall, then turned to face me. "Jade," he paused, wincing. "I told you Zander's okay, but-."

My heart clenched, "but you lied?"

Danny shook his head, "he's not dead but he was injured."

I gasped and reached up to clutch my heart, "what?"

"He's going to be okay," ScatterBrain quickly said, trying to reassure me. "You should have seen him Jade, he was-."

"We're lucky he was here," Danny interrupted before Scatter Brain could finish.

"What happened?" I whispered with tears in my eyes.

ScatterBrain took in a breath, "we weren't prepared for the attack, but we should have been. The Vultures had been too quiet ever since-."

"Kovach," I nodded recalling the story Zander had told

me.

"He told you?" Danny asked with a raise of his eyebrow.

"Of course, should he not have?"

"No, it just makes things a lot easier, that's all." Danny shrugged but I felt as if he wasn't being honest. But ScatterBrain continued talking before I could think too much of it.

"Zander always has his knife close by, I typically have a gun," he shrugged when I raised my eyebrow. "Welcome to the life, Jade. Anyways," he quickly said seeing my impatient expression- I just wanted to know what happened to Zander. "His knife isn't much match for guns so he had to get to The Clubhouse as soon as he could as we have a stash of weapons there.

"On the way he ran into one of The Vultures that seemed to have sneaked on to the property through the trees. As you know we usually have a Prospect guarding the building but since we were celebrating nobody was there. Lucky for Zander this guy didn't have a gun on him and he was able to take him out fairly quickly with his knife." I gasped, shocked at hearing this even though I shouldn't have been.

"The Professor is a badass, Jade," ScatterBrain stated. "Once he returned with the weapons we were able to retaliate. Unfortunately," here ScatterBrain trailed off and looked grim, "while he was retrieving the weapons Yankee tried to be a hero and-."

"No," the tears that had been stinging my eyes fell.

"He risked his life, sacrificed it really. It should have been me who was shot." Danny admitted solemnly.

"God," Vetta hissed quietly, leaning up to kiss Danny's cheek.

"Yankee died a hero," Danny stated.

"But Zander-."

"He saw Yankees body laying on the driveway," ScatterBrain continued, "and knew if it was left there, his body would be trampled. He lifted his gun and just kept pushing the trigger as he ran towards the body, wanting to save it. Miraculously he managed to hit many of the Vultures who were within range, but it wasn't without a price.

"One of them fired back and he went to dodge it- stabbing himself in the leg with his own knife which he obviously still had in his one hand. The good thing is he managed to hit the guy by returning fire and he rescued Yankee's body in the process. Scarlet will need to give him some stitches, and he may be limping for a little while as Six Inch had, but ultimately he'll be okay."

"Oh my god." I felt weak, clammy, and was sure I was pale from shock. But Zander was okay, he was alive- but Yankee wasn't.

"He's taking Yankee's death pretty hard," Danny added in a soft voice. "He's been out of the game for so long- he needs you, Jade."

"You should go," ScatterBrain urged.

My entire body was shaking but I nodded, taking a few wobbly steps until I was able to find my footing and walk a little more calmly. Glass covered the house from a few broken windows, windows that two of The Prospects were already working on covering up with boards. They nodded at me as I passed them but I didn't return the greeting, too focused on getting outside and finding Zander.

However, when I crossed the threshold and stood on the wrap around porch my stomach clenched and rolled; I had to swallow a few times to ensure bile wouldn't rise in my throat. Blood was all over the ground in puddles and members of The Club were working on moving two bodies away- bodies of men I didn't recognize. There were a few abandoned bikes which I assumed belonged to the members of The Vultures who had been killed here today. Killed. By Zander.

Zander had killed people today. For some reason it was that single fact that was making this difficult for me. Yes, he'd killed Eric Kovach that first night and it hadn't seemed to bother me then, but this was different. This was an attack on The Club. Yankee had died. Any one of us could have been killed, and Zander killed not just one man, but three by the sounds of it- and saved Yankees body in the process.

Who was he? Who was this guy, firing off guns and killing people? It certainly wasn't the man I'd fallen in love with, that's for sure.

Or was it?

I made my way slowly towards The Clubhouse needing time to wrap my brain around everything that had happened; I knew Zander needed me and was waiting for me, but I wasn't ready to see him yet. I'd already been filled with doubt and confusion just hours before all of this happened- and this only intensified my anxious feelings. What made this the most confusing for me is the fact that just days before- this morning even- I had been so certain, so sure, that this was what I wanted. I was so set in my own mind that I went through the horrible tests that ultimately inducted me in as an associate to The Club. So what changed?

"Ali." I blinked, realizing I'd managed to make it all the way to The Clubhouse unconsciously and was now standing in the doorway. Zander was seated in a chair, his leg propped up on a bale of hay that had been opened. Scarlet was dividing up a few pills and proceeded to hand one to Zander. My eyes went wide as he popped it in his mouth and swallowed it.

"Zander-."

"It's morphine," Scarlet explained, not taking her eyes off of Zander's leg, which I now saw was surrounded by torn and bloody fabric. "To help with the pain. The knife got you good, it's a deep cut."

"I-," I couldn't take my eyes off of what Scarlet was doing.

"Ali, look at me." Slowly I drew my eyes up his body to his face. It was pale and he was wincing as he waited for the drug to kick in. "How are you?"

I swallowed, my mouth opening and closing a few times. I didn't know what to say to him. "I don't know," I finally whispered hoarsely.

He nodded as if he understood. "I-" he broke off in a hiss as Scarlet dabbed at his leg.

"Sorry," Scarlet mumbled. "The morphine should kick in any second."

Zander nodded, holding his breath for a few seconds before letting it out slowly. "Ah, that's better." He didn't flinch as Scarlet began to sew his leg up, his eyes on me. "I'm sorry you had to go through all of this."

"Not your fault," I mumbled, crossing my arms uncomfortably.

"You look like you need a smoke," He reached into the inner pocket of his Cut

and withdrew a pack, holding it out for me. I accepted it, grateful, as I lit one first for him, then for me.

"I hadn't expected to witness an attack like that," I admitted after a moment. "It- caught me off guard."

"Understandable." Zander blew out a cloud of smoke. "It was inevitable, though. We've told you, this life is unpredictable and dangerous."

"I tried to warn you," Scarlet stated quietly as she finished the stitches. She glanced up at me, a solemn expression on her face. "Didn't I?"

"You all did," I agreed, dropping the cigarette on the ground and stomping on it. "But nothing could have prepared me for it."

Scarlet began to wrap a bandage around Zander's leg as he studied my face. I think he knew something was wrong, that this whole situation had put me off, but he didn't want to discuss it in front of Scarlet. Instead he waited until she was finished nursing him back to health, popped another morphine pill, and stood, unsteadily, on his feet.

"You shouldn't go to work tomorrow," Scarlet stated as she packed up her supplies. "You should really stay off the leg for a day or two, and-."

"Not an option," Zander muttered. "I called in on Friday for Jade's initiation, I can't call in again tomorrow. Besides, I sent in my resignation today- it wouldn't look good not to show up."

"Zander," Scarlet tried but he shook her off.

"I'll be fine, Scar." He leaned down and kissed her cheek. "Thanks for fixing me up."

"Anytime," she mumbled. Zander began to limp out the door but I glanced back at Scarlet who just shook her head and zipped up her bag. "Go. He's acting like he's okay, but he's not."

"Thanks Scarlet," I whispered giving her a tight smile, then rushed out to catch up with Zander, which was fairly easy since he wasn't moving very fast. "Zander wait."

He glanced back at me, "I need to help the guys clean up."

"No, you need to rest."

"Jade," he sighed, and once again the use of my nickname from him made my stomach twist.

"Ali." I stated firmly.

"What?"

I sighed and shook my head, "you keep calling me Jade, Zander! Do I go around calling you 'Professor'? No, because that's not who you are to me. Is that how you see me though, Zander? Am I just 'Jade' to you now?"

He blinked, looking very confused. "I don't understand-?"

Just like that, I lost it. "You've transformed me into this other girl, Zander! After everything that's happened here- from the tests, to this outfit, to the attack today- all of these things have made you see me as this other person. This- girl- you created out of your Wildest Dreams, this girl who I've slowly transformed into, and I don't know if I want to be her Zander. I don't know if I want to be the kind of girl who thinks it's normal to clean up blood off her boyfriend, who thinks it's okay to have her boyfriend carry a knife hidden in his boot, who's boyfriend has no problem murdering innocent people!"

"Innocent," Zander hissed angrily. "Those men would have killed you- in fact, they did try and kill you! Did you not see that window shatter as you ran inside the house? They were aiming for you!"

"That's besides the point!" I snapped as my heart began to race. "You killed three people, Zander, and you don't even seem bothered by it! How am I supposed to be okay with that?"

"You said it yourself, Ali," he emphasized my name, nearly yelling it. "You could accept all of this because it meant being with me! You wanted this. You wanted me!"

"I still do," I cried. "I-," Tears began to fall from my eyes as I reached up to wipe them away, angrily. "I love you Zander, but-."

"But what?" He asked, sounding angry himself. "But what, Ali?"

"But I think I need some time to- absorb everything that happened." He scoffed, looking away. "I'm scared, Zander. What happened today- terrified me. I was shot at, Yankee was killed, and you were stabbed!"

"I stabbed myself," Zander pointed out.

"You stabbed yourself while shooting and killing three other men, injuring countless others, and protecting the dead body of your fallen soldier. That's- that's a lot to take in." I wiped more tears away as I sniffled. "I think I need a few days to wrap my head around everything- away from The Club."

"But Ali-."

"I want to go back to Baysin with you," I interrupted. "Tonight."

"What?" Zander bit his lip, "I wasn't going to go tonight."

"Please Zander," I begged, taking a step forward. I knew I looked hysterical with tears and makeup running down my face, my hair was probably a mess, and the beautiful silky green dress was full of wrinkles. I lowered my voice to a whisper and heard it break as I repeated, "please."

"Okay." He nodded reaching out for me. I hesitated for only a moment but allowed him to pull me in close, wrapping me in his arms, and melted into his embrace as more tears stung my eyes. He pulled back for a second, reaching up to wipe the tears gently with his thumb. "Tomorrow we'll have to return though, to pay our respects to Yankee."

I forced a watery smile, nodding my head as I said, "okay." He didn't know I was lying, didn't know I had no intentions of coming back any time soon. I needed space, distance, time to think away from everyone and everything. I knew it was going to get me into trouble, knew I'd lose the respect I'd so carefully gained from Danny- but it was what I had to do in order to gain clarity.

Besides, I wasn't an actual member of The Club and I didn't really need to be present, did I?

CHAPTER 17

Zander dropped me off at the hotel where I retrieved my car and drove to my grandmother's house- or was it my house now? She was gone, my dad was gone, and I was the only living relative left with access to it. However, as Zander had pointed out to me earlier that day I wasn't eighteen yet and therefore couldn't legally take possession of the house, no matter how much I wanted to.

I could still sleep in it though. Nobody had to know my father was gone, nobody had to know I was staying in the house by myself. Zander didn't even know where the house was. I was safe here. It was the perfect place for me to think about my life, the choice's I'd made recently, and what I was going to do about it.

I thought I'd fall asleep quickly after everything that I'd been through that day, but despite the fact I was exhausted my brain wouldn't settle. I kept going over the events that took place- starting with Zander and I's conversation that morning, to the gifts that afternoon, leading up to the whole 'Jade' issue, and the attack on The Club. When I finally did fall asleep it wasn't peaceful, images of unknown faces with guns rushed through my head and I'd wake up what felt like moments later, but was really hours, covered in sweat and panting.

I finally dragged myself out of bed around nine thirty

the next morning, not feeling rested at all. As I poured myself a cup of coffee my phone rang. I hesitated to grab it, but when I saw Gina's name on the screen I became curious- I'd been ignoring her calls and messages for weeks until she finally gave up and stopped contacting me, so why was she suddenly calling me after days of silence?

"Hello?" I asked hesitantly, afraid she might start screaming at me.

"Oh my God," she shrieked. I flinched, moving the phone away from my ear for a moment. "Ali! I'm so happy you answered. Are you okay?"

"Yeah, I-."

"I know your grandma died, and I'm so so sorry I wasn't there for you! But you didn't tell me when the funeral was! Then you started ignoring my calls and wouldn't answer my messages. God, I was so angry! Mr Thorn said you were taking some time off school to grieve, which was totally cool and everything. I've been asking around and your duties have been taken care of. The yearbook is almost done! The school paper was printed, and many blog posts have gone up on the school website. Prom tickets went on sale and I made sure to buy you two, just in case.

"You've missed so much gossip though! But none of it is as big as what I heard today. I knew you'd want to know, so I just had to call and tell you that-."

"What?" I asked. Gina's rambling seemed pointless but the build up had my heart beating in anticipation, I almost felt like a normal teenager, wanting to hear the latest gossip of my friends.

"Mr Dionne quit! He's finishing off the month and then he's done! Mr Hottie, Ali! Mr. D! Our English teacher."

"What?" I don't know why the news surprised me so much, considering I already, in fact, knew about it. Maybe it was because I hadn't expected Gina to find out so quickly, maybe it was because I expected her gossip to be about the cheerleader and the quarterback breaking up after three months of dating, or maybe it was because hearing Gina tell me this made everything that much more real. "Do- do we know why?"

"Nobody's been able to find anything out," Gina said. "But, he is limping!"

"Who?"

"Mr Dionne! C'mon Ali, keep up."

"Is he okay?" I asked as I sipped my coffee.

"He's fielding everyone's questions. But there's a rumour going around that he rides a motorcycle, I bet he got in an accident or something. He was off on Friday, nobody knows why! Suddenly he's here today, quitting his job and limping? I mean, it's all a little suspicious, don't you think?"

"Yeah, it is," I mumbled trying not to sigh.

"How come you don't sound interested in all of this?" Gina whined. "C'mon Ali this is big news! The school's buzzing. Everyone's forgotten about Nick's album, and those pictures of the two of you- all anyone can talk about is Mr Dionne!"

"That's great, Gina." I set my mug down and sighed.

Gina let out an irritated breath. "Okay, I get it. You're probably still bummed out about your grandma, right? That's why you took another week off of school?"

"Yeah," I agreed, swallowing. Gina always made the situation with my grandma sound like it was nothing to worry about.

"I know something that'll cheer you up!" she paused, building suspense, then, "I have tickets to Shattered Life's show this Friday night! I was going to take this guy I met last weekend, but he's being an asshole and avoiding me, so I thought why not take you? I know you're not Nick's biggest fan but you've been in such a glum state lately and I thought it might help to cheer you up a little bit! It's in Forest Glen, about an hour away from here, but they're playing an arena show, their first one! I have front row seats and-."

"I'll go."

"Really?" Gina broke off, sounding surprised.

I nodded, not that she could see me. "Yeah, it'll be fun." I knew it was a risk to go to the show. The last time Nick had seen me I was drunk, took off with Yankee and Butch, and ditched my father at Shakers. Had that really only been a week ago? It seemed so much longer. But this was the perfect opportunity to do something fun, something that would take my mind off of everything and help me forget about the mess I'd made my life into. It also was an excuse to avoid going to The Club this weekend, as I was sure I'd be having a few drinks at the show- I knew I'd need them to get through it- and therefore would be too hungover to drive to Riverton on Saturday.

"Oh Ali, I'm so happy you said yes! This will be great. We haven't hung out in forever and-." I let Gina drone on for a few more minutes, making agreeing sounds whenever she paused to take a breath but not really paying attention to what she was saying as I sipped my coffee and lit a cigarette. Finally I heard the sound of the school bell in the background. "Oh shit, gotta go. Math class. I'll text you later and we'll arrange details, 'K? Bye Ali!" she hung up before I could respond and I sighed, set down my phone, and finished my coffee and smoke.

I was already regretting Friday night.

That night I had to turn off my phone. Zander had called me numerous times throughout the day- all of which I ignored. He sent me message after message asking me if I was okay, reminding me to meet him at five so we could ride to The Club together for Yankee's memorial, and expressing his worries when I continued to ignore him. It wasn't until Danny's call came through at six that I finally decided to shut down the phone completely, sitting in silence, a bottle of vodka on the table in front of me. I hadn't touched it, not yet, but I was heavily debating it.

That's when I realized I'd become just like my father after all. I didn't have a problem with drugs, but I certainly had a problem with alcohol. How long had it been since I went a day without a drink? Whenever I was at The Club, it was normal to have a drink or two. Going out with my dad, he'd bought me drinks. Sitting here, with no reason to have one, I was tempted to chug the entire bottle, by myself.

Angrily I reached out and swiped the bottle away. It landed on the floor with a thud and rolled out of sight and I broke down in tears, crumpling into a ball on the couch. All my life I'd tried to avoid turning out like my father, my brother- but in the end it didn't matter. I was an addict. Just like them.

But you're not, a little voice in my head whispered. *You don't rely on the alcohol to function. You just enjoy a few drinks every now and again. Is that really such a problem?* I lifted my tear stained face and stared at the bottle on the ground. *You're going through a very hard time right now. Your life has been completely turned upside down. A drink or two isn't going to hurt you, it's going to help you.* The voice was right (although now I know it wasn't), I realized. I wasn't an addict just because I enjoyed a few drinks every now and then. Besides, a drink or two would help settle my nerves and maybe I'd get a decent sleep tonight. That wouldn't be such a bad thing, right?

Slowly I got off the couch and crawled across the floor until I reached the bottle. With shaking hands I opened the lid and gulped three mouth fulls, sighed, then twisted the lid back on. Instantly my nerves started to seize; I set the bottle back on the table and lay down on the couch, letting the alcohol settle the buzzing in my brain until all that was left was darkness.

I was afraid to turn my phone on the next day. As the screen lit up I closed my eyes and held my breath, waiting for the inevitable signal that I had messages. Sure enough it began to vibrate, and didn't stop for almost two minutes as message after message came in. I knew I was in trouble, knew they were pissed, but I had done what I had to. They didn't know how I was feeling, they didn't realize how terrified I was to be at The Club right now. It had all been too much, too fast. I just needed some time, that was all. Or that's what I kept telling myself, anyway.

I skipped the text messages knowing it was the voicemails I needed to hear; with bated breath I hit play and waited.

"Ali, please answer the phone. I have to leave for Riverton in five minutes, I can't be late."- Zander.

"Alessaundra, this is getting ridiculous. C'mon, talk to me."- Zander.

"I'm getting on my bike now. If I show up to The Clubhouse without you-" he sighed. "Please just call me back."- Zander.

Then finally...

"I don't know what your problem is, Jade, but you better get your ass up here to The Clubhouse. Fuck sakes, woman, Yankee gave his life protecting me, you, and the entire Club. The least you could do is put whatever problems you have aside and pay your respects to him!"- Danny.

"There are going to be some serious consequences for this. We put our trust and loyalties into you and this is how you repay us? You can bet your ass, Alessaundra Campbell, you will regret not coming here today."- Danny.

That last message had me swallowing in fear. He'd only ever used my real, full name in times of seriousness: like my initiation. I gulped, hitting the last message.

"Ali, I don't know what's wrong, I don't know why you aren't answering my calls, or why you didn't show up tonight but- well, Danny's pissed. The Club isn't happy, and- I'm worried, Ali. Please, just call me back."

With tears in my eyes I deleted all of the messages and flopped back on the couch, staring up at the ceiling. I didn't bother reading the texts, but deleted those as well without even opening one. What was the point? They'd probably just say the same thing as the voice mails had.

When my phone started ringing again I jumped, almost afraid to answer it, but it was Aunt Patty's name on the screen and not Zander or Danny's. I hesitated before answering it: I hadn't heard from or spoken to Aunt Patty since grandma's funeral. She'd reached out a few times, seeing if I was okay, but I hadn't answered her, too caught up in everything that had been going on. I hadn't reached out to anyone in my life, except for the members of The Club. I'd isolated myself to only them. No wonder I was feeling so disconnected.

"Hello?"

"Oh Ali," My Aunt sounded so relieved to hear from me. "I hadn't heard from you or your father in so long, I was getting so worried! I wasn't sure if you'd be in class or-."

"I actually took an additional week off. I just needed a few more days."

"Of course. So how are things, with you and your father? Is he there?"

"No, uh, he's out right now."

"Oh." She paused. "He is still- clean- isn't he, Ali?"

Aunt Patty sounded so concerned for her brother and it made me feel even worse to have to lie to her. "He's fine Aunt Patty. We've been- bonding?" I groaned silently to myself. "It's been great."

"I'm so happy to hear that! I was going to ask if you wanted to join us for dinner some time this week? The girls miss you so much, Ali! But," she paused, "I know you said he's doing better, but I'd appreciate it if you didn't invite your father. With his past- I'm just not ready to have the girls around him quite yet."

I closed my eyes against the guilt I was feeling. "No problem Aunt Patty. I'm sure he'd be too busy anyways."

Aunt Patty said something in return but I didn't hear her as my phone beeped indicating another call was coming in. I pulled my phone away and saw Zander's name on the screen. My heart began to pound as I licked my lips, nervously. "I gotta go, Aunt Patty. I'll see you later this week." Before she could answer I hung up, ignored Zander's call, and turned off my phone again.

This was going to be a long week.

A long week it was. I stayed hidden in the house ignoring my phone, watching boring movies on TV, and praying time would go by faster. Every time I heard a noise outside I'd jump, thinking The Club had found me somehow. I was too afraid to leave the house, choosing to order pizza for dinner and eating the leftovers for breakfast and lunch.

I chanced leaving only once, when I went to my Aunt's on Thursday night. I had the weirdest feeling I was followed at one point, even thought I heard the rumble of a motorbike down the street. Since I was heading out with Gina the next day I decided to stay there for the night, much to the twins' happiness. They even insisted I sleep in their room and I obliged, making a bed on their floor with blankets from my bed upstairs. I figured, if I was being watched there was no way they'd sneak into my Aunt's house to try and grab me, especially not if I was with two innocent five year old girls.

I had trouble sleeping that night. Every time I started to drift off my eyes would spring open thinking I was hearing footsteps out the window, the rumble of a bike engine, or the jiggle of a door handle. In the morning when my Aunt went to take the girls to school I paced around the living room, blinds closed tight, heart pounding, and waiting to see if someone would come barrelling through the door- but nobody did. Perhaps I was being overly anxious and paranoid. Was it possible The Club truly had no idea where I was?

Aunt Patty went to work around ten, leaving me alone in the house. I'd warned her I was going out with Gina and she was pleased to hear we were going to see Nick; I think she secretly still hoped he and I would get back together.

I spent the day in my room wondering what I should wear to the show. I'd brought my boots, which were hidden in my car and wondered if I should wear them? I could match them with my ripped jeans and a tank top, leave my hair a little wavy like Nick always liked it, and apply a light, natural looking layer of make-up? One thing I knew for sure, I couldn't- wouldn't- wear the leather jacket. But I had become so accustomed to wearing cowboy boots everyday that it felt a little strange not to have a pair on my feet. I glanced down at the flats I was currently wearing and made the decision to yes, wear the boots. It didn't have to mean anything, right?

Gina was skipping her last class so she could be here by two and we'd be on the road before the traffic hit. We were planning on grabbing a quick dinner and then heading to the arena for the show, which started at six thirty. Gina promised she'd do all the driving and swore she'd only have a drink or two, and no more than that. I didn't care. If Gina got drunk, I'd just find a hotel room for the two of us, but I certainly wasn't staying sober tonight.

When Gina picked me up she stared at my outfit with raised eyebrows. "Since when do you wear cowboy boots?" She asked as I buckled my seat belt.

I shrugged, flicking my hair over my shoulder. "A few weeks now."

"You've never worn them to school."

I stared at her blankly, "so?"

"Whatever," she shrugged, pulling away from the driveway and heading towards the highway. "So Mr Dionne was asking about you."

"What?" I whipped my head around to stare at her as she switched lanes, picking up speed. "Why?"

"He asked if I'd heard from you, and wanted to make sure you were okay. He's the faculty advisor for the yearbook and shit, right?"

I nodded as Gina rolled down her window, pulled a cigarette out of her middle console and lit it. I did the same, blowing the smoke out of the crack in my own window. "What did you say?"

She shrugged, "I said you were fine and that you'd be back on Monday. You are returning to school on Monday, right?" She glanced at me, looking concerned.

"Yeah," I said as I exhaled a cloud of smoke. "I guess I am."

"He seemed worried you were gonna drop out or something. I laughed in his face, as if you'd ever drop out of school."

I forced a laugh as I flicked my cigarette out the window. "Yeah, crazy."

"He really seemed concerned though Ali. It was kind of sweet." Her soft smile widened, "I think he likes you."

"What?"

Gina laughed, "I'm only bugging you! I mean, he does like you but so does every other teacher in the school! You're a straight A student, never hands in assignments late, and always shows up to class- with the exception of these last few weeks, but they get that. You could probably stop showing up to school, miss every single exam, and still pass all of your classes. Me? I'll be lucky to pass any of mine and graduate with everyone else."

My heart sank, "Gina, are your grades really that bad?"

She waved her hand flippantly. "Who cares. I'm going to beauty school, I don't need top grades, I just need to pass."

A moment of silence passed as I considered what Gina had just told me. I bit my lip and turned to her, hesitant. "Did you tell Z- Mr Dionne that we were going to the show tonight?"

"No." I stared at her, a little surprised. She shrugged. "I figured it would be better not to mention you were going to a concert when you're supposed to be grieving still. I thought it might look kinda bad, like you were just taking advantage of having time off of school, or something."

I sighed, feeling a sense of relief as Gina took an exit, driving off of the highway. We passed the sign to Forest Glen, Gina following directions from her phone until she pulled into a parking lot down the road from the Arena. We got out of the car, paid, and began to find a place to have dinner.

I forgot how fun Gina could be to hang out with. We ordered drinks, shared a few appetizers as a meal, and then made our way to the arena for the show. Gina had me laughing like I hadn't laughed in months. She had all of the school gossip (including, as I expected, the head cheerleader and the quarterback breaking up after three months) and filled me in on everything I'd missed for the past two weeks.

She told me how everyone had been talking about Nick and I, thanks to those damn pictures taken of us at Coffee Cafe, and said that the rumour mill was buzzing for days after the album dropped, especially when I didn't come to school. Once the news broke about my grandmothers passing, though, people stopped talking out of respect for me, which I think surprised me more than anything else she'd said. I never thought the other kids at school cared all that much for me, but maybe I was wrong.

"Did you tell Nick we were coming tonight?" Gina asked as we took our seats. I was carrying two vodka sodas while Gina had a beer, her last drink of the night, she said.

I sat down crossing one leg over the other as I took a large sip of my drink and shook my head. "Uh uh. I didn't tell you about seeing him play last week."

"What?" Gina's eyes went wide. "Spill. Now."

I sighed, regretting saying anything as I finished my first drink, setting the cup under my seat. "Okay. Well, Nick showed up at the funeral and gave my dad tickets to this exclusive show he was playing at Shakers and-."

"You were there? I heard that show was amazing! I wanted tickets so bad but wasn't able to get them." She groaned.

"It was okay," I shrugged.

"Uh oh, what happened?" Gina wasn't as privy as Nick had been about my father. All she knew was that he was only around sometimes, but she'd never really asked for details so I didn't feel inclined to tell her about that. Instead I said, "Nick- sang to me. In a way that made me uncomfortable and-."

"And what?" Gina was on the edge of her seat, taking a sip from her beer. "What?"

I sighed, "he came up to me at the end of the show and I may have- lost it on him, and walked out."

Her eyes went wide and her mouth dropped open. "No way! Oh God Ali, your life is like- a dream!"

I could hear the envy in her voice and, for a split second, I considered telling her all of the dark secrets I kept deep inside- Zander, my father, The Club- but knew I could never reveal those to her. Instead I pressed my lips together and inhaled deeply, trying to settle my pounding heart.

Luckily the lights went down and the opening act came on before Gina could ask me any more questions. I wasn't very interested in hearing them so I excused myself, said I had to hit the bathroom, and instead made my way to the bar for another two drinks before actually going to the restroom.

By the time the opening act was over I'd made my way to three of the bars in the arena, visited the bathroom twice, and was carrying two more drinks back to my seat. Gina was checking her phone and turned to face me when I got back. "You missed the entire opening act!"

I shrugged, "I'm not here to see them anyways."

"They were pretty good," Gina pointed out, sliding her phone into her purse. "How was the line to the bathroom?"

I raised one shoulder, taking a sip of my drink. "They were getting busy, but best to hit em now, before the show starts."

"Right." Gina swung her purse over her shoulder. "Be right back."

"Hey Gina!" I called as she started to walk away. She glanced back at me and I held my cup in the air. "Will you grab me another drink while you're out there?"

She bit her lip, looking worried but nodded. I sat down, finished off a drink, and turned to face the stage. A large curtain with the band's name SHATTERED LIFE was covering their equipment. Gina was right in the fact that this was their first arena show, and it was totally different than any of the small theatres or clubs they'd played before. The arena probably had about ten thousand occupants and I couldn't help but wonder if Nick was feeling anxious to be playing to such a large crowd.

Pulling my phone out I hovered over the power button, almost turning it on so I could text him- but I thought better of it. If I turned my phone on now I was sure I'd be slammed with texts and calls from Zander and Danny, and I didn't want to deal with those right now. Instead I slid it back into the back pocket of my pants, finished my other drink, and waited for Gina to return with another for me.

Gina got back just as the lights went down again, thrusting the drink at me. "The line was insane!"

"You only got me one?" I asked with a raise of my eyebrow.

"You only asked for one," she pointed out. "God, Ali."

"Sorry," I mumbled, taking a large sip.

"Don't you think-." Gina started but before she could finish a loud note from Kevin's electric guitar sounded, Aaron beat on the drums a few times, and the curtain opened, revealing Nick standing under a single spot light. The crowd went wild and I flinched as the girl standing next to me lost her mind, her piercing voice echoing loudly in my ears.

Nick took the microphone off the stand. "Thank you Forest Glen, it's good to be here tonight! We are Shattered Life and welcome to the show!" The crowd screamed louder as more notes were played by Kevin and Aaron. Nick began to bob his head a few times, and then broke out into song as he opened with Rage.

Around me girls were dancing, Gina was swinging her head, and everyone was shouting- but me, my eyes were focused on Nick who kept scanning the front row until his eyes landed on me. His smile, which had been soft as he sang, widened as he belted the next line loudly. I wasn't sure how he knew I was there, or even how he was able to spot me in a crowd of ten thousand people, but of course he found me, he always seemed to find me.

They sang a few songs and took a break while some dancer came out and put on an 'intermission' show to keep the crowd entertained. I excused myself to the bar, Gina watching me worriedly as I left. I knew she was concerned about how much I was drinking, but these vodka soda's were weak, and after weeks of drinking straight vodka it was going to take more than a few mixed drinks to get me drunk.

The girl sitting next to me followed, getting into line behind me, and gushing about the show. "Oh my God, aren't they amazing? I swear Nick, the lead singer, keeps staring at me! He's so hot, don't you think?" she sighed, dreamily. "How long have you been a fan? I discovered their early EP's like years ago. I fell in love with Everlasting and was so disappointed they never included it on their album! It never made sense to me why they didn't, you know? It was their biggest song! Not to mention I was crushed when they released Come Back To Me, cuz you just know Ali was who he wrote Everlasting about and-."

I rolled my eyes and tried to ignore her as I walked up and ordered myself two more drinks. The bartender eyed me a little wearily and I tried to make sure I didn't stagger as I waited for her to hand me my drinks. She did, but I could tell she was doing so reluctantly; I wouldn't be able to order any more from her.

The girl behind me only ordered a beer and ran to catch up with me as I started down the stairs. "I never got your name, by the way! I'm Sally. You know, you look kinda familiar, have you been to a lot of their shows? I've been trying to follow them to as many as I can and- oh my god, they're coming back!" She shoved past me, causing me to spill both of my drinks on the floor. I growled, my eyes narrowing as I flicked my hands to get as much vodka off of them as I could; luckily they didn't splash onto my clothes, but now I was drinkless and annoyed.

Sally smiled at me as I got back to my seat swinging her head to the music. Gina forced a smile, but I just stared at the stage stony faced. I noticed a few security guards around us now, standing by the front of the stage- had they been there the whole time? I didn't think so, but they seemed to be hovering close to me. Gina shrugged, continuing to dance to the music.

As Nick slowed things down and went into Everlasting Sally screamed, grabbing my arm in excitement. "Oh my God, I love this song!" I flung her off of me, her hand flailing up and hitting me in the face. Something stung by my eyes and I whirled, raising my hand to- what, I wasn't sure, punch her? Slap her? I never got to find out. A security guard was on me instantly, pinning my hands behind my back. I tried to struggle, heard the music on stage falter, and when I glanced up, Nick was looking right at me, his expression disappointed.

I stopped struggling, letting the security guard turn my body away. When I looked back at Gina to see if she was following I saw her pointedly ignoring me, watching the stage but obviously not hearing the music. I sighed, waiting for the guard to lead me outside; I was surprised when he guided me backstage instead.

"We've been asked to escort you into the band's dressing room," he stated in a firm voice. "Nick had a feeling you'd do something and he doesn't want the cops involved."

"This was Nick's idea?" I asked, somewhat surprised as the guard opened the door to the room. Inside I saw a comfortable looking couch next to a mini-fridge, there was a vanity table with lights, and a door led to a bathroom, which reminded me I desperately had to go.

"He saw you from the sideline," The guard mumbled. "You're Ali, right?"

"Yeah."

"I'm Donny, Nick talks about you a lot." The guard stretched his hand out for me to shake and I grasped it a little hesitantly.

"So who are you?" I asked. "Are you Nick's bodyguard? The Band's? Or the arena's?"

"I work for the band as a whole," Donny stated, closing the door and standing in front of it, blocking it. "But I spend the most time with Nick."

"So they're still doing that, are they? Acting like the band is Nick's, and not a team effort?" Donny hesitated but nodded. "Poor Kevin and Aaron."

"They seem okay with it."

I raised an eyebrow in disbelief, "are they going to say that to me when I ask them about it?" Donny shrugged. "That's what I thought."

"You may as well make yourself comfortable," Donny said, subtly changing the subject. "There's another forty five minutes left of the show. If you turn the TV on you can view it."

I walked towards the bathroom and flicked on the light- it was fairly large with a full tub and shower. I looked over my shoulder and said, "I've heard these songs more than enough times. But thanks Donny."

I helped myself to two beers from the minifridge while I awaited Nick to be finished with the show. Finally, after what seemed like hours, he entered with Kevin and Aaron trailing behind. They sounded like they were arguing about something.

"-not my fault. What was I supposed to do-?"

"Ignore it," Kevin growled.

"You messed up too," Aaron pointed out. "It wasn't just Nick and-."

"Oh shut up." Kevin yelled. "I'm so sick of-."

Donny cleared his throat and the three guys stopped at the same time, glancing first at him then over to me. I raised my beer towards them in a cheers. "Hello boys."

"Ali." Nick said, taking a step forward.

Kevin rolled his eyes, "great, she's here too."

"Why is she-?" Aaron asked, looking at Nick confused.

Nick sighed, "I asked Donny to bring her back here rather than escort her out and potentially get her arrested."

Aaron and Kevin blinked and groaned. "Nick, man-."

"Why?"

"I'm sorry," Nick said. "But-."

"After what happened last time?" Kevin asked angrily. "You went on and on for days about-."

"I know."

"And yet here she is again."

"I can hear you, you know." I finished the last sip of my beer and crushed the can, tossing it on the table.

"And she's drunk." Kevin shook his head. "Nick have you lost your goddamn mind?"

"I just need to talk to her, please." He lowered his voice and whispered something that I couldn't hear. Whatever secret he was saying I didn't want to know; I reached for the fridge to get another beer but stumbled, falling onto the couch with a moan. It was oddly comfortable here and I closed my eyes as the door closed. I waited for footsteps but didn't hear any, had they left me alone? Peeking one eye open I saw Nick standing there studying me unblinkingly.

"What?" I mumbled, my voice muffled by the couch.

He shook his head as he finally took a few steps towards me. "What's happened to you, Ali?"

"Nothing."

"Ali," he sighed sadly and I felt him sit down on the couch beside me. His hands cradled my head, turning it towards him. I squinted my eyes open. "You are not okay."

"I'm fine."

"Okay," he raised a hand to his forehead for a second before dropping it to his knee. "If you're so fine, why are you wasted?"

"I'm not wasted!" I heard my words slur.

"Really." His voice was flat.

"I only had a few." I tried to protest.

"This isn't like you Ali. These past few weeks- you've changed. I saw it that first day, at Coffee Cafe, there was just something different about you. At your grandma's funeral, you seemed so sad and wouldn't talk to me, someone you've known for years- yet this guy, who you probably had only known for a few weeks was able to comfort you in your time of need? Then at the show last week you ran off with these two- gang members, who I also happened to see outside of the funeral house? And now you're getting in fights!"

"Battle wound," I smirked, pointing to where there was a small scratch on my cheek, just under my eye. "I think the chick was wearing a ring."

Nick groaned, "you're not taking this serious at all, are you?"

"You're taking it a little too seriously." I moaned as I rolled trying to sit up. Nick placed his hands under my armpits and helped heave me until I was sitting. I flopped back against the couch, rolling my head towards him and grinning. "You looked hot on stage, by the way."

"Ali," He groaned.

"Do you remember the day we first met?" I asked him in a soft voice, my eyes closing. "I was in ninth grade, you were a senior, and I walked in on you playing your guitar in the cafeteria at eight thirty in the morning. You were singing Have You Ever Seen The Rain by CCR and I was mesmerized by your voice and the way you plucked the chords so effortlessly. I couldn't help but clap when you finished-."

"I was so surprised," Nick added in a quiet voice. "I hadn't realized anyone was watching."

"What can I say? Whenever I had a test I was always sure to arrive early and get a few extra minutes of studying in. I got the best grade on that test, thanks to you and the songs you played while I studied. I loved listening to you play, and the next day, under the tree-."

"I asked to kiss you," he grinned.

"Just like you wrote in the song."

"Yeah," he sighed. "Exactly like the song."

My head fell, landing to rest on Nick's shoulder. I felt him stiffen for a moment before he slowly raised his arm to rest across my shoulder. I snuggled in, sighing happily and feeling more relaxed than I had in awhile. I often referred to Nick as a neglectful boyfriend who had been more concerned about his band and record deal than me, but the truth was he had been a pretty good and caring boyfriend, and being in his arms felt like home.

I turned my head at the same time he glanced down at me and I was suddenly overcome with the urge to kiss him. I tilted my head up, stretching towards his mouth, pursing my lips and closing my eyes. His mouth was a breath away from mine, and I felt his exhale on my face as he sighed and pulled away. My eyes sprang open.

"I can't Ali." He looked like he was having an internal battle with himself as he rubbed his eyes with his palms.

"Can't?"

"I'm sorry. But, aren't you seeing-."

Reality crashed over me and my stomach turned, guilt weighing down on me. "Oh my god." My stomach continued to turn and I stood up, stumbled, then rushed to the bathroom, falling into the wall once before finally making it to the toilet and emptying it's contents. I heard Nick's footsteps, felt his hands pull my hair back away from my face, and kneel down beside me.

He didn't say anything as I vomited, but he stayed by my side the entire time until I was finished, feeling weak with sweat beading on my forehead. "Do you have a place to stay tonight?" he whispered to me as I sat against the door, my head thrown back. I shook my head, not trusting my mouth to open. I heard him sigh, "you do now."

"What-?" I groaned, clamping my mouth closed again.

"I have a room, you can stay with me." My eyes sprang open and I went to protest but he held his hand up to stop me. "You can't drive home, Ali, and I'm not letting you get on a bus, not like this. I'd rather sacrifice my bed and sleep on the floor, as long as it means you're safe."

Tears brimmed my eyes and began to fall. I'd forgotten how good Nick truly was to me, forgot how sweet and caring he could be, forgot how well he treated me- when he wasn't focused on the band. Nick wrapped his arms around me, cradling my body. "It's okay, Ali," he whispered, bending down to kiss the top of my head. That only made me cry more.

I had so many tears built up inside of me, and sitting here, on the bathroom floor with Nick and the sour smell of vomit in the air, I let them fall. I cried tears for Zander. I cried tears for Nick. I cried for my father. I cried for my grandmother. I cried because I was afraid and I cried because there was nothing I could do about it. I cried for everything in my life I no longer had control over. I cried until I had no more tears left to cry and Nick stayed with me, a comfortable and reassuring presence, the whole time.

I woke up on a comfortable bed, surrounded by pillows, and wrapped in a white duvet. The room was unfamiliar but I could tell, just by looking around, that it was a hotel room. My head was pounding and I pulled the blanket over my head with a groan wanting nothing more than to go back to sleep. A sound below the bed had me flinging the blanket off of me as I sat up and stared at the bundle on the floor: Nick.

I thought I was in a hotel room because Gina and I had decided to crash, but now the events of the night before came flashing through my head- getting drunk at the show, trying to fight some random fan-girl beside me, getting escorted out by security and led to Nick's dressing room, making a move on Nick, vomiting in front of Nick- but how did I end up here? That part was still unclear to me. My last memory was sobbing on the bathroom floor.

Someone pounded on the door and I jumped, my heart pounding: as always my first thought these days was, *did The Club find me*? But as the pounding continued a voice started calling out, "Nick, man, open the door!" I glanced down at the floor where Nick continued to sleep- I'd forgotten how deep a sleeper he was- but I recognized Kevin's voice so I slid out of bed, thankful to discover I was still fully dressed, and opened the door to the room.

Kevin stood there, mouth open, hand raised, and speechless for a moment as he tried to make sense of what he was seeing. He blinked then finally seemed to realize his mouth was wide open and snapped it shut, slowly lowering his hand back to his side. He still looked uncomfortable though as I leaned against the doorway, crossing my arms and raising an eyebrow, waiting for him to say something.

Finally he cleared his throat. "Uh, hi, Ali."

"Hey."

"Uh, is Nick around?"

I flicked my head, letting my hair swing behind my shoulder as I shrugged. "He's still sleeping." Kevin nodded and turned to go but I called his name, stopping him. "Wait." I bit my lip, suddenly feeling nervous. Kevin had always been a good friend to me and I didn't like how angry he seemed to be about everything. "I'm sorry, if I did anything to hurt the band, you know, after-."

Kevin sighed and shook his head, "it's not your fault, Ali."

"Actually, it kind of was. I cheated on Nick, Kevin. I know that must have caused some issues for a while there."

Kevin nodded taking a few steps until he was leaning against the door frame as well. "Nick was pretty bummed out for a while there. I worried we wouldn't get the album completed in time. They wanted a song, and we couldn't give them one, until-."

"Nick channelled his pain into one."

"Yeah. Aaron and I- we weren't sure if we should release the song. I mean, it was good- it is good- but we know how you felt about the fame portion of the band and we didn't want to hurt you."

"I appreciate that."

"But Scotty- he insisted, and you don't go against your manager, Ali. It's just not done."

I nodded, "I'm not mad- not anymore, anyways. I mean,

it was just a song-."

"But then it turned into an album." Kevin pointed out, looking regretful. "Nick just kept utilizing his pain until he'd written half a dozen songs- and Scotty thought they were masterpieces. It was Scotty's idea to name the album after you, Ali. Not Nick's. You should know that."

"I'm liking this Scotty guy less and less," I mumbled irritably. "And I think I've only met the guy once."

"He's a bit of an asshole," Kevin agreed. "But he's good at his job. I mean look at us, we played an arena last night!"

"I'm happy for you guys." I lowered my voice, "but do you ever feel like Scotty is putting Nick in the spotlight more than you and Aaron? This was all of your band, not just Nick's and-."

"Scotty is just trying to help us, and you have to admit, Nick was the one who started the band, Nick's the one who writes most of our songs, Nick-."

"That doesn't mean you should be pushed aside like you're nothing."

Kevin bit his lip and nodded, "we're doing what we have to do, Ali."

"It just doesn't seem fair." A moment of silence passed and I glanced at Kevin, my eyes zeroing in on his left hand. "How's Jocelyn, anyways?"

Kevin grinned in that soppy way people in love smile at each other. My heart clenched as I realized I hadn't seen Zander smile at me like that in weeks. "She's good. Almost done university, graduating with honours. I don't know how she's managed to do all of that work in the middle of all of this chaos but-."

"It must be hard to have you gone so much."

Kevin nodded, "it is, for both of us. But she understands, and she's happy for me. She knows how important this is for us. Speaking of which, though, I should get back to my room. When Nick wakes up, have him call me, okay? I need to touch base with him about a few things."

"Okay, I will. It was nice to see you Kevin."

Kevin smiled a little sadly, "it was good to see you too, Ali."

I closed the door with a sigh, resting my head on it and shutting my eyes. It had been nice to talk civilly with Kevin, to find out he didn't actually hate me, and despite the fact he wished it was different he really was okay with the way things were with the band. I felt a wave of sadness as I realized that if I hadn't screwed up and cheated on Nick, I would have been around for all of these decisions, and maybe, just maybe, things would be different for everyone.

"He just wants to know if he and Jocelyn have time to go to dinner tonight. We play a show tomorrow that's a few hours North of here. If he and Jocelyn hang out tonight he's going to have to drive himself to the show in the morning."

I jumped at Nick's voice and spun around, watching as he sat up on his bed of blankets and pillows, stretching his arms up. He was shirtless and I found myself staring at his chest and the tattoo that ran down his ribs- EVERLASTING, written in an old English font. He saw me staring and glanced down. "Do you remember when I got this?"

Gulping I nodded, "right after you released the song to iTunes and got your first one hundred downloads."

"Who would have thought the song would blow up like it did, eh?" he grinned. "By the way, I see you finally got yourself a tattoo- what does it mean?"

My eyes widened as I remembered I was in a tank top, The Clubs mark on display for everyone to see on my back. It had been stupid of me to not wear a sweater or a jacket or something to cover up the mark. Anyone could have seen it, I could have put myself and Gina in danger. How could I have been so stupid and reckless?

"It's nothing," I muttered trying to act nonchalant about it. "Just- nothing."

"It can't be nothing," Nick stated, reaching for his shirt and pulling it over his head, mussing his dark hair. "You always said you wouldn't get a tattoo unless it meant something important to you."

"Just forget about it, Nick."

His face dropped, "this has to do with that gang, doesn't it?" He stood up, placing his hands in his pockets. "Talk to me, Ali. What's happening with you? Did you mark yourself as one of theirs? Have you joined a gang? Are you hiding from them? Whatever it is, I can help you." With every sentence he spoke he took one step towards me until he was standing right in front of me, his voice soft and quiet. "Please let me help you Ali."

Tears had sprung to my eyes again- I was so sick of crying- as I shook my head. "You don't understand, Nick. You can't help me. Anything you do, could get you killed. I-." I broke off as I wiped some tears away. "Please, Nick, please, just stop asking me questions. Please."

"You're scared Ali," Nick stated sadly, and I saw a few tears glistening in his eyes. "What have they done to you?"

"They haven't done anything but accept me into their lives," I mumbled through the tears. "You don't understand Nick, you just don't!"

"Then help me understand, Ali. Please."

I shook my head quickly, wiping more tears away. "No. I won't put you in that position Nick. I can't risk your life, not for me."

"You're scaring me Ali," Nick breathed softly.

"I'm scaring myself," I admitted, sniffling. I shook my head, "I just need to go home, Nick."

"How are you going to do that, Ali? Gina left, before the show even ended, I should add. I take it she drove you here?" I nodded, reaching up to wipe my face. He sighed. "Look, I can drive you. I have my car and I-."

"You have your car?" I asked, surprised. "But why-?"

He shrugged, "sometimes I need space from the others. When I don't feel like driving it, Donny's more than happy to get behind the wheel. He often accompanies me in my car anyways, just in case."

"You'd drive me all the way to Baysin, then turn around and head all the way North?" I felt more tears well in my eyes at his kindness and the love he still clearly had for me. How could he still love me after all this time, after everything I'd done to him, after I'd clearly changed into someone he couldn't recognize?

"I'd do anything for you Ali," he stated seriously, taking my hands in his as more tears fell. "You should know that by now."

I nodded, "I do, Zander, I do." Nick blinked, leaning away from me and dropping my hands quickly. At first I didn't realize what was wrong, what I'd said to make him so upset. "Nick? What's wrong?"

He took a step back, putting distance between us. "Is that his name, then?"

"Who's?" I asked, still confused.

Nick shook his head and let out a big breath. "Your boyfriends. You-."

Still confused I stopped to think about the conversation we were having, Nick had said he'd be there for me, that he'd do anything for me, and I'd said-. I groaned. "Fuck, Nick, I-."

"Forget it, Ali," Nick looked at me sadly. "I was caught up in the moment, and even I forgot- that's to say, I just was hoping- never mind, it doesn't matter. The fact is, you're seeing someone, and you shouldn't be here with me, right now. I'm sure he's probably wondering where you are, anyways."

"Nick I-." I tried to apologize again but Nick cut me off, reaching for his keys that were sitting on the counter next to the door.

"We should get going. I have to be back here by three to pack up my things and check out. Got everything?" I swallowed and nodded, patting my pockets to make sure my ID was still there and grabbed my phone off of the counter where it sat as well. Nodding Nick reached for the door and opened it. "Let's go."

It was a quiet drive all the way back to Baysin. Nick seemed lost in thought and I didn't know what to say to make him feel better, or if there even was anything, in fact, to say. I'm sure these last twenty four hours were the weirdest he'd experienced, leaving him confused and full of questions. Questions I wanted to answer for him, questions I wasn't even sure had answers.

As we pulled onto the exit to Baysin I spoke for the first time in over an hour. "Do you mind if we stop at Coffee Cafe? I could really use a pick-me-up."

Nick nodded, switching lanes so we could turn left instead of right, towards Novella and my favourite coffee shop. I felt like he wanted to say something, but every time he'd open his mouth he'd close it a second later with a sigh, choosing not to say anything instead.

Finally he pulled into the parking lot. "I need to use the restroom so I'll just run in okay?" They were the first words he spoke, and they weren't exactly heartwarming.

"Okay." Once again he did that thing where he opened his mouth to say something but closed it, clenching his jaw, and nodded as he opened his door and exited the car. I sighed, leaning my head back against the headrest and closing my eyes, anticipating the rush of caffeine that would soon be flowing through my veins.

Flipping down the mirror I studied my reflection, wincing at the scratch under my eye and the dark circles that surrounded it. Just as I was about to flip the mirror back up I spotted something in the distance that made my heart start to beat quickly- a motorcycle with someone in a black helmet, sunglasses, and leather jacket- Cut, I corrected myself. My heart leapt thinking, at first, that it was Zander. If there was anything I'd learned from my slip up with Nick, it was that I still loved and cared for Zander, despite the fear and uncertainty I was currently feeling.

But as I jumped out of the car and turned excitedly,

ready to run across the parking lot and throw my arms around him, the guy took off his sunglasses and glared at me. I froze, my heart starting to bang harder in my chest, my excitement turning to fear. It wasn't Zander who was waiting for me; it was Danny.

He raised his hand and used a single finger to gesture me forwards, a cold and angry expression on his face. I gulped but knew I had no other choice but to walk over there; my legs trembled and I prayed I wouldn't stumble and fall. I stopped five feet from him and the bike, swallowed against the dryness in my mouth, and tried to look him in the eye but it was hard with his eyes piercing me so intensely.

"Where the fuck have you been?" Danny snarled.

I ignored him, crossing my arms over my chest. "How did you find me?"

Danny smirked, "I knew you'd show up here sooner or later. This is your favourite coffee shop after all, isn't it?"

My heart sank in betrayal. "What else did Zander tell you about me?"

Danny chose not to answer that. "Do you have any idea how much trouble you are in? You missed out on Yankee's memorial! You ignored calls, directly from Zander and myself- your Presidents! You-."

"I am not a member of this Club, Danny." I snapped. "You are not my President, you are not-."

"You have marked yourself as An Associate. You have sworn to be loyal to us!" Danny was trying to keep his voice quiet, and it only made it sound more dangerous, sending shivers down my spine. "You are as much a part of this Club as Scarlet or Vetta, even The Prospects for fuck sakes- as part of The Club as Zander was when he was a Weekend Warrior. We accepted you, brought you into our hearts, made you a part of our sacred family- and this is how you repay us?" As angry as Danny was I could see the hurt that he carefully hid behind his eyes.

"I'm sorry, I just-."

"What?" he growled.

"I got scared." I admitted dropping my arms to my side. "The Vultures- the attack-."

Danny scoffed, "you smuggled drugs into a police inhabited club and faced down a dangerous drug dealer- and an attack on The Club by The Vultures scared you?"

I bit my lip, glancing towards Coffee Cafe where I could see Nick at the counter ordering our drinks. I sighed, turning back to Danny. "I just needed some time."

"Well you had it. Now get on the bike, you're coming back to Horse Shoes with me." It wasn't a request and I knew it, but I couldn't just leave without saying goodbye to Nick, not after everything he'd done for me.

"I just-."

"Get on the bike, Jade." I swallowed, but was secretly thankful to hear him call me Jade, rather than Alessaundra. "Now."

I heard the door to Coffee Cafe open and saw Nick exit, notice my absence from the car, and look around the parking lot to find out where I was. As our eyes locked, his went wide as he spotted me talking to Danny. He seemed so unsure of what to do- I'm sure from a distance, he thought it was Zander standing with me and was afraid to approach. If only he knew how safe he truly was to keep his distance.

"If you go over there, there will be some serious consequences Jade." I looked back at Danny. The threat was very clear in his voice.

"But I-," I licked my dry lips.

"No buts. Get on the bike."

"Okay." I finally whispered, my shoulders slumping in defeat. "Please, just don't hurt Nick."

Danny didn't say anything, just picked up his helmet and handed it to me. As I put it on my head and clipped it under my chin I looked back at Nick, who I think saw the fear and uncertainty in my eyes, even from a distance. He began to march over quickly, the coffee tray still in his hands. Danny saw him and growled, wrenching my arm and pulling me onto the bike behind him. I tripped but managed to swing my leg up.

Nick got to us just as Danny was starting the bike. "Ali! Ali, are you okay?"

"Go away, Nick," I shouted as Danny revved the engine. "Please, just go!"

"I'm going to call the Police," Nick stated, reaching for the phone in his pocket, his eyes on Danny.

"No!" I cried. I heard Danny growl again as he put the bike in gear. "Nick, don't, please."

"Ali!"

"Goodbye, Nick." I wasn't sure if he heard me, though, over the rumble of the engine as Danny revved it and took off, causing Nick to jump backwards and drop both coffees. Holding on tight to Danny I looked backwards one last time and watched as Nick faded into the distance, praying he wouldn't actually call the Police, hoping he'd understand and go home, where he'd be safe: I could never forgive myself if something happened to Nick because of me.

"Alessaundra." As soon as I got off of Danny's bike Zander was there, pacing, as if he had been waiting for us. I knew there was no way Danny could have informed him we'd be on our way but he was waiting nonetheless. He reached into his pocket and withdrew a pack of smokes, lighting one and passing it to me. Danny nodded at him and walked away without another word but I knew he had more to say to me.

Zander was quiet as the two of us stood in the parking lot smoking our cigarettes. I wanted to talk, but wasn't sure what I should say, and I also felt it was important that he make the first move. He discarded his smoke and immediately lit another, inhaled deeply and finally spoke as he exhaled. "What the hell happened to you Alessaundra?"

I dropped my cigarette on the ground and twisted my foot to put out the smouldering end as I sighed. "I got scared."

"You missed Yankee's memorial. You promised me-."

"I know."

"Ali," Zander let a breath out of his nose, "I don't think you truly understand what you have done. The Club- they don't trust you anymore. They- they're angry."

I lifted my head up as I exhaled another deep breath. "I know, I screwed up."

"You didn't screw up." I dropped my head and looked at him in surprise. "You fucked up. Royally. The Club may never trust you again."

"I just needed some time," I defended, kicking a rock on the ground and watching it roll across the driveway. "The Vultures- the attack-."

"We could have helped you, Ali." I stuck my hands in my back pocket. "We're supposed to be a family, you're supposed to be able to trust us- trust me." I heard the hurt in his voice and when I finally turned to look at him I could see a few tears shining in his eyes. "You didn't tell me. You ignored me. You reached out to Gina but wouldn't answer my phone calls and-."

"I needed to feel normal again Zander. I needed to feel like- a teenager! Do you have any idea how hard it has been for me? I know I have only myself to blame for choosing this life. You gave me so many chances to step away, Scarlet warned me time and time again but I was too blind, too overcome with my feelings for you to truly stop and think about what it would mean for me to turn myself over completely to you and promise myself to The Club. Once it happened though- I was overwhelmed. Everything seemed to happen at once and then when The Vultures attacked-." Tears were in my eyes now- was I ever going to stop crying? "That attack sent me over the edge. I lost it, Zander. I lost myself. I needed to step away from everyone and everything and just think."

"And did it help?" I knew it was hard for Zander to hear me admit all of this but he was exhibiting an insane amount of patience, trying to remain calm as I talked, and I was beyond thankful for that. It was far easier to explain when someone wasn't yelling at you.

"It helped," I admitted, taking a step towards him. Until now neither one of us had reached out to touch the other. We'd kept a bit of distance, respecting the other's space. Now, though, I needed to show him exactly how I was feeling. He stood still until I was right in front of him, staring up into his blue eyes. "I love you Zander, and that won't ever change. Throughout all of this you are the one thing that has remained the same.

"I won't lie to you, though. I enjoyed being a normal teenage girl the past few days. I got to spend time with my family, hang out with a friend, and attend my ex-boyfriends concert." Zander's eyes narrowed slightly and I reached for his hands, squeezing them. "Yes, Zander, I went to Nick's show. I got drunk, almost got in a fight-," here he glanced down at the scratch by my eye. "Gina ditched me, Nick had security escort me backstage so I wouldn't get into any more trouble, and I crashed in his hotel room while he slept on the floor. Nothing happened with Nick, Zander, I swear." I assured him. "But what did happen was I realized just how badly I wanted to be with you. Nick was telling me he'd be there for me if I needed help and you know what I did? I called him by your name, Zander, called him you because in my heart I knew that the only person who will ever truly be there for me, who could ever really protect me- is you.

"I hate that it took all of this for me to realize that Zander, and I'm sorry I put you through so much uncertainty this past week. It wasn't fair to you and it wasn't fair to The Club, but I'm ready now, truly, one hundred percent certain that this is where I belong."

Zander squeezed my hand tightly but his eyes were sad, his mouth drawn down in a frown. "I really wish you would have talked to me about all of this first. I don't think you truly understand what you've done here, Ali." He let out a long breath and closed his eyes as if he were in pain. "Look at it from the perspective of The Club. You come along, lie your way into The Club- and yes I know that's my fault as much as it is yours-," he quickly inputted before I could open my mouth to protest. "But the fact still remains that you lied, and not only did you lie but they fell for the lie, trusted the lie- trusted you. You became a part of this Club, seemed unafraid of every obstacle thrown your way, and then when the truth was revealed you were put to the test and passed each and every one of them as if you truly belonged. They accepted you for everything that you were and inducted you into The Club as an associate, going as far as to mark you as one of our own, present you with gifts as a show of appreciation and love for you.

"Then you turn your back on us, stop showing up, ditch the memorial service of a hero, and go radio silent. You ignored text messages, turned off your phone so we couldn't call you, and even went as far as to leave town so we couldn't find you. Nobody knew if or when you were coming back- and they lost trust in you. Danny and I took it in turns to drive around Baysin, going to your favourite spots in town, hoping by some miracle we may run into you there."

"So that's how Danny knew where to find me, and why you were waiting for us." I interrupted, finally understanding.

Zander nodded. "I'd been pacing that parking lot every day Danny was out searching for you, praying that that would be the day he returned with you. The Club were getting reckless; ScatterBrain was insisting we send out a search party and start calling in favours. Butch wanted to hunt you down himself, and even The Prospects were starting to get angry with the whole situation. There was talk, Alessaundra, that if you didn't show up by the end of this weekend-." He broke off, biting his lip. "I don't even want to tell you what they were suggesting."

My heart was beating quickly as I licked my lips. "They hate me, don't they?"

"They're not happy, no."

I sighed finally letting go of Zander's hands and stepping away, turning my body so I could take in the entirety of Horse Shoes- looking at the barn where Marbles and Rocky lived, the old farmhouse, and even The Clubhouse which I could hardly see but knew it was there. I turned back to face Zander, setting my face determinedly. "How can I prove to everyone that I still belong here? How can I earn their respect back? How can I show them that they can still trust me?"

"I don't know Alessaundra," Zander stated quietly. He gazed off in the direction of The Clubhouse. "You may never regain it from them. I hate to say it, Ali, but they may never trust you fully ever again."

I blinked feeling my eyes burn. "I fucked up."

"You did."

I bit my lip, forcing the tears to remain in my eyes. "What do you want me to do about school Zander? Gina told me you sent in your resignation, it's official, everyone knows and your last day is May 1st."

"It is." He agreed.

"I was thinking about going back on Monday," I stated slowly. "I think a return to routine will help, a bit of normalcy- you know?"

"I think that's a good idea." His short answers were starting to bother me.

"But is it the right choice? Should I be around here more? Make a statement that I am serious about being a part of The Club?"

"I can't tell you that, Ali," Zander finally said, turning to look at me. "That's something only you can decide. However, if you do choose to go back to school- I would highly recommend we ride in together, at least for this coming week until I finish. That way The Club can be rest assured that you are, in fact, where you say you're going to be, and will return with me that same evening."

"Like a child," I mumbled. "And then what do we do, once you finish work?"

"And then," Zander shrugged, reaching for another cigarette, lit it, and handed it to me before lighting his own. "We can only hope you've gained a little bit of their trust back by next weekend so you can be trusted to go to and from school by yourself."

I felt completely isolated. None of the members of The Redneck Devils would talk to me, but they were more than happy to glare at me whenever they saw me. Even Scatter-Brain, whom I thought I'd been close to, wouldn't talk to me. I felt horrible, I felt sad, I felt abandoned.

Zander had gone to talk to Danny when we'd finished our conversation and I was basically ordered to go to our room and stay there until he returned. Scarlet had embraced me in a hug when I walked in the door but Vetta shot daggers at me through her eyes and stormed out of the house. But even though Scarlet was happy to have me back she was keeping her distance from me, probably worried about upsetting The Club if she was too kind to me.

To make things worse I was forbidden from helping Scarlet cook or clean and was told to just sit on the couch and await some sort of direction, not that any came. I wanted to help Scarlet, wanted to do something to help The Club- but I couldn't. There was nothing for me to do but sit there, be quiet, and look pretty. How was this going to help me gain respect from The Club again?

"Obedience," Scarlet whispered to me as she vacuumed the carpet. "You're following orders without complaint, obeying even the most ridiculous requests- it shows them you will do whatever it takes to get back in their good books."

"What else can I do?" I begged her but she shook her head, pressing her lips together to keep her mouth shut. She'd already said too much and wasn't going to risk getting caught saying any more.

I'd never experienced time move so slowly- not even during the attack when we were locked away. Was it really still only Sunday? Had it only been a day since Danny had forced me to return? I couldn't help but wonder if Nick had tried to contact me, or if Gina was worried about me, or if even Aunt Patty had called to check in. Zander had taken my phone from me though, which only made this feel more like a punishment.

Around noon, Vetta stormed into the house, glared at me, then went into the kitchen to speak to Scarlet in hushed tones. I couldn't hear them but I could see Scarlet's face as she frowned, replied, and continued to look worried. Vetta was waving her arms around, trying to make a point, but refusing to speak in louder tones than a whisper. Finally Scarlet nodded, looking displeased. Vetta, though, looked very smug as she walked past me, giving me that look again and storming out of the house.

Scarlet sighed as she resumed making lunch for The Club. I opened my mouth, closed it, bit my lip, then blurted. "Is everything okay?"

Scarlet paused, a few pieces of lunch meat in her hand as she looked up at me. "Jade, I-."

"Whatever that was about, Scar, I want to help."

Scarlet set the meat down on the sandwich and folded the bread together, cutting it. Finally she said, very quickly so that it sounded like one big word, "The Club is planning on patching over The Prospects and wants to throw a big party for them."

"Oh." I wasn't sure how to feel about that. "But why- why does that upset you?"

Scarlet sighed and finished packing up the fixings she was using. She glanced around hesitantly to make sure no one was around, then, lowering her voice, she said, "things are very confusing right now, Jade. Your loyalty is up in the air, and The Prospects, I don't trust them, not completely. But, since I'm not a patched member nobody cares what I have to say, and-."

"One of The Prospects always looks at me like he wants to kill me." I started slowly, gazing off into the distance. "He makes me feel uncomfortable and-."

"Link." I turned back to look at her. "Abraham, but he's already got a Road Name that The Club refers to him as. Danny, in particular, thinks he's a good fit for The Club."

"Of course he does," I mumbled to myself.

"Look, Jade," Scarlet dropped her voice even lower as she took a few steps towards me. "I'm very worried about what's going to happen here. Patching over new members means the votes can change and-," she swallowed, looked around again, then dropped her voice some more. "They've been in Church all day, on and off, discussing you, The Prospects, and everything- right now Zander has enough pull to keep you safe. But if they patch over new members-."

"The vote can change." I stated, my voice hollow as my heart pounded.

"Zander will do whatever it takes to protect you but-."

"He may not be able to stop them." I finished for her, swallowing a lump of fear that had formed in my throat. Zander had warned me that Danny was unpredictable and had a hard time trusting people. My betrayal- for lack of a better word- must have intensified that feeling for him. Danny had grown to like me, respected me, even trusted me... and I turned my back on that. I fully believed Danny would have already killed me if it wasn't for Zander; how long could Zander continue to protect me from his brother and the rest of The Club?

"Zander won't let anything happen to you, Jade. He may be angry, hurt, and disappointed- but he still loves you."

Tears blurred my vision and I nodded, reaching up to wipe them away. "I know. Thanks Scarlet."

We heard the noises outside at the same time, the sound of footsteps and voices as The Club approached the house for lunch. Scarlet quickly moved back to the kitchen and started plating the sandwiches, and I turned back to stare at the wall, begging the tears to stop before anyone found me crying: I couldn't afford to look weak in front of The Club.

Zander and I got up early Monday morning and took his bike from Riverton to Baysin, stopping at The Golden Daylight to switch to his truck, then drove to school together. He didn't say much to me; he hadn't been saying much to me all weekend. The silence was starting to worry me, and as we pulled into the deserted school parking lot I decided I had to say something.

Zander slammed his door shut and I quickly exited his truck, rounding the front and called his name. His eyes looked weary as he turned to look at me. I was nervous, my heart beating rapidly in my chest as I took another step towards him. "I hate this. I hate you not talking to me, I hate the uncertainty, I hate the fact that things are going on around me and I can't even lend a hand. I hate that it feels like you're angry at me and that it seems like there's nothing I can do to fix it. I know I got myself into this, Zander, but I hate that it's even happening, at all. Please, Zander," I begged, tears shining in my eyes, "please talk to me."

I heard him sigh, watched him bite his lip, saw his eyes squeeze shut for a second- he looked like he was having an internal battle with himself. Finally he stormed forwards, drawing his arms around me and pressing his lips to mine in a hungry kiss. I gasped, surprised as his lips moved against mine forcefully and felt his tongue slip into my mouth.

I was panting when we broke apart and Zander lowered his forehead to mine, closed his eyes and took a deep breath in. I felt his body relax and instantly I did as well. Scarlet's words echoed in my head as we held each other for a moment *He may be angry, hurt, and disappointed- but he still loves you.* "I love you Zander," I whispered with tears in my eyes. "I love you so much."

"I love you too."

I drew him in for a hug, holding his body close to mine, grabbing him tightly and never wanting to let go. However, we were in the middle of the staff parking lot and at any moment someone could pull in and see us. We seemed to realize this at the same time as we moved apart, distancing ourselves, but not without holding onto each other's hands for one moment longer than we should have.

Finally our hands slid apart and Zander grabbed his bag, walking into the staff entrance and leaving me standing there by myself. My hands were shaking a little with nerves as I brushed my hair back out of my face and smoothed it down, took a deep breath, and started off towards the main entrance of the school.

If Zander and I had cared to look a little more closely during our exchange we would have seen that we weren't alone and that there was, in fact, someone else in the parking lot who had seen us embrace. If we'd been a little more diligent we would have noticed the car parked at the back of the lot. But we were too caught up in the moment and ultimately doomed ourselves.

CHAPTER 18

Every morning that week Zander and I had the same routine: ride in on the bike to The Golden Daylight, transfer to his truck, and drive to school together. If we were running a little late Zander would drop me off a couple blocks away and I would walk the remainder of the distance, so we weren't arriving together, but if we managed to get out of bed at six in the morning we'd make it to the school before anyone else and go our separate ways only to meet back up in homeroom and play our respective roles of student and teacher. I was thankful we only had to do this for a few days because it was the most challenging thing I'd ever had to do.

After school I'd swing by the print lab to check on the yearbook progress, collect articles and blog posts, and meet with the Student Council when I had a spare moment to check in about Prom details- apparently over a hundred tickets had already been sold. These meetings couldn't last long, of course, for Zander and I were expected back at The Club by dinner. Luckily most of the work on the yearbook was complete, as Gina had said, and everyone seemed to be getting along fine without me.

At Horse Shoes nothing had changed. Zander would spend hours in The Clubhouse with the rest of The Redneck Devils before coming into the house, late in the evening and giving us no time together. He'd even had to go on one evening run with ScatterBrain and Butch, returning around midnight- that next morning was one of two times he'd dropped me off a few blocks from school so we wouldn't be seen showing up together, and even that had been risky.

I was happy when Friday rolled around: Zander's last day at school. The last day we had to hide our relationship, the last day we had to pretend, the last day we had to lie. Gina made a sappy announcement in class that day- she still hadn't spoken to me all week- and everyone cheered and clapped as Zander got a little emotional. I knew he was going to miss the job and the students, he was an excellent teacher after all, but he was doing what he had to do for both him and The Club.

The day went by surprisingly fast and when the bell rang I rushed to the print lab. The yearbook was due at the end of today and I wanted to look it over one last time before submitting it to Mr Thorn. I'd dismissed the committee the day before, thanking them for their service and help these last few weeks and assuring them I'd get the file sent away. They trusted me, I was Alessaundra Campbell after all- the girl who does no wrong.

I wasn't expecting Zander to come to the lab that afternoon, thought he'd be too busy packing up his desk and classroom, so when the door opened and he walked in I was pleasantly surprised. I looked up at him as I hit send, forwarding the file to Mr Thorn for his approval, as he strolled over to stand next to my desk.

"This is where it all began, do you remember?"

I grinned, thinking back to when Zander and I had first agreed to start dating all those weeks ago. "Who would have thought we'd end up where we are now?"

"A lot has happened to us," Zander agreed, reaching down to rub my shoulders. I moaned and relaxed into his hands, melting as he massaged the tension away. "But through it all, Ali, one thing has remained the same."

"Oh yeah?" I murmured, "and what's that?"

"The connection we have," he stated simply, leaning down and pressing a kiss to the hollow of my shoulder. "There has always been something about you, Ali, something that drew me in, held me there, and refused to let me go. Through everything that connection hasn't changed, if anything it has only strengthened.

"I know you are feeling a little lost right now and that The Club is making you feel lonely, but you need to know you are not alone. All you need to do is hold on a little bit longer, Ali. They'll come through, I promise you."

Zander's hands slipped down to my arms and I swung around to face him, tilting my face up to his. "I love you, Zander." He leaned down and pressed his soft lips to mine and I moaned as his tongue slipped out accessing my mouth with ease. I reached up, grabbed his hair and pulled him closer to me, pressing my body into his.

I didn't realize that Zander hadn't locked the door, never anticipated someone would walk in and catch us- but as the door swung open Zander and I jumped apart, whipping our heads around to stare at the person who'd just trespassed on our moment.

Mr Thorn stood there with his face pale, his eyes wide, and mouth hanging open as he sputtered in surprise. He was speechless as he stared at the closeness of our bodies, our swollen lips, and the way our hands were touching each other. Slowly his pale face began to redden and his hands closed into fists. He slammed the door of the print lab closed and took a deep, centering breath but when he spoke his voice was shaking. "Th-this- wh-what- I don't-."

"Mr Thorn." I stood up quickly from my chair and stepped away from Zander and towards Mr Thorn raising my hands defensively. "Please, Mr Thorn. We can explain."

"Explain?" His voice sounded faint. I was worried he was going to pop a vein as it stuck out, throbbing, on his forehead. "How can you p-possibly explain this?"

I glanced at Zander, but the look I saw in his eyes scared

me- they were narrowed to slits and his mouth was drawn in a straight line. He looked very tense, his shoulders stiffening as he stood up straight.

"You see, the thing is-."

"You're going to let us go, Charlie." I blinked, taken aback as I turned to look at Zander. "You're going to let us go and you aren't going to tell anyone about this."

Mr Thorn started sputtering angrily again, his face turning from red to purple. "L-let you go? You can't be s-serious!"

"He's not," I interjected but Zander just chuckled and it sent a shiver down my spine.

"It's my last day, Charlie. What are you possibly going to do?" He reached for my hand and went to pull me towards the door, past Mr Thorn's shaking body.

Mr Thorn wasn't going to let this slide, though. He finally seemed to find his voice as he saw how serious Zander was about leaving, raised his finger, which was still shaking slightly, and screamed. "You are in violation of- countless rules and regulations, Zander! It doesn't matter if today is your last day or your first. Relationships with students are strictly forbidden, especially if that student is not of age. Tell me, Alessaundra, have you turned eighteen yet?"

Mr Thorn knew I hadn't, he knew my file better than anyone else at this school. "No," I admitted quietly. "Not for two more weeks."

Mr Thorn looked smug for a moment but his smile faded, his lips drooping until he was frowning. "This doesn't just affect Mr Dionne, Alessaundra. This will have a major impact on you and your future." He paused for a moment to let that sink in, not that I hadn't already thought of the consequences. Finally he asked, "How could something like this happen?"

Zander was still so tense and anxious. I gave his hand a squeeze then let go, taking a step towards Mr Thorn. I knew what Zander was worried about, but I had to make Mr Thorn understand. "We met during midterms, before Zander was even a teacher here. We- we fell for each other instantly, we had so much in common. But when we returned from spring break- and I discovered he was my teacher-"

"You should have reported it that instant!" Mr Thorn interrupted.

I took a calming breath, "Zander insisted we end things, he didn't think it would be right for us to continue dating, but I-." I licked my lips, "I pursued him. I didn't let him give up on me. Don't you see, Mr Thorn, this is entirely my fault. I should have listened to Zander when he said we couldn't be together, I should have accepted that we couldn't continue a relationship right now, but I liked him too much, and I couldn't let him go. Please don't punish him for my mistakes, Mr Thorn. Please."

Mr Thorn shook his head sadly, "I hear everything you are saying, Alessaundra, but be that as it may Zander still took advantage of an underage student and I have no choice but to report it to the authorities."

He pulled out his cellphone and my heart stopped as I gasped for breath. He was going to call the police, he was going to report us, he was-.

"You need to get out of here," Zander mumbled quietly, grabbing my arm and shoving me towards the door. "Now. Go to The Club, tell them what happened, warn them. Ali, if the police find out who I am-."

My lip quivered in fear as I jumped into his arms, brought his face towards mine, and kissed him hard. "Whatever happens, remember me in your Wildest Dreams," I whispered against his mouth. Then I grabbed the keys he handed me and ran out the door. Mr Thorn yelled after me but I didn't stop, didn't listen. I had to keep running, I had to get to the truck, I had to get to The Club. I had to warn them.

I had tried calling Danny the entire eighteen minutes it took me to get to Horse Shoes- I was speeding, yes, but I couldn't waste any time. Zander was in trouble. I skid to a stop in the parking lot spraying tiny gravel rocks with the wheels and flung open the door. I wasn't sure if Danny was going to be in The Clubhouse but it was the only place I could think of to check. Bikes were lined up outside and I was fairly certain the entire Club was inside, everyone- except for Zander, because he was in trouble.

The Prospects were the only ones in the barn when I opened the door and I knew what that meant- the rest of The Club had to have been in Church. My heart was pounding and my breath was coming out in short gasps as I panted, the three men turning to look at me, weapons raised. When they saw it was me two of them lowered their weapons, but not Link. Link continued to raise his hand gun and aim it at me.

"You don't belong here. Get out."

I raised my hands defensively. "I need Danny- The Prince- now! It's an emergency."

"Get out," Link snarled. "Club business."

My voice shook as I stepped towards him slowly. I eyed the only motorcycle in the room and I recognized it as the one I'd learned to ride on- the one time I rode by myself. "You don't understand, it has to do with Zander."

Link switched the safety off the gun and the click echoed throughout the room. "I'm not asking you again-."

"Please!" I screamed, panicked, my voice ringing out loudly. Link snarled and I'm fairly certain he would have shot me, without a second thought, but the door to The Club's meeting room swung open and ScatterBrain stormed out, looking angry.

"What is going on-." He stopped as he took in the entire situation, me standing there shaking, Link with a gun pointed at me, and no Zander to be seen. "Jade, what is it? What's wrong?"

"It's Zander," I gasped, tears now rolling down my face in relief. "He's in trouble."

Now Danny was there- he must have heard everything. "Where is he? What happened?" His voice was loud and demanding and I flinched, my knees going weak.

"Mr Thorn," I panted, "caught us- at school, and-."

"Mr Thorn? Who? What are you talking about?"

"The Principal at the school. He saw us- threatened to call the police- he has Zander!"

"Fuck," Danny growled raising a hand and slamming it against a hay bale that was next to him. "You," he rounded on me, pointing. "This is all your fault!"

"I-," I stammered stepping backwards, away from him. "No, Danny, I didn't-."

"Prince," ScatterBrain murmured, "c'mon man, you can't blame her for this."

"I warned you all," Danny shouted rounding on The Club. "I warned you that she would get us into trouble, and look, because of her our other president could be hauled away by the cops! If they get a hold of him- if they find out who he is- that he is one of us-"

"We're all going down," Butch growled.

"What are we going to do?" Link asked, a snarl on his face. I gulped, taking another step back, afraid of the looks that were coming over everyone's faces. I was too far away from the door to run, but the bike- the bike I'd only ridden once- they couldn't possibly stop me if I took off on that, could they?

"We have no choice," Danny stated. "We need to take care of the problem." The problem. Me. I was the problem. Danny wanted to take care of me, and Zander wasn't around to save me.

Like one The Club turned to face me- only one person seemed against it: ScatterBrain. He stood off to the side, eyes wide in fear and surprise, mouth hanging open as I began to back up until I reached the bike. Danny walked to the front of the group reaching back for something- a weapon, it turned out, as Link pressed the hand gun into his palm.

"I'm regretful it has come down to this," Danny stated sounding solemn. "You've given us no choice, though. If the cops do, in fact, have my brother it's only a matter of time before they turn up at our doorstep, and it's all because of you."

"Please, Danny, think- Zander, he needs you. If Zander finds out-." I was rambling, words spewing out of my mouth in fear.

Danny shook his head. "I had my doubts about you this entire time, Jade. You had me believe, for one split second, that you could be trusted. I let my guard down and look what happened. You led the cops right to us!"

"No, Danny-."

He raised the gun, aiming the barrel right at me. I didn't give myself the chance to think as I spun, grabbed the handle bars of the bike, and swung my body onto it. The keys were in the ignition and my hands acted on their own accord as I started the engine and took off- I could never tell you, now, how I had been able to do it or how I was able to escape, but somehow I managed to get out of that barn unharmed, even as gunshots rang out behind me.

I knew I'd be followed, though, had no doubt they'd be seconds behind me: and they were. I'd just pulled onto the main road when the sound of multiple bikes echoed behind me. I panicked as my brain caught up to me- what was I doing? I'd only driven a bike once, what made me think I could do this? How far would I make it before I crashed? And why wasn't I wearing a helmet?

Gun shots echoed again and I ducked my head, trying to keep control of the bike. I recognized the turn that was coming up though- the S bend where the road twisted and turned. I remembered Zander telling me to lean into the turn, the first time I ever rode up with him, but as I approached the first curve I saw a car approach on the other side of the road. Gunshots rang out and I panicked, tried to move into the curve, but felt the bike tilt instead.

I screamed, closed my eyes, and held on to the bike as my body began to fly off of it. I felt the impact as I hit the ground, and then nothing but darkness.

CHAPTER 19

My head was pounding, there was something attached to my hand, and I could feel something stuck to my arm. I blinked, slowly opening my eyes to see an IV sticking out of my left arm and what appeared to be a heart monitor connected to my index finger- the beeping from the machine was relentless and making my head hurt even more as I groaned and rolled my head to the side.

I gasped as I saw someone sitting in a chair gazing out the window. My first thought was Zander but as my eyes focused on the person and he turned to look at me, I realized the guy had dark hair, not sandy blonde and my heart sunk. However, despite the fact I was disappointed it wasn't Zander sitting in that chair, I still felt relieved to see it was Nick, and not somebody else: like Danny.

"Hey." Nick turned his head and saw I was conscious, jumped out of his chair and rushed to the bed. "How are you feeling?"

"Sore," I moaned trying to sit up. Nick reached out and helped me until I was propped against some pillows. "What are you doing here?"

"My Aunt called me," he shrugged. "She's head of the Emergency Department, remember? She requested a private room for you and everything."

"Oh right." I wrinkled my eyebrows together, thinking, but it only made my head hurt more. "What happened?"

"I was hoping you could tell me that," Nick mumbled sitting on the edge of the bed. I'd never seen him look so serious in my life; his eyebrows were furrowed and low with a big wrinkle between them as his eyes squinted, mouth drawn in a straight line. "It was those guys, wasn't it?"

"Nick," I sighed, closing my eyes. "Please- not now."

"Do you even know what happened to you, Alessaundra? They tried to kill you! An eye witness saw a pack of bikes shooting guns at you; they say you were riding a motorcycle yourself, and when you went to round the corner you lost control of the bike. You're lucky to be alive, Ali. What were you thinking? You weren't even wearing a helmet." I blinked, tears in my eyes to see Nick also fighting back his own tears. He didn't look so serious anymore, now he just looked sad. "You could have died, Ali."

I lowered my head and felt the tears leak from my eyes and drip down onto my hands. I sniffled and reached up to wipe them away when the door opened. My heart jumped, hoping it was Zander, but it wasn't. It was Nick's Aunt, the nurse who worked here at Baysin General Hospital. She smiled softly when she saw me awake, but frowned when she saw the tears.

"Are you in pain, Ali? I can up your meds, or-."

"No," I shook my head, which only made my head hurt more. "Well, I have a headache, but other than that I feel fine."

She frowned, studying the monitor and screen for a second. "I'm going to remove your IVs and take off the heart monitor. However, I will go fetch you some Tylenol 3's for the pain." As she worked she glanced between Nick and I, then said, "you're very lucky, you know that Ali? Not many people can be thrown from a motorcycle and come out of it without a broken arm or leg."

"I don't feel so lucky," I mumbled reaching up to touch my head. I felt a bandage where my temple was.

"You hit your head hard," she stated, "we've been monitoring you for concussion symptoms, but other than that you should be able to be released by morning. You cut your arm, here," she pointed to where another bandage covered my arm, "and scratched up your leg there." She lifted the blanket and showed me bandages around my leg. "You may have a limp for a few days but it's better than a broken leg you can't even walk on."

Without another word she left, leaving Nick and I alone again. I looked back over at Nick. "Are you mad?"

"Mad?" Nick raised his eyebrows in surprise. "Why would I be mad?"

"Because of this," I gestured at all of my injuries. "I was reckless."

"Yeah, but was it entirely your fault, Ali?" I pressed my lips together, refusing to answer him and he sighed. "Okay, I get it. You can't say anything. But why are you still protecting them?"

"I'm not-." My words were cut off as the door to my room swung open again and this time Zander rushed in. He took one look at me, saw the bandages that covered my body, and froze; I thought I saw tears glisten in his eyes but Zander has always been so strong and hid his emotions well.

"Alessaundra," his voice broke and I swallowed, waiting for him to make another move. "Are you-?" His eyes fell on Nick and he stopped, a flicker of annoyance crossing his face. "What are you doing here?" He knew who Nick was, probably recognized him from all of the photographs that had circulated weeks before.

"I'm here for Ali," Nick stated, his voice sounding cold. "You and your people- you did this to her."

"Not me," Zander growled. "I'd never-."

"It was Danny," I stated, trying to break up their argument. Zander looked over at me. "He thought- he thought I betrayed The Club. When Mr Thorn caught us and threatened to call the cops-."

"Danny blamed you." Zander nodded. "I know."

"You know?" I asked, my voice shrill. Then I remembered-, "Wait, how did you get away from Mr Thorn, Zander?"

"ScatterBrain called me the second you left on that bike." Zander shook his head, "I couldn't believe it when he told me. Charlie had already been on the phone to his superiors, reporting what had happened. His next call was to the police. When I got that call I knew I had to get out of there- knew I had to help you, save you if I could. I won't lie to you Ali- I threatened Charlie, and I'm sure he's only going to use that against me as well, but I had no other option. It was the only way I could get out of there."

"You threatened him?" I asked, then glanced down, noticing, for the first time, his cowboy boots. "Your knife-?"

"I always have it on me, Ali." Zander nodded.

I let out a big breath and closed my eyes against the pain in my head. "What happened next?"

"By the time I got away from the school and called ScatterBrain back, he told me what had happened. Danny sent Butch, Six Inch, and Link after you. ScatterBrain had tried to follow but Danny demanded he stay behind, he knew that despite everything that had gone on ScatterBrain still trusted you- he would have saved you, and with me out of the way he wasn't going to risk ScatterBrain interfering.

"ScatterBrain disobeyed orders though, Ali. Danny underestimated how loyal ScatterBrain is to me, and when Danny turned his back on him ScatterBrain hit him over the head with his gun, knocking him out. He didn't want to kill Danny, just needed him out of the way so he could help me- help you. It worked. ScatterBrain was able to get on his bike and race out of there, just in time for him to arrive at the crash site. The Club were trying to shut up the witness, but ScatterBrain stepped in. If he hadn't made it there in time, there would have been no witness, no one to save you- you'd be dead right now, Ali."

"ScatterBrain saved my life," I whispered.

Zander nodded. "He sacrificed a lot to save you, Ali."

Nick, who had been sitting quietly for the telling of the story, finally snapped. He turned to Zander, face beat red from anger, and raised his hand to point his index finger at him. "This is all your fault. You and your little- gang! If it wasn't for you Alessaundra wouldn't be sitting here in a hospital bed, if it wasn't for you, Alessaundra wouldn't have almost died, if it wasn't for you-."

"I know," Zander growled angrily. "You think I don't already know that?"

"What are we going to do, Zander?" I asked, trying to get their attention off of each other and back on to me before they could start tearing each other's heads off.

Zander took a breath, trying to calm himself. "There's nothing else for me to do, Ali. Danny's gone too far, he crossed a line- made a decision to get rid of An Associate without even consulting with me! I have no choice, I have to end him."

My eyes went wide as I gasped, my mouth parting open slightly in surprise. I licked my lips then said, "and when you say 'end him', you mean-?"

"Yes, Alessaundra." As serious as he was about this choice, I saw the sadness hidden behind his eyes. He was trying not to show how much this decision was affecting him, but it couldn't be easy to decide you had to kill your own brother.

"Zander, you can't, he's your brother." I don't know why I was defending Danny, but I knew if Zander didn't think this choice through completely he'd regret it.

Zander shook his head. "It doesn't matter Ali."

"Zander-." I paused, and suddenly there were tears in my eyes. "If you do that, if you go there, and-." I gulped, blinking furiously as everything fell into place in my head.

"I have to, Ali." Zander leaned forwards and pushed his forehead against mine. "I'll remember you, Alessaundra. I'll remember you in my Wildest Dreams, in my most beautiful reality, and as everything I needed you to be." He pressed his lips quickly to mine then stood up and marched towards the door, where he stopped and glanced back- but he didn't look at me, his eyes were on Nick who seemed speechless. "Take care of her." Before either of us could say anything he stormed out, slamming the door, and leaving us in silence.

Nick turned to me, confusion written all over his face as tears flooded down my cheeks. "What does he mean, take care of you?" But I couldn't answer him, couldn't bring myself to get the words out. I knew what Zander was telling me in that moment, though- when he faced Danny there could only be two outcomes: either he was killed, or he killed Danny and would become the one and only President of The Club, and he didn't want that life for me. There was no other option, he had to let me go, and Nick was the best person for me right now. My heart broke and tears continued to pour from my eyes as I curled into a ball on my bed.

Half an hour later, after Nick's Aunt had returned to give me a few Tylenol's and check my vitals, my headache had disappeared, but I was far from feeling pain free. I was restless, but wasn't allowed to leave my bed. Nick, who still didn't fully understand what had happened earlier had gone to get coffee, hoping it'd help ease my worries. But he didn't understand that nothing would.

Finally I grabbed my phone and dialed ScatterBrain's number, praying he'd pick up. On the third ring he did, sounding surprised and unsure. "Jade, I seriously don't have the time to talk right now." I could hear screams and shouts in the background.

"What's happening, Markus?" I asked, dropping his nickname for the first time in almost two months. "Has it been done?"

"No," ScatterBrain mumbled. "It's only just begun."

"Put me on speaker. I need to hear it." I begged. I didn't think he would and was therefore surprised when everything became that much louder and clearer to me.

Danny's voice was the first one to ring out, loud and

clear. He sounded furious, his words slurring together in anger. "I warned each and every one of you that she couldn't be trusted and do you see how right I was? Do you see what she has done to this Club? She's divided us, split us down the middle! How can we function if we can't even stand together?"

"That's no excuse to kill her," Zander snapped, just as loudly. I could picture the two of them, in the middle as the other Club Members encircled them, and having a face to face screaming match. I could see Zander standing with his knife, Danny with a gun, waiting for one of them to make the first move.

"You have made too many bad choices," Danny growled. "You have made too many mistakes!" I heard the sound of flesh hitting flesh, and what sounded like a body hitting the ground, then someone spat. "I'll kill you for that." It was Danny. "You should hand over your Cut now, while you still have the chance to walk away alive."

"You don't get to make that choice," Zander snarled. "Isn't this what you wanted, Danny? Me by your side, sharing the role, making decisions together?"

"I must have been crazy to think we could make this work."

"You're right. This could never work. Only one of us can be President, Danny."

"And you think that should be you?" Danny yelled. "You think you've earned the position after everything you've done to this Club, after all the lies you've told to protect your little girlfriend?"

When Zander spoke next I could picture the smirk that crossed his face. "My choices of the past don't matter. All that matters is what's going to happen right now. I won't get voted out, you'd need a unanimous vote for that and you'd never get that. The only thing left to do is fight."

"To the death." Danny growled. "Are you sure you want to risk that?"

"I'm not afraid of you Danny." Zander stated firmly. "Not

after what you did. You tried to kill An Associate, without even voting on it, without discussing it with me!"

"She knew too much, Zander!" I flinched, his voice blaring into my ear from the phone speaker. "You know the rules, brother. When someone knows too much and can't be trusted any further, then they need to be taken out. She broke our trust, she was disloyal, and she almost exposed us through you! There was no other choice left but to get rid of her. Besides, we had an agreement! If at any time you can't make it to Church my vote would count for two! We had Church, you weren't there, the vote passed!"

Zander's voice shook with rage as he said, "but you never gave her a chance. She was my girlfriend, Danny! She would have come around!"

"We don't know that," Danny snarled. "We couldn't take that risk. She had to be taken care of!"

Zander spoke over Danny. "And that rule was put into place while I was a Weekend Warrior, Danny, before I stepped into my role as President, and you know it! You were just bending the rules, trying to make them suit your needs, like you always do. You say Alessaundra couldn't be trusted, but the only person who can't be trusted here is you."

There was a moment of silence and then I heard what sounded like a body hitting another body, the sound of a scuffle, a gunshot, moans, groans, cheers- I couldn't keep up with what was happening. Too many bizarre images kept flashing through my head as I pictured the possibilities of what these sounds meant- the only thing I knew for sure, in that moment, was that the fight had begun, Zander and Danny were facing each other, and only one would come out of it alive.

With shaking hands I ended the call, unable to listen to any more of it. My cheeks were wet from tears I hadn't even realized I'd been crying and I threw my phone across the room, watching it hit the wall and fall to the ground. It was almost worse, though, not knowing, not hearing- not being there.

Sobs overcame me and I curled into my pillow as I cried, praying that Zander came out of this alive.

CHAPTER 20

I only had to stay at the hospital for the night so they could monitor the mild concussion I had, indeed, obtained from the accident. When Nick returned, he brought Aunt Patty with him- turns out my emergency contact information hadn't been updated and my grandmother's name and number were the only one's in the system. Nick thought Aunt Patty ought to know what was happening and had stopped in to tell her.

When Aunt Patty rushed into the room she had tears in her eyes and her mouth was quivering. "Oh Ali," she cried. Her eyes stared at the bandages that were visible. "How did this happen?"

I licked my lips, trying to think of what to say. "Do- do you remember that guy I said I was seeing?" Aunt Patty nodded, using a tissue to wipe her eyes. "He- he drives a motorcycle and he tried to teach me how to ride it. We- we got in a fight, and I wanted to leave, but I didn't have my car so I- stupidly- jumped on his bike, and-."

"You crashed," Aunt Patty cried. "Oh Ali."

"Not one of my brightest moments, I'll admit."

She laughed softly through her tears. "I'm just so thankful you're okay. Have you called your father, does he know?"

I hesitated again then sighed as I admitted, "Dad's gone,

Aunt Patty. He's- he's been gone for weeks." Aunt Patty opened her mouth in shock. "I'm sorry I didn't tell you, I just- I just wanted to be alone for a little while."

"It's okay," Aunt Patty whispered as she wiped her face. "Oh, by the way, Mr Thorn called me today, but I missed his call. Do you know what that could have been about?"

My heart started to pound as I lowered my head in shame- it was time to come clean about this as well, she'd find out soon enough anyways. "The guy- I said I was seeing-," I broke off as my hands began to shake. I swallowed hard, then raised my head to look Aunt Patty square in the face. "He was Zander Dionne, my English teacher."

Aunt Patty gasped, looking faint. "Alessaundra!"

"I know," I quickly said, "it sounds bad, but it's not what you think Aunt Patty! We met before he was my teacher and we-."

"I don't want to hear it," Aunt Patty shook her head, looking at me like I had three heads. "Who are you, Alessaundra Campbell, and what happened to the girl who'd never lie- who used her head?"

"She changed," I admitted softly. "She lived through hell for most of her life and she finally decided she didn't want to pretend anymore. I have tried for so long to be good so that I wouldn't end up like my father- but I can't do it anymore Aunt Patty. It's so exhausting, trying to be good, and I-."

"I want you out of my house," she breathed. There were still tears in her eyes but she no longer looked sad, now she looked angry. "I- I have an obligation to care for you for two more weeks and then I want you out. You promised me you'd be a good role model for my daughters, but this- this is unacceptable, at least to me. Dating a teacher? I won't have someone like you around my girls!"

"I understand," I whispered looking down at my hands, my thumbs twisting together nervously. "But Aunt Patty-," before I could finish I heard the sound of the door closing and sighed, glancing up to see she'd left. Nick came in moments later, handing me a coffee. Grateful I took a sip and made a face.

"Decaf," he stated, "my Aunt said the caffeine may not be a good mix with the pain meds. What happened with your Aunt? She looked pissed."

"I told her the truth," I shrugged, taking another sip of my coffee. It didn't taste as bad by the third sip. "At least, as much of the truth as I could."

"She didn't take it well, huh?"

"Nope." I traced the lid of my cup with my finger. "She's kicking me out, Nick. Two weeks."

"Your birthday." I nodded. "Isn't that what you've wanted though, Ali? Ever since you were forced to live with her, all you've ever wanted was to live in your grandma's house by yourself."

"I can't afford the bills, Nick. I don't have a job."

"Glenda would hire you in a second at Novella." Nick pointed out.

"True." I sighed, setting down my coffee. "How did I screw up so badly Nick?"

"You're seventeen, Ali. You're supposed to make mistakes."

"Most seventeen year old's don't fall for their teacher, get involved in a Bike Club, and risk their lives by riding a motorcycle without a helmet or the experience."

"You're right, they usually wait until they turn eighteen for that." I chuckled softly at Nick's lame joke. "Seriously though, Ali, we all make mistakes in life. All we have to do is learn from them. That's why we're given these obstacles in life. They make things hard, but life wouldn't be fun if it was easy, you know?"

I smiled softly at him, drying my tears on the bed sheet. "When did you get so wise, Nick?"

"I've always been wise, Ali."

"Not like this."

"Maybe I learned from my own pain." He grinned at me

and I looked down in shame. "Hey, it's okay Ali. I know why you did what you did, and I'm honestly thankful for it. I got a number one signal, an album in the top ten, and a sold out tour. The only thing I don't have is someone to share that success with." He sat on the edge of my bed and grabbed my hand, squeezing it.

"I don't know if I'm ready for that yet," I admitted in a soft voice.

"That's okay," he assured me, still holding my hand softly in his. "Just know that I'll be here for you, even if you're not ready to be with me again. Ali, you're going to need someone on your side- you know you won't be able to avoid the Police, right? Mr Thorn- he would have had to report this, they'll come looking for you, asking questions, and-."

"I know." This time I squeezed his hand, showing my appreciation. "Thank you Nick."

"I just need to know one thing first," Nick turned his body so it was angled more towards me. "How did this even happen, Ali?"

I took a deep breath and delved into the story of how Zander and I met. I knew it had to be painful for Nick to hear but he listened, holding my hand, gasping in a few places, snarling in others, but always supportive. When I finished tears were once again streaming down my face and I leaned into Nick for support. He smoothed the hair down at the back of my head, kissed my temple and whispered, "I am so sorry, Ali. You know I would never do that to you, right?" I looked at him with bloodshot and swollen eyes. "I'd never put you in harm's way, I'd never force you into anything you wouldn't be comfortable with. I love you, Ali- I always have, and when you're ready, I'll be here to help you put your life back together again."

Instead of answering him I leaned my head onto his shoulder, wiped my nose with a tissue, and let out a long, soft sigh. I didn't know what was going to happen next, but at least I'd have someone by my side when I had to face it.

I was released the next day from the hospital and sent home to rest. I wasn't allowed to attend school until my concussion was fully healed so I stayed in my bedroom at Aunt Patty's while Nick kept me company when he could. I knew Aunt Patty wasn't pleased about this, but she was doing her best to stay out of my business. As for not going to school I wasn't too broken up about it. I knew Mr Thorn had reported Zander and I, and therefore there would be rumours spread, and I wasn't ready to go back to being the talk of the school. Maybe I never would be.

Nick postponed a few tour dates, much to Kevin and Aaron's annoyance, but once they heard what happened to me they understood. Scotty, on the other hand, was pissed, blaming Nick- and me- for blowing thousands of dollars on lost bookings and tickets. Nick told me not to worry about it, that he'd take care of it.

And Nick and I? I couldn't define what we were, not yet anyways. It'd only been two weeks since I'd been released from the hospital, two weeks of confusion and uncertainty, waiting to see what would happen next. He was there, though, by my side the entire time, a familiar presence that filled me with hope. It was hard to think of him as anything other than a friend right now though, not with Zander still so fresh on my mind.

I hadn't heard from Zander since that day in the hospital. When I'd thrown my phone at the wall I'd broken it and had to get a new one. Nick was super helpful with that but it meant I'd lost all of my contacts, which was maybe for the better. I had no way of contacting Zander, or Scarlet, or even ScatterBrain. It was like I was starting fresh, anew. Until Gina called me to tell me Zander had been arrested.

Gina and I hadn't spoken since the Shattered Life concert, but when she heard the rumours about Zander and I she started digging- turns out we'd been seen that Monday morning in the parking lot- by Mr Thorn. He'd tried to forget about it, pretended it was a simple hug between teacher and student. However, on Wednesday he was running late to school and saw me get out of Zander's truck, two blocks from school. Again, he tried to make excuses- maybe a student simply needed a ride to school? That kiss, though, was the final piece to the puzzle and he couldn't ignore it any longer. He'd had no choice but to report Zander and I- and after Zander threatened him, he made sure Zander would be given everything he was entitled to.

The day Gina called me I was packing my bags, collecting my things so I could move into my grandmother's house- my house. I'd already talked to Glenda and she was willing to give me a job at Novella, just as Nick had predicted. Everything seemed to be working out- until it wasn't.

"He was arrested?" I asked dropping the books I was carrying into a box on my bed- at least now I knew he won the fight and wasn't killed by Danny after all. "How do you even know this?"

"I know everything," Gina answered flippantly. "Apparently he's been staying at The Golden Daylight Hotel and Spa, you know that fancy hotel downtown? The Police caught him as he was coming out of the building, arms loaded with bags like he was attempting to leave town. They say he was dating a student," she prodded, and now I knew why she'd called to tell me. She wanted clarification. "They say he was dating you."

I sighed, sitting down on my bed. "It's true, Gina," I finally admitted. "We'd been seeing each other for weeks."

"What?" A long period of silence followed that single word; I'd never known Gina to become speechless.

"It's a long story."

"So all this time," Gina started, "I've been talking about how hot he was, making jokes about hooking up with him- all that time you were dating him?"

"Yup." Another silence fell. "I'm sorry I didn't tell you Gina."

"No," now she sighed, "I get it. It's just- I thought we were friends, Ali. I thought we could tell each other everything. I thought we trusted each other. It's no wonder you seemed to change so much these past few months, you've been keeping a major secret and I- I'm sorry for being such a bitch to you."

"Thanks Gina," I replied softly, smiling. "And rest assured, we are friends. There's just some things friends can't share, you know?" *Like the fact that our teacher wasn't just a teacher but president of a Bike Club.* I hated to keep even more secrets from her, the only friend I really had, but there was no way I could tell her anything about The Redneck Devils. Some secrets had to stay that way.

"I'm happy to hear that Ali. Oh, and by the way? Happy birthday." I thanked her and hung up the phone, glancing at the bottle of vodka that was sitting on my nightstand. Old habits die hard, I thought, as I reached for the bottle and took a slug- just one shot, to celebrate this occasion.

It didn't take long for the Police to find me after Zander was arrested. I had been expecting it, but it didn't make things any easier. I answered their questions to the best of my ability, trying to keep myself from being labelled an accomplice to The Redneck Devils. However, in the end, it was the police and the prosecution that brought it up.

"Are you aware, Miss Campbell, that Mr Dionne has ties to a bike club named The Redneck Devils? Remember, you have sworn an oath to tell the truth."

My hands were shaking as I looked at them, their eyes staring into mine intensely, unblinkingly. I sighed knowing I had no other choice. "What do you want to know?"

We spent hours in the interview room at the Police station. They wanted to know everything- Zander's history with The Club, my involvement, the events that took place while I was at their headquarters. I couldn't simply tell them all of that in an interview, there was far too much information. I wasn't even sure how any of this was relevant to Zander's arrest, since he was taken in for statutory rape and sexual exploitation. But I complied with their questions, even if it meant turning my back on The Club- I'd already been dismissed as An Associate, I had no loyalty ties left.

It hadn't been easy though. There were a lot of circumstances I had to consider, but finally I decided that the only way I could be one hundred percent honest was to write about it.

So, here you have it. My truth, my story, my side. Exactly how it happened through my eyes. We were too consenting people who met one morning in a bookshop and fell in love. We tried to stay away from each other, tried to end things, but the connection between us was too strong and we couldn't do it. Maybe if I'd known about who Zander truly was I never would have considered a relationship with him- or maybe I would have? I'll never know.

One thing is for certain, though. By submitting this statement I am ratting on The Club. I am releasing all of their secrets to the Police and putting my life at risk. They'll never forgive me for this and I can guarantee they'll come after me. Especially if Zander is in prison. But it's a risk I have to take to save myself, and after everything I've done and everything I've been through these past few months I deserve to be a little bit selfish.

CHAPTER 21
PRESENT DAY

I stop writing to read over the last few lines I wrote. I bite my lip, wonder if I should change it, but decide to keep it. I feel hands touch my shoulders, massage them gently.

"Are you done?" Nick asks me. His hands feel warm and I roll my neck to encourage him to keep rubbing.

"Just about." I look back at the computer and hit save, then move the mouse, click a few times, and open an email to the prosecutor. "Here goes nothing," I mumble as my heart begins to race. I attach the file and hit send then let out a deep breath as Nick's hands move from my shoulders, down my arms, and then I feel his lips on my neck.

"I'm proud of you," he mutters against the sensitive skin there, sending shivers down my spine, but I don't reply. I just sit there and stare at the screen, where a tiny notification is telling me **Message Sent**

CHAPTER 22

I sit at the kitchen table with a newspaper in front of me, gazing at the big, bold, headline. **Male Teacher Accused of Sexual Relations With Student**. I sigh as I bring my cup of coffee to my mouth, downing the last few drops, then I place the cup on top of the Newspaper, where Zander's face is displayed largely.

"You shouldn't go," Nick's voice makes me jump; I hadn't heard him come into the kitchen. He kisses my cheek, then walks to the coffee pot and makes his own cup, reaching over to refill mine. I smile at him, gratefully.

"I know," I say quietly as he places my cup back in front of me. "But I have to."

"I can come with you."

I shake my head, "no, you can't. You have a show tonight. Sound check is in three hours. Scotty will ban me from future shows if you cancel this one too."

"Yeah maybe you're right," Nick sighs. "You shouldn't have to do this alone, though."

"I'll be fine." I reach over for his hand and squeeze it. I'm still not sure what exactly Nick and I are but we've been living together for the past few weeks now, when he's not out touring that is.

"I'll have my phone on. Call me if you need to talk." I

smile again, thankful to have him by my side. If nothing else he's been the one constant being I could count on throughout this whole ordeal.

I walk through the front door security with bated breath- I wasn't supposed to be there. Zander had been let out on bail, forced to remain at Horse Shoes with the promise to attend his First Appearance, which was today. He wasn't allowed to contact me, wasn't allowed to be anywhere near a school or a park, or anywhere underage children may appear, causing Horse Shoes to close down their business, temporarily.

I have to know what will happen though, and I can't trust the newspapers to be honest about it. Security lets me pass and I walk towards the courtroom, take a seat in the back, and stare at the front, waiting for Zander's appearance. I'd been warned that if his case went to trial I may be asked to speak as a witness; I didn't want that, so I had to come and see for myself what the outcome will be.

I sit there for an hour and a half until, finally, Zander's name is called. He walks in with a lawyer, stands in front of the podium, and awaits the judge to speak. I can't take my eyes off of him; he looks amazing in his suit, with his hair short and his beard trimmed. A thousand memories flash through my head as I look at him, wanting nothing more than for him to turn back and see me, but also terrified of what would happen if he did.

The judge asks him a few generic questions: his name, the charges, and his understanding of why he is there. The judge looks at the paper in front of him, study's it for a moment, then looks back at Zander through round glasses. "How would you like to proceed with this case, Mr Dionne?"

Zander turns his head a bit to look at his lawyer who nods, a slight incline of the head- but I saw it. I hold my breath as Zander opens his mouth. "I would like to plea, your honour."

Plea? Zander's going to plea guilty? But why would he do that? How would that help him? Then I realize- if Zander plea's, the case goes away, it never goes to trial, and no additional evidence can be used against him. Zander's only crime would have been dating a student, and The Redneck Devils would be left out of it. It's smart, I admit, but it doesn't make watching him plea any easier.

The judge asks Zander a few more legal questions, all of which Zander says "yes" to. My heart is beating loud, I feel like the entire courtroom can hear it as I await the judge's declaration. Finally the judge leans forwards and asks Zander, in a clear voice, "how do you plea Mr Dionne?"

I'm holding my breath again, waiting for the inevitable, and when he says it I feel like my heart stops, at least for a moment. "Guilty, your honour."

The judge nods, gazes at his notes again, and declares. "You are sentenced to six months in prison and twenty years on the Sexual Offenders List, with an immediate withdrawal of your teaching credentials. I hope you enjoyed teaching, Mr Dionne, because I doubt you'll ever get another job like that again." He bangs his gavel and Zander walks away with his lawyer- but not before looking back, directly at me, in the crowd. He knew I was there, knew the whole time. I felt frozen to my seat as I close my eyes and let a few tears fall.

I return to my house to find it empty and wonder what I should do next? It seems surreal that it is over: Zander was in prison, The Club was safe, and I could forget about this chapter of my life. But what was next for me?

I never returned to school. I couldn't face my classmates, my teachers, or Mr Thorn after everything I'd done. I knew my grades would suffer because of it, but I didn't care; there were other ways I could earn my high school diploma. The hardest part was denying my acceptance to University- without a high school diploma they'd never allow me to attend. All of the grades I'd worked so hard to earn and all of the work I'd done on the Student Council and the yearbook seemed to be for nothing. Four years of my life I'd never get back. Not to mention I wouldn't go to Prom, which happened to be tonight, much to Gina's dismay. All that work to plan the perfect Prom and I wouldn't even get to enjoy it.

However, Nick had asked me if I wanted to join him on the road and I was highly considering it. I'd even taken to playing the guitar again, learning new chords, and writing my own songs. What else was there to do when you were living with a musician?

I walk to the couch, pick my guitar up off the stand, and start plucking away at the strings. Quickly a melody forms and a poem pops into my head and before long I have a song.

Maybe I did the wrong thing
And maybe I made mistakes
But I don't deserve to feel this way
You're better off without me
And I'm better off without you
But how could we end up this way
Maybe we could have changed it
Worked it out differently
Maybe you and I could still be living happily
What if I hadn't said it
What if you didn't know
Could we still be together, nobody knows
Maybe someday you're gonna realize
You shoulda looked and opened up your eyes
We could have stopped the fight and we could have stopped the tears
Now we're stuck with memories for so many years
You and I aren't meant to be
Tell me why couldn't I see
We are wrong it was not right
All that left was for us to fight
Maybe one day we'll meet
Crossing paths on the street

Who knows what the future holds
For us

As I continue to play I can't help but think about my relationship with Zander. He and I had never had a perfect relationship and maybe inside I had known it was going to end one day, but the thing about life was you never knew where it was going to take you, so may as well enjoy the roller-coaster of a ride it provides.

We had done some crazy things these past few months, things I never would have imagined I'd do in my Wildest Dreams. However, I'd done them, and now I had to live with it and the scars they left me with- both inside and out. But scars were stories, stories I'd tell so others could learn from my mistakes, and maybe that wasn't such a bad thing. Maybe it would be good for me. Who knows? Only time would tell.

CHAPTER 23

1 year later

Zander

Killing his brother had made him cold and hard but those kinds of emotions were necessary for him as leader of The Redneck Devils. It hadn't been easy, he'll admit to himself, to stick that knife in Danny's neck and watch him bleed out. But all the rage and pent up emotions he felt towards his brother after he tried to kill Alessaundra left him no choice. He had to do it.

He wasn't sure if Danny would have actually killed him. He knew his brother had been angry and felt betrayed, but to actually kill him over that? It was unlikely. Danny had just wanted Zander to submit to him, and at worst hand in his Patch, but he wasn't willing to do that. Not after his brother had tried to kill Ali.

When Zander stuck that knife in Danny's neck, Danny had looked at him incredulously, eyes wide, a gurgling sound escaping him as he tried to say something in response. His hand had grasped the handle and, with his final strength, pulled it out causing the blood to spurt out quickly as he dropped to his knees, and then fell to his face. Zander's Cut had been covered in blood but in his world that was a sign of honour- the dirtier the Cut, the better- but he had had to burn his black cowboy boots along with Danny's body.

Of course Danny's death meant that he, Zander, was now President of The Club and that his entire life now revolved around The Club and their business in drugs- after he got out of Prison, anyways. He was surprised at how quickly those six months had gone by- thanks to the help of The Satans and some of his fathers old friends he had protection behind the stone walls.

He had to leave ScatterBrain in charge of The Club while he'd been away as he was, rightfully so, his right hand man, his Vice President- The Club hadn't seen a VP since his father had run The Club and he enjoyed having a sense of normalcy back. However being away meant he was out of the loop; there was only so much information that could get passed on to him while he was behind bars and that was one part he hadn't enjoyed. Not that there was much The Club could do at the time, but since getting out six months ago he'd worked alongside his Club to come up with new ways to smuggle and export drugs.

Thanks to Alessaundra's statement the Police knew about the hay bales, knew about the horse races, and decided that Riverton needed a larger Police presence. They built a station a few miles down the road from Horse Shoes and frequently drove by to check on things, much to The Club's dismay. They were lucky, though, that the Police couldn't use any of the information Alessaundra had provided them with- since the case involved Alessaundra as a minor they'd now sealed those records and they couldn't be accessed or used for anything, except the intended case they were filed for, a case which was now closed.

However, she had still cost The Club a lot of trouble, and if he hadn't been in the position to stop them he knew the rest of the members would have hunted her down and killed her by now. But he was their President and as much as they hated it, they couldn't act out against him. Alessaundra was safe, for now.

He'll admit he still loved her. How could he not? The girl was spectacular and handled the situation she had been thrust into with more grace than he ever had dreamed of. She had adapted to The Club so easily, as if she had been born to be a part of it, as if she belonged there. She bonded easily with everyone and they had all loved her. She had even given her pledge as an Associate to The Club, permanently marking herself as one of them- a mark she had yet to cover up. He couldn't deny that if she showed up on his doorstep tomorrow, he was sure he'd take her back without a second thought, and that thought scared him.

When he saw her at his court appearance he wondered what it meant but he didn't have the opportunity to ask for he was immediately taken away. But that had been a year ago, and he'd done a lot of thinking since then. He knew it had been stupid to date her as his student, but even more reckless to bring her around The Club and introduce her to the life of The Redneck Devils. He'd lied to his family, his Club, to the people he cared the most about- but love made you do some things you weren't proud of, and right now he was about to do another one of those things.

Of course he'd been keeping tabs on her, he had a lot of connections after all. He knew she had finished her high school credits by taking online classes, he knew she was back together and touring with Nick, and knew she was making money writing promotional articles and reviews on Shattered Life. It just so happened that their next stop was in Baysin, and Zander was going to be there.

Zander stood across the street at his truck watching as ScatterBrain and Butch walked towards Shakers, the club Shattered Life was playing at that night. He'd heard about this club, knew that the band had played there a lot while they were starting up, recognized it as the club where Alessaundra had seen the band play after they debuted their first album, and knew that Butch had been there that night. He expected this to be easy, but he was wrong.

There was a line up all around the club, mainly girls dressed in their shortest skirts and most revealing shirts, but some of those girls were accompanied by their boyfriends. ScatterBrain and Butch bi-passed the line, shrugged their Cuts as they approached the bouncer, and crossed their arms to look intimidating. Zander couldn't hear what was being said but he saw the bouncers mouth moving quickly, gesturing at the pair almost angrily. So, they'd been warned. Smirking Zander shrugged off his Cut and thrust it into the crack of his truck window before marching towards where ScatterBrain and Butch were currently making a scene with the bouncer.

Butch's voice was loud and angry as he pointed at the bouncer. "-who we are? If you don't let us in-."

"I do know who you are, and it's exactly that reason why I can not grant you access. I'm sorry but it's out of my hands." The bouncer raised them in defence, shrugging. "Now, I'm going to have to ask you to leave or else I'll have no choice but to call the cops, and I'm sure you don't want that."

ScatterBrain growled while Butch cracked his knuckles. Zander had wanted to see how far the bouncer would go, if he could be manipulated into letting them in, but he wasn't backing down. There was only one thing for him to do. "Hey," he called out approaching them. "Is there a problem here, gentlemen?" He crossed his arms in front of him, careful not to let any significant tattoos show that may give him away- he'd added a few to his body since being released from prison- and raised an eyebrow at ScatterBrain and Butch. The pair exchanged looks, noticed the lack of Cut on Zander's back, and faced him turning their backs on the bouncer.

"Stay out of this," Butch growled.

"It doesn't concern you," added ScatterBrain.

Zander glanced at the bouncer, "should I call the cops?"

The bouncer raised his eyebrow, "I was debating that myself."

"Why you little-," Butch raised his fist to Zander but

ScatterBrain reached out and grabbed a fistful of his Cut, pulling him back. "Let go of me."

"Save it," ScatterBrain murmured, glaring at Zander. "He's not worth it."

Butch growled angrily but let ScatterBrain lead him away, past the line of nervous looking girls, and to their bikes across the street. Zander watched as they got on, started their engines, and drove off. Only once they were out of sight did Zander turn back to the bouncer and shrug. "What was that all about?"

The bouncer shook his head, "I'm under strict orders- no one wearing a leather vest and bearing the name Redneck Devils are allowed in tonight."

"Those are pretty specific rules," he pointed out.

The bouncer shrugged, "just going by what I'm told. But, hey, thanks for the help." The bouncer reached over for the door and opened it. "Are you here for the show?"

"Yeah, thanks." Zander grinned, waved to the bouncer and stepped into the club feeling confident. Now Zander knew why there was such a large line outside- inside, the club was packed. Thumping music played and girls spun around the dance floor in the middle of the room. There was a stage on the far wall with drums and guitars already displayed, just waiting for the band to come on. Girls mingled around, smiling at him, winking, and tossing their hair over their shoulder. He was flattered, but he wasn't here for just any girl; he was only here for one.

He made his way to the bar and sat on an empty stool, gestured to the bartender for a drink, and accepted the shot of vodka that was passed to him: he had once been a whisky man, but Alessaundra had turned him into a fan of vodka. He took it, gestured for another, then turned to scan the crowd. He'd just thrown back his second shot when a voice spoke from behind him. "You shouldn't be here."

Sighing Zander set the shot glass back down on the bar and looked at who'd spoken. "Say's who?"

Nick didn't answer. Instead he said, "how'd you get past the bouncer? He had specific orders to keep you and your- people- out of here."

Zander grinned as he took his third shot. "Next time you may want to provide them with pictures."

Nick narrowed his eyes at him and said threateningly. "I can have security on you in five seconds."

Zander chuckled, "is that supposed to scare me?"

"What's the point of staying? I know you aren't here to see us play. What do you think is going to happen? Do you think she's going to- to- to see you standing there and come running into your arms so you can live happily ever after? You let her go, man, and now she's with me."

His smirk caused Zander to laugh. "Is that what you're afraid of, Nick? Is that why you banned me and my friends from coming here tonight? Are you worried that that exact thing might happen? You're nothing compared to me, *man*." He mocked.

Nick narrowed his eyes, "If you don't leave I'll call the cops. You'll be arrested- you'll go back to jail."

Zander howled in laughter, "for what? Watching a show at a club?" He reached for the shot the bartender had poured him and threw it back, his eyes moving past Nick to someone standing behind him. Long dark hair, jade green eyes, wearing a dress with a cardigan over top of it- it was Alessaundra. He blinked a few times then set the shot glass down on the bar, turning to look at Nick again. "Fine. I'll leave. Drinks are on him," he added to the bartender, pointing at Nick. "Have a good show."

Zander got up and headed for the door, confident that Alessaundra would follow. He went out the smokers entrance which was empty, lit a cigarette, and inhaled deeply as he counted to himself. Ten seconds later the door opened again and there she was, dark hair swinging as she stepped outside and crossed her arms over her chest. She stared at him for a moment, waiting for him to say something, but when he didn't she sighed. "Why are you here?"

Zander tilted his head up and exhaled a long breath of smoke. "I thought that would be obvious. I wanted to see you."

Alessaundra shook her head, exasperated. "Why now?"

He smirked, exhaling another breath. "You had to have expected this. It's the first show Shattered Life has played in the vicinity all year."

"We did," she agreed. "Which is why we asked the bouncer to keep any Redneck Devils out."

"Clearly that didn't work."

"Clearly," she drawled unamused. "I guess next time we need to provide the bouncer with pictures."

"That's exactly what I said." Zander grinned, dropping his cigarette butt on the ground next to a pile of others. "No wonder we made such a good couple- Zander and Ali, The Professor and Jade."

Alessaundra groaned. "Jade is dead, Zander. I'm nineteen now, I have no use for a fake ID." She reached into her purse and grabbed a smoke, then searched around for a lighter.

"Jade will never be dead, not to me." Zander watched as she became frustrated, unable to find one, so he grabbed his heavy silver one with The Redneck Devil logo on it, and handed it to her. She hesitated a moment then snatched it quickly, lighting her smoke with it before dropping it back into his open hand. "Thanks," she said reluctantly. Zander lit himself another smoke and the two of them stood there in silence, inhaling and exhaling until their cigarettes were done. Finally Alessaundra sighed and said, "you're different, Zander."

"So are you," he noted.

Ali shook her head, stomping out her smoke. "Am I really though? Or is this who I've been all along? Maybe the Ali you knew was a different Ali, an Ali I made myself into in order to be with you? But this Ali, right here, is the Ali I've always meant to be- it's the same Ali who was with Nick before she met you."

Zander laughed softly. "Bullshit."

"What?"

"I said, that's bullshit."

"But it's not," Ali insisted. She grabbed a handful of her hair in frustration. "Don't you see, Zander? You never really knew me! I mean, how could you have? We dated for like a week before you brought me up to Horse Shoes and made me lie about who I was! I had to create this- whole other persona! I was never truly myself with you Zander."

Zander watched as she released her hair. "I knew you better than anyone ever could have," he finally stated as she paced back and forth down the small alley. "And if you turned yourself into someone else, that's on you, not me! I was only trying to protect you, can't you see that?"

"You were protecting yourself." Alessaundra countered.

"I loved you!"

"You only thought you did!"

"We were in love!" he emphasized angrily.

"But I wasn't really me."

"That doesn't change the way you felt." Zander strolled over to her, grabbed her arms and stared into her eyes. "You keep saying you were some made up person? Would some made up person have faced a drug dealer in front of a room full of cops? Would a made up person have hopped on a motorcycle with no training and learn how to ride it? Would a made up person have made friendships with every member of The Club?

"The truth is you loved it, Alessaundra. You loved me and you loved The Club. You loved the thrill, the danger, and the unpredictable outcome of it- and you loved who you were with us. Sure, you may have gotten scared for a moment there, that night The Vultures attacked, and I don't blame you for that. But the fact is you came back and were determined to win the entire Club over again. You, Alessaundra. You."

Alessaundra was breathing heavily now. "I only came back because I was forced to. I was terrified of all of you!"

"If you were so terrified of us you never would have

marked yourself as one of us." These next words came out of Zander's mouth calmly, quietly, and he watched as Alessaundra swallowed, her neck jumping. "A mark you still bear on your back."

Alessaundra started to struggle to get out of his hold but Zander released her only enough so he could pull her cardigan off. A ripping sound echoed through the alley, leaving Ali standing in only her dress. Alessaundra gasped, reaching for the torn fabric, but Zander refused to let it go. "Give it back to me," she cried, jumping up for it, but Zander only held it higher.

She stopped jumping, folded her hands into fists, and began to pound on his chest angrily- but Zander hardly felt a thing. He finally let go of the torn cardigan, watching the fabric float to the ground, and grabbed a hold of her fists, forcing her to look up into his face. Tears were starting to stream down her face as she struggled against his hold. "Let go of me," she groaned out through clenched teeth. She raised her foot and tried to kick him, but missed.

Zander had had enough and backed her up until she was against the wall, causing her to gasp in surprise as her back crashed into it. "Never put your hands on me," Zander stated quietly, sending fearful shivers down her spine.

Alessaundra whimpered, "You're crazy."

"Six months in prison does that to a man." Zander grinned.

"I can't believe I ever went out with someone like you," she panted as her heart began to pound in her chest.

Zander started laughing maniacally. "Admit it, Alessaundra. You love this. The danger, the thrill- it's more action than you've received in a year! I can hear your heart pounding in your chest, I can see the flush on your face, the desire in your eyes. You want this."

"No," she cried, "no I love Nick!"

"Maybe," Zander smirked, "but you love me too." He leaned down and placed his mouth to hers even as she tried to move away from him, but it was no use. As soon as his lips touched hers Alessaundra forgot about everything- the trial, his arrest, and the fact that he was now President of The Redneck Devils. Everything escaped from her mind the second Zander's soft lips pressed against hers- and just like that she was seventeen again.

Zander's hands wound up into her hair, pulling her body closer to his with an intensity that shocked even him. She responded accordingly, her hands moving up towards his hair, clinging and grabbing to it as she tried to get as close to him as possible. She moved her hands to his neck and he moved his down her back to grab hold of her bottom. Zander's teeth nibbled at Alessaundra's lips and she moaned. They were both panting heavily lost in each other, until Alessaundra shoved Zander away harshly.

"No." She placed one hand on the wall behind her to steady her weak legs and raised the other one to point accusingly at Zander. "No, I won't do this to him, not again."

"Are you seriously going to stand there and tell me you want to choose the musician over me?" Alessaundra nodded her head, lips pressed tightly together. "Can you honestly stand there and tell me you don't miss the thrill of it all? The unexpected danger? The anticipation of not knowing what's going to happen next? Are you honestly going to be happy living a life of tours, music, and predictability?"

"At least my life won't be in danger."

"But what about Scarlet? And ScatterBrain? They were your friends! How can you turn your back on them so easily?"

"Scarlet was different, and Markus-."

"They are as much a part of The Club as I am," Zander stated pointing at his chest. "As much a part of The Club as you were. We're a family, Alessaundra, and you can't have one without the other."

Tears welled in Alessaundra's eyes again and he watched as she blinked, trying to stop them from falling. Finally she whispered, "why can't you just let me be happy, Zander?"

"Happy?" His voice was flat. "You call this low life happy?" She nodded. "But all you are is a groupie."

Alessaundra's mouth dropped open, offended as she gasped. "A groupie? Well, I'd rather be a groupie than a back warmer any day."

Now it was Zander's turn to be offended. "You know you were more to me than that."

"Oh really? Then what was I to you, Zander?"

"You- you were-," he stuttered trying to find the words. "Everything!" he finally screamed. "Don't you see that Alessaundra? You were everything to me! Do you think I would have risked my job for some chick who didn't mean anything to me? Do you really believe I would have risked everything for some girl I just wanted to have a fling with? Do you honestly think I would have brought you around The Club, flaunted you, if I thought you were good for nothing other than keeping my back warm while I rode? Do you think I would have done any of that for someone who didn't matter?"

Alessaundra was quiet for a moment, reaching up to wipe a tear from her cheek. She sniffled as she quietly said, "If I was everything to you then why did you let me go so easily?"

Zander closed his eyes as he took a breath. "If you love someone set them free. If they come back they're yours, if they don't they never were."

"Zander-."

"I was trying to keep you safe Alessaundra," he stated in a low voice. "I knew that if I let you stay with me something terrible would have happened to you."

"But you told me to go back to Nick. You said-."

"I needed you to be safe. Somebody had to look out for you if things didn't go right with Danny. If Danny had killed me, he would have come after you again. I had to stop him, Alessaundra. I had to save you. You can understand that, can't you?"

Alessaundra was quiet for a long time then, her eyes on his. She studied his face- the five o'clock shadow he used to have had once again grown out into a beard. His blue eyes, while still striking, looked distant and cold. There was a scar above his eye he never had before and his hair was gelled back in a style she didn't recognize. Zander had changed a lot this past year, but she knew there were differences in her too.

Finally she took a small step forwards and grabbed his hand, holding it tightly in hers. "I can't go back to you Zander. I'm sorry." The tears that had been glistening in her eyes began to fall in earnest now, her throat constricting as she said, "I can't be in that kind of atmosphere. It's not who I am."

"But it is-." Zander insisted clutching her hands tightly, but Alessaundra shook her head, interrupting him before he could finish his sentence.

"I keep trying to tell you, Zander. That's not who I am, or at least it's not who I want to be. I'm sorry but we can't be together Zander. It was too hard. It's best if we never see each other again."

Zander opened his mouth to say something but before he could the door to The Club opened and Nick walked out. He saw Ali, with her hair a mess, her cardigan torn off, and tears streaming down her face holding hands with Zander. He turned to Zander, face contorted in rage as he took a step towards him.

"You son of a bitch," Nick growled. He raised his fist but Ali stopped him, rushing over and grabbing his arm to lower it. He glanced at her, confused, as she shook her head.

"Don't," she pleaded. "Please."

Alessaundra knew that Nick would never win in a fight against him and he smirked as Nick lowered his hand, instead wrapping it around her waist. "I was worried about you," he stated in a quiet voice. "You missed our entire set."

"I'm sorry." She leaned up and kissed his cheek. "But I had to talk to him."

Nick glanced at Zander with a scowl. "Why?"

"You know why," Ali said softly.

He closed his eyes as if he were in pain but nodded, rubbing Alessaundra's back soothingly. "Are you okay?" he whispered. She nodded and he looked back towards Zander. "You should leave."

"I'm not finished here."

"Yes we are." Alessaundra stated sadly. "Please Zander, just go home." When he didn't move she sighed, grabbed Nick's hand, and turned towards the door. Nick opened it and gestured her inside but she stopped on the threshold and glanced back at him, looking sad. "Goodbye Zander."

Zander watched as the two of them went back into the club without another word. He considered going back in himself, but what good would it do him? Clearly she'd made her choice, and she wasn't going to change her mind about it.

As he exited the alley he pulled out a cigarette and walked towards his truck. ScatterBrain was back, leaning against the drivers door as he waited for him. "How'd it go, Prof? Is our prized gem returning to us?"

"Nope," Zander said as he inhaled. On the exhale he added, "she chose the musician."

"Really?"

Zander shrugged as if this decision didn't bother him. "She wasn't exactly Club material, anyways."

ScatterBrain paused, taking the last drag of his smoke before tossing it on the ground, then casually stated, "That's a bunch of bullshit and you know it. You can be honest with me, man. There's no one else around. You can tell me what you really think."

Zander shook his head, "it is what it is. See you at The Club?"

ScatterBrain nodded and got on his bike again, taking off. Zander stopped and looked back at Shakers, frowning. He knew he had to let Alessaundra go, it was the only way he'd be able to move on. It was clear that Alessaundra wasn't the best companion for him while he was in this position. He knew she was right, he had changed. He'd changed a lot. Murder does that to people. Could he ever be that guy she met in the bookstore? Could he go back to being that kind stranger who bought her a book? Maybe. But he didn't think so. Too much had happened since then. He wanted to be that guy, for her, but he wasn't and he knew that now.

Zander pulled away from the curb and drove towards Riverton, thinking of everything that had happened since that day he met Alessaundra. He had shown her so many things, so many new experiences, things she never would have thought of, even in her Wildest Dreams- and that would be enough for him. For now anyways- he was sure this wasn't the last he'd seen of Alessaundra Campbell, and he looked forward to the day that they'd meet again.

ACKNOWLEDGEMENT

First I want to acknowledge NaNoWriMo- National Novel Writing Month- for without the motivation to write 50,000 words during the month of Novemeber every year I never would have sat down to write and rewrite this book.

Next I want to thank my husband for his continued support, for there would be days when all I would do is sit and write for hours on end. Thank you for sacraficing your time for me and for lending me your support over the last few years.

To my family, and friends, who have encouraged me time and time again to publish my work, even without reading it. I can never thank you enough for believing in me.

And to anyone who picks up and reads this book- thank you. The very fact you were willing to read my work means everything to me. Alessaundra and Zander's story is not over yet. Stay tuned.

ABOUT THE AUTHOR

Vanessa Karkheck

I've been writing for many years, but never had the courage to publish. Wildest Dreams began in 2013 for NaNoWriMo and went through many re-writes before I managed to get it to the exact place it was meant to be.

I am 30 years old and live in Kitchener Ontario, Canada with my husband, daughter, and dog. When I'm not writing I'm teaching little people how to learn through play!

Manufactured by Amazon.ca
Bolton, ON